Ru

"It's just that I saw Carlston at the theater last night."

"Carlston?"

"William Standfield, the Earl of Carlston." Andrew's voice had hardened. "You probably wouldn't know the story—it was at least three years ago, when you were at that school."

The name did have a familiar ring. She had heard it in one of those whispered cautionary tales that her friends had shared. "Didn't he kill someone?"

"His wife. The Countess of Carlston, formerly Elise de Vraine." Andrew paused, his face softening. "Everyone knows he killed her, but no body was found and so he was never tried. Still, the King turned his back, and no one would receive him after that. The rumor was that he went to the Continent."

"And now he has returned," Helen breathed, imagining a black-cloaked figure sweeping up innocent girls.

"Trying to worm himself back into society," Andrew said caustically. "He'll do it too. He was with Prinny at the theater, and Brummell always liked him."

Helen's image of a dastardly abductor disappeared in a wave of logic. "He would hardly be making off with housemaids if he is trying to reestablish himself."

"True, although there was talk that he'd attacked a maid, too, as well as Lady Elise." With a jerk of his wrist, Andrew spun the billiard ball across the table. It slammed into another with a sharp crack, sending both ricocheting into the cushions. "He should not have come back."

OTHER BOOKS YOU MAY ENJOY

Bitterblue	Kristin Cashore
Eon	Alison Goodman
Eona	Alison Goodman
Fire	Kristin Cashore
The Half Bad trilogy	Sally Green
The Legend trilogy	Marie Lu
Rebel of the Sands	Alwyn Hamilton
The Rose & the Dagger	Renée Ahdieh
The Wrath & the Dawn	Renée Ahdieh
The Young Elites trilogy	Marie Lu

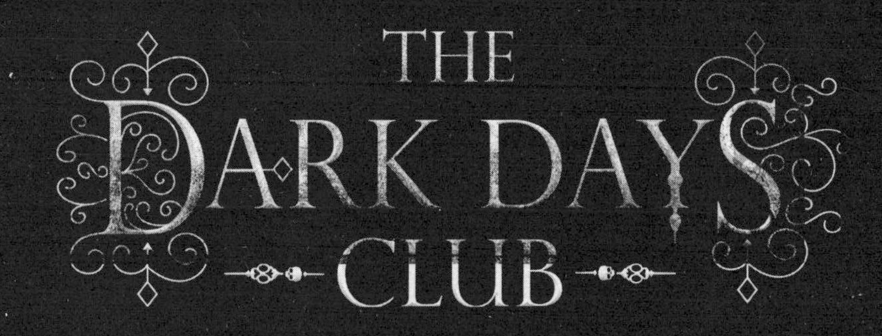
THE
DARK DAYS
CLUB

ALISON GOODMAN

THE DARK DAYS CLUB

speak

SPEAK
An imprint of Penguin Random House LLC
375 Hudson Street
New York, New York 10014

First published in the United States of America by Viking,
an imprint of Penguin Random House LLC, 2016
Published by Speak, an imprint of Penguin Random House LLC, 2017

THE LIBRARY OF CONGRESS HAS CATALOGED THE VIKING EDITION AS FOLLOWS:
Goodman, Alison.
The Dark Days Club / Alison Goodman.
pages cm—(Lady Helen ; book 1)
Summary: "In April 1812, as she is preparing for her debut presentation to Queen Charlotte, Lady Helen Wrexhall finds herself in the middle of a conspiracy reaching to the very top of society, and learns the truth about her mother, who died ten years ago"—Provided by publisher.
ISBN: 978-0-670-78547-6 (hardcover)
[1. Courts and courtiers—Fiction. 2. Conspiracies—Fiction.
3. Secrets—Fiction. 4. Supernatural—Fiction.
5. Charlotte, Queen, consort of George III, King of Great Britain, 1744–1818—Fiction.
6. London (England)—History—19th century—Fiction.
7. Great Britain—History—1800–1837—Fiction.]
I. Title.
PZ7.G61352Dar 2016
[Fic]—dc23 2015006792

Speak ISBN 9780142425091

Printed in the United States of America

1 3 5 7 9 10 8 6 4 2

To my mother, Charmaine Goodman,
who gave me my first Georgette Heyer book to read
and started my lifelong passion for all things Regency

THE DARK DAYS CLUB

In 1810 the British King, George III, descended into a melancholy madness from which he would never recover.

In 1811 his son, the Prince of Wales—fat, frivolous, and forty-nine—was declared his regent, and given care of a country that was at war and in deep recession. The new Prince Regent, or "Prinny," as he was commonly known, immediately gave a sumptuous party for over two thousand members of the upper class, which set the tone for his regency: nine years of staggering extravagance, relentless scandal, and the constant threat of rioting and revolution.

In 1812, Prinny had been regent for one year. Britain was on the brink of war with America, and in its tenth year of almost continuous war with France and its emperor, Napoleon Bonaparte. None of these countries, however, knew there was another, even older war being waged: a secret battle that had started centuries before against a demonic horde hidden in plain sight across the cities, towns, and villages of the world. Only a small group of people stood in the way of this multitude and its insidious predation upon humankind.

London, late April 1812: a month that had seen violent civil unrest, savage battles on the Continent, and the rumblings of aggression from the new American nation. It was also the month in which Queen Charlotte—after a two-year hiatus—returned to the practice of holding drawing rooms for the presentation of young ladies into high society. A battleground of a different kind.

One

Wednesday, 29 April 1812

IN THE SUN-WARMED quiet of her uncle's library, Lady Helen Wrexhall spread the skirt of her muslin morning gown and sank into the deep curtsy required for Royal presentation: back held straight, head slightly bowed, left knee bent so low, it nearly touched the floor. And, of course, face set into a serene Court smile.

"Your Majesty is correct," she said to the blue brocade sofa doing duty as Queen Charlotte. "I am the daughter of Lady Catherine, Countess of Hayden."

Helen glanced sideways at her reflection in the glass-fronted bookcase that lined the wall: the best place in the town house to view the whole of her tall self. The curtsy was good—it should be, after so many weeks of practice—but she sounded far too surly. She tried again.

"Yes, Your Highness, I am indeed the daughter of Lady Catherine."

No, too jaunty. She rose from the curtsy and dropped the folds of her gown, opening her fingers into long spreads of frustration. Her aunt had told her to find a tone that acknowledged her connection to Lady Catherine but also maintained a dignified distance from it. A great deal of meaning to place upon a few words. She backed a few steps away from the blue silk bulk of the substitute queen. Flanking Her Majesty were two matching brocade armchairs: the princesses Mary and Augusta. Helen eyed the makeshift Royals, already sensing disaster. Tomorrow she would be curtsying to the real Royal ladies, and there could be no room for awkwardness or mistakes. She had to have an answer ready about her mother, just in case Queen Charlotte mentioned the infamous Countess of Hayden.

It did not seem likely. Ten years had passed since Helen's mother and father had drowned at sea. Surely Lady Catherine would not be on the mind of a queen burdened by a mad husband and a profligate son running the country to ruin. Helen pressed her palms together. Even she could not remember much about her mother. Lady Catherine's name was only uttered as a reproach in her aunt and uncle's house, and her brother never mentioned their mother anymore. Yet that morning at breakfast, Aunt Leonore had suddenly told Helen to practice a graceful answer to a possible Royal inquiry. Perhaps the Crown never forgot a noblewoman whose name was shrouded in rumor. Especially when those rumors were wound tight around the word *treason*.

One more time, then. Helen held up the edges of her gown and glided into the low obeisance.

"Yes, Your Majesty. My mother was Lady Catherine."

That was better; the less said, the smaller the chance of making a mistake.

Helen lifted her face to receive the Royal kiss on her forehead, rose from the curtsy, then gathered up her imaginary train and backed away from the sofa—the most difficult maneuver in the whole Court Presentation. Lud, she hoped she did not trip or lose control of her curtsy tomorrow. It was the first official

Queen's Drawing Room since the King's madness had returned two years ago, and there had been a desperate scramble by mothers to secure their daughters a place on the presentation list. Aunt Leonore—who had lost her own daughter and only child at birth—had been at the forefront of the rush, and Helen had duly received her summons from the Lord Chamberlain. What if she wrecked the whole enterprise by stumbling? For a moment she saw an image of herself sprawled on the polished Palace floor, the huge old-fashioned hoopskirt standing up around her like a frigate in full sail.

Helen sat on the sofa and slumped against the stiff cushions. It was no good dwelling on possible mishaps; she had done all that she could to prepare for the day. Her dance master had drilled her interminably on every movement of the ceremony. He'd even brought in his dainty wife to demonstrate how to slip a porcelain *bourdaloue*—shaped, amusingly, like a lady's slipper—up under the hoop of her Court gown in case she needed to relieve herself during the long wait to be called. Now *that* was a difficult maneuver, Helen thought, her unruly sense of humor rising into a smile. Especially in a screened corner of a Royal stateroom. What if someone dropped one? Her imagination conjured the sound of smashing porcelain and the stink of warm spreading piss.

No, that would not be so funny. And she, for one, was not going to tempt fate. Tomorrow morning she would drink *nothing.* At least, nothing after her cup of chocolate.

On that sensible resolution, Helen turned her attention to the stack of ladies' magazines her aunt had left on the gilt side table—an unsubtle reminder to find a riding dress she liked. She picked up the new edition of *La Belle Assemblée* and curled her legs under herself on the sofa, tucking the hem of her gown around the soft soles of her kid leather slippers. Aunt would take a fit if she saw her sitting in such a graceless way, but she felt so twitchy—so unbecomingly lively—that it was best to keep herself folded up as tight as a new parasol.

It was a bad case of presentation nerves. Nothing more.

She stared fiercely at the magazine as if it could rid her of the knowledge that these *nerves* had appeared long before any thought of her presentation. They had started at least six months ago, just after her eighteenth birthday, a deep energy that made her follow her curiosity beyond the bounds of propriety. She had made midnight forays into her uncle's study and his private papers; paid breathless visits up to the silent attic stacked full of chairs; even danced a lone, wild reel in the billiard room. All, she had to admit, for no reason beyond the thrill of it, and the need to rid her body of this unseemly vigor.

The other explanation for her nerves sat at the back of her mind like a hundredweight: her mother's blood. Although never said aloud by her aunt and uncle, the fear that she would have her mother's wild streak had sat heavily upon their faces when they first took her in. Even then, when she was only eight years old, the implication had been clear to Helen—she must be on guard against her own nature. After all, it had been her mother's reckless pursuit of intrigue and excitement that had killed her and her husband, leaving their two children orphaned. Helen thought she had escaped that legacy of restless energy. She had read Mr. Locke and found his radical philosophy—that men created themselves from the sum of their own experiences and choices—far more amenable than the idea of a predestined nature. So, she told herself firmly as she turned pages, this worsening of her nerves did not mean she was like her mother. It was just a normal response to the prospect of curtsying before the Queen.

She lingered for a moment at a fascinating article about mythology, then resolutely flipped to the fashion pages, stopping at the illustration of an impossibly elongated woman in a bright green riding outfit. Helen clicked her tongue. Apparently, the fashions for spring 1812 were to be more military than the army itself. The taste for black braid and frogged clasps had run wild.

"Barnett, where is my niece?" Aunt Leonore's voice carried through the town house hallway to the library.

Helen jerked upright. According to the gilt clock on the mantel, only twenty minutes had passed since Aunt had left to view the latest caricatures at Ackermann's Repository. It was usually a two-hour expedition; something must have happened. She heard the butler's lower tones directing his mistress to the library, and then the increasing volume of her aunt's voice as she approached, talking as if she were already in the room. Helen swung her feet to the floor. Three quick flicks smoothed out the telltale creases in her muslin. She positioned the magazine on her lap and gave one last tug at the high waist of her bodice.

The double doors opened halfway. Barnett stood for a stately moment in the gap—a well-judged pause in which a person could uncurl herself. But for once Helen was ready. His eyes met hers in warm collusion, then he pushed the doors fully apart and stepped aside. Aunt Leonore entered midsentence, still clad in her scarlet pelisse, working one blue glove from her hand, and trailed by Murphett, her lady's maid.

". . . you will not credit this, my dear, but I am sure it is the truth. I would not have given it a moment's notice if only Mrs. Shoreham had the telling of it, but I met Lady Beck, and you know I have the highest faith in her . . ." Aunt Leonore paused, searching for the right accolade.

"Her spies?" Helen supplied. She sent a quick glance of thanks to Barnett as he bowed and quietly backed from the room, drawing the doors closed.

Aunt Leonore stifled a smile. "You know very well I was not thinking such a thing. Her *prudence*." She held out the glove.

Murphett promptly stepped forward to drape it over her arm.

"So what did the prudent Lady Beck tell you?" Helen asked, her curiosity sparking.

For an instant Aunt Leonore's excited smile locked into a strange, stiff grimace. It was such a brief pause in the quicksilver of her expressions that Helen almost missed it. She focused more closely on her aunt's face: the grimace was gone, replaced by a tiny sideways pull of her mouth and a drawing around the eyes. Some kind of unhappy realization, quickly hidden. Helen knew she was right—reading expressions was her one true accomplishment. When she concentrated properly on a face, her accuracy was startling and a little disturbing. It certainly made her aunt and uncle uneasy, and they had forbidden her to voice her observations about anyone, especially themselves. Girls were meant to paint screens, sob out ballads, and play the pianoforte, not see through the masks of polite society.

"It is very cold out today," her aunt said. "I hope we do not have another spring like last year."

The abrupt change of subject silenced Helen for a moment. Aunt was definitely hiding something. She tried again. "What did Lady Beck say to bring you back so soon?"

Her aunt started work on the other glove, her eyes finding *La Belle Assemblée* on Helen's lap. "Did you find a riding habit you liked? We must discuss the design with Mr. Duray this week if we want it before the Season truly starts."

The tightness around her aunt's mouth—a clear refusal—stopped Helen asking a third time. She would wait until Murphett left the room.

"I have found nothing I like," she said. "The gowns this Season are all so overdone." She wrinkled her nose, belatedly remembering that she had resolved not to do so anymore. She knew it was not her best feature, being a little on the long, narrow side, but then Helen was painfully aware that almost everything about herself was on the long, narrow side. As well as being much taller than average, she was *scarecrow*-thin—according to her older brother, Andrew—although her friends assured her she was celestially slender. Even so, Helen had a mirror, and she knew she was a Long Meg who definitely did not look adorable when she wrinkled her nose.

Aunt Leonore pulled the second glove free. "You would dress yourself like a Quaker if I let you."

Helen held up the magazine, still open at the offending illustration. "But look, at least twenty-five frogs on the bodice alone. Is it too much to ask for a dress that won't scare the horse?"

Aunt Leonore gave her loud cackle—the one that had earned her the title Lady Laugh amongst her friends and Lady Hee-Haw amongst her enemies. "Not this Season, my dear. It is all military flimflam."

"Bonaparte has a lot to answer for," Helen said. "First Europe, and now our fashion." She flipped the magazine closed and rested it on her lap.

"You really do have your mother's grim sense of humor." Aunt Leonore lifted her chin as Murphett unbuttoned the bodice of her pelisse. "God rest her soul."

Helen kept her eyes down, feigning interest in the magazine cover. It was best not to show any response to the rare mentions of her mother, especially those concerning shared traits. They were never meant as compliments.

"Promise me you won't make such deplorable jests at Almack's," her aunt continued.

"No jests," Helen promised dutifully, but could not help adding, "Perhaps I should not speak again until I am married."

Her aunt gave a soft snort. "That would certainly help my nerves." She held out her arms, and Murphett deftly pulled the scarlet coat free. "No, my dear, I don't want you to be silent. That would be just as bad. Promise me you will have some proper conversation ready for your dance partners. And make your little quips less political. It does not do for a girl your age to be so aware." She settled on the sofa next to Helen.

"Will that be all, my lady?" Murphett asked.

"Yes, thank you."

As Murphett curtsied and exited, pulling the doors closed, Aunt Leonore's face sagged into the worn pathways of her fifty-four years. She tweaked and smoothed the folds of her blue walking dress, the rearrangements bringing a waft of rose perfume from the fine crepe. Helen saw the fussing for what it was—procrastination—and studied her aunt's features again. A mix of sadness and anxiety.

The sadness disappeared, replaced by irritation. "Do stop staring, Helen."

Helen picked at a loose thread in the binding of *La Belle Assemblée*. "What is troubling you, Aunt? Something has taken the excitement from your news."

"You read me, didn't you?" her aunt said. "You know your uncle and I have asked you not to do so."

"I am sorry. I could not help seeing it."

Aunt Leonore sighed, part resignation, part concern. "I suppose I cannot hide the truth; it will come to your ears soon enough. When I came in, I suddenly recalled that you have more than a passing acquaintance with Delia Cransdon. The news is about her, I am afraid. Now, I do not want you to get upset. Tomorrow is such an important day."

Helen stopped pulling at the thread, her hand stilled by a sudden sense of foreboding. While Delia was not her closest friend—that special place belonged to the Honorable Millicent Gardwell—she was nonetheless one of Helen's cronies from her year at Miss Holcromb's Select Seminary. "Delia is not ill, is she?"

"Worse," Aunt Leonore said, pity drawing down the corners of her mouth. "Three days ago, she ran off with a man by the name of Trent, and there has been no marriage."

Helen's breath caught in her chest. If it was true, Delia was ruined. "No. That is not possible."

Or was it? Helen thought back over the last few months, and had to admit she had seen despair growing in her friend's eyes. Delia had made her debut the Season before last, but had received no offers of marriage. She had none of the essential *three*—beauty, high connections, or fortune—and, at twenty years of age, knew she was coming to the end of her opportunities. She had even confided in Helen and Millicent that all she could see ahead was spinsterhood and its associated humiliations. Had that bleak future forced her to run away with a man who was little more than a stranger? Helen shook her head.

"I cannot believe Delia would do such a thing. Lady Beck must be mistaken."

"Her housekeeper had it from the Cransdons' cook," Aunt Leonore said, sealing the truth of the matter. "It seems Delia and this Mr. Trent were discovered in a public house, in Sussex, of all places. You know what that means, don't you? Sussex is in the opposite direction to Scotland—they were not headed toward the border to be married." She clasped her hands together, the pressure pushing purple into her knuckles. "I suppose I must tell you all, since it will be the talk tomorrow. Lady Beck says your poor friend was found covered in blood."

"Blood!" Helen rose from the sofa, unable to sit quietly alongside such terrible news. "Was she hurt?"

"Apparently not."

"Then whose blood was it? Mr. Trent's?"

"My dear, prepare yourself," Aunt Leonore said softly. "The

man committed self-murder. He used a pistol, in front of Delia."

Suicide? Helen closed her eyes, fighting back the horror that rose like bile into her throat. The worst crime—the worst sin—of all, and Delia had witnessed it. Unbidden, her mind conjured a vision of her friend's face splattered with blood, mouth open wide in an unending scream.

"And there is something more," her aunt continued, rescuing her from the terrifying image. "A groom from the public house vows he saw Mr. Trent through the window, lit from within as if he had those new gas candles under his skin. He says Mr. Trent"—her voice lowered into breathy significance—"must have been a ghoul."

"Ghouls do not exist, Aunt," Helen said sharply, finding comfort in the solid ground of rationality. She did not share her aunt's fascination with the demons and ghosts of Gothic novels. Yet the shocking image of blood and fear still resonated through her bones. She walked across to the front window and stared out at the everyday activity on Half Moon Street, as if seeing the row of town houses and the aproned oysterman delivering his barrels would somehow rid her of its grisly echoes. Poor Delia. How she must be suffering.

"Did she ever say anything about Mr. Trent?" Aunt Leonore asked. "He did not seem to have any connections, and no one has any knowledge of him. It is all very strange. One could even say unnatural." She clearly did not want to give up the idea of supernatural intervention.

"Delia never mentioned a Mr. Trent," Helen had to admit, "and I'm sure she would have told me if she had a suitor. It cannot be more than a fortnight since I saw her last." She made a quick count back to the last pre-Season assembly they had both attended. "No, it has been over a month." She turned from the window. "I saw her despair growing, Aunt. I should have called on her more often, but I have been too busy with these silly preparations."

Even as she uttered the word *silly*, Helen knew it was a misstep.

Aunt Leonore drew a deep breath. "They are not silly preparations. Tomorrow must be perfect in all ways. *All ways.* Come back here and sit down. I have nightmares of you loping around like that in front of the Queen."

Since every move in the presence of Queen Charlotte was strictly controlled by the Palace chamberlains, Aunt Leonore's horror was not going to come to pass. Nevertheless, Helen returned to the sofa and lowered herself onto the very edge of the seat. Perhaps if she sat very still, her aunt would not be compelled to launch into another lecture about the importance of a young lady's Court presentation.

"Preparation is the key to elegance," her aunt continued, "and although we may not be beauties, we can be celebrated for our elegance. It lasts longer than beauty and . . ."

Helen clenched her hands in her lap, trying to squeeze away the urge to spring up and pace the room as her aunt talked. Poor Delia must be beside herself.

". . . aside from a girl's wedding day, her presentation is the most momentous day in her life. It is a declaration to society that she is a woman and ready to take on a woman's responsibilities. Are you listening to me, Helen?"

"Yes, Aunt."

Of course she knew that her entrance into society was important. Yet the initial excitement of stepping into the wider world had long been overshadowed by the fact that it was all aimed at her own marriage. Not that she was against marriage—quite the contrary. It brought with it a household and the greater freedoms of a married woman. No, what grated was her uncle's intention to arrange her betrothal by the end of the year, as if an alliance in her first Season would prove that his good *ton* had finally overcome the taint of her mother.

Perhaps she was being singular again, but she wanted more than just one Season to meet the men of her circle. At present she could claim only one truly congenial acquaintance amongst them—her brother's closest friend, the Duke of Selburn—and while he was very personable, one man of near thirty years of age was hardly a full exploration of possible life mates. It seemed patently obvious to Helen that no one's real character could be discovered in a few months of balls and parties—even with her special talent to read expressions—yet that was how many matches were made. Millicent, who had also secured a place on the presentation list, had no qualms about a quick betrothal, but poor Delia had understood Helen's stance. Indeed, when they were all at Miss Holcromb's—three years past now—it had been Delia who had always tempered their daydreams with the knowledge that once a choice of husband was made, it was final. There could be no appeal to law or family.

Helen straightened at the memory of Delia's caution. What had made her friend forget her convictions and rush into such an unfortunate and tragic alliance?

"Aunt, I cannot reconcile this with the Delia that I know," she said, turning the conversation back to the plight of her friend. "I cannot understand it at all."

"No one can know the secrets of another person's soul," Aunt Leonore said. "Perhaps she was unbalanced by her feelings."

"Delia is not the kind of girl to be sent mad by love," Helen said. She looked at the clock again. It was only a quarter past two—still time to make a call. "I know you want me to rest, Aunt, but may we call on the Cransdons? Please. Delia must be distraught."

"I am sorry for your friend's unhappy situation, Helen, but you cannot associate with her now. You must know that."

Helen sat even straighter, this time in protest. "I cannot abandon her."

"You are a sweet girl, but the family has already left for their estate. I could not sanction a visit anyway. Not now." Aunt Leonore pressed her hand over Helen's, the chill of the spring day still on her skin. "You do understand that it is best that she is removed to the country. Her fall is the talk of the town: staying here would be intolerable for her poor family. She would be the object of every quiz's gaze and society's disgust."

"I will not let her think I've turned my face," Helen said.

Aunt Leonore glanced at the closed doors and lowered her voice. "Write her a letter, then. I can allow that. And I will make sure your uncle franks it before he hears of the scandal."

"But, Aunt, Delia was going to come to my ball. And she was to make up one of my party at Lansdale for Michaelmas."

"I am afraid that is all in the past."

"Please, say she may still come to Lansdale."

"Good Lord, child. After this, your uncle would not hear of it."

"Surely we have enough credit to survive a visit from one girl," Helen said, unable to hold back the sharpness in her voice. "On Uncle's own estate."

"I am thinking of you, Helen. I cannot allow you to be associated with such wanton and ungodly behavior."

"But in country society she will not be—"

"I am sorry." Helen saw real regret in the slump of her aunt's shoulders. "You cannot afford to be associated with *any* scandal. You know why."

Helen bowed her head. She did know why: the daughter of Lady Catherine would be watched by the *beau monde* for any sign of bad blood. Even by association.

"You do understand, don't you?"

"Yes, of course."

Aunt Leonore patted her hand. "You are a good girl. I have always said it."

They both looked up as clattering hooves sounded on the narrow street outside. A smart phaeton passed recklessly close to their front window, two straining grays in the traces. For a moment the brash eyes of the high-seated driver connected with Helen's, his wild exhilaration leaping across the well-ordered room. Helen found herself leaning forward as if dragged into the wake of such abandon. What if she just ordered one of her uncle's carriages and caught up with Delia on the open road? A mad idea, but it flared hot for a moment in her veins.

"Someone should put a stop to such wicked driving in Mayfair," Aunt Leonore said, glaring at the now-empty street. She gave Helen's hand one last squeeze. "Write the letter, but do not dwell on your friend's disgrace, my dear. You must put it out of your mind."

"I will try," Helen said, and, as she had done many times in the last few months, quelled the inner fire that rushed through her body. Although she did not want to admit it, she could not escape the thought that it was her mother's blood that burned within her, nor the fact that it seemed to be getting stronger.

Two

A few hours later, Helen was in her bedchamber finishing the letter to Delia at the drop desk of her mahogany secretaire, when a knock sounded on the door.

"Come," she said, still intent on writing the final sentence in the dwindling light.

Hugo, the first footman, entered and bowed. He placed a newly trimmed oil lamp on the mantel, then crossed the room toward the sash windows to close the inner shutters against the press of night. As he passed the desk, Helen was sure she felt his eyes fix upon her letter. She looked up, but he was already at the far window, reaching for the heavy brass shutter latch.

Pulling the page closer, Helen tapped the excess ink from her pen and made her signature, the usual flourish of it somewhat subdued.

It had been a difficult letter to write: what words could bring consolation after such a devastating mistake, especially when the facts were so few and the story had become embroidered with the supernatural? In the end, Helen had decided to barely mention the event, instead choosing to reassure Delia of her own regard. It was no small pledge: steadfast friendship with a ruined girl was not going to add to Helen's good *ton*. She knew her aunt would prefer that she cut the connection completely, but until that was said aloud, she would continue to write to her friend. It was the only support she could offer while under the guardianship of her uncle, Viscount Pennworth.

A sprinkle of sand across the wet ink, a quick tap and shake of the page, and the letter was ready to be folded and sealed. Helen chose a wafer from the little drawer within the secretaire, dampened it on a sea sponge, and fixed the ends of the paper together. She turned the packet over and wrote the directions to the Cransdons' estate, leaving a space for her uncle's free-post frank.

All done, for what it was worth.

"Hugo," she called.

He stood at the gilt wall sconce lighting the last candle with a long taper. "Yes, my lady?"

She held out the letter. "Make sure this goes to my aunt, please. Not Lord Pennworth."

He snuffed the taper's wick between his finger and thumb—a sidelong glance checking that she saw the show—and crossed the carpet between them. With a bow, he took the letter, but his attention was not on the task or on Helen. His eyes were turning over the contents of the secretaire—her only private space—but it was too late to close the desk hatch. His bland expression had already tightened into sharp interest. She knew what he had found: two tiny portraits propped against the back of the inner shelf. The matched miniatures of her mother and father, painted by the great Sir Joshua Reynolds.

Abruptly, she stood, blocking his view.

"That will be all, thank you," she said.

"My lady," he murmured, but she could hear the smug elation in his voice. He had snatched a juicy morsel of gossip for the servants' hall.

As he left the room, Helen took out the portrait of her mother, as if to reclaim it from the footman's sly gaze. Lady Catherine had specifically bequeathed both miniatures to her, along with the secretaire, yet her uncle had nearly denied her possession of the precious paintings. He had flatly refused to have any images of his sister-in-law and her husband in his house. It was only Aunt Leonore's intervention that had allowed Helen to keep the portraits in her chamber, on the understanding that she would not openly display them.

She cradled the small oval pendant in her palm. The miniature always surprised her with its weight—probably the glass covers set over front and back, and the substantial gold frame, although the edging was not solid, but a delicate filigree with a plain gold loop at the top for a chain. Ten years ago, on the long nights when she had fiercely studied the little portrait to stop herself from crying, she had discovered that the gold tracery held a motif: a tiny flame repeated over and over. If it had any special meaning, it was long gone with her mother, but it made a pretty design.

Reynolds had painted Lady Catherine on ivory, using the precious substance to re-create the luster of the Countess's pale skin. Rich auburn hair, dressed high in the old manner, and large blue eyes dominated the oval face that, with its decided chin, was more handsome than beautiful. Reynolds had also captured something of Lady Catherine's famed daring in his masterful depiction of her clear, challenging gaze.

Why did she betray England?

Helen turned over the little frame. She had heard so many different rumors about what her mother had supposedly done—some had her spying for Napoleon, stealing state documents, seducing generals and selling their secrets—none of which her aunt and uncle would confirm or deny. They simply refused to talk about the subject. Even Andrew did not know the truth. Or if he did, he would not talk about it either.

With a gentle fingertip, she traced the woven swath of hair pressed underneath the glass at the back. Two colors—dark red and bright blond—were worked into a tight checkerboard pattern. Her mother's and father's hair entwined for eternity.

She took one of her own carefully contrived ringlets and inspected it with a frown. By no stretch of the imagination could anyone call her hair auburn. It was brown. Helen dropped the ringlet. She might not have her mother's fiery hair, but she did have the same pale skin, and her chin was just as decided. That, as far as she could see in any mirror, was the extent of her inheritance from Lady Catherine. She bent to replace the miniature on the shelf.

What about the strange energy that coursed through her?

The thought stopped Helen's hand. Could her mother's blood be blamed for all her restlessness? Or was it her own wayward nature? Neither option brought any comfort. Forcing the disquiet from her mind, she carefully replaced the miniature beside its companion.

The sound of a door opening along the hallway turned her attention outward. Lately, her hearing had become more acute—a baffling but useful development. She heard the door click shut, quick footsteps, and the scrape of an opening drawer. Her maid, Darby, had arrived in the adjoining dressing room to prepare the evening toilette.

Reassured, Helen picked up her father's portrait. It also had the flame motif worked into its gold frame, but this time it was fashioned as the loop to hold a chain or riband. There was no woven hair under the glass at the back—just plain white silk. Helen contemplated the painting of Douglas Wrexhall, sixth Earl of Hayden. It was like looking at an image of her brother: the same golden hair, broad forehead, and firm mouth. Andrew had inherited all their father's good looks, but—according to Aunt Leonore in her more exasperated moments—none of his good sense. Then again, their father had been a married man at twenty-one, whereas Andrew, who had just come of age himself, had made it clear he was in no hurry to enter the matrimonial state.

It had been a month since Andrew had attained his majority, and during that time a tantalizing question had gathered momentum in Helen's mind. Now that her brother had control of his fortune and no immediate desire to marry, could he be persuaded to set up a town house for them both? At present he took bachelor lodgings at the Albany, but if he had his own establishment, it would be well within the bounds of propriety for his sister to keep house for him. She would be an excellent hostess, too, and it would save her from Uncle's ready disapproval and Aunt's fussing. She could even ask Delia to stay for the Season; be of *real* service to her friend. Helen chewed her bottom lip. It would answer everything—if Andrew were willing. He was to dine with them that evening; she could ask him before they were called to table. It was a bold scheme, but it was worth a try. Not just for herself, but for poor Delia, too.

Satisfied with her plan, she replaced her father's portrait and sent up her customary prayer for the two missing members of her family—*Keep their souls safe*—although, in truth, she still felt the unfairness of her parents' demise. Why had the raging sea taken them, yet spared their small crew? There was, of course, no answer to that question, just as there was no answer to why Lady Catherine had gone against crown and country. If she had not done so, maybe she and Helen's father would still be alive today. Maybe she would be sitting here, in this room, reassuring her daughter that she'd be at her side throughout the ordeal at the Palace tomorrow. As she should be.

Helen lifted her shoulders and let them drop, trying to shake off the reemergence of her old, childish anger. No use railing against the dead. Neither resentment nor yearning brought them back.

She picked up the portrait of Lady Catherine again. It really was very small—no larger than a gentleman's fob watch and half as thick. Easy to hide. If she truly wanted some essence of her mother at her presentation, she could carry it and no one would be the wiser. Granted, it was a sentimental idea. Maybe even a little superstitious. Yet wasn't it natural for an orphaned daughter to want some remembrance of her mother at one of the most important moments in her life?

The strict rules of presentation dress did not allow anything but a fan to be carried, so hiding the portrait within a reticule was out of the question. Nor could she slide it inside her skintight gloves. Could it be slipped into her décolletage? She looked down at her narrow chest. Unlike the day dress she was wearing, her presentation gown required long stays that had to be laced tight across the bosom, and the neckline was cut very low. There would not be enough room. Besides, there was something just a little unseemly about hiding her mother in such a place.

Perhaps she could conceal the miniature in her hand as she made her curtsy to Queen Charlotte. Helen curled her fingers around it. No, it would not work. She would already have her fan in one hand, and the other had to be free to manage the long train and dreaded hoop. The miniature would be too easily dropped. Unless she attached it to her fan. It was a Vernis Martin—a rare gift from her uncle—with room enough between the painted ivory sticks to thread some cotton. She could hang the miniature from it and keep it nestled in her palm.

Did she dare?

Helen sighed. No, she did not. Her aunt had put too much effort into the smooth success of her presentation, and such a breach of propriety, if discovered, would be poor thanks for all that dear lady's hard work. And if Uncle found out, he would be furious. She did not want to see that triumphant look that said, *You see? She is cut from the same black cloth as her mother.*

Yet she could not quite give up the idea of her mother's presence blessing the day.

Her hand closed around the portrait again. She would take it to her dressing room and hide it amongst the things on her table. Lady Catherine could, at least, be present for the toilette tomorrow.

She shut the desk hatch, turned the lock, and pulled the key free. A quick glance over her shoulder at the adjoining door confirmed that Darby was still in the dressing room. Helen ran her fingers along the lower edge of the desk and found the tiny groove in the banded wood. One firm press followed by a flick to the right, and the small spring-loaded compartment swung out. She had found it on one of her many explorations of the secretaire. Helen slid the key into the shallow slot and pushed the holder home, her mother's portrait clasped in her other hand.

A soft knock sounded from behind the adjoining door: Darby's announcement that it was time to dress for dinner. Helen stepped back from her desk.

"Come."

"Good evening, my lady," Darby said, emerging from the dressing room with an apricot gown draped across her outstretched arms. "Are you ready for your hot water?"

The girl was surrounded by a pale blue shimmer—like tiny ripples in the air—that followed the generous contours of her body. A soft, glowing outline. Helen squeezed her eyes shut. She had obviously worked far too long at the letter to Delia. Lud, she hoped she did not need spectacles. She opened her eyes and shook her head, but the shimmer was still in place. Perhaps it was the migraine. Her aunt suffered greatly from them, and often spoke of seeing strange lights before the terrible headache arrived.

She finally focused on her maid's face. Darby's eyes were swollen into red-rimmed distress, and the soft contours of her mouth had disappeared into a tight line. She had been crying, and Jen

Darby was not one for easy tears. Something must have happened downstairs.

Helen knew that ever since she had promoted Darby from junior maid to the exalted role of lady's maid six months ago, some of the more senior housemaids had been waging a campaign of petty meanness against the girl. To make matters worse, neither Murphett nor Mrs. Grant, the housekeeper in charge of the female staff, had done anything to stop it. Neither approved of Jen Darby's advancement to the exclusive ranks of the upper servants. In their opinion she was far too big—"like a lumbering ox," Mrs. Grant had commented once, when she thought Helen could not hear—and did not have the proper daintiness or Town polish required for a lady's maid. Helen had to admit that Darby was not the most delicate of creatures, but she had far more important qualities than mere refinement: a quickness, for instance, that matched Helen's own, and a bright curiosity. It had only been Helen's obstinate refusal to accept any other candidate that had swayed Mrs. Grant to allow the promotion. Such a leap in status without due cause, the formidable housekeeper had been heard to mutter, went against the natural order.

Ignoring the faint blue shimmer, Helen rose from her chair. "Are you quite well, Darby?" she asked as the maid laid the gown on the four-poster bed.

"I'm very well, my lady. Very well, thank you," Darby said, but the last of her words rose into the squeaky gasp of a held-back sob.

"I'm glad you are so well," Helen said. "If you were any more well, you might break down altogether." It prompted a tiny smile, as she knew it would. "Please, tell me what is wrong," she urged.

Darby bowed her head for a moment, gathering herself, then looked up with the frankness that had been another reason why

Helen had raised her so high. "My anxiety is not for me, my lady. It is for Berta. One of the housemaids."

Helen recalled the girl: a new Bavarian émigré, long-limbed and darkly handsome, with a habit of holding her hand over her mouth when she spoke. She usually lit the morning fires in Helen's rooms, but had not done so for the last two days. "What is wrong? Is she ill?"

"No, my lady," Darby said. "She has disappeared."

"Disappeared?" The word sounded ominous. "When? Why wasn't I told?"

"It happened two days ago. Lady Pennworth told us not to say anything to you. Not before your presentation, anyway." Darby's earnest gray eyes met Helen's in a moment of sudden apprehension. "You won't tell her I said anything, will you, my lady?"

"Of course not. But do you think Berta has run away?"

"It is what they are saying—Mrs. Grant and the others downstairs—but her lockbox is still in the room she shares with the kitchen maids."

Helen nodded. Even the lowest servant had a lockable box for his or her belongings; the circumstance would have to be dire for it to be left behind. She turned Lady Catherine's portrait over and over in her hands, trying to find a reasonable—and unalarming—explanation for the abandoned box. None came to mind. She looked up to find Darby's attention fixed on the gold miniature.

"It is a likeness of my mother," Helen said.

"Yes, my lady. I can see the resemblance."

"Not much of one, I think," Helen said quickly. She closed her hand around it. "It seems unlikely that Berta would leave her belongings."

Darby took a steadying breath. "I don't believe Berta has run away at all, my lady, but Mrs. Grant has told me that I am to say no more about it. The search is over, and that is that." She squared her shoulders as if bracing against the sin of opposing the housekeeper. The shimmer followed the movement.

Helen blinked hard, but the phenomenon still did not shift.

"I would swear on the Good Book that she would not run away," Darby added. "Her mother relies upon her wages."

"You think she has come to some kind of harm?"

"I don't know. She went out of the house on Monday morning—an errand for Mrs. Grant—and no one saw her after that. The others are saying she's taken her looks to Covent Garden for better money. But she is a good, God-fearing girl, my lady. I am sure she would not do so."

Helen knew she should feign ignorance of the notorious grid of streets where hundreds of courtesans plied their trade. Yet such delicacy would be of no use to Berta. "Did the search for her take in the Garden? Does she have a father to make inquiries?"

"She has only her mother, up north, I believe. My lord did send out Hugo and Philip to look for her when she was missed." Darby gave a small shrug, an eloquent opinion on the footmen's diligence. "Philip said that he spoke to a lad—a page—who saw something at the same time that Berta disappeared. . . ." She faltered.

"What did he see?"

Darby wrapped her arms around her body. The shimmer curved around the new hunched contour. "I am not saying there is any connection, my lady."

Helen caught the wary note in her voice. "You can tell me," she said. "Whatever it is."

"The boy told Philip he saw a coach. A *gentleman's* coach."

"You think she has been taken by a gentleman?" Helen stared at her maid. Surely that was not possible. Then again, if the tales Andrew told about some of his friends were true, it was more than possible. Helen closed her eyes: if Berta had indeed been taken, she was lost to all decent society.

"I don't know what to do, my lady. Do you think the Runners would help?"

Helen did not. Her uncle said the Bow Street Runners were not much better than the criminals they chased, and the alternatives—the thief-takers for hire—were even worse. In a case with no clear crime, involving only a housemaid, Helen doubted the Runners would bother to investigate. By any measure of decency, it was her uncle's responsibility to find his servant. And there was no surety that she was actually missing. She might have decided the Garden was more lucrative after all.

"Is there any possibility that Berta *did* run away?" Helen asked. "Perhaps she was not happy. Or maybe she did want more money. For her mother."

Darby stepped back, her face freezing into the impassive mask of service. "I am sorry, my lady. I should not have bothered you," she said stiffly. "Please forgive me." She turned to the dress on the bed, smoothing out the silk.

Helen closed her fingers even more tightly around the miniature, wretchedly aware that she had not lived up to some expectation. Was it her own or Darby's? The failure sat like a cold stone in her chest. But what could she do? She could not even visit a friend who was in need. Helen opened her hand and looked down at her mother. Lady Catherine's clear blue gaze seemed to hold a rebuke.

"I do not disbelieve you," Helen said.

"Everyone else does, my lady." Darby's voice was small. "They think she is just another fallen girl. But someone has to keep looking for her, don't they?"

"Yes, of course," Helen said. Yet what could Darby do? If Berta had run away to Covent Garden, she was beyond help. And if a gentleman was involved, a mere lady's maid could not confront him. No one would listen to a servant above a gentleman or, worse, a nobleman.

"I will ask my brother," Helen finally said. "If it is, indeed, a gentleman, maybe the Earl has heard something amongst his acquaintances."

Darby pressed her hands to her tear-streaked cheeks. "Thank you, my lady," she said, dipping into a curtsy. "I was certain you would know what to do. Thank you."

"He may know nothing," Helen warned.

"Yes, my lady. But something is being done for Berta, and that makes me so much easier. I feared she would just be forgotten."

"That will not happen," Helen said. "I promise we will find her, however long it takes."

She smiled reassuringly and headed into the dressing room, the rashness of her words weighing heavier and heavier with every step. Why had she made such a pledge? It was going to be almost impossible to locate one girl amongst all the other forgotten girls in the ravenous maw of the city.

Helen knew about the dangers outside her door. Every month she read the "Incidents Occurring in and near London" in *La Belle Assemblée*: a blood-curdling list of all the local murders and cruelties set out on the pages straight after the fashion forecast. At Christmas the papers had been full of the shocking Ratcliffe Highway murders, the brutal slaughter of two innocent families described for weeks in gore-soaked detail. And now, in *The Times*, there were daily reports of savage attacks by those calling themselves Luddites: desperate working men destroying the new machinery destined to replace them, and setting upon their employers with clubs and guns. All of the gruesome accounts confirmed that a frightening and ever-present savagery lived in the dark shadows beyond Half Moon Street.

Three paces took Helen past the green chaise longue to the mahogany dressing table. She rubbed her eyes, glad to be free of the unsettling shimmer. Whatever the problem with her sight, it seemed only to occur around Darby. Perhaps the phenomenon was confined to living things. Although, of course, Hugo had not shimmered. Nor, come to think of it, did her own body. If she was of her aunt's turn of mind, she would believe the source to be supernatural, but she was more inclined to invoke Mr. Mesmer's magnetism or Mr. Galvani's animal electricity. Helen shrugged away such whimsical theories—it was most likely fatigue.

A survey of the neatly arranged pots and brushes and bowls on the dressing table found only one suitable hiding place for the miniature: the space between the edge of the mirror and the white potpourri bowl set before it. She propped the portrait in place and stepped back, a crescent of gold frame and her mother's challenging eyes just visible.

By all rights, she should tell Darby that Berta's disappearance was Viscount Pennworth's concern. That it was not appropriate for young ladies or servants to become involved in such grave matters.

"Darby?" she called. "There is something I must say."

Her maid reappeared in the doorway, no longer surrounded by blue. It must have been fatigue after all. "Yes, my lady?"

"I think—" Helen stopped, fancying that she felt a painted gaze upon her back: a tiny press of disappointment. "I think I will wear the cream gloves, not the apricot," she said.

Appropriate or not, she had made a promise to find Berta, and she would keep her word. And, in the end, Darby was right: no one else was going to look for a maid who might have strayed from the path of virtue. Especially not Uncle Pennworth.

Three

WITH HER EVENING toilette finally complete, Helen opened her bedchamber door and checked the third-floor corridor. Empty. She'd have to hurry if she was to catch Andrew alone before they sat down to dinner. There would be no opportunity to speak privately otherwise: Berta's disappearance and the possibility of setting up their own house could hardly be discussed at the table, and Andrew would be obliged to linger over port with Uncle long after she and Aunt withdrew. This was her one chance, at least for a week or so. She lifted the hem of her satin underdress and ran toward the staircase, only the portraits of her uncle's ancestors witnessing the breach of propriety.

At the top of the stairs, she peered down into the depths of the central foyer. Luck was still with her; no one was about. Out of habit, she counted the steps on her rapid downward journey, coming to a breathless stop on number forty-two, the first-floor landing. A strong smell of roast beef had risen on the warm air from the basement kitchen, mixing with the waxy smoke of the evening candles. Dinner must be very near service.

Opposite, the drawing room doors were closed. Was Andrew already caught inside with Aunt and Uncle, or had he taken refuge in the billiard room, as usual? Helen leaned over the banister and listened. From below came the muted clash of kitchen pots, the throbbing night song of her aunt's canary, and, just faintly, the click-clack of billiard balls. Aha. Helen smiled and, hitching the hem of her dress even higher above her ankles, ran down the last twenty steps.

At the bottom, she rounded the banister straight into the path of Philip, the second footman, struggling to straighten his powdered wig. His hands snapped to his sides.

"My lady!" He dipped his head, the wig a little askew atop his copper hair, and stepped smartly back against the wall.

"Philip!" She looked up through the balustrade at the closed drawing room doors on the floor above. "Are my aunt and uncle down yet?"

"Yes, my lady. They have sent me to request Lord Hayden's company."

Lud, it was later than she thought: Aunt and Uncle would be looking for her next. Helen edged sideways, behind the rise of the staircase. "Lord Hayden is in the billiard room, is he not?" she whispered, waving vigorously for Philip to join her concealment.

It was no easy task for either of them, since Helen was close on five-foot-nine and Philip was over six-two, having recently been hired to match Hugo in both stature and—as her aunt often remarked—shapely calves. An important requirement, Helen had observed blandly to Millicent, as the footmen's red and gold livery was quite tightly fitted.

"He is, my lady," Philip said, obediently sidestepping along the wall. His blue eyes were watery, and there was an awkwardness about him that was not usually present. Another victim, perhaps, of the seasonal cold that was running rife through the household.

"Philip, can you"—Helen paused, knowing she was putting him on the spot—"can you dally? It will be worth your while."

"For how long, my lady?" Helen saw the real question in the dilation of his eyes: *How much?*

She opened the metal clasp of her reticule and fished inside, her fingers closing on the flat round of a farthing. "Make it ten minutes," she said, dropping the coin into his gloved palm. "I don't want to get you into trouble."

"Ten minutes." He bowed, the coin already inside his waistcoat pocket.

"And, Philip," she added, "Darby tells me that you spoke to the page who last saw Berta before she disappeared."

His hand went to his cravat. "Yes, my lady." He looked up through the rungs of the balustrade, his voice lowering into an even softer whisper. "That is, my lady, we were told not to worry you with it."

"It will worry me even more if I do not have the facts."

Philip curled his tongue over his top lip. Helen waited as he pondered his dilemma, the churn of thoughts obvious from the furrow on his freckled brow. By rights, he should follow the wishes of her aunt and uncle, but he was leaning toward the call of future farthings. "The boy was running an errand in Berkeley Street," he finally said, his eyes flicking down to her reticule. "He saw a coach pull up beside Berta, but he couldn't remember much about it. That's all, my lady."

"Did you press him?"

"He's the Holyoakes' page over in Berkeley Square. A good lad. I'm sure he told all he knew."

Helen nodded. "Thank you, Philip. And, remember, if anyone asks, I'm not down yet."

"Of course not, my lady."

She pulled her shawl more securely over her arms, then headed sedately into the corridor that led to the back of the town house. As soon as she turned the corner, she ran for the billiard room.

She slowed as she approached the closed door, frowning at a faint sense of unease. Although she had not read any falseness in Philip's face, there had been something in his expression that had rung sour. The only thing that came to mind was a slight distance. . . . Yes, a lack of interest about Berta's situation. In all fairness, it was not surprising. The man was unwell, and Helen had heard that some of the staff were wary of Berta's foreignness. Yet it raised a doubt about the rigor of Philip's interview with the page: it would not have had the concentration of true concern. If the page had held something back or neglected an important detail, Philip would probably not have noticed.

Admittedly, no one else would be able to see such hesitations or concealments in the same intense manner that she could. How many times had she observed the secret truths etched into the faces of those around her? Truths that were often in contradiction to the handed-down wisdom of society. She had seen keen intelligence in Lady Trevayne's black footman, the swift rise of lust in a visiting vicar, and even a look of soul love between two men. Sometimes such knowledge shook her, but she could not ignore the evidence of her eyes. Nor could she refuse to use her ability to help another in distress. If her promise to Darby was to have any value, then she would have to interview the page herself and make her own judgment.

Now, all she had to do was work out a way to manage such an intrusion upon a household with which she had no acquaintance.

She paused at the door of the billiard room, intent upon another intrusion. This was a male sanctum, and while she was not expressly forbidden to enter, it was understood that a lady would not venture inside. One quick glance at the empty corridor, a rap on the door, and she was over the threshold.

Inside, the air smelled of cigar smoke, candle wax, and claret, the pungent mix locked into the room by the heavy wood paneling, thick red rug, and lack of windows. The long figure of her brother was bent over the far cushion of the billiard table, his cue poised before a ball. He looked up from the green baize, gave a quick smile of welcome, then returned to his contemplation of the shot.

"Hello, sprite," he said, sliding the cue between his fingers to line up the angle. "Come to play stick with me?" Snorting at his own joke, he slammed the cue tip into the ivory ball. It cannoned into a red ball, sending it spinning into a corner pocket. "Did you see that? Selburn couldn't do better. What do you say?"

Since Helen had never seen her brother's friend, the Duke of Selburn, play billiards, she resisted commenting on the shot and said instead, "I need to talk to you." She closed the door. "Alone."

Andrew walked out from behind the table, eyeing his next shot. "You'll catch the devil from Uncle if he finds you in here."

"He won't." Helen waved away the consideration with a bravado hand.

She took in her brother's outfit with guarded approval. For the most part, he followed the dictates of Mr. Brummell—the acknowledged leader of fashion—with regards to his attire: superb tailoring and subdued colors to create an understated elegance and heroic shape. Andrew's evening jacket was of Spanish blue and cut to make the best of his athletic stature, his satin breeches were impeccably fitted, and his crisp white cravat cascaded in a fall of intricate folds. But he had faltered with his waistcoat: pea-green and embroidered with a riot of blue and pink flowers. It seemed that Andrew, like the Prince Regent, had a weakness for bright satin and embroidery, two things definitely not within Beau Brummell's philosophy.

"I do like that jacket," Helen offered, overlooking the waistcoat. Nothing pleased her brother more than a compliment on his attire.

He brightened. "Weston. Fine, isn't it." He patted one closely fitted sleeve. "You look very well too, sis. Are you all set for tomorrow?" He looked around the room as if he had lost something. "There," he said, tipping the end of the cue at a small box on the mantel. "For you."

"Really?" Helen was momentarily diverted.

"Just a fal-lal for the big event." He grinned, obviously enjoying her surprise.

It had always been easy for Helen to read her brother's expressions. Unlike herself, he allowed every emotion he experienced to play across his face. Such openness had made it very easy for her to beat him in their childhood card games, but also to know when he had needed time alone or a sympathetic ear. She skirted the billiard table and picked up the gift. A red Morocco case that, if she were not mistaken, was from Rundell, Bridge and Rundell—the very best. She glanced across at her brother; his grin had widened with anticipation.

"Go on, open it," he urged.

She slid the two tiny brass hooks free from their catches and lifted the lid. Inside were four gold-and-diamond hairpins wrought in the shape of laurel wreaths. The diamond clusters flared in the candlelight as Helen ran her finger across the finely sculpted pins. They would do beautifully at the back of her coiffure, holding in the lace lappets and huge ostrich plumes that the Queen insisted every woman wear at her Drawing Rooms.

"Oh, Andrew, they are lovely. Thank you."

"Aunt told me what you needed. Mind you, *I* chose 'em." He bent over the table again, lining up his shot. "So, what's all the hush-hush about?"

Helen lingered for a moment more, tilting the box to watch the diamonds shimmer, then resolutely shut the lid. "Drew," she said slowly, "do you think you will set up your own establishment here in London soon?"

Andrew straightened, resting the end of his cue on the rug.

"Now, that's a loaded question if ever I heard one. Has Aunt got in your ear again about me marrying?"

"No, not at all." She hesitated, suddenly confronted by the indelicacy of what she was about to ask. "In truth, it is about me marrying. Or not marrying, as it were."

"What are you gibbling about?" Andrew said. "*Not* marrying? I thought marrying was all you girls ever thought about. Don't you want to be mistress of your own household?"

"That's just it—I do want to be mistress of a household. *Your* household."

She watched him pass through perplexity, reasoning, and finally into understanding, his brow clearing as he came to her point. "You certainly are one for the deep game. All the freedoms of a married lady without the husband, hey?"

"It has been done before," Helen said, catching a note of dismissal in his voice. "Many girls act as hostess for their widowed father or an uncle."

Andrew nodded. "Yes, but not often for a brother. At least, not at your age. It's usually spinsterish old cats who take on the job. You know I'd end up acting your chaperone instead of you acting my hostess." He raised his eyebrows, inviting agreement, but Helen stonily resisted. With an amused smile, he added, "You're an heiress, sis, and not bad-looking. You're going to get offers. In fact, I'm going to have to beat 'em off with a stick." He jabbed the end of the cue at an imaginary suitor. "No need to get yourself into a pucker."

Helen lifted her chin. "I am not in a pucker." She turned the jewel box over in her hands, weighing her brother's buoyant mood against her own disquiet. Andrew was not one for tackling difficult subjects. He was likely to withdraw if she mentioned their mother, but he needed to understand. "Aunt is afraid the scandal will affect my chances of marrying well."

"Really?" He grinned. "I can't say I've felt any effect in that area."

"That is because you are not the *daughter* of Lady Catherine," Helen said flatly. Their parentage had never been a burden for Andrew—he was, after all, the seventh Earl of Hayden, with vast estates and good looks that excused all. No, it seemed that corruption only passed through the female line. "Aunt told me this morning that I should distance myself from Mother should the Queen mention her tomorrow."

Andrew rolled one of the red billiard balls under his hand. "I doubt the Queen would say anything," he said, but the teasing humor was gone from his face.

"True," Helen said. "Still, denying Mother feels wrong. Don't you agree?"

The silence felt ominous. "You should do as Aunt says," Andrew finally said. "She knows about these things. Mother forwent our loyalty. The less we are associated with her, the better."

She met the flint in his eyes. "Do you really mean that?"

"Yes." He looked away, making a business of placing the red ball back into position. "You must think of yourself now."

His broad shoulders had rounded over. He was already drawing into himself.

"Well, then, I will take your advice and think only of myself," she said brightly, coaxing him back. "Let me be your hostess. It would be such fun—we could hold dinners and dances, and I would have a chance to talk to people properly and find someone I like. Aunt is a dear, but she does hover over me. And Uncle would have me take the first man who comes along. Think of it, Drew. You wouldn't have to stay in those nasty rooms. Always a clean bed and good food. Aunt has taught me how to manage a household beautifully."

And, Helen thought, observing the dark shadows under her brother's eyes, she might be able to stop him from burning himself to a frazzle. Even she had heard he had been frequenting the worst gaming hells and taverns.

Andrew shook his head. "Aunt and Uncle wouldn't have it for a minute."

Admittedly, it was a sticking point. "They would if you asked them," she said firmly.

"I doubt it. And I get good food at my club. I'm sorry, sprite, but I'm not in any hurry to set up."

Helen pulled out her trump card. "It would stop Aunt from pressing you to marry. At least for a while."

Andrew eyed her with respect. "It might, at that."

"Please, Drew." She could see by the little knit between his eyes that he was wavering. "Please."

He frowned up at the ceiling as if its ornate plaster rose and chandelier might hold the answer to her request. "I don't think it will come to it," he finally said. "Aunt is worrying for no reason. You'll have your Season and you'll meet some fellow who'll suit you and the family just right, and that will be that." Helen opened her mouth to protest, but he hurried on. "If, by a slim chance, you aren't buckled by the end of the year, we can talk again." He held up his hand. "Not promising anything. Just saying that I know you, and if you haven't got an escape route, you get all lathered. We can talk again at Christmas. Does that suit?"

It did not suit at all. Michaelmas was well before Christmas. Poor Delia would be stuck in Sussex for all of the London Season. "But, Drew—"

His mouth tightened. "We'll talk at Christmas."

"But it will take months to find a suitable—"

"We'll talk at Christmas. That's my offer. Agreed?"

Andrew did not often stand firm, but Helen knew this was one of those rare times. She would have to wait.

"Agreed," she said, forcing a smile. Andrew held out his hand.

She shook it three times, as they used to when they were children, and added, "There's something else, Drew. I've had some rather troubling news. Darby, my maid, has told me that one of the housemaids has gone missing."

Andrew shrugged. "That's Uncle's concern, not yours." He reached into the table's side pocket and pulled out another red ball, positioning it on the baize. "You're not having another fit of *noblesse oblige,* are you?"

Helen folded her arms, ignoring the jibe at her failed effort to save Jonathan the footman's position after he'd been accused of stealing wine from the cellar. He had been cleared of the charge, but their uncle had still dismissed him without a reference. "Darby has come to me with a problem," she said crisply, "and I want to help."

"Well, she shouldn't have come to you. Ought to have known better." Andrew fixed her with a stern gaze. "You can't help everyone. Like I said, it is Uncle's concern."

"Yes, but they think the maid has gone—" Helen waved in the general direction of Covent Garden.

"They think she's gone Cyprian?"

Helen nodded, unfazed by the vulgar term. "Darby says it is not possible. And there is a witness who claims the girl may have been taken by a gentleman. In his carriage." She saw that information register on her brother's face. "Have you heard anything, Drew? Any rumor?"

"Sounds like hum to me." He slid the cue through his fingers, a thought shifting his jaw.

"You do know something. Tell me," Helen demanded.

"It's just that I saw Carlston at the theater last night."

"Carlston?"

"William Standfield, the Earl of Carlston." Andrew's voice had hardened. "You probably wouldn't know the story—it was at least three years ago, when you were at that school."

The name did have a familiar ring. She had heard it in one of those whispered cautionary tales that her friends had shared. "Didn't he kill someone?"

"His wife. The Countess of Carlston, formerly Elise de Vraine." Andrew paused, his face softening. "She was lovely. French. Escaped the Terror as a child, then had the bad luck to run into Carlston. Everyone knows he killed her, but no body was found and so he was never tried. Still, the King turned his back, and no one would receive him after that. The rumor was that he went to the Continent."

"And now he has returned," Helen breathed, imagining a black-cloaked figure sweeping up innocent girls.

"Trying to worm himself back into society," Andrew said caustically. "He'll do it too. He was with Prinny at the theater, and Brummell always liked him."

Helen's image of a dastardly abductor disappeared in a wave of logic. "He would hardly be making off with housemaids if he is trying to reestablish himself."

"True, although there was talk that he'd attacked a maid, too, as well as Lady Elise." With a jerk of his wrist, Andrew spun the billiard ball across the table. It slammed into another with a sharp crack, sending both ricocheting into the cushions. "He should not have come back."

Helen struggled to identify this new harsh edge in her brother's voice. Anger? No, it was more like bitterness.

A knock on the door made them both turn.

"Come," Andrew said.

Philip entered and bowed. "My lord," he said, keeping his eyes on Andrew. "Lord and Lady Pennworth request that you join them in the drawing room."

"Thank you. Has Lady Pennworth been asking for Lady Helen, too?"

"I have not seen Lady Helen," Philip said woodenly. He withdrew, closing the door behind him.

"Are you bribing the servants again?" Andrew asked. He placed his cue back into the mahogany rack on the wall.

"Perhaps it *is* Lord Carlston," Helen said, ignoring the question. "Do you think he is capable of abducting girls so blatantly?"

Andrew walked to her side and, with a small bow, held out his arm. "Let's go up before Aunt starts missing you."

Helen placed her hand on his elbow. "But do you, Drew? Do you think he is capable of it?"

"I think Carlston is capable of anything," Andrew said, leading her toward the door. "For God's sake, don't go spreading some half-baked idea that he's abducting housemaids."

"Then promise me you'll keep an eye on him."

"I'll do no such thing," Andrew said. "I'm not having anything to do with the man."

Helen looked up, ready to press her request, but his expression stopped her words. She had never seen such dislike on his face. Lord Carlston must be vile, indeed, to cause such violent feelings in her good-natured brother.

"I want you to stay away from him too," Andrew continued. "I know what you are like when you have the bit between your teeth, but Carlston is dangerous." He stopped their progress and looked squarely into her eyes. "I am not funning, Helen. Remember what he did to his wife."

"I won't go near the man," she promised.

Of course, she added privately, that did not mean she couldn't watch Lord Carlston from a safe distance away.

Four

Thursday, 30 April 1812

At half past nine the following morning, Helen stood in the middle of her dressing room, arms held up and spread out to either side over the waxed calico-and-whalebone hoop tied at her waist. The wide frame dragged at her hips for a moment as Darby tugged the heavily embroidered white silk petticoat over its expanse. It was only the first of the four layers that made up her presentation gown, but Helen already felt weighed down by the volume of cloth and outmoded hoop.

How had her mother and aunt ever worn such cumbersome things every day? Or, indeed, endured the pain of the old-fashioned headdress required for Court?

She dug her forefinger under one of the stiff pads of false hair that supported the heavy plume of ostrich feathers, and found a space between the layer of hairdresser's grease and the hard web of pins. Gently, she levered a few away from her scalp, easing the tight pull on her own hair. That felt better. The movement sent a waft of oily jasmine pomade into the warm air. She coughed, setting the hoop into a small sway.

"My lady, please," Darby pleaded, looking up from straightening the hem.

Helen steadied the silk-encased hoop with the flat of her hands as Darby smoothed one last fold into place. The girl was frowning with concentration, the tip of her tongue between her lips like a six-year-old at her letters. Last night Helen had told her that the Earl had no certain knowledge of Berta's disappearance, and Darby had received that news with fortitude. Still, her sadness was obvious beneath her fierce focus upon the toilette. Particularly since she had agreed with Helen that the Earl's only suggestion for a perpetrator—Lord Carlston—seemed to be based more upon his own dislike than any firm fact. And, of course, if Lord Carlston was involved, there would be little chance of recovering Berta. Helen tucked in her chin at the thought. *Dear God, protect the girl from such a man.*

Darby rose from her knees. "Bring the satin, please." She waved over the two housemaids who stood waiting with the white, high-waisted dress decorated with lavish panels of silver embroidery, its neckline thickly bordered with pearls.

Darby's soft commands deftly marshaled their efforts, and the next three layers—satin dress, translucent tulle skirt, and embroidered net skirt sprinkled with more pearls and glass spangles—were successfully thrown over the plumage and hoop. Finally Helen threaded her arms through the cutaway white velvet bodice that held the train, and Darby secured the tiny pearl buttons and large diamond buckle under her bust.

"Finished, my lady."

Darby stepped back. They looked at each other and smiled.

The maids spread the train behind Helen: a four-foot sweep of white velvet and silk worked in more pearls, glass beads, and silver-embroidered flowers.

"It's so beautiful, my lady," whispered Tilly, the younger of the two. "It's like lookin' at a frozed-up stream, all shimmerin' like."

The other girl, Beth, nodded her dark head enthusiastically.

"Tilly, you were not asked for your opinion," Darby said. She took Helen's right hand and carefully worked the long white kid glove over her fingers.

"No, it is all right." Helen smiled at the young housemaid. Tilly's comment was not just lip service—sincere admiration brightened her eyes. "I think it looks like a frozen stream too."

With both skintight gloves smoothed into place, Helen took the few steps to the mirror. She had, of course, practiced wearing the hoop, and the toilette had been rehearsed, but neither she nor the maids had seen the whole effect until now. What struck her most was the expanse of skin above the pearl-encrusted neckline. The gown was off the shoulder and cut very low, as Court required, and the thick pearl border drew attention to the pale smooth hemispheres of her breasts. She could not stop looking at those two curves, far more exposed than they had ever been before. There was something very unsettling about such an exhibition of one's self. And yet, something rather satisfying.

"It is a little ridiculous to pair a high-waisted dress with a hoop, don't you think?" she murmured, although the magnificence of her costume and hair took the bite from her words. She had to admit that she felt a little splendid.

"Helen."

It was her uncle's voice from behind the door that led to the hallway. She turned swiftly from the mirror, setting the hoop rocking. Three startled pairs of eyes met her own.

"Go," she whispered to Darby. The girl hastened to the door and opened it a little way, dipping into a curtsy.

"Is my niece able to receive me?" Uncle demanded.

Darby's eyes cut back to her. Reluctantly, Helen nodded.

"Yes, my lord." Darby drew the door fully open.

Lord Pennworth's heavyset figure was clad in a sober green morning coat, and an old-fashioned gray powdered wig emphasized the blue pouches of skin beneath his eyes. The other two maids curtsied.

"So, child, you are in all your finery," he said, scrutinizing her for a long moment, his voice glutinous with catarrh. "Everything overdone as the Queen demands, I see. An affront to good taste and modesty."

Helen felt heat rush to her face, although she should have expected such derision. It was her uncle's often-expressed opinion that the Queen's Court was merely a gilded marketplace of overdressed women trading in unholy gossip.

Lord Pennworth's views on women, and unholiness in general, were often expressed, both at home and in public. He was an admirer of the evangelical Hannah More, although unlike that moderate lady, his own particular brand of piety was made of choler and spit. His vehement campaigning against the bawdy houses had captured the attention of the caricaturists, who had rechristened him Lord Stopcock in their savage cartoons. On one of her midnight forays into his papers, Helen had found a published engraving of him by Cruikshank. She had been forced to stuff her fist in her mouth to stop from laughing at the uncanny depiction of him as a cockerel: huge barrel chest thrust out, round eyes bulging, and florid face colored in the bloated red of the coxcomb drawn atop his head.

"Uncle, I was not expecting you." Helen dipped into her own curtsy and made a quick search of his face as she rose: his small, dry-skinned mouth was pursed into a tight bud, the sure sign of a lecture.

"Leave us," he told the servants.

After another deferential bob each, the two housemaids hurried from the room, but Darby's agonized eyes met Helen's for an instant before shifting to the miniature still half visible from behind the potpourri bowl. Neither of them was close enough to hide it from view.

"You too, Darby," Uncle ordered.

Darby curtsied again and followed the other girls.

Helen estimated the distance to the dressing table: a few steps and her hoop would block any view of it. That is, if she could get there before her uncle's keen eye did. She made to move, but he was already over the threshold and occupying the center of the room.

"Your aunt tells me that she instructed you to prepare an answer for Her Majesty should she question you about your mother."

"Yes, Uncle."

"Show me."

She sank into the low Court curtsy, eyes kept firmly away from the draw of the portrait. "Yes, Your Majesty, my mother was Lady Catherine."

Her uncle's gray brows twitched inward. Perhaps she should have put more mildness into the tone. "I would hope that you would not look so boldly at Her Majesty." He gestured her up with an impatient hand.

"No, of course not."

He took a step toward the dressing table, his hands rubbing together in a dry scrape. Surely he would see the miniature.

"Uncle, has any progress been made in finding Berta?" She smiled to temper the suddenness of the question. He was looking at her blankly, but at least it had pulled his attention away from the table. "The missing maid," she prompted.

He grunted. "I have done as much as my duty demands. The girl has gone, and that is that."

"But, Uncle, she has left her lockbox—"

He held up his hand. "It is not your concern. Your duty is to present yourself with proper dignity today." He settled back onto his heels, arms crossed. "I have been thinking long on this matter of comment about your mother. It is unlikely that Her Majesty will make mention. However, I feel sure that you will encounter impertinences from other women at the palace, and afterward at the various enjoyments of the Season. You must ignore them if you can. If you cannot, then you may say this." He cleared his throat with a wet rasp of phlegm. "'My mother drowned at sea, and it was the best outcome for all concerned.'"

Helen's body locked. "I beg your pardon, sir?"

He repeated the words, each one pressing more and more breath from her body. *Best outcome?*

"One should always stay with the truth in these circumstances," he added. "Say it, child. And don't be mealymouthed. If you show your weakness, they will descend upon you like a pack of harpies."

Helen licked her lips. She could not form the words. No, she *would not* form the words. The realization straightened her shoulders.

"Quickly, now. Let me hear you say it."

"Please, Uncle, I cannot say that."

He did not move. Helen searched his face again: his mouth had bunched into tight displeasure. She felt three hard heartbeats measure the ominous passage of time. Finally he drew in a deep breath through pinched nostrils. "This is your ignorance and youth speaking, and no doubt the excitement of the day. Now, repeat the words."

Helen swallowed, her parched throat shriveling her voice. "Forgive me, Uncle, but I cannot think my mother's death was the best outcome."

For a moment he stared at her, skin turning scarlet and a vein in his forehead pulsing into a thick blue ridge. "Is that so?" He thrust his face so close, she could smell the beef on his breath and see the yellowed rims of his eyelids. "Would you rather your mother had been tried and beheaded? The great Lady Catherine, head hacked from her body, the mob ripping at her hair for souvenir?" He drew back. "You are not a dull wit, girl. Even you must see it was the best outcome for the family."

Helen fixed her eyes on the carpet, trying to block the foul image of her mother's headless body slumped over the block, blood pouring over pale spine and sinew—the execution reserved for a treasonous Peer.

He blew out a disgusted breath. "And, I must say, that is fine thanks to your aunt for all her care. She loves you as a daughter, and now you say her tender devotion to you was a bad outcome?"

"No. I did not mean that at all, Uncle."

"You do not know *what* you mean. You speak without thinking, like all of your sex." He took an angry step away. "I cannot stop you from attending this Drawing Room, but, by God, if you cannot do as you are told in public, I *will* stop you from appearing at any other ball or rout." He rounded on her again. "And I will stop the preparations for your ball. I won't have any more disgrace—large or small—associated with this family."

She knew he meant every word: it was in the narrowing of his jaundiced eyes. Aunt Leonore would not be able to smooth this breach as she had smoothed so many before. No, if Helen wanted any freedom, any life beyond the house, she would have to comply. However much it galled.

"I am sorry, Uncle," she said, forcing a placid tone. "Please forgive me."

He sighed with heavy forbearance. "I must remember that, for all your finery and height, you are still a child. You must allow me to lead you in these matters until you are in the care of a husband. Now, rehearse the words and remember to say them with the dignity of your position."

Haltingly, Helen said, "'My mother drowned at sea. It was the best outcome for all concerned.'" The words burned the back of her throat.

"It will need more practice." He paused. "I see that you think this is harsh. But it is for your own good. Your aunt and I do not want you to suffer for your mother's misdeeds. You must show the world that you are steady and modest at every opportunity."

"Yes, Uncle."

"Your aunt expects you downstairs in a few minutes." He gave one last glance over her ensemble. "You are too tall and bare-boned for beauty, Helen, but you do have some presence. If you do not slouch, and are mindful of what I have said, I am sure you will be a credit to the family."

He strode out, his progress down the hall marked by the phlegmy clearing of his throat. Helen looked up at the ceiling, fighting back the tears that stung her eyes. She would not cry.

"My lady, are you all right?" Darby stood at the bedroom doorway. She had obviously circled around to listen, but Helen did not care.

"We must keep going, Darby, or we will be late." Helen picked up a silver hairbrush to focus on something—anything—other than the words she had been forced to utter.

Her hands were shaking too hard to hold the brush. She let it drop from her gloved grip onto the table, her eyes finding her mother's portrait. Lady Catherine's living actions might have been shameful, but to say that her death was the best outcome went against all decency. All civilized feeling. Helen pressed her hands together. She would not say it again. Ever. And, moreover, she would honor the loving mother whom she had known for eight years; the mother who had taught her to ride, who had lobbed new apples at her to catch in the orchard, and who had patiently led her through the steps of a cotillion.

She picked up the miniature, her hand finally steady. Yes, her mother would come to her presentation after all.

"Darby, where is my fan? The Vernis Martin."

She felt lightheaded. Could she really smuggle her mother's image into the Palace? Attached to the very fan that her uncle had given her as a presentation gift?

"Here, my lady." Darby passed her the long mother-of-pearl inlaid case.

Could she? Uncle's bloated face loomed in her mind again, his meaty breath hot against her face as he spat those terrible words: *best outcome.*

Yes, she could.

Juggling both box and miniature, she lifted the hinged lid and dug out the fan. One flick and it was open. The ivory sticks were painted with a pastoral scene of sheep and their shepherd asleep under an oak tree, and varnished with the distinctive Martin green-bronze lacquer. The decoration ended a few inches from the head of the fan, where the sticks were gathered into the diamond-set rivet. She ran a gloved finger along the cream arc of unpainted ivory. There was hardly any space between the sticks, but she could force some thread between two. She cupped the miniature in her palm—it really was quite heavy. She would need something more than just thread.

"Darby, find me some riband," she ordered.

"What color?" Darby ducked to rummage through the work-box beside the chaise longue.

"It does not matter." She held her finger and thumb a few inches apart. "But at least this much."

Darby pulled out a piece of blue riband. "Will this do, my lady?"

Helen took the offered length with a decisive nod. She opened her hand to show the miniature.

"Help me tie this to my fan."

Five

KEEPING THE MINIATURE hidden was proving harder than Helen had imagined. The bump and bustle of so many people making their way along the Palace corridor made it almost impossible to move without using both hands to steer her hoop through the melee. It was no easy task to keep hold of gown, train, presentation card, fan and attached miniature all at once.

"For goodness' sake, don't bunch your dress so tight," her aunt said, noticing her death grip on the spangled net. "Here, let me carry something for you."

Before Aunt could reach for her fan and the hidden miniature, Helen handed over her presentation card. Thankfully, their arrival in the crowded State Room diverted any further offer of help.

"It is going to be a tedious wait," Aunt said. "The visiting dignitaries will be received first. Still, we should start making our way toward the presentation chamber now. I don't want to push our way through the entire guest list when your name is called."

Although it was just past noon and the day was bright, a huge crystal chandelier blazed overhead, the mass of candles adding to the oppressive heat in the room. At the far end, Palace officials milled in the doorway of the Grand Council Chamber, readying themselves for the proceedings. Helen ran a quick eye over the paintings that lined the walls: portraits of Kings, Queens, and one particularly handsome pastoral. By Ricci, if she was not mistaken. A pity she would not have the chance to view it properly.

"I think I see a clear space near the door," Aunt Leonore said loudly in her ear while graciously acknowledging the apology of a gentleman who had set her lilac gown swaying. "Keep close to me, my dear."

Helen nodded, her hold on the miniature finally secure enough for her to start searching for Millicent. The multitude of shifting gowns and undulating feathers—a dizzying array of pastel pinks, soft purples, white, cream, stately blues, and sudden yellows—made it almost impossible to focus on any one person. Particularly one diminutive blonde amongst so many other diminutive blondes dressed in the paler shades of presentation. Delia's name suddenly rose up through the chatter, a snide laugh following it. Helen turned to glare at the perpetrator, but whoever it was had already moved past.

"Can you see Millicent?" she asked her aunt.

"La, child, I can barely see who is three in front of us."

They moved another foot or so forward. Helen, with her superior height, noted a break in the crowd: a wide space had been left around a dark-haired man standing before the huge marble mantelpiece. She caught sight of his face for a moment: young, but made harsh from some kind of suffering, with a savage intensity in his eyes as he scanned the room. There was a coiled quality to him as well, for all his loose-limbed height.

"Let us stop here," Aunt Leonore said, drawing Helen's attention from the tall gentleman to a space beside a blue chinoise urn in the center of the room. "The doorway is too densely packed now."

Her aunt stepped into the newfound gap and eyed a lesser-ranked lady and her protégée who had also taken refuge there. The two ladies curtsied, and the younger one, in her haste to make room, bumped her white tulle hoop into a nearby gentleman, sending him into a little hopping jump. Helen smothered a smile: the poor man was as red as his garters.

"Perhaps Lady Gardwell and Millicent have not yet arrived," Aunt said.

Helen looked over her shoulder to the fireplace again. The man had been joined by another. It took a moment for her to fully recognize the new arrival: not quite as tall as his companion, and fair-headed, his coat a plain and elegant blue amongst all the bright embroidered silks and lace. Good Lord, it was Mr. Brummell, Andrew's idol. Helen took in the fine cut of his coat, the harmony of his white waistcoat and pristine neckcloth; he made everyone else seem overdressed. He was certainly worthy of his unofficial title, Beau.

"Aunt, look who is here. Near the mantel."

Her aunt found the hearth, her mouth pursing. "Now, that is something to behold. Mr. Brummell does not usually attend Drawing Rooms. I suppose it is because the Prince Regent is expected."

"Whom does he stand beside?"

"That, my dear, is the Earl of Carlston," her aunt said, lowering her voice. "I had heard he was back from the Continent. What gall to come here."

So this was the man Andrew disliked so much.

"He is the one who killed his wife, is he not?" Helen whispered. And perhaps the one who had abducted Berta. He was smiling at something Brummell had said, but with no mirth in it, and his eyes were still hunting the crowd. She could readily believe he would take an innocent girl.

Her aunt gave a small gasp. "Oh no, he is looking this way." She turned her shoulder. "My dear, do not give him the satisfaction of your attention."

Helen reluctantly averted her eyes, but she had the distinct impression that her aunt had expected the Earl's notice. She risked another glance. Lord Carlston was once again in conversation with Mr. Brummell. As he spoke, he shifted his shoulders and she saw a moment of pain cross his strong features. Other than that, his face was curiously unreadable.

"For goodness' sake, stop staring at him," her aunt said. "Come, let us look for Millicent." She surveyed the room, her hand on Helen's arm as if to restrain her from turning again. "Aha, there she is, behind Bishop Meath."

She pointed her fan toward a long window swagged in opulent red velvet overlooking the Royal gardens. As the cluster of people before it separated, a familiar gold-blonde head came into view. It was cocked to one side in an attitude that could have been called charmingly quizzical, but Helen recognized it as a prelude to Millicent giving a setdown to someone she had deemed an idiot—no doubt the young fop in canary yellow who was standing before her and her mother. Millicent, for all her semblance of sweet prettiness, did not suffer fools.

In that uncanny way that one person's regard can create a silent summons for another, Millicent turned her head and saw Helen, the barely concealed impatience on her face brightening into pleasure. Her dress, thoroughly discussed with Helen months before, was a magnificent cloud of cream net and tulle, shot through with gold thread and embroidered with vines of gold and green leaves. Helen knew that the needlework alone had cost fifty guineas. As Millicent had acidly remarked during one afternoon spent studying the Court fashion plates, "The most impoverished must put on the best show."

Touching her mother's thin arm, Millicent nodded a curt farewell to the fop and steered Lady Gardwell toward them. Helen smiled; not even presentation to the Queen could quell her friend's busy nature, nor rally her mother's gentle helplessness. Lady Gardwell was extremely short of sight, so her eyes never fully focused. It gave her face a permanently anxious expression, and seemed to have prompted an equally hazy approach to life.

Helen flexed her wrist, shifting the miniature into a firmer position against her palm. Her paper-thin kid glove was damp with perspiration, and stuck to her skin. There were too many bodies in the room, filling the air with an overpowering stink of stale perfume and sweat, not to mention the heavy anticipation that seemed to press down upon everyone like black clouds on a thundery day. She searched her friend's face: Millicent appeared outwardly calm, but Helen could see the tiny signs of fear. It was not surprising—so much had been placed upon their one minute before the Queen. No doubt she herself had the same tight eyes and jaw.

Aunt Leonore flipped open her fan and waved it, sending a pulse of warm air across the two of them. "Lud! That shade of blue does not suit Lady Gardwell at all," she whispered as Millicent and her mother approached. She received their curtsies with a gracious smile. "Lady Gardwell and Miss Gardwell, what a pleasure to see you again."

Millicent's mother smiled a timid greeting. "Lady Pennworth, it is such a crush, is it not?" Her soft voice was barely audible above the high hum of conversation. "And, Lady Helen, how well you look today."

"Won't you stand here, by me?" Aunt Leonore said kindly. "This hustle and bustle is so tiring. Now, tell me, how is Sir Giles?"

As the two older ladies engaged in halting conversation, Helen drew Millicent aside.

"Have you heard?" she asked, bending slightly to accommodate her friend's smaller stature and wide hoop.

"You mean Delia?" Helen nodded. Millicent's mouth quirked

sideways into dismay. "Of course, it is all over town. She must be so distressed. To actually see him do it."

"I have written to her, but Aunt and Uncle won't let me do more."

"It is the same with me." Millicent frowned. "Did she mention this man to you? She mentioned no one to me."

"Nor me." Helen touched her friend's arm. "Millicent, I feel I should have done something. I saw her despair, but I did not act."

"Nonsense. Delia has always been prone to melancholy. Even *you* cannot know what is wholly in another's mind." Millicent shot a glance at Aunt Leonore. "What about Michaelmas?"

Helen shook her head. "I tried, but they will not let me invite her. You will still come, though, won't you?"

"Of course." Millicent's quick smile of reassurance faded. "But I don't think either of us will see Delia for a long while."

They were both silent for a moment. Helen pressed her fingertips hard against her mother's portrait. Her aunt was still engaged with Lady Gardwell. Could she risk showing it? "Millicent," she whispered, her heart beating hard. "Look." She opened her hand, giving a glimpse of the miniature, then snapped her fingers shut.

Her friend gasped. "I cannot believe you have brought that here." She studied Helen's face, a crease of concern between her brows. "I may not have your ability to read expressions, but I can see something has happened."

Helen gave a tiny shrug.

"Your uncle?"

She tucked in her chin.

Millicent nodded her understanding. "Well, don't let him find out you carried it here. I want my best friend at my ball."

"He won't. It is just . . ." She stared down at her closed hand. "My mother is not here."

"Yes," Millicent said. "Yes, I know." She flicked open her fan, waving it briskly as if she could fan away Helen's despondency. "I feel as if I will jump from my skin at any moment. I wish it were all over. Tell me some news that will keep me from conjuring visions of tripping over my train or bungling my curtsy."

"I have just the thing," Helen said, allowing her friend to shift her mood. "Look behind me. Do you see that dark-haired man over there, standing by the fireplace?"

Millicent peered across the room. "You mean the one headed over here, with Mr. Brummell?"

Even as Helen turned, she felt her aunt's hand close around her arm. "Helen, dear, I believe Mr. Brummell is heading our way. Remember to smile."

"Is that Lord Carlston with him, Lady Pennworth?" Millicent's mother asked, squinting. Her voice rang uncharacteristically sharp.

"I believe it is, Lady Gardwell." In contrast, Aunt Leonore's tone had a sudden wariness.

"You are related to him, are you not?"

Helen felt the air chill markedly between the two women. Both had smiles fixed upon their faces.

Lady Gardwell finally broke the loaded silence. "I would not want my daughter or myself to be in the way of a family reunion," she said. "Please excuse us. *Bonne chance*, Lady Helen." She sketched a quick curtsy to them both. "Come, Millicent, I see an acquaintance ahead."

She caught her daughter's hand and pulled her into the crowd. Helen stared after them, Millicent's bewildered backward gaze meeting her own astonishment. "Related?" Helen said as she lost sight of her friend. "We are related to him?"

Aunt Leonore touched the diamonds at her throat, her color high under the powder on her cheeks. "Well, not directly by blood. He is your uncle's second cousin. I had hoped he would have the decency not to claim the connection."

So, Lord Carlston was related to her uncle. She could readily believe it; both men seemed to look upon the world with disdain. "Why did no one tell me?" she asked. "Does Andrew know?"

"Yes, but it is hardly a connection that we are falling over ourselves to acknowledge. And who knew the man would come back? We all hoped he had gone for good." Her aunt grabbed hold of her arm again, the jolt shifting Helen's grip on the miniature. "Don't waste your time thinking on Carlston, my dear. It is Mr. Brummell who is important. It is he who can make you all the rage. Remember, charm and modesty. And smile!"

Helen barely had time to do so before the two men stood before them. Mr. Brummell bowed, cool appraisal on his attractive face. He had broken his nose at some point, and the slight flattening disrupted the symmetry of his features. In Helen's opinion, it added a certain manliness, saving his good looks from blandness. Aunt Leonore gave a nod of acknowledgment that set her plume shivering. "Mr. Brummell, how lovely to see you again."

Helen felt a ripple of movement around them. People were edging back with sidelong glances. Were they moving away in deference to Mr. Brummell, or disgust at Carlston? A quick survey of the surrounding faces gave the answer. It seemed Mr. Brummell's famous influence was not enough to make Lord Carlston palatable. Not yet, anyway.

"It is always a pleasure, madam," Mr. Brummell said, bowing once more. Helen felt herself under his appraisal again, his curiosity evident in the slight lift of his brows. Then, with an elegant hand, he indicated Lord Carlston. "Lady Pennworth, may I present the Earl of Carlston."

Aunt bent her neck in frigid acknowledgment. "Lord Carlston."

The Earl inclined his head. "Madam."

Lord Carlston was handsome, Helen conceded, in a hard, angular way that made the men around him seem somewhat effeminate.

Yet there was a ruthlessness to the set of his mouth that was decidedly repellent. His skin was unfashionably tanned—both Andrew and Aunt had mentioned he had been on the Continent—and the brown of his eyes was so dark that it merged with the black pupil, making their expression impenetrable. It was very disconcerting and gave him a flat look of soullessness, like the eyes of the preserved shark she had seen in the new Egyptian Hall. Helen lifted her bare shoulders against a sudden chill. How apt. There could be no soul in this man: he was a murderer. And possibly an abductor. She wrapped her fingers more firmly around the head of the fan and the miniature. Just in time, for her aunt was turning to introduce the men.

"My dear, allow me to present the Earl of Carlston and Mr. Brummell. Gentlemen, this is my niece, the Lady Helen Wrexhall."

Helen dipped into her curtsy but did not lower her eyes as modesty decreed, instead studying Lord Carlston as he bowed. He was studying her just as closely, his gaze far too penetrating for politeness. For a long moment they observed one another. Well, he could look with those dark shark eyes all he liked. He would not find much in her face either.

"Lord Carlston, Mr. Brummell," she said, rising from her curtsy and sweeping an aloof glance over them both. Andrew might have warned her to keep her distance from his lordship, but she could hardly embarrass her aunt by refusing the introduction. And it was an excellent chance to read the man. "I am pleased to make your acquaintance."

Carlston was still watching her closely. "Lady Helen, it is indeed a delight," he said. "Particularly since we are related."

"Distantly," Aunt said, her mouth small.

Carlston smiled, and it held all the superiority of his rank. "And yet irrefutably."

Aunt Leonore's mouth buckled tighter. Mr. Brummell cleared

his throat. A sign to Carlston of some kind, for the Earl immediately swept a calculating gaze across the far side of the room. Helen was sorely tempted to look in the same direction, but it would mean too pointed a turn. Whatever he saw prompted no expression on his face. Lord Carlston gave away nothing.

He fixed his gaze on her again and smiled. Helen fancied it was the look of a wolf before it leaped. "Lady Helen, I see that you carry a Vernis Martin fan."

She clenched her hand around the fan rivet and miniature, her own smile stiffening into a rictus. Of all things, why did he ask about her fan? Her free hand found the base of her throat, as if its span could hide the flush of heat that rose into her face.

"I am a great connoisseur of fans," he added.

"Really? Of fans?" She kept a stranglehold on her own. "And do you have much cause to use them?"

Mr. Brummell's shoulders shook as if he was suppressing a laugh. "Yes, do you, Carlston?" he asked.

Aunt Leonore widened her eyes in warning. "Helen, dear, I am sure Lord Carlston merely has an interest."

"I do, madam." He was lying—no doubt of it—although he gave none of the usual telltale signs of deception. No rapid blink or hard swallow. "Would you allow me to inspect your example, Lady Helen?"

"It is nothing out of the ordinary, Lord Carlston," she said, rallying a smile as false as his own. Why was he so insistent? But she could not pass the fan over. What if her aunt's quick eye found the portrait? "I'm sure it can be of no interest to such an expert."

"A Vernis Martin is always out of the ordinary, Lady Helen." He held out his hand.

Helen lifted her chin, meeting his challenge. *No,* she thought savagely. *No, I will not.* For a moment she saw something surprising in those shark eyes. Sympathy. Was he playing some game?

"Helen show Lord Carlston your fan," her aunt ordered.

"I cannot believe you are serious, sir," she said, trying to conjure the same teasing tone that Millicent used with her many admirers. "I feel sure you are funning with me."

"You will find that I am always serious, Lady Helen."

"Show him, my dear," her aunt hissed, the real message plain in the tilt of her head: *Show him the fan so that we may be rid of him.*

He extended his hand toward her, his gaze steady and infuriatingly indifferent. He knew she could not refuse him. The discourtesy would be unforgiveable, and her aunt would probably wrench the fan from her grasp and give it to him anyway. So be it. Raising her chin higher, she pushed the riveted end into his hand, pressing the miniature into his palm. She drew back her shoulders, ready for discovery. Aunt was going to be furious.

He flicked open the sticks, the curve of his large hand cradling the end, shielding it from sight. She drew in a steadying breath. Any moment now. He bent his head to study the painted panorama. Why was he waiting? He could obviously see the miniature—he had it in his hand—but he was not reacting. In fact, he was keeping it hidden.

"A very pretty fan," he said, but she saw the tiniest of creases between his dark brows. If she had to hazard a guess, underneath all that implacable control, Lord Carlston was aghast.

He looked up, the weight of his silence drawing all attention to his next words. She stayed as still as possible. If she did not move, perhaps he would just give it back.

"Was this represented to you as an original Vernis Martin?" he asked.

Helen exhaled. A reprieve. But why?

Her aunt drew herself up, all pinched indignation. "I will have you know that the fan was a gift from her uncle, Viscount Pennworth."

"A lovely gift," Carlston said blandly.

He closed the fan with a snap and passed it back to Helen. Even as she took the end, she knew it was too light. The miniature was gone. Had it fallen? She glanced down, but it was not on the floor. A piece of blue riband was still caught between the sticks. Sliced clean. He must have cut it off, but she had seen no knife. Her fingers closed convulsively around the rivet. Was he looking for some kind of vaporish response? Well, he would not have it. She forced indifference into her face and saw another flicker in those dark eyes. Amusement. A surge of hot fury caught her in the chest. Why was he doing this? It did not make sense.

"I believe we must make way for others who wish to make your acquaintance, Lady Helen," he said, bowing. "It has been a pleasure."

He was leaving. With her mother's portrait. No!

"Lord Carlston, I do hope you will visit us," she blurted, stopping his withdrawal. Beside him, Mr. Brummell paused in his own bow, eyebrows raised at her impropriety. "I mean," Helen continued doggedly, "will you do us the honor of calling on us tomorrow? Since we are *family*." She dragged up a smile as tight as a fist.

"Helen!" her aunt said.

The amusement deepened in Lord Carlston's eyes, bringing a sudden warmth to their flat scrutiny. "Since we are *family*, Lady Helen, I would be delighted to call tomorrow. As would Mr. Brummell."

Mr. Brummell smiled, but Helen could see the irritation buried within it. "Yes, a pleasure, madam. Until tomorrow, then."

It seemed that even the mighty Mr. Brummell bowed to Lord Carlston's will.

"Tomorrow," Aunt Leonore echoed faintly.

The two men withdrew, the crowd parting around them.

Helen clenched the fan, keeping track of Carlston's straight back through the shift of bodies and undulating feathers. Never before had she felt such a strong desire to slap someone. Or worse, to scream her outrage.

"What on earth has possessed you?" Aunt Leonore demanded. "The last thing we need is a call from that man. Your uncle will be most aggrieved."

Andrew would be unhappy too—she had not kept her distance. But it went against all rightful feeling to let Carlston walk away so smug and victorious.

"He will bring Mr. Brummell," Helen said shortly, watching as that gentleman's fair head bent to look at something in Carlston's hand. *Her* miniature.

"Well, there is that," Aunt conceded. She brightened. "In fact, you have held Mr. Brummell by your side for a good ten minutes. There can be no question of your success now."

Helen nodded, but her attention was once again fixed on Lord Carlston. Instinct told her he would look back. He would not be able to resist gloating. There—he was turning. And for once his expression was easily read.

Anticipation.

~

As an earl's daughter, Helen numbered as one of the privileged *Entrée* company, and so was called into the Royal presence first, along with the others of noble and diplomatic rank. As she and her aunt made their way through the crowd to the Grand Council Chamber, she saw Mr. Brummell again across the room, conversing with Lady Conyngham, the famous dark-haired beauty who Aunt had wagered would be Prinny's next favorite. Lord Carlston, however, was nowhere to be seen. Stealthily she rose onto her toes to view the entrance hall far behind them. Perhaps he had gone.

Hopefully he would be finished with his strange game tomorrow and return her miniature when he made his morning call. A game was the only explanation she could find for his behavior. Why else would he take the miniature and not give her secret away? Unless he was unbalanced. Even so, that did not explain Mr. Brummell's complicity. She shook her head, as dizzy from the unanswered questions as from the prospect of finally making her curtsy to the Queen.

"Helen, stop making yourself taller." Aunt Leonore caught her arm and tugged her down from her toes, then steered her firmly toward the open doors of the Grand Council Chamber.

A last glance found Millicent near the windows, waiting for the general company to be called. She was scanning the crowd too. *Look to the left,* Helen silently urged, *look to the left.* Finally Millicent did. Helen saw her smile and lift her hand, like a benediction, and then she was obscured by the plumes of the other *Entrée* girls and their sponsors.

It was an easy step across the threshold of the Grand Council Chamber, and yet Helen felt as though she had crossed an abyss. The sudden rise of tension in the room was almost tangible, like a thickening in the air. A large fire in the grate—a concession to the Queen's advanced years—added to the stifling atmosphere. The chatter of the State Room was gone, replaced by soft whispers and the rustle of silk as those with the *Entrée* ranged themselves around the throne.

"Remember to keep your chin up," Aunt Leonore whispered, passing back Helen's presentation card. "And don't wobble. You occasionally wobble when you sink into your curtsy. And when you gather your train, do it in one movement. Don't flail your arm around like a fish on a hook."

"I wobble?" How could her aunt be telling her that now?

"You will do well," Aunt added. "I'm sure you will do well."

The clear tones of the Lord Chamberlain cut through the muted conversations to announce the start of the presentations. Helen watched a dark-haired girl pass by, train draped over her arm, thin face set with concentration. The throne, overhung with a red velvet canopy, was surrounded by a wide semicircle of courtiers and guests blocking any view of the Queen or the Princesses Mary and Augusta. Another immense crystal-drop chandelier hung from the ceiling. Its glow and the watery sunlight through the windows shimmered across the diamonds that circled necks and wrists, and cast the noble gold lion and unicorn above the throne into sharp relief. It was all quite dazzling.

An usher approached and bowed. "Lady Pennworth, if you will please join the other sponsors," he said, indicating a group of pale-faced ladies at the edge of the semicircle. His attention shifted to Helen. "My lady, please follow me."

Another neat bow, and he led her across the carpet to a cluster of twenty or more girls, all in pale satins, pearls, and bugle beads. Aunt Leonore was already in the midst of the sponsors, her rank shifting a few of the lesser ladies into tight-mouthed retreat.

Helen suppressed a smile and took her place beside a plump girl in billowing white tulle heavily bordered with pink silk rosebuds. Her round face was flushed and slightly dewed with perspiration along her carefully curled hairline—the poor girl was close to combusting with the heat. A name hovered at the edge of Helen's memory. Elizabeth. They had been introduced at a pre-Season assembly. She saw the same recognition brighten the girl's protuberant blue eyes. Yes, Lady Elizabeth Brompton. Called Pug behind her back for those eyes, but also for her relentless good nature.

"Lady Helen." Lady Elizabeth dipped into a curtsy.

Helen ducked her head and murmured a response, aware of the retreating usher's bloodless lips pursing in disapproval at the exchange.

"Gad, I swear I will faint any minute now," Lady Elizabeth continued in an overloud whisper. She cooled the large expanse of her décolletage with a vigorous flapping of her own presentation card. "It is so hot in here, but I dare not open my fan. Isabelle Rainsford over there"—her plumes tilted toward a girl with tear-reddened eyes—"opened hers for a moment, and a flock of chamberlains descended upon her like ravens upon a carcass. 'Twas most entertaining." She leaned closer, her voice finally dropping to an undertone. "Apparently, Her Majesty is irritated by the flapping."

"I am glad you warned me," Helen said, wondering if she should mention that a white card used as a fervent fan might irritate Her Majesty just as much. She decided against it. Lady Elizabeth's color was so high that she probably needed the extra air. She looked down at her fan, the tiny piece of blue riband still caught between the sticks. Carlston's theft of her miniature was an outrage, but at least she no longer had to worry about concealing it from her aunt. Or juggling it along with her hoop and train as she made her curtsy before the Queen.

Before the Queen.

A cold realization crawled across her scalp and along her bare shoulders. Good Lord, if the miniature had still been attached, she would now be holding the portrait of a suspected traitor in the Queen's presence. How could she have been so stupid? Only seeing her own path, like a blinkered coach horse. She felt the sudden press of a hundred accusing eyes upon her, but when she looked up, the room was unchanged: all attention still focused on the throne, the ushers crossing the carpet in their age-old trajectories. Was that why Carlston had taken it? Helen frowned, trying to fit such a benevolent motivation to the man. No. He had taken it for his own reasons, and she would wager they were not chivalrous. Still, he had saved her from her own foolish shortsightedness.

Lady Elizabeth leaned closer, her whisper hot against Helen's ear. "I believe you are a friend of Miss Cransdon's, are you not?" Her eyes bulged even more with curiosity. "Miss Delia Cransdon?"

Helen braced her feet a little more deeply in the thick carpet. "I am."

"Is it true what they are saying? That she ran away with a man who killed a tavern maid and then himself?"

A tavern maid? The story was building into a massacre. "I have heard no such thing," she said, allowing the firm denial to cover both crimes. "Who told you such a story?"

Lady Elizabeth's stubby hand flapped. "It is all about the room. So, it is not true, then?"

Helen was saved from an outright lie by the arrival of a young usher at Lady Elizabeth's elbow. "My lady, if you will follow me."

"Finally," she whispered, adjusting her train over her arm. "See-ho, away!"

Helen watched Lady Elizabeth's hoop set into an ungainly swing as she hurried to keep up with the usher. For all her rompish ways, Pug was not known to be a tattle-monger. Yet she had seen fit to repeat the tavern story. It did not bode well for Delia. Nor did the addition of a murdered tavern maid to the tale. Of course, it might not be an addition: perhaps Aunt had not heard all of the story. Helen glanced across at the group of sponsors. Her aunt was in close conversation with another lady, but Helen's attention was caught by the expression on a face behind them—a fine-boned lady with dark hair who watched Aunt with hard intensity and a frown that spoke of distrust. She must have felt Helen's attention, for she looked up, but her eyes slid away.

Helen turned back to the presentations. Lady Elizabeth was next in line, her fingers picking at the rivet of her fan as two gentlemen-in-waiting busied themselves around her plump figure. The younger man lifted the folds of the heavy train from her arm and spread it on the floor behind her in a sweep of white damask and pink silk rosebuds. The older, his eyes fixed on the activity before the throne, kept Lady Elizabeth in place with a tilt of his gray-powdered head. The poor girl's high color had paled into a mosaic of pink-and-white blotches across her chest and face. *At least it matches her gown,* Helen thought, then immediately felt uncharitable. Pug was not to blame for the tattle-mongers' zeal. At some unseen sign, the older gentleman stepped back and bowed, opening up the pathway to the throne. With name card held out stiffly, Pug took a deep breath, cast one last look back at her train, and marched forward.

And so it was for all the girls ahead of Helen. At first she watched each preparation—the deep breath, the nervous check of the train—but after six girls had disappeared into the gap and reemerged radiant with relief, she found her attention turning inward. What if the Queen actually did ask about her mother? Her heart took up a hard rhythm, each beat rising into her throat. And her innards seemed to have pushed themselves low into her bowel. She concentrated on one of the gold fleurs-de-lis that bordered the carpet, and slowly deepened her breath through the damp constriction of her stays. A long exhale helped steady the dizzy lightness in her head. There was still time for one last rehearsal of her answer, but the words she had practiced for the Queen were gone. She could not even remember how to start. All she could see in her mind was her uncle's bloated face snarling, *Best outcome.*

"My lady, if you will please follow me."

No. She was not ready. What if she wobbled?

"My lady?"

Helen focused on the polite face of the usher. A glimmer of impatience crossed his sallow features.

"Yes, of course," she murmured, and forced herself forward.

Ahead, the two gentlemen-in-waiting broke apart from a whispered exchange.

"Lady Helen, may I present Sir Desmond Morwell," the usher whispered, indicating the older gentleman. "And Sir Ian Lester."

The two men bowed. Even through her fear she noted the weariness in the older man's face and the younger one's flicking of finger against thumb. They had a long day ahead of them.

"Allow me to take your train, Lady Helen," Sir Ian said, lifting the heavy drape of satin from her left arm. The release of weight brought a settling of cooler air. A moment of reinvigoration. She could not help but look behind as he spread the broad sweep out on the carpet.

"Please have your card ready for the Lord Chamberlain," Sir Desmond said. For all his weariness, he had a gentle face beneath the old-fashioned gray-powdered wig of office. And large brown eyes—absurdly large for a man—that lent him an air of great kindness. "You may start your walk to the throne once he has announced you."

She met his level gaze and found a measure of calm in his matter-of-fact tone. Thousands of girls had done this without catastrophe. So could she.

Sir Desmond bowed and stepped away, opening the path to the Queen.

One after another, curious faces turned and whispered. Now she understood the need for that deep breath, that one last look at the train. She walked forward, chin up, although every part of her longed to look down at the swaying brush of her hem. What if she tripped? She passed through the crowd, the blur of faces suddenly focusing into one familiar smile: the Duke of Selburn, her brother's friend, his plain, long-boned face transformed into a lifeline of warm support. Always so kind, and now winking to give her some courage. Next to him, the stately Lady Cholmondeley. She smiled too. And, of course, Aunt Leonore. Dear Aunt, with her teeth clamped into her lower lip and a prayer in her eyes.

Helen handed her card to the Lord Chamberlain.

"The Lady Helen Wrexhall," he announced.

The throne seemed so far away. The two Princesses stood behind their mother like pale shadows, their famed beauty lost against their mother's presence. Helen caught an impression of gray hair dressed high, abundant blue ostrich feathers, and powdered jowls, and then all her attention was on crossing the carpet before the assembled world. Fifteen steps: she counted them. She reached the throne, stopping on the dull mark in the thick pile that had been flattened by so many other slippered feet. She had never seen Royalty this close before.

Her Majesty had become stout, like her son, and the tragedy of her husband's long illness had etched deep lines into her face that dragged at her mouth and creased her forehead into grim sufferance. Her famous snuff habit was stained into the edge of her broad nostrils, the yellowed skin visible beneath thick powder. Yet her widely spaced eyes were bright with interest, and she leaned forward, expectantly.

Helen tucked her left knee behind the right and lowered herself into her curtsy, head bowed. It was smooth, no wobble. She exhaled—Aunt would be happy. At eye level, the gloved Royal hand clasped the carved armrest. A rustle of blue silk and Her Majesty's corsage, stitched with gold stars and sprinkled with brilliants, came into view as she bent to give the Royal kiss. Helen raised her face into a sweet smell of cloves and a flash of diamonds on age-spotted skin. Then the gentle press of dry lips on her forehead.

"You are the daughter of Countess Hayden?" Her Majesty asked in a pitch so low that it was little more than warm breath against Helen's skin. She had asked, after all. Helen's throat closed. All she could do was nod.

"Child, do not believe everything they say about your mother."

The soft words wrenched Helen's gaze upward. For one long moment she was caught in the intent, pale stare of her Queen. What did she mean? But there were no clues in the sagging face above. It wore the impenetrable mask forged from a lifetime at Court. Her Majesty drew back and nodded a gracious dismissal. Or was it a nod of satisfaction?

A gentleman-in-waiting ducked behind Helen and deftly gathered her train, bundling it over her arm in a billow of satin. It took all of her focus to bow her head to the Princesses and the Queen, rise from her curtsy, and back away from the throne.

Six

Friday, 1 May 1812

Aunt Leonore twitched the thin pages of *The Times* into a sharp snap and placed the open newspaper on the breakfast table. "So galling," she muttered.

Helen collected a soft brioche from the silver serving basket offered by Barnett and let the comment pass. There had already been two other such mutterings. She broke open the roll and breathed in the sweet, yeasty warmth. There was something so comforting about the smell of fresh bread, and she needed some comfort after a sleepless night spent reconstructing her encounters with Lord Carlston and the Queen. She still did not know why Carlston had taken her miniature. Nor what the Queen had meant by her extraordinary statement. It had sounded like an obscure denial of Lady Catherine's treason. Yet Helen could not be sure, and she could hardly ask Her Majesty for clarification.

Still, if there was any chance that her mother had been unjustly accused, it was her duty to discover the truth. Perhaps she could even redeem her mother's name.

She busied herself away from those foolish hopes by cutting a square of butter. She would not even know where to start. And what if she did start, and found that the reality was worse than the rumors? A few years ago she'd had a taste of the harsh truth from Andrew: he had told her that some of those times when Mother had joined them suddenly at Deanswood Hall had actually been enforced retreats to the family estate to avoid the heat of a new scandal.

Aunt stabbed a piece of toast into her cup of tea, but did not lift the sagging result to her mouth. Instead she turned back to the offending page: a description of the previous day's Royal Drawing Room. "So galling," she said again, "to be overlooked for the Prince Regent's evening party." She dropped the soggy toast onto her plate. "It is your uncle's doing, you know. If he was not so outspoken about the degeneracy of the Carlton House set, we would have been invited."

Helen looked up from buttering the roll. It was unusual for Aunt to risk criticizing Uncle, even in the relative privacy of the small breakfast room.

"You knew we were not invited weeks ago," she pointed out.

"It does not make it any less humiliating." Aunt closed the newspaper. "Now that you are presented, we should have had our rightful invitation. At least the list of those who attended has not been published. It would be beyond bearable if one's name was missing." She pushed her plate away. Barnett stepped out from beside the service bureau and removed it. "And now we have to deal with a call from Lord Carlston, which is not going to add to our *ton*. Even with Mr. Brummell's ameliorating presence."

Aunt's look across the table was plain: *Your fault.*

After dinner last night, the entire household had heard Lord Pennworth's heated views about Lord Carlston's intended visit booming from the drawing room. It had taken Aunt a full half-hour to calm him down, and it was only Beau Brummell's sponsorship of the man that had finally swayed Uncle to accept the visit. Even he acknowledged the importance of the Beau's approval to a girl's social success. He had made it clear, however, that he would be at his club when Lord Carlston made his appearance.

Helen took a bite of the brioche, letting her full mouth save her from the necessity of an answer. Lord Carlston's visit was indeed her fault, but she did not feel any guilt about it. Not at all. She was going to get her miniature back and have an explanation, although how that was going to be achieved was not yet clear. Surely, as a gentleman, he would just return it. She took another bite and chewed reflectively. Perhaps not—he had shown very little evidence of gentlemanly behavior thus far.

Aunt picked up the top card from the stack of invitations that had arrived in the early mail. "We have, at least, been invited to the King's birthday ball." She flexed the thick paper between finger and thumb. "You never told me what the Queen said to you."

Helen lifted a dismissive shoulder. "I was so nervous, I hardly took it in. Just a pleasantry, I think."

She had made no conscious decision to keep the Queen's statement a secret. Yet when Aunt had first asked what Her Majesty had said, Helen had hedged the answer. And now she had done it again. Perhaps it was childish, but she could not bear to think of her aunt picking apart this unexpected championing of her mother. It was her revelation, and hers alone.

Aunt observed her nervously. "Did Her Majesty say something harsh?"

At least here she could tell the truth. "No, not at all." She leaned over the table and read the engraved lettering on the next card. "The Howards' on the third? Do we go?"

"There is not much else on offer, so I think we will. I have heard that Lord Byron will be attending."

"Really? I cannot wait to see him," Helen said. "I hear he is an Adonis."

Millicent had already seen the celebrated poet and reported, rather too extensively, on his physical charms and excitingly surly nature. Helen wondered what her friend would make of Lord Carlston's strange behavior. Well, she would find out soon enough: the Gardwells were to accompany them to the park on Sunday for promenade.

Aunt snorted. "Lord Byron is a good-looking boy, I will grant you that, but I mislike this whole business with Caro Lamb. It is all becoming so public."

Helen nudged the card aside to read the next. "Aunt, look. Lady Jersey has asked us to make up a party that goes to Vauxhall Gardens on Tuesday. Are we to go? I love the Gardens."

"Of course we shall accept. One can hardly refuse a patroness of Almack's, although I fear we may be an afterthought, since her card is so late." Aunt took an irritated sip of tea. "Still, afterthought or not, we will go. We may have secured an Almack's voucher for the whole of May, but we need Silence's continuing sponsorship if you are to be ensured a voucher for June, too."

Helen looked up at her aunt's use of the sour nickname bestowed upon the patroness of the exclusive club for her habit of ceaseless chatter. "I thought you liked Lady Jersey."

"I do. I just mistrust this sudden interest in you. She is mercurial, to say the least, and the last thing we need is for her to take offense at something ridiculous and refuse us entry to Almack's."

Helen smiled: even with Lady Jersey's unpredictable nature, a night at the pleasure gardens was something special. She shifted the card aside to show the one beneath. "And here is Millicent's ball for the nineteenth."

"That one goes without saying," Aunt said. "I wonder if we should ask Carlston to your ball now, since you have seen fit to draw him into our sphere."

Helen hurriedly took another bite of brioche. Her ball had been scheduled for the twenty-sixth to take advantage of the light of the full moon, but it was also the anniversary of the day that she and Andrew had learned of their parents' death. Usually, she spent it in private memorial, recalling those few memories that she still managed to hold close. Not this year, however. Apparently, such an activity was maudlin; her aunt had announced it was time to replace it with happier memories. Perhaps she was right. Yet it still felt like a betrayal, and Helen could not face the ball's preparations with quite the enthusiasm that Aunt expected. The inclusion of Carlston, however, would certainly add a *frisson* to the evening. She tried to picture her uncle receiving him, but even her lively imagination could not conjure it.

She swallowed her mouthful. "Uncle would not be pleased."

"True. Yet there is a very good chance that if Carlston comes, Brummell will too. It seems the Beau is intent on bringing the man back into society." Aunt returned the Royal invitation to the stack. "If that is the case, Brummell might very well make us his last ball of the evening." She tapped the white tablecloth meditatively. "We must try to ensure that happy situation. Have you finished your part of the guest list yet?"

"Not quite."

"Then that will be your task for the morning." Aunt brushed crumbs from her hands, a surreptitious glance downward also checking the front of her citron morning gown. "Your uncle wishes me to engage another housemaid, and so I must write to the registry office. After that we shall review your list." A flick of a finger expelled an errant crumb from her bodice.

"Are you replacing Berta already? But she has only been missing four days."

"How do you know about Berta?" Aunt waved away her own question. "Of course, the servants." She cast a reproachful look at Barnett, then turned her irritation back to Helen. "It does not matter how many days she has been missing; we cannot afford to be short-staffed for your ball. And you know as well as I do that your uncle will not have her back in the house should she return. She has proved herself unreliable." Aunt paused, struck by a thought. "I shall write to the Heathcotes and the Leonards. They may know of a girl. It is far better to hire on a recommendation from someone you know, Helen. Remember that when it comes time for you to hire."

"But surely we can't leave it at that," Helen said. "Darby says Berta spoke about a mother up north. No mother should be left wondering what has happened to her daughter."

Aunt sighed. "That is true enough. But I don't see what we can do. Your uncle has ordered her things to be packed up and another girl to be hired."

Her things packed up? Helen suddenly saw a way to further her promise to Darby. Not a particularly honorable way, but it might provide a clue to where Berta had gone.

"Barnett, where is Berta's lockable box?"

The butler stepped forward. "Mrs. Grant has moved it to the housekeeper's room, my lady. For safekeeping." The last was said with a gentle note of censure; he knew where she was heading.

"What do you propose to do?" Aunt asked. "Open it?"

"Yes." Helen shot an apologetic glance in Barnett's direction. "She may have something in there with an address for her mother writ upon it."

"My dear, one does not open a servant's private box."

From the corner of her eye, Helen saw Barnett's high-bridged nose dip in agreement. "If Berta does not return, then the box must be sent back to her mother," she countered. "Don't you agree?"

Aunt patted Helen's arm. "I know you mean well, and there is virtue in your argument, but it has not come to that yet. We will wait to see if Berta returns. If she does not, Mrs. Grant can open the box."

"But what if she is in trouble? We could help her."

"It is not your place to go rummaging through the poor girl's belongings, and I can't see that it will help her in any way." Aunt signaled to Barnett. He stepped smartly behind her chair and pulled it out as she rose.

"It might give us an idea of where she has gone," Helen persisted.

"What is the most important thing I have told you about a well-run servants' hall?"

"'A well-run servants' hall requires vigilance from the lady of the house, but not direct interference,'" Helen dutifully quoted. "But—"

"Exactly." Aunt walked to the door. "Mrs. Grant is in charge of the female staff. She will know what to do." She looked back. "You must not trespass on Mrs. Grant's dominion. You know how difficult it gets if she is upset. I will see you in the drawing room with your guest list."

Helen pushed away her plate. "Yes, Aunt."

As Barnett opened the door, Helen remembered another, more useful piece of information about the well-run servants' hall. At night the butler's pantry was always locked to secure the valuable plate. The housekeeper's room, however—like the other servants' rooms—was never locked.

HELEN SPENT THE rest of the morning finishing her part of the list, then sitting with Aunt in the drawing room and discussing each potential guest. Not all survived the dissection, although Helen successfully argued for the lowly Miss Taylor, another friend from her seminary days.

At around noon Barnett served a light luncheon of meat and fruit. Helen took only an apricot and a slice of ham. How could she eat when she was about to face Lord Carlston in a battle of wits?

She soon withdrew to her dressing room to change into her afternoon gown in readiness for that battle. After much pacing back and forth in front of her clothes press, she finally decided to wear her new favorite ensemble: an apple-green velvet bodice over a white satin underdress. A pair of lace fingerless mitts, dyed to match the velvet, completed the outfit. One last pat to her hair in the mirror—braided and curled around a high Grecian knot by Darby—and she was ready to receive Lord Carlston and his amused shark eyes.

"What if he does not give the miniature back, my lady?" Darby asked, demolishing Helen's hard-won composure. "What if he does not mention it? What if he does not even acknowledge taking it?"

They were all questions Helen had asked herself, with no answers. She had told Darby the whole story during her morning toilette—before family prayers and breakfast—but it seemed that her maid only now realized the full awkwardness of the situation. A realization that had arrived with full force for Helen at two that morning.

"He must have some compelling reason for taking the portrait, and I'm sure he will want me to know it," Helen said. She observed her certainty in the mirror. It looked almost real. "Otherwise, he would not have agreed to the visit."

"Unless he was just being polite, my lady," Darby said, returning the extra hairpins to their silver box. "Or he wants to torment you."

Yes, there was that, too.

Helen turned away from the discomfiting thought to face her maid with another uneasy subject. "I have had an idea on how to find Berta."

Darby looked up eagerly.

"No, wait. You will not like it. I am going to search her lockbox." She acknowledged Darby's gasp with an apologetic lift of her hand. "I know, it is a dreadful breach, and my aunt has not given me permission to open it. But there may be a clue inside. I feel I must look."

The broad lines of Darby's face seemed to narrow. Although Helen had not meant it to be so, her idea had suddenly become a test of the girl's allegiance. Was Darby *her* maid, or her aunt's servant? She had never asked Darby to directly disobey Aunt before. Of course, the girl had taken it upon herself to tell Helen about Berta and had even helped her tie the miniature to the fan, but that was nothing compared to choosing Helen's wishes above the direct orders of the mistress of the house. If it were discovered, she could lose her position without a character reference, which would make it almost impossible for her to find work again. Yet here she was being forced to make a choice, all for the sake of a fellow maid. Would she feel obliged to inform Aunt of the lockbox plan, or would she keep Helen's secret?

Darby closed the silver pin box with a snap and turned it over and over in her competent, square hands. The pins shifted back and forth against the sides, the sound like the roll of a drum.

"It has been moved to the housekeeper's room," she finally said. "How will you get it?"

Helen exhaled, surprised at the intensity of her relief. "I will go down after everyone has retired."

"Then I will go, too. You will need someone to keep watch."

Helen shook her head. Allegiance was all very well, but she did not want Darby to risk direct participation. "I cannot allow that."

Darby's soft mouth compressed into obstinacy. "I involved you, madam, when I knew it was not the proper thing to do. I will accompany you." The stubbornness lifted into a shrewd smile. "I have great faith in your ability to move around the house without being heard."

So she knew about the midnight forays. "Obviously, I was not completely unheard," Helen said dryly.

"Only by me, my lady. My room is next to the staircase, and the top step squeaks." Darby met her gaze solemnly. "It is no one's business but your own."

"Thank you," Helen said slowly. A small thrill settled in her chest. To Darby, her decision to roam the halls at night was not the act of a naughty child, but that of a lady about her own business. It had not been business of any consequence, to be sure, but now she had something real to do. Something important. And, she had to admit, she liked the idea of Darby's company. "We must find a way to open the box so that Mrs. Grant will not suspect it has been breached. Could we pick the lock, do you think?"

Darby cocked her head. "There is no certainty that it will open, my lady. However, Berta's box is only made of deal, like my own, so if we are careful, we should be able to lever it open without splitting the wood. I did so with mine when I misplaced the key, and if the lock lever is not damaged, it can be pushed back into service. A flat piece of metal will do the job."

"Can you find such a tool?"

"Yes, easily."

"Good, then do so." And although they were alone, Helen lowered her voice. "We go tonight."

~

WITH ONE CAMPAIGN planned, Helen hurried downstairs to fight the other.

Her aunt was already in position in the drawing room. She, too, had changed into a new gown—a stylish purple-and-black stripe—and sat primly by her tambour frame, hook in hand. Sally, one of the senior maids, stood in readiness behind the tea table, which had been set with a large silver urn and matching tea caddy worked in a riot of rococo grapes and shells. Aunt had come armored with the Paul de Lamerie service.

Helen crossed to the right-hand window and peered down at a carriage-and-four edging along the narrow street. A number of pedestrians hurried across the cobbles to the safety of the higher paths on each side. As she watched, the unmistakably tall and well-dressed figures of Lord Carlston and Beau Brummell strolled around the corner. An even larger man in a good-quality coat, with the golden brown skin of warmer climes, followed them but kept his distance, hat brim pulled low over his eyes. Lord Carlston turned and spoke to him, a wave of his hand sending the giant across the road, opposite the house. It was obviously his man.

"They are coming, Aunt."

"Then for goodness' sake, step away from the window and take up your work. We must not look as though we are waiting for them."

Helen sat on the yellow silk sofa that was strategically set opposite the doorway and pulled out her embroidery from the workbag at its side. The cushion-size piece of linen with its dense, half-filled design of pansies had acted as her fine work for over a year now, and was not likely to be finished any time soon, not with Andrew's constant demands for rolled-hem cravats and linen shirts. Still, it was a pretty piece and had often, in times of excruciatingly dull conversation, saved the day by becoming a subject of discussion. She pulled the needle and scarlet thread free from its mooring in the cloth.

Three stitches were placed before the knock sounded and the double doors opened. Barnett crossed the carpet, silver salver in hand, bowed, and offered its contents to Aunt. She picked up the two cards set upon it, scrutinized the embossed lettering on each, replaced them, and nodded. "We are at home."

Barnett withdrew, closing the doors behind him.

"We must hope that they keep their topcoats on," Aunt said. "Although I would not put it past Carlston to claim the family connection and stay longer."

Helen nodded as if she agreed, but a coats-on call would give her only fifteen minutes or so to extract her miniature. That is, if Lord Carlston had actually brought it with him. And that would just be the start of the difficulties.

Another knock. Helen resolutely lowered her eyes to her work and positioned another stitch. She heard the doors open, and saw the arrival of Barnett's buckled shoes and two sets of highly polished black topboots.

"Lord Carlston and Mr. Brummell, my lady," the butler announced.

Without looking up, Helen placed her work neatly on the small round table beside the sofa, gathered her skirts, and stood. Finally she raised her head, her expression composed into one part boredom, two parts polite indifference. He would find no anxiety in her face.

She caught a moment of those dark eyes—still amused—and then Lord Carlston and Mr. Brummell bowed. Although they had handed their hats, gloves, and canes to Barnett at the front door, both still wore their coats. Fifteen minutes, then.

Helen dipped into her curtsy in concert with Aunt. The first hurdle was to somehow find a way to engage Lord Carlston in private conversation.

"Mr. Brummell and Lord Carlston. How pleasant to see you again," Aunt said.

Inwardly, Helen winced at the petty misranking. Wry appreciation twitched Lord Carlston's mouth, then was gone.

"Lady Pennworth." Mr. Brummell stepped forward. "And Lady Helen. I hope we find you well. But I see that you are both in good spirits."

"We are, thank you," Aunt said, a graceful hand indicating her permission for them to take the two chairs opposite her own.

As her aunt sat, Helen returned to the sofa and picked up her work again. A quick glance up from the linen gave her an image of Carlston's profile, framed by his high shirt collar and white neckcloth, and then she was back positioning a stitch. All her impressions from the day before were reinforced: he was handsome but repellent. There was still that savagery in the lines from nose to mouth, and every plane of his face was angled and definite, as if the sculptor had abandoned all idea of curves except for the lower lip and a wave of dark hair that fell across his forehead.

"Do you not agree, Carlston?" Mr. Brummell asked in an obvious effort to draw the Earl into the conversation.

"Indeed," Carlston said pleasantly. "No doubt missing the Prince Regent's gathering last night has helped you to remain so remarkably fresh."

As his meaning penetrated, Helen saw her aunt stiffen. She herself was torn between horrified amusement and a strange kind of triumph that he had noted their absence.

"It was a tedious night," Mr. Brummell said quickly, casting a quelling glance in Carlston's direction.

"Will you take tea?" Aunt asked.

"No, we do not stay long," Lord Carlston said. Brummell closed his eyes for a moment, probably in despair at his friend's manners.

"That will be all, Sally," Aunt said, dismissing the maid.

"Lady Pennworth," Brummell said into the silence. "I see a fine array of Sèvres in that corner. As you know, I am also a keen collector. Would you be so kind as to show me your pieces?"

"With pleasure, Mr. Brummell," Aunt said. To the uninitiated ear, her voice was serene, but Helen heard the tremor of rage. Aunt rose from her chair and, with a pointed turning of her back, led Mr. Brummell over to the arrangement of porcelain set on a table along the far wall.

Helen watched him pick up a sky-blue teacup and study the pattern. If she were not mistaken, he had deliberately drawn her aunt to the other end of the room. Was this Lord Carlston's way of engaging *her* in private conversation?

It seemed that it was, for his lordship suddenly rose from his seat and crossed to stand before her, a half step closer than courtesy dictated. She smelled the fresh scent of plain soap. He must be one of those who followed Mr. Brummell's dictate that men should smell of nothing more than good washing and clean air. Helen realized she had swayed a little forward. She sat back. It had to be said that plain soap was a much better fragrance than the far-too-popular and overspiced Imperial Water.

"Your stitching is very fine," he said.

A swift search of his face found only polite attention. As usual, he was giving nothing away. Including, she thought with a sting of irritation, her miniature. There would be no gentlemanly return of her property.

"Thank you," she said, and glanced across at her aunt and Mr. Brummell. Both still had their backs turned. Time to make the first strike. "I would wish, though, that my talents lay more in the accomplishment of painting."

His dark brows lifted in inquiry. They were set at a slight diabolic angle, she decided.

"And if you had such a talent," he asked, "what would you paint?"

She smiled without teeth. "Miniatures."

He met her smile. "Too heavy-handed, Lady Helen. Shall we try again? This time with subtlety."

She bowed her head and jabbed her needle into the linen. He thought her without subtlety, did he? She yanked the needle through the cloth. Well, she would not play his game.

With deliberate tranquility, she put aside her work, looked squarely up into his face, and said, "The portrait is mine and I want it back. Be so kind as to return it, Lord Carlston."

"Ah, the direct approach." He reached into his coat pocket and pulled out her miniature. Gold filigree flashed, and then his fingers closed around it. "What possessed you to take it to the Palace?" There was nothing pleasant in his voice now.

Helen bridled; he had no business talking to her like that. "I do not have to answer to you, Lord Carlston."

"You do if you want it back."

The flat statement silenced her. She wanted to fabricate a lie just to spite him, but found nothing. It would have to be the truth. "I wanted some remembrance of my mother at my presentation."

"Your mother was a traitor. Did you not think of the consequences?"

Heat rose into her cheeks. "No, not until it was too late." She clamped her gloved hands together until the force pressed the pattern of lace into her skin. "It was foolish, I know. Did you take it to . . . help me?"

"No."

"Why, then?"

"I was once acquainted with your mother."

Helen stared up at him. He could be no more than five and twenty: he would have been a mere youth when her mother had died. "How did you know her?"

He cast a thoughtful glance across at Aunt. "I suspect your family does not speak often of Lady Catherine."

"No, my mother is not a frequent subject of discussion," Helen said stiffly.

"I see." He drew back slightly. "You must have a commanding view of the street from your windows."

Perplexed by the sudden turn in conversation, Helen nodded, but her mind was still fixed on his claim to have known her mother. Was this man her pathway to the truth?

She stood, driven upright by the possibility, but he was already walking toward the windows, his attention on Aunt and Mr. Brummell. As if feeling his lordship's stare, Mr. Brummell turned slightly, a silent question directed over the high starched points of his collar. Helen caught the infinitesimal shake of Carlston's head and the flick of his hand. It was true, then—Lord Carlston *did* have some kind of command over the powerful Beau, beyond even the normal demands of his higher rank. Mr. Brummell obediently returned to Aunt, pointing out another piece of porcelain for discussion.

Carlston stopped before the far window. Some part of Helen noted that it placed him out of the peripheral sight of the others, and the odd clarity of that observation made her pause. Then she was halfway across the room before she acknowledged she was following him.

He raised his hand, and she saw the miniature flat against his palm. Did he expect her to jump for it? Uncertain, she stopped, stranded between the sofa and the window. He glanced over at Mr. Brummell and Aunt again, then drew his hand back. His fingers closed around the portrait. Even as she thought, *He's going to throw it,* he whipped his hand forward and hurled the small missile at her with brutal strength. A blur of gold streaked toward her head. She snatched it out of the air a moment before it hit her forehead, the stinging impact against her palm muffled by the lace of her mitt.

God's blood, how had she done that? It had felt so easy and natural. She opened her fist. The glass front was unharmed, her mother's portrait safely intact.

The Earl's deep sound of satisfaction brought her head up. All of his expression was centered in a fierce light in his eyes: exaltation.

She clenched her fist around the miniature and closed the distance between them, propelled by rage. "How dare you—"

"Have you opened it yet?" he asked, stopping her midsentence. His mask was back in place.

"What?" She stared down at her hand again. "It does not open."

"Take the time to look," he said. "If you do not, it will be a cardinal sin."

"My dear, what are you doing?" Aunt's voice wrenched her around.

"I was just pointing out an amusing situation on the road below," Lord Carlston said smoothly. He walked past Helen, drawing Aunt's attention away from the fact that they had been standing too close together. "I also see that Lady Chawith has drawn up in her carriage. We will take our leave of you, madam." He bowed then turned to Helen. "It has been a pleasure."

Mr. Brummell bowed and murmured his own compliments. The two men departed, leaving a bemused silence in their wake.

"Well," Aunt said. "That was abrupt."

Abrupt and infuriating. Helen tightened her grip around the miniature, longing to open her hand and check for a catch—not that she believed there was one. Surely she would have found it by now.

A knock made them both jump. Was he back? No, it was only Barnett with silver salver in hand. He walked across to Aunt and bowed, offering Lady Chawith's unmistakable flamboyant blue card.

"Did she see Mr. Brummell depart?" Aunt asked him.

"Yes, my lady."

Aunt smiled. "Then, yes, we are at home."

Seven

A RELENTLESS PARADE OF visitors kept Helen in the drawing room all afternoon, the miniature hidden in the workbag at her feet, pulling at her attention like a magnet. When their last guest, Lady Beck, finally stood to leave, then remembered another piece of scandal about Lord Byron, Helen felt as though she might howl with frustration. Eventually, however, the woman made her stately way downstairs and Helen, with a swift excuse to Aunt, headed in the opposite direction, taking the stairs at a disgraceful two at a time, workbag clasped to her chest.

She closed her chamber door behind her and listened for Darby in the dim cool room. Beyond the eternal grind of carriage wheels on the gritty clay of nearby Piccadilly and Curzon Street, all was quiet. The candles and hearth had not yet been lit for the evening, and the last of the dour afternoon light made gray shapes of her bed, writing desk, and chair.

"Darby?"

No answer: her maid was elsewhere.

Good.

She crossed to the window, lace-clad hand deep inside her workbag and groping for the miniature. Two fingers hooked around the smooth, cold oval. She pulled it free from a tangle of cottons and held it flat on her palm and up to the pale daylight.

Take the time to look.

Helen frowned at the gold filigree and the memory of Lord Carlston's commanding manner. Insufferable man. Had he already opened it? The possibility deepened her frown. She was not even sure she believed him.

She turned the frame on its edge. A faint seam in the gold indicated that the two halves—portrait side and woven-hair side—were fixed together rather than being one whole piece. It could, possibly, open. She ran her fingertip around the seam. No catch; not even an indentation. She held the portrait at eye level, tilting it toward the fading light. Perhaps opening it involved prising the glass cover off the front or back. Yet both seemed to be clamped in place by a surrounding ledge of gold. Surely he did not mean breaking it? Helen shook her head, as much to deny the possibility as to refuse the action. She ran her finger over the filigree border. Perhaps a catch had been embedded somewhere in the delicate gold lacework. It seemed improbable; she had stared at it for hours in those early months after her parents' death. Even in her grief, she would have noticed. Nevertheless, she squinted into the layer beneath the filigree. Nothing obvious.

Take the *time* to look, he'd said. And then something about cardinal sin.

On reflection, it was an odd comment, since it was unlikely he was Catholic. Her aunt would have surely mentioned such a family disgrace in the same breath as the murder. Helen made a soft sound of inspiration. Lord Carlston was still at his games. *Time* and *cardinal sin* must be clues.

She studied the gold frame again. There was no obvious reference to time on it—no clockface or hands. And there was definitely no reference to cardinal sin. Perhaps the clue was just "cardinal." A cardinal's miter? A cardinal bird? Perhaps he meant the cardinal directions: north, south, east, west. Was that too simple?

She studied the motifs worked into the border. The small gold flames at the cardinal positions did not appear any different from those around them. Still, it was worth a try. She pressed the flame at the north position. Nothing happened. The obvious direction would be clockwise, since he had mentioned time. She slid her fingertip to the east position and pushed. Something moved beneath the filigree.

Good Heavens, he was telling the truth.

She jabbed at the remaining two flames. There was a small shift under each, and then the portrait slid slightly to the side, as if swinging on an axle that had been fixed at the top.

Helen let out her breath, suddenly aware that she had been holding it. All this time, there had been a hidden compartment and she had not known; a compartment made for her mother.

She pushed the portrait to the side and peered into the base. A reflection of her own eye stared back. A mirror. She looked more closely. A mirror covered in some kind of glass. She tapped it and the sound was dull. Not glass, something heavier. She dug her fingernail into the edge, but it did not lift. No other hidden compartments. The whole mechanism seemed very elaborate for just a mirror. As far as Helen could recall, Lady Catherine had not been vain, so it was doubtful that she would carry a portrait of herself around, let alone one with a mirror inside. What was its purpose, then? Espionage? It was the rumor that she had heard most often: Lady Catherine as spy for Bonaparte. *Napoleon's harlot.* The possibility swept over her in a sick chill. She had once asked Andrew if it could be true—finally voicing the terrible fear—but he had just walked away. She had never raised the subject again, but doubt had taken root. Still, this was no proof. And the Queen herself had warned against the rumors that had wrapped themselves around her mother's name.

With a careful finger, she guided the portrait back into place. A press of the gold border locked the mechanism into one piece again. Of course, she was assuming that her mother had commissioned the unusual interior. Perhaps it had been someone else. Her father? She glanced across at her secretaire. Maybe his portrait had a secret compartment too.

It took only a moment to retrieve the key and unlock the desk hatch. As always, her father's handsome face looked out from the inner shelf. She replaced her mother's miniature and picked up the portrait of Lord Hayden. It did not have the weight of her mother's and, when held to the light, showed no seam around the edge. Nor were there any flames on the smooth gold border, save those shaped into the loop at the top. Helen twisted and pulled it. Nothing. She pressed the four cardinal points for good measure, but the portrait did not shift. Unless there was another way to open the plainer frame, only her mother's miniature had a mirror set inside. But what did that mean? And why did Lord Carlston want her to find it?

A knock on the door jerked her hand down to her side, her father's miniature hidden in her fist.

"Wait," she called. "Who is it?"

"Hugo, my lady," the muffled voice answered, "to light the night candles. And Tilly, to stoke the hearth."

"One moment."

She placed her father's portrait back on the shelf and locked the desk hatch again. The key was quickly back in its niche and the compartment pressed home. All was as it should be. Hugo and his sharp eyes would have nothing to report this time.

"Enter," Helen called, stepping away from the desk.

~

DARBY ARRIVED TO dress her for dinner as Tilly finished stoking the hearth in the bedchamber, the new flames giving some warmth to the chill of early dusk. Hugo had already lit the candles, closed the shutters, and departed with a sidelong glance at the writing desk.

As soon as the door closed behind Tilly, Darby asked, "Did Lord Carlston return it, my lady?" Her face was pink with anticipation.

"Yes," Helen whispered, "but by the most unusual method."

She motioned Darby through to the dressing room and pointed to the hallway door; anyone could be listening. Darby crossed over, opened it a crack, and then closed it again, nodding. All was clear.

"He threw it at me," Helen said. "With *all* his strength."

"Threw it?"

Helen nodded. "But not only that—I caught it. It was as if someone else's hand reached up for it."

"I cannot believe he would throw something at a lady," Darby said. "How did he know you could catch it?"

Helen was struck by the question. "He couldn't have. Even I didn't know."

"Did he say why he had taken it?"

"No, although he made it clear it was not an act of chivalry." Helen picked up her silver hairpin box and upended it onto the dressing table, the pins spreading across the polished wood in a pattering clatter. Although a little larger than the miniature, the box had a similar weight. "Here, throw this at me. I want to see if I can do it again."

Darby stared at the offered projectile, then backed away. "No, my lady, I can't!"

"Yes, you can. It's all right; I've asked you to do it. You won't get into trouble."

"But what if it hits you?"

"Then it hits me. But we must hope I can catch it again." She smiled. "Or at least duck."

Her maid took the box. "I don't like doing this, my lady."

"Think of it as an investigation using the methods of natural philosophy."

Darby frowned. "Isn't that godless?"

"No. All I'm saying is that we are going to prove whether or not I can catch the box in the same way I caught the miniature."

"But it is very heavy and hard," Darby said, weighing it in her hand. "Perhaps we could start with something softer." She looked around, fixing on the chest of drawers. "I could roll up a pair of gloves."

Helen shook her head. "It won't have the same heft or speed as the miniature. We will use the box."

With grim resignation, Darby clasped it more firmly. "As you wish, my lady. Are you ready?"

"No, don't tell me. Just throw it, like he did."

Drawing back her arm, Darby pitched the box into a high lob that sailed up toward the ceiling and then lazily arced down to Helen. It dropped, unsatisfyingly, into her hand.

Darby clapped. "Well done, my lady."

"No, not like that." Helen crossed the carpet and pressed the box back into her maid's hand. "Throw it at me with all your strength and as fast as you can. When I'm not expecting it."

"But you *are* expecting it," Darby said.

That was true. Helen walked to the other side of the room again. "All right. I shall start dressing for dinner and then, at some point, just throw it at me. As if you mean it."

It was a most exciting toilette. The first missile came as Darby turned from retrieving a fresh pair of silk stockings from the chest of drawers. Although the vigor behind the throw was still too timid, it caught Helen stepping out of her petticoat. Nevertheless, her hand flew up and caught it mid-arc. After some patient urging, Darby's next throw was far more energetic. It shot out from behind the door of the clothes press, and Helen found herself leaping up from the dressing table chair, clad in only her fresh chemise and stays. The box slapped into her hand at the top of her ascent, and she added a twist on the downward journey to land facing Darby. It was all fluid reflex, a stretching of muscle and judgment that felt new, but at the same time as if it had always been in her bones.

"Did you see that?"

"I did, my lady. You are like a cat."

They both laughed.

"Make it more difficult," Helen urged.

Darby nodded, her gray eyes bright with the challenge. "Watch out, my lady. I will not hold back."

She was as good as her word: the throws came quick and hard. Some were aimed at Helen's head, some at her feet, and a few even aimed at her back. And each time, Helen scooped and spun and leaped, catching the box with smooth certainty.

Finally Darby threw a particularly fast and nasty pitch at the back of Helen's head as she viewed her finished toilette in the mirror. She saw it coming—a blur in the glass—and did not even turn around, using the reflection to judge the right moment to raise her hand and grab the box before its sharp edge slammed into her scalp.

"Oh, my lady, that is . . ." Darby faltered.

"Unusual," Helen whispered.

"Yes." Darby nodded vigorously. Helen lowered her hand, the box caged in her fingers, and looked at the reflection of her own wide eyes. How could she do this? It was obviously no freak occurrence—she was able to do it over and over again—yet she had never shown any particular aptitude in the shuttlecock and bat-and-ball games she had played as a child. And even this past Christmas, when Andrew had tossed her a bonbon during a riotous game, she had dropped it. That would not happen now. An uneasy correlation formed in her mind: this new ability and the strange restless energy that had been building within her.

She needed to talk to Lord Carlston. Whatever this was, he seemed to know about it. She gripped the silver box, trying to still the sudden trembling in her hand. Silently, Darby came and adjusted a curl that had come loose, her hand resting against Helen's shoulder in a brief moment of reassurance. Helen met her eyes in the mirror. Darby's face had the same mix of wonder and confusion that was in her own. But there was also something else: wariness.

"Don't mention this to anyone, Darby."

"I won't, my lady."

In the reflection, she saw Darby cross herself.

HELEN AND HER aunt and uncle were engaged to dine at Lord and Lady Heathcote's that evening—a May Day celebration. Dinner started at the fashionable town hour of eight and, as usual, was a drawn-out affair, made especially tedious for Helen. She'd had the misfortune to be placed between a Mr. Pruit, who insisted on delivering a sermon about the evils of dance, and old Sir Reginald Danely, whose pouchy eyes and tooth-sucking attention were reserved for the meat. Neither gentleman offered any distraction from the turmoil of her thoughts. All she could think of was the miniature and her mother and that feeling of . . . *rightness* when she had stretched and leaped to catch the box. And every question that she asked herself—*How can I do this? Why can I do it? Is there a link to Mother?*—seemed to lead back to Lord Carlston. She was sure he had answers. Yet, maddeningly, she had no way of knowing when she would have the chance to demand them from him.

Did she dare write and arrange an encounter? Although only a new acquaintance, he was a distant relative, and she could argue that it was in the realms of propriety: admittedly, the far realms of propriety, considering his reputation. The bold idea made her put down her forkload of salmon. Her aunt and uncle would not accept that argument, nor would they let such a letter leave the house. If she did write, she would have to send it secretly, by Darby or the penny post. She picked up her fork again and took a mouthful of the delicately herbed fish. It would be a big risk: keeping a secret from the servants was almost impossible. She trusted Darby, but her uncle had his own spies, and he would, no doubt, come to hear of it before she had even finished writing the address. Such a transgression would have her packed in a minute and exiled to Lansdale, his country estate, to sit in solitude until he arranged a marriage. The possibility turned the salmon to ash in her mouth. She would have to find another way.

Finally the footmen laid out the dessert course—an extensive selection of pastries and sweets from Gunter's. From the other end of the table, where her uncle and aunt sat, Helen could hear snatches of a heated debate about the terrible Luddite riots: apparently, more weaving machines had been destroyed in Lancashire, and a factory owner killed. At her end, however, the conversation had dwindled into remarks upon the food and snide gossip, neither of which interested her in the least. That was, until Lady Fellowes mentioned the Ratcliffe Highway murders.

"Have you heard the rumors?" she said to Mr. Beardsley at her side and Lady Dale beyond. "It is said there was another murderer involved in those heinous Ratcliffe killings, and that he is still at large."

Although the conventions of polite dining dictated that Helen confine herself to those sitting to her left and right, she picked up a peach and, on the pretext of peeling it, focused her attention on the conversation opposite.

"No," Mr. Beardsley said breathlessly, in a peculiarly girlish manner. "How awful." He gave an extravagant shudder, hands pressed to either side of his thin powdered face. "I still have nightmares from the descriptions in the papers."

Mr. Beardsley's theatricality held no charm for Helen, but she did sympathize with his horror. The reports of the Ratcliffe Highway murders had stayed in her mind as well.

Two innocent families—seven people in all—had been brutally bludgeoned to death in December. One of the victims had been a three-month-old baby, little Timothy Marr, whose head had been nearly severed from his tiny shoulders by a vicious slice to the throat. The description had pierced Helen with a cold understanding: there were monsters in the world, for surely only a monster could kill an infant with such brutality. The Marr family had been drapers, and Mr. and Mrs. Marr, their apprentice, and little Timothy had been killed just after their shop had closed for the night. The newspapers had reported that there had been so much gore that it was impossible to pick a way through the narrow premises without slipping and sliding on the blood. Then, just twelve days later, the Marrs' neighbors, Mr. and Mrs. Williamson, and their servant girl had met the same gruesome fate in their tavern—bludgeoned, throats cut, and Mr. Williamson's hand all but hacked off. It was not unusual for the papers to report bloody murders, but none had been like this before: savage, motiveless killings of respectable people who had no ties to the criminal world. It felt as if decency itself was under attack. This second killing spree made it clear that a madman was on the loose. The Home Office—responsible for public protection—ordered an investigation and assigned Bow Street Runners to the case. Thankfully, an arrest was quickly made: Mr. John Williams, a seaman. Helen, alongside all of London, had breathed a sigh of relief that the foul murderer had been found. Yet he was never brought to trial, robbing the city of final justice by hanging himself in his jail cell.

Lady Dale shook her head. "Do not take any heed of the stories, my dear Mr. Beardsley. It is mere scaremongering by the penny press. John Williams was charged with the murders, and his suicide confirmed his guilt." She arched an eyebrow at her two companions. "But have you heard the latest? We have our own murderer back amongst us. Lord Carlston has returned."

At his lordship's name, Helen's attention sharpened even more.

"Oh yes," Mr. Beardsley said, face vivid with the new subject. "So handsome. So *séduisant*." He gave another shudder, this time of delight. "Mrs. Delacomb was pushing her daughter at him last night. I swear, she was ready to lay the girl out on a platter for the man. Doesn't she know what he did to his last wife?"

"Honoria Delacomb would push that bran-faced girl at the Devil if there were a chance he would marry her," Lady Dale said. "She would think Carlston a fine catch—never mind that slight taint of murder."

Lady Fellowes sniffed. "Well, I would not give a dog I liked to the man." She reached for a peach. "Although," she added, her plump hand hovering over the fruit, "one could argue that Miss Delacomb *is* very much like a bulldog." She chose a cream-filled pastry instead.

Mr. Beardsley giggled. "It is a lost cause, anyway. No sign of Lady Carlston was ever found and, by law, a missing person is not deemed dead until seven years have passed. Mrs. Delacomb will find that his lordship is still officially married for another three years, at least."

Lady Fellowes gave a snort. "Oh, please, I must have the joy of telling Honoria that piece of intelligence."

Lady Dale allowed a small smile. "I doubt that Miss Delacomb has any of the charms that would tempt a man like Carlston, legally or not." She took a contemplative sip of red wine. "Nevertheless, there are plenty of girls out there who would, and I, for one, do not like the idea of him moving amongst them. Without his wife's body found, he may be legally untouchable, but I think we all agree his heart is black with sin. I knew him and dear Elise before all the ugliness, and from what I can see, his sojourn on the Continent has not changed him at all. If anything, he is even more cold and vicious." Lady Dale shook her head, the false curls on either side of her narrow face bouncing in disapproval. "I could never understand why Elise chose him. She was such a sweet girl, and the dear Duke of Selburn was intent upon her too. Do you remember? It was before the old Duke, his father, died. Selburn was still Viscount Chenwith at the time."

Helen, who had long finished peeling the peach, looked up at that. She had not known that Selburn had wanted to marry Carlston's wife. Was that why Andrew—ever loyal to his friend—disliked Carlston so much and would not speak of the family tie, even to his sister?

"I remember that the Duke took a horsewhip to Carlston over it," Lady Fellowes said. "Such a scandal!"

"Yes, but as I remember it, Carlston took the whip off him and beat the Duke near senseless," Mr. Beardsley said with another delighted shudder. "Brute of a man."

Helen gasped; no wonder Andrew wanted naught to do with Lord Carlston. Her soft exclamation caught the attention of Lady Fellowes. The woman's small eyes fixed glassily on her for a moment, then a nervous lick of her lips announced that she had recalled Helen's connection to Carlston. With a loud clearing of her throat and a flutter of plump fingers, she said to no one in particular, "What an excellent array of fruit. Don't you agree?"

THE DINNER BROKE up at around one in the morning, but the carriage ride home was far longer than usual, delayed by the last of the rowdy May Day revelers clogging New Bond Street. Helen's uncle sent both Philip and Hugo to clear a path for the coach, but even with their commanding height and obvious red livery, it took the footmen twenty minutes to perform the task.

It was nearly two by the time Helen entered her bedchamber. As always, Darby was in the dressing room. She was mending by the light of a candle, but on Helen's entrance immediately set the linen petticoat aside and rose to curtsy. Small lengths of white thread clung to her brown-checked gown, and she absently brushed at them as she took the night candlestick from Helen and placed it on the dressing table.

"Was it a pleasant evening, my lady?" she asked, gathering the cream shawl from Helen's shoulders. Three deft folds and it was laid on top of the chest of drawers.

"Uneventful," Helen said, passing over her reticule. "I was at the dull end of the table."

She held out her hands for Darby to work the lemon kid gloves from them. As her maid untied the right riband, Helen studied her face for any sign of her earlier wariness. None seemed to be in evidence, yet something was on the girl's mind. Perhaps she was having second thoughts about their plan.

Darby glanced up. "Was the food delicious, my lady?"

Helen nodded. Darby always liked to hear about the dishes that had been served. "There was a good plate of new season asparagus dressed in almond butter, and a chine of well-roasted spring lamb." She stretched out her fingers as the second glove was pulled off. "And the desserts were from Gunter's. I had ice cream and a rather wonderful tartlet with strawberries on top."

"Ice cream!" Darby gave a soft grunt of appreciation. "What flavor was it?"

"Raspberry."

"Yet it is not even the season," she marveled. "Did it taste very much like the fruit?"

"Exactly like it." Helen watched her stow the gloves in the top drawer. "Tell me, Darby, are you still willing to open Berta's box with me?"

Surprise wiped the late-night fatigue from the girl's face. "Of course, my lady. What makes you think I would not?"

"I think my ability to catch things has unsettled you." Helen quirked her mouth to show she shared the disquiet.

Darby picked up the folded shawl, smoothing it. "I must admit it has occupied my thoughts all evening. Forgive me for saying so, but what your ladyship did was not natural. It made me wonder what or who was behind such a strange gift. But I know you are a good person, so I trust that if it has purpose or meaning, then it is from the hand of God and not the Great Deceiver."

Helen stared at her maid. The hand of God? What a startling thought. "That is quite a pronouncement."

Darby met her gaze squarely. "Yes, it is." She bent to open a lower drawer.

A sudden fear caught Helen. What if Darby's trust was misplaced? What if the extra energy and sudden dexterity were, in fact, the work of the Devil? Perhaps her uncle was right: she was destined to descend into her mother's unholy ways.

No, she was not like her mother. Admittedly, she also fell short of her uncle's ideal of female virtue—it was so hard to be that irreproachable mix of innocence, modesty, and unquestioning obedience—but such a failure did not make her an instrument of Hell. After all, she went to church and took Communion every week. If she were an instrument of Hell, surely she would not be able to accept the Host. At the very first touch of sanctified wine or bread, she would have dissolved into flames and howls and sparks of sulfur.

Helen wrapped her arms around herself, the relief of such logic resolving into the amusing image of their vicar dousing her infernal flames. Reverend Haley was a neat man: he would be greatly irritated by such an untidy show of fiendishness. Yet even that diverting vision could not quite shake the new anxiety that burrowed into her mind like a wasp into a beehive. If anyone had lost grace and become an instrument of Hell, it was Lord Carlston; the one man who seemed to have the answers she craved. What did that say about her ability?

Darby saved her from that unhappy line of thought by withdrawing a thin, flat length of metal from the bottom drawer. She held it up. "For the box, my lady."

A hoof rasp—what a clever thought. "Well done, Darby. That should do the job."

"I went down to the mews straight after you left and took it when the groom wasn't looking," Darby said. "See, I was always intending to go with you." She offered the rasp, an expectant look on her face.

Helen took the file and held it up. Although it tapered at the end, it seemed rather thick. "Are you sure it will fit in between the lid and the base?"

Darby exhaled, her hand flat against her heart. "Oh, my lady, what a relief. You are not possessed."

"I beg your pardon?"

"The rasp is iron, and those of the demon and faery worlds cannot abide iron. It burns them if they touch it." She smiled broadly at Helen. "I am very glad it has not burned you."

Helen contemplated the cold metal in her hand—trial by iron—and gave a small hollow laugh. "What would you have done if it had?"

Darby shrugged. "I had not got that far. I was sure it would not, my lady."

Helen handed back the rasp. "I appreciate the confidence." It was an absurd country superstition, yet she could not help gathering a little comfort from it. It did not, however, quite dispel all her doubt. She crossed the room, trying to walk the unease from her mind and body. "We will wait until the house retires, and then make our way down to the housekeeper's room."

And so they waited. Darby picked up her mending again. Helen settled on the chaise longue and turned her mind firmly away from the awful possibility of being an instrument of Hell. Or Heaven, for that matter. Instead she tried to concentrate on a plan to meet Lord Carlston—perhaps he rode Rotten Row, and she could happen upon him during the promenade hours—and at the same time listen for signs that the household had finally gone to bed. She heard the soft tread of one of the housemaids climbing the stairs to the garret, and a little later, the sound of Barnett checking the ground-floor doors and shutters. After that, the house seemed to settle into itself. Eventually even the street noise died down into the occasional rumble of a late-returning carriage.

When she finally heard the clock downstairs chime three, she rose and whispered, "Check the hallway."

Darby crossed to the door, opened it a crack, and peered out. She gave a reassuring nod and ducked back to retrieve the iron rasp from the mantel.

Gathering her gown, Helen stepped softly into the dim corridor and peered up through the balustrade at Mrs. Grant's door on the half landing above. Far too close for comfort. The door was firmly closed, but even so, Helen suppressed a shudder at the thought of being discovered by the housekeeper. It had always been her main anxiety on her midnight forays—Mrs. Grant would be quick to report any misdemeanor to Aunt. And this time there was more at stake: she had involved Darby. Mrs. Grant would be even quicker to report an upstart housemaid raised too high. Helen bunched her gown more tightly. Maybe she should send Darby back.

At that moment, Darby emerged from the dressing room and shut the door. Only a sliver of brightness from under the doorway brought some shape to the dark corridor and lit the excitement on her maid's face. Helen stood still in the gloom, warring with herself. It was not fair to put her at such risk. Yet it felt right to have the girl by her side. A strange thing to admit.

"You must go back," Helen whispered.

The excitement on Darby's face drew down into a frown. "No, my lady. This is for Berta."

It was true: this was no silly night wandering. They had an important purpose. With a nod, Helen led the way to the staircase.

They paused at the top and peered down the switchback of stairs. The second and first floors were dark. The only light came up from the ground-floor foyer: the night lamp outside the front door shone through the high fanlight window, patterning the marble floor with a crescent of lacework. Helen held her breath and listened, but no sound rose. The house seemed at rest. It was time to go down.

She avoided the squeaky top step and landed lightly on the one below, glancing back. With a smile, Darby followed. They made their way slowly down the three flights to the foyer, their steps muffled by the thick carpet runners. At the bottom, Helen crept toward the back corridor, intent on reaching the kitchen stairs at the rear of the house, the route she had always taken to wheedle a cake from Cook. A hiss from Darby turned her around.

"We can take Mr. Barnett's stairs, my lady." She pointed down the narrow, uncarpeted extension of the main staircase.

Helen had only a rough map of the servants' quarters in her mind. Even so, she knew the stairs ended just behind the butler's pantry, and the housekeeper's room—their goal—was well beyond it, near the front of the house. She also knew that Barnett slept in a small room adjacent to his pantry to protect the valuable plate. Hopefully he was a deep sleeper.

She paused at the top step and contemplated the dark stairwell. The basement had very few windows, and none along the corridor. Without a candle, it would make more sense for Darby to go first—her duties took her down there every day. Helen made a soft sound of self-reproach. It was neither Darby's place nor her responsibility to take the lead.

"Keep close," Helen whispered, and, with more confidence than she felt, descended into the darkness, her grip sliding along the smooth, worn wood of the balustrade.

The steep spiral of steps sighed and creaked under their cautious descent. Darby took her at her word and stayed on her heels the whole way down. As they neared the bottom, Helen slowed their momentum to an even more careful creep. The darkness felt as if it had its own texture: a dense, thick wrapping of black. Helen could barely see the last few steps as she made her way down to the cold stone floor.

The damp air in the corridor smelled of boiled wool and meat fat. It even tasted greasy, settling at the back of Helen's throat like a dose of oil. She felt her way along the plaster wall until her fingers found a corner. A chilly draft swirled around her ankles, bringing with it a whiff of the servants' privy and the horse stink of the mews. Ah—the passageway to the side yard. She led the way across, her groping fingers finding the smooth guide of the opposite wall.

A few more steps along the corridor brought her fingertips up against the frame of a doorway: the butler's pantry. Door open. If Barnett heard them pass, all was lost. Beside her, Darby sucked in a hard breath, obviously coming to the same conclusion. No candle was alight within, but that did not mean Barnett was asleep. Through the door, she could see a narrow window set high in the wall, a gray rectangle against the darkness, but there was not enough light to reach the corridor. She strained to hear if there was any movement in the room. Yes, something was making a noise. Low and deep. A snore? It came again: a rough, rhythmic snort. Helen held her own breath, waiting. There it was again. Definitely a snore. She grabbed Darby's sleeve and edged past the door, wincing as the girl's half boot scraped the stone. Had Barnett heard it too? She pulled Darby along, praying for the next snore. Finally it sawed through the silence.

Helen could just make out the corridor's end: a faint outline of the front basement door, its top and bottom silvered with pale light from the lamp high on the street above. It was enough to show her their destination: the shadowy door to the housekeeper's room.

Darby saw it too, or perhaps she just knew they were close, for she quickened her step.

Unlike Barnett's door, this one was firmly closed. Helen grasped the cold metal handle and slowly turned it. What if Mrs. Grant was still inside? The wild thought came too late: the mechanism had already clicked. The door swung inward. Helen stood on the threshold, taking in the terrain, Darby peering over her shoulder. Two front windows allowed enough street light to carve glimpses of detail out of the shadows: the glint of gold lettering along book spines stacked on a desk; a curve of hearth bricks above the last red embers of an evening fire; the ghostly shape of a chemise on a drying rack. And all around, walls filled with shelves of china that shone in cold catches of gleaming white.

But, thankfully, no Mrs. Grant.

"There it is," Darby whispered, pointing to a box under the desk. "I noted it while at tea this evening."

"Find a candle," Helen said. "I'll get the box." With one last glance back up the dark corridor, she shut the door.

Berta's lockbox was not big. Nor was it heavy, Helen thought with surprise, as she pulled it out from under the desk. There could not be much in it. Darby turned from the fireplace, the flame from a taper bringing soft illumination to the room. Even in that small light, it was obvious that the box was cheap: the deal had not been finished well or even varnished, and the brass lock was badly fitted in the facing of the lid. Helen tapped it. Loose, too. Maybe it would just come apart. She dug her fingernails into the crack between lid and base and lifted, but it stayed stubbornly fast.

Darby kneeled beside her, tin candleholder in hand. "My lady, be careful of your nails," she murmured. "Here, let me open it. I have had some experience."

"No, I will do it." If it ever came to recriminations, at least Helen could truthfully say that *she* had broken open the box. She slotted the end of the rasp into the gap beside the brass lock.

"You will need to slide right and then up, my lady," Darby said, demonstrating with the taper. The flame trailed through the air, leaving a momentary path of instruction.

Helen steadied her grip on the rasp then wrenched it to the right and firmly up. A little too firmly—something cracked. She froze.

"Oh no," Darby whispered. "The wood has split."

Helen pulled the rasp free. Carefully, she lifted the lid. "At least it is open."

Darby was right: the lock had torn free of its moorings and splintered the wood. Helen poked the sharp slivers back into place, but it was obvious the lock could not be pressed back into use.

"What are we going to do, my lady?"

"Search for a clue," Helen said. She could sense the future calamity of the broken lock, but there was no point in retreating from their immediate task. "Hold up the candle."

Darby obliged.

Inside the box, laid across the top, was a white cotton chemisette with a modest ruffle at the neck and a few clumsy pin tucks down the front.

"That's her Sunday best," Darby said softly.

Helen gently lifted out the bodice insert and placed it on the carpet, suddenly feeling the burden of handling the girl's belongings. How would she feel if someone broke open her writing desk and pawed through her secrets?

Next came a blue dress-length of dimity, not yet made up. The cloth was coarse under Helen's fingers, but the bluebell print was pretty. Beneath it, a few treasures had been carefully laid out: a cheap copy of Mr. Scott's *The Lady of the Lake*, three old entrance tickets to Vauxhall Gardens pressed between a folded piece of paper, a length of green riband, four farthings in a heart-shaped tin box, and a Bible.

"There are no letters," Helen said, surveying the pitiable array of items. "Did you say her mother lived in the north? Surely she would write to her daughter?"

Darby shrugged. "She probably doesn't have the learning for it."

Most likely, but it was disappointing to find no address. Helen slipped the Vauxhall tickets from their paper shield. They were years old and a little dirty—probably found on the ground and kept for the pretty artwork. With a sigh, she slid them back into their cover.

After all that effort, they had discovered nothing that might help locate Berta.

She picked up the Bible. It was bound with black leather: quite a handsome edition for a housemaid. Maybe it had been a gift or a prize, which meant there could be an inscription inside that noted the place of origin. She opened the cover and flipped to the frontispiece. No inscription, just Berta's name. She ran her thumb across the gilt edging, fanning the pages. They stopped and parted about halfway through, caught on something inserted within. Two thin cards. She pulled them out.

It took a moment for the image on the top card to make sense.

"What is it?" Darby leaned over, the taper in her hand shedding more light onto the abomination. "Holy Father!"

The drawing showed a naked woman lying on a bed, legs akimbo, a group of men eyeing her through their raised quizzing glasses. A familiar signature was scrawled at the edge.

"It is by Rowlandson," Helen said in disbelief, that fact almost as shocking as the image. "How could he draw this? He has exhibited at the Royal Academy!"

She turned to the next card. Not by Rowlandson, and even more obscene. A naked woman on her knees with a man, hugely rampant, bent over her, like a stallion covering a mare.

"Why would Berta have such things?" Darby sat back on her heels. "Oh, my lady. Maybe I was wrong. Maybe she *has* gone to Covent Garden."

For all her sickened horror, Helen could not stop looking. Of course she had seen depictions of the male member on the Greek statues at the British Museum, but none of those had been so large and *upstanding*. Was this truly the human act?

"My lady, you will make yourself ill looking at such filth. Put them away."

Helen jammed the cards back between the pages of the Bible and shoved it into the box. Her hand hovered over the leather cover. No, such things should not be housed in the Holy Book. She slid out the cards and quickly inserted them between the pages of *The Lady of the Lake*. "We must go, Darby."

Her maid nodded emphatically. Together they feverishly repacked the rest of Berta's belongings, closed the box, and pushed it under the desk.

"What will we do about the lock?" Darby asked.

"I don't know," Helen said, rising to her feet. She just wanted to be away from the room—away from the drawings—as fast as possible.

With the candleholder back on the mantel and the taper snuffed out, Helen led the way into the corridor. They retraced their steps, the reassuring sound of Barnett's snores following them to the staircase. As they climbed toward the gray gloom of the foyer, Helen looked back. For an instant she thought she saw a figure—a dense, man-shaped darkness—standing at the recess that led to the yard. Then she blinked, and it was gone.

Eight

Saturday, 2 May 1812

BOTH MISTRESS AND maid were quiet the next morning as Helen dressed for family prayers. Darby tried to raise the subject of the cards, but Helen held up her hand, stopping any discussion. They were all she had thought about for three restless hours before she had finally fallen asleep. She needed to set them aside, at least until the shock and the strange uneasiness they had brought in their wake had found a place to sit within her mind.

Thankfully, the day planned by her aunt did not offer many opportunities for quiet contemplation. They started at the cloth warehouses, shopping for dress-lengths to take to Madame Hortense and a woolen for Mr. Duray, the habit maker, and then on to an exhausting round of visits, culminating in a small private supper ball at the Lindsays'. During the rather long evening, the images did intrude upon her again, but each time, she firmly pushed them out of her thoughts and concentrated on her conversation and dance steps.

It was not until Sunday morning at church that the images returned in full worrying force.

Reverend Haley's sermon was a vigorous denunciation of

unholy entertainments—the dangers of lewd plays and masquerade balls—but his constant use of words like *naked* and *flesh* brought back stark flashes of those black ink bodies. Helen saw them when she kneeled on the small prayer stools beside Aunt and Uncle. She saw them as she sang, "When I Survey the Wondrous Cross." And she saw them from her seat in the family box as she looked at the memorial stones set into the church wall. It was as if the foul images had finally blossomed into their full meaning, like a dark bruise upon her mind. And they had left her with equally troubling questions. Darby had asked the obvious in the housekeeper's room: Why would a young maid like Berta have such obscene things in her possession? Perhaps it had been a mistake; she had lent her Bible to another who had hidden the cards within to make mischief. Or maybe they had been given to her, although they were hardly a decent man's token of regard. The other possibility—that Berta really was depraved and had followed that depravity to Covent Garden—haunted Helen in the coach all the way home to Half Moon Street.

As was Uncle's custom, he joined Helen and Aunt for Sunday luncheon before he retired to his club. He had long conceded the necessity of allowing his wife, and now Helen, to attend social events on Sundays—the Season did not stop for the Sabbath—but he insisted upon the family dining together after church to maintain the sanctity of the day. It was never an easy meal for Helen, and that afternoon it seemed even more fraught than usual. Perhaps it was the horror of those cards overlaid by the shock of her uncle's convivial mood.

"I am glad to hear from your aunt that your presentation went well, Helen." He smiled over a fork laden with cold beef.

Helen hurriedly touched her serviette to her lips, hiding a surprised swallow of trout mousse. "It did, Uncle. Thank you."

"And the Queen spoke to her too, Pennworth," Aunt said.

"With no mention of Cath—" She trailed off, realizing her mistake, then recovered with a bright "with no mention of awkward connections."

He grunted, chewing reflectively. "I am glad to hear it. Let us hope the Court harpies will follow Her Majesty's example and leave that episode in the past." He waved his empty fork at Helen. "You see, my dear, our good reputation and your mild behavior has rehabilitated your position. It even has the Royal approval." He grinned.

For a moment Helen was nonplused, then she realized he was being playful. She quickly positioned a smile. "Yes, Uncle."

He nodded, satisfied, at his wife. "It was well done on our part, Leonore."

Aunt straightened under the unusual praise. "Indeed, Pennworth."

Helen stared down at the row of beans on her plate.

"And did you enjoy your evening beside Sir Reginald at the Heathcotes' the other night?" her uncle continued. She recalled the silent old man at her left who had plowed through the lamb and venison dishes.

"He seemed quite taken with the meat," she said, then caught the widening of Aunt's eyes, and pressed her lips together against further observations.

Uncle paused in his own spearing of another slice of beef. "He is a widower twice over, you know," he said, glancing at Aunt. "He mentioned he may be looking to wed again."

The delicate trout in Helen's stomach hardened into a lump of stone. Sir Reginald was approaching sixty.

Aunt's eyes fleetingly met Helen's: another warning not to speak. "I am not so sure, Pennworth. He is only a baronet."

"Good stock, though." Uncle extracted a piece of gristle from between his teeth. "And a bit of bad history wouldn't put him off. It might with others, you know, even with the Queen's graciousness."

"That may be, but you know Sir Reginald has been forced to sell a good deal of his estate. And it is near Nottingham, where those terrible Luddites are shooting people."

Helen looked down at her plate again. Clever Aunt. She had brought up the one subject that Uncle could not leave alone.

"True," he said. "The blackguards are rioting all over the country. I read in *The Times* yesterday that they are placarding the town streets in Nottingham and offering a reward for the mayor, dead or alive. Dead or alive, by Jove! They should all be strung up immediately, or it will end like the French Terror twenty years ago."

"I'm sure they will be stopped, my dear," Aunt said mildly.

The conversation moved on to Uncle's disgust at Reverend Haley's veiled stance on the matter—"The damned man is almost certainly a secret supporter of the workers!"—but Helen barely heard the diatribe. In her mind was a vision of old Sir Reginald leaning in to kiss her, his fleshy mouth and gravy breath looming closer and closer. And then, before she could stop it, an even worse image of Sir Reginald bent over her like the man on the second card. She pressed her hand to her mouth, hiding the rise of revulsion. Uncle was already looking for a quick betrothal, and he was not looking high. Aunt might have diverted him from the idea of this match, but there would come a time when she did not dislike the candidate so much. What then?

Helen picked up her glass and took a large mouthful of chilled wine. But even that could not quite wash away the imagined kiss and repugnant vision of old Sir Reginald.

~

AFTER LUNCH SHE slowly followed Aunt upstairs to the drawing room, impatient with the prospect of sitting through another three hours of reading or sewing or writing letters until the time came for the afternoon promenade in Hyde Park. Usually Helen either rode her mare, Circe, or drove herself and Aunt in the tilbury along Rotten Row. Today, however, Millicent and Lady Gardwell had arranged to collect them on their way to the park, and since the Gardwells could no longer afford to keep a London carriage, it was to be a stroll through the verdant pathways. Not as much fun as riding, but still an excellent opportunity to talk privately with her friend about the strange events of the past few days. Before that, however, there was the afternoon to fill.

With a sigh, Helen picked up *The Mirror of the Graces*—a newly published guide to good dressing—and settled onto the sofa. She had just reached the author's pronouncement that it was a woman's duty to be ornamental, but only as a way to enhance the beauty of a virtuous spirit, when the clock struck the longed-for hour. Aunt rose from her letters and signaled that it was time to dress.

"Do wear that new spotted cambric petticoat with the amber tunic, my dear," she said as they parted at the landing. "It is a fine enough day for it, and you can pair it with the sea-green Cossack coat."

Obediently, Helen donned the ensemble and met Aunt downstairs again. It felt like another age before Philip finally opened the drawing room doors to announce that Lady and Miss Gardwell had arrived. The young footman's pale skin was flushed with anticipation. Helen stifled a smile. He was to accompany them to the park, and his excitement was understandable. After all, walking out in the fresh air amongst so much natural beauty—and so much female beauty—was a daily drawcard for a good number of London's men. Of all ranks.

With their outerwear buttoned high, and bonnets tied tight against the wind that routinely barreled along the busy expanse of

Piccadilly, the small party set off toward Hyde Park Corner. Helen took Millicent's arm and forged ahead, trying to find a moment of privacy, but the older ladies kept pace, no doubt spurred on by the wind that still held an edge of winter.

"Girls," Aunt said from behind. "Do not walk so fast, please. Such speed is undignified."

Gritting her teeth, Helen slowed, catching Millicent's eye. Would they never get a moment to talk alone?

That moment had to wait a little longer. When they arrived at the park gates, it was well into the promenade hour, and the place was thronging. It seemed that the first fine Sunday for weeks had prompted most of London to venture out. The paths were filled with a shifting parade of defiant spring colors and lightweight cloth flapping in the breeze. Helen caught Millicent's arm and pulled her back as a lady in a flounced purple habit rode across the path on a lively bay mare, heading toward the start of Rotten Row. A good number of riders and carriages were already on the gravel-and-tan riding track, and the mare danced sideways as the woman tried to urge it into the sedate procession. Helen clicked her tongue in disapproval. The woman had a bad seat and a heavy hand; she should be on a more docile mount. A groom rode behind her, but he seemed more concerned with eyeing the maids on their half-day off than with his mistress's safety.

Sunday was the most democratic day at the "Lungs of London," with those of the lower stations, like the giggling maids, coming to walk in the same open spaces as the *beau monde.* Helen always thought it such a fascinating mix: the Quality eyeing each other's fashions, the scandalous demimonde with their bold eyes and revealing gowns, the middling families in their respectable best, and the house servants flirting on the lawns. But it also made for some impertinences, such as the two young city men gawping at Millicent as she lifted her hem to step over a deposit of horse dung.

Helen gave the taller of the two a haughty stare and pulled her friend toward the path that led to the Serpentine. From the corner of her eye, she saw a well-dressed older gentleman in a navy-blue greatcoat and black high-crowned beaver watching them from a small hill that rose toward the river. He seemed vaguely familiar.

"My dears," Aunt called. "Not that way. We will walk beside the Row."

Helen tucked her arm back into Millicent's and obediently adjusted their direction, her velvet reticule swinging from her wrist.

The path beside Rotten Row was so crowded that it was almost uncomfortable and, more to the point, offered no privacy. Helen and Millicent veered around a knot of men who had clustered at the fence to watch a black stallion go through its paces, their opinions of its gait loud in the crisp air. The two girls managed to find a moment of clear path beyond them, but then the young family ahead slowed and they found themselves in the midst of three crying children. With a smile and a nod, Helen quickly steered Millicent into a space between an old gentleman who hummed to himself and a pair of ladies walking arm in arm. She heard her aunt's raucous laugh pierce the air, but the sound seemed far too distant. She looked over her shoulder. Aunt and Lady Gardwell were still near the start of the path, exchanging pleasantries with the Cholmondeleys.

"Oh no," Helen said. "I thought they were right behind us."

"We shall have to wait," Millicent said. "We can't go beyond their sight."

Helen cast around for a solution, and found one beside the fence. A muddy patch had kept a space at the railings clear of spectators. "Let's wait over there," she said, leading her friend off the path to the pocket of privacy. "They can still see us, and we can talk properly without being overheard. Two buns for the price of one."

"If we don't get sucked into the mud first," Millicent said, lifting her hem and stepping cautiously over the grass. "Look, my boots are already stained."

"We can go back to the path if you want," Helen said. "It's just that it's been an age since I've spoken to you without someone hovering over us."

"I know." Millicent dropped her hem with a shrug. "Tell me truly how your presentation went. I managed a good curtsy, thank goodness, but I fumbled my train as I backed away. I got such a fright. How did your curtsy go?"

"Very well," Helen said, glancing over her shoulder again. Aunt and Lady Gardwell had not yet moved on. She dropped her voice to a near whisper. "Millicent, you won't believe it, but before we went into the Grand Council Chamber, Lord Carlston stole my mother's miniature."

Her friend frowned. "What do you mean, he stole it?"

"He cut it loose from my fan."

"Never!" Her friend's horror curled into a delighted smile. Millicent did love to be shocked. "Why would he do such a thing?"

"I don't know. But there is more. He made a morning call and gave it back to me, but not in the way you would expect." She paused for dramatic effect. "He threw it."

Millicent gasped. "Threw it! Is he mad, like they say?" She grasped Helen's arm, bringing them even closer together. "Did he explain his actions?"

Helen looked into her friend's eager face and felt a strange hesitation, as if she had suddenly come upon an unexpected crossroad in a well-known path. Only a moment ago she'd had every intention of telling Millicent all about Lord Carlston and his strange behavior. She had always shared her secrets with her friend—big and small. But now it did not seem so straightforward. Did she really want to explain Lord Carlston's knowledge of her mother?

Or the strange mirror in the miniature? And suppose she told Millicent about her unusual dexterity, and came up against the same wariness that she had seen in Darby? Most troubling, could she really burden her friend with what she had found in Berta's lockbox? No, that last would be unforgivable. In any case, how could she possibly describe such things out loud?

"He gave no reason for taking it," she finally said. It was the truth, but not the entire truth. For such a small betrayal, Helen felt an inordinately large sense of foreboding. With seven little words, it seemed she had stepped onto a new path—one that left Millicent behind—and something told her she could never turn back.

Millicent clutched her arm even tighter. "Oh my goodness, you don't think he is trying to fix his interest in some strange way, do you? No, that would be impossible—he is still considered a married man. Tell me exactly what he said."

"Really, it was nothing," Helen said. "I think he must be mad, as you say." She looked across the riding track, desperate for a change of subject that would stop the jab of regret. She found Pug Brompton, riding past on a sturdy gray mare. "Look, there is Lady Elizabeth." She raised her hand, receiving a wave of Pug's whip in response. "I spoke to her while we were waiting to be presented. She knew about Delia and Mr. Trent. But not only that—she said she'd been told that Mr. Trent had also killed a maid."

"I heard that too, from Cecily Cartwright," Millicent said indignantly. "People love to embellish a scandal."

"Has Delia written to you at all?" Helen asked.

"No. I suspect her parents will not permit her."

On that grim forecast, they paused for a moment, their conversation stifled by the arrival of a lady and gentleman next to them. Millicent fixed on something further along the path. "Look! Is that your brother with the Duke of Selburn?"

Helen followed her gaze. Two familiar tall figures stood at the mouth of a smaller path that branched off toward the lake. "I think it is." She smiled at the unexpected pleasure: Andrew did not often attend the promenade.

The two men were stylishly dressed for the occasion, Selburn in a particularly handsome olive green topcoat with a brown hat. A good combination, Helen thought, for a fair-skinned, fair-haired man like the Duke.

He saw them first and, with a word and tilt of his cane, drew Andrew's attention away from a dashing lady driving a phaeton on the Row. Her brother waved, and at Helen's acknowledgment, the two men strolled toward them. As they drew up, Helen and Millicent curtsied.

"Good afternoon, Your Grace. I believe you are acquainted with Miss Gardwell," Helen said. "Hello, Drew."

Both men bowed.

"A delight to see you again, Lady Helen, Miss Gardwell," Selburn said.

"Is Aunt with you, sis?" Andrew asked. "Or are you two gallivanting on your own?"

Millicent giggled. "I have never been accused of gallivanting, Lord Hayden."

"Gallivanting is quite the thing these days, Miss Gardwell, don't you know?" Andrew replied.

Helen looked over her shoulder, easily locating Philip's red livery beside the Row fence, and thus her aunt. She and Lady Gardwell had not made much progress along the path. "She is over there, standing by that red curricle, speaking to Lord and Lady Heathcote."

Aunt was obviously checking their location too, for she had turned to scan the crowd. She saw them and, with a smile, flicked her hand, waving them onward.

"Your aunt seems to think we should walk on," Selburn said. "Shall we?"

He offered his arm to Helen. Her brother immediately offered his to Millicent, murmuring a comment that Helen did not catch. She heard her friend giggle again. Now, there was an interesting possibility: Drew and Millicent. No, she had to stop such thoughts—there was nothing more certain to kill a budding interest than an overly enthusiastic sibling.

She laid her hand on the crook of Selburn's arm, and together they started along the path, falling into line with the other strolling couples and families. It promised to be an entertaining walk: in those few times when she had talked to the Duke beyond the polite chitchat of the ballroom, he had proven himself a man of good sense and easy humor. Nor had she forgotten the kindness he had shown in that illicit wink at her presentation.

"And how do you feel now that you are presented to Her Majesty and the world?" he asked, as though picking up her thoughts. "Any different?"

Helen glanced up, smiling into the warmth of his hazel eyes. It was a pleasure in itself to walk with a man who stood a good head taller than herself. "But of course," she said. "I am immediately ten times more sage and knowledgeable."

"I thought as much," he said gravely. A lady coming the other way, in an orange pelisse and rather overdone chip hat, bowed to him. He returned her salute. "It is amazing how a minute before Royalty can change one's essential nature, don't you think?" he added.

"Imagine what two minutes could do," Helen said.

Selburn smiled. She watched his mouth, liking the way it curled up at the very ends. It was too thin to be thought handsome, but it had a pleasingly firm cast. "I can assure you," he said, "that two minutes, or even two hours, in the Prince Regent's company does little for oneself, or for anyone else, for that matter. He is not a man of intense decision."

A quick rejoinder rose to Helen's lips, but she hesitated. This was where Aunt would caution her to step back from the satirical and stay within the sweeter confines of a young lady's conversation. But the remark was already on her tongue and its spice too delicious. "But that is not true, sir. I have heard that His Majesty can order six waistcoats from his tailor in less than a minute."

Selburn laughed. "I stand corrected," he said appreciatively. "If you are not careful, Lady Helen, the Misses Berry will hear of you and press you to attend their salon. They like collecting wit and intelligence, and then where would you be? Labeled a bluestocking in your first Season!"

He thought her witty enough to be invited to the famous salon? Helen lowered her eyes lest her gratification be too obvious. "There would be no need for them to press, Your Grace. It would be an honor to attend."

"Then, if you will allow, I shall mention your name."

Helen bowed her agreement, feeling a flip of excitement in her stomach. A tantalizing image of herself in conversation with luminaries such as Sir Thomas Lawrence or Mr. Scott or even Mrs. Radcliffe flashed through her mind.

"Do you often attend their salons?" she asked.

"I do. It is a most free society and one that—"

Under the tuck of her fingers, she felt Selburn's relaxed stance suddenly stiffen. He stopped walking, his eyes on the Row, his long jaw tight. A turn of her head brought the reason into sharp focus: Lord Carlston, riding along the fence line toward them on a big, heavy-boned chestnut of at least eighteen hands, the horse mincing with playful freshness. The Earl's seat was as elegant as his finely tailored navy-blue coat and pale buckskin breeches, and he had a light hand that still managed to keep the animal under control.

As he neared, Carlston slowed his mount from a trot to a walk and nodded to Helen. She glanced at the Duke's stony face, remembering the gossip at Lady Heathcote's: he had taken a horsewhip to Carlston and had it turned upon him. Tension prickled across her skin. What was she to do? Acknowledge Carlston and so force his company upon the Duke, or cut him, and potentially lose her source of information? She stood still, caught within her indecision. With a wry lift of his eyebrow, Lord Carlston shifted his attention to Selburn. Helen saw the Duke's fist clench the silver top of his cane. For a long moment the two men eyed each other. The patent dislike in their silent battle brought Andrew to a bristling halt beside Helen and even stopped a few strangers on the path.

A ripple of noise further along the Row—shrill shouts and the stamp of hooves—cut through the hostility. Carlston turned in his saddle, breaking the standoff with Selburn. Beyond him, Helen saw the cause of the panic: a small bay horse rearing at the other side of the wide track. The animal came down hard, then bucked, and even before Helen saw a flash of purple cloth, she knew the woman with the heavy hands had lost control of her mount. The bay reared again, this time breaking into a rocking gallop that sent the woman flying off its back. She landed on the track in a billow of purple silk, the wheels of a curricle narrowly missing her leg. Her groom leaped off his own mount and pulled her to safety. Free of any hold on its bridle, the bay made for the fence. Good Lord, it was coming straight at them, Helen realized. If it took the fence into the crowd, it would trample everyone in its path.

In her mind, she saw each separate action needed to contain the beast, like a magic lantern show clicking through its pictures. *Click*: three strides to the fence. *Click*: a vault to clear it. *Click*: intersect the animal's path. *Click*: a lunge to catch the bridle and bring the horse's head down. She could feel the whole sequence imprinted in her muscles: a future certainty building into the necessity of action. It was hot in her veins, searing through the voice in her head shouting that a lady did not run, did not leap, did not lunge for a horse. Did not. Did not.

She dropped her reticule and caught up her hem. Beside her, Selburn threw his cane to the ground. Three fast steps took her to the fence, Selburn a moment behind. She saw his shocked glance as they both reached for a handhold on the wooden paling. She steadied herself to leap, but as every part of her forged upward, she was suddenly wrenched back to earth by a brutal grip on her shoulder.

"Helen!" Andrew's hand closed even harder, pulling her away from the fence.

In a blur, she saw Selburn vault over the barrier and run toward the horse, past Carlston, who was watching it all from his mount.

"For Christ's sake," Andrew said in her ear, dragging her back a few more stumbling steps. "Are you mad?"

She tried to rip her arm free, but his weight anchored her to the ground. She turned in his grasp and saw Selburn catch the bridle and bring the horse to a shivering, dancing stop.

"What do you think you are doing?" Andrew wrenched her around again. His face, so close, was flushed with effort and fury. "Everyone is watching."

Helen blinked, the unused energy in her body surging into a wave of nausea. She swayed, knees buckling. Andrew's hold changed from restraint to support.

"I don't know," she said, gasping. "I'm sorry. It was the horse—I wanted to help the horse."

"Help? How could you have possibly helped?" He glanced at the small crowd that had gathered around them. "Come, I'll return you to Aunt. You must go home. Compose yourself."

With a hand firmly between her shoulder blades, he ushered her onto the path, glaring at a plump woman who tut-tutted behind a blue-gloved hand. Helen burned with humiliation.

"You don't look at all well," Millicent said, hurrying to her other side. She searched Helen's face, frowning at what she found. "Here, lean on me." She smiled sweetly at Andrew, her voice rising enough to carry to the onlookers. "Lord Hayden, your sister is not well. Perhaps you could fetch her reticule? She dropped it in the excitement."

Andrew bowed as Millicent urged Helen forward. "It's all right." Millicent patted her arm, her voice dropping to a whisper. "Not many people saw. Most eyes were on the horse."

Helen looked over her shoulder, searching for Selburn. He was leading the bay back to its rider, who, it seemed, had come to no harm. He bowed and passed the reins to the groom, the lady thanking him with fluttering hands and exclamations, the coo of them reaching Helen across the short distance. It was true: Selburn had been most heroic. Although not in any danger. In fact, none of them had been in any danger. The realization came in a dizzying collision of what had just happened with what would have happened. She clutched Millicent's arm for support. Somehow she knew, with absolute certainty, that the horse had lost its momentum by the time the Duke had reached it, and would have shied from the fence anyway. And before that, she had seen in her mind's eye exactly how to stop the beast.

How could she have known all that? Yet it was as certain as the hand on the end of her arm.

She looked wildly around the park, forcing herself to focus on a group of children. There, that boy playing with the hoop: it would collide in less than five seconds with the gentleman inspecting a flower, sending his hat flying into the bushes. With her heartbeat hard in her ears, she saw her prediction play out, the gentleman clutching futilely for his headwear. She focused again. Beyond the children, a young lady walking briskly with her mother would misstep and fall in less than three seconds. Helen gave a small moan as the girl staggered and sprawled onto the ground. How did she know it would happen? Holy star, could she prognosticate now?

She felt a prickle across the nape of her neck—a gaze that was more than just curious—and turned around. Further along the track, Lord Carlston watched from the saddle. His expression was unreadable: a flat observation that held no emotion. She lifted her chin. Why did he just sit there, looking? He had not even attempted to stop the runaway horse.

He smiled—not at her, she realized, but at some private satisfaction—then pulled on the rein and turned his mount, urging it back into the procession. Helen watched his back as he rode away, unable to shake the frightening impression that he knew more about her—far more—than she did herself.

Nine

Aunt leaned across the footwell of the coach to peer into Helen's face. The cabin's two outside lamps did little to illuminate the darkness of the quarter-moon night.

"Are you sure you are up to this?" she asked, raising her voice over the grind of the wheels. "You look pale. If you are not well, we can always turn around. It is only the Howards after all."

"What? And miss seeing Lord Byron?" Helen forced a playful note into her voice. She added a reassuring smile. "I am perfectly well, Aunt. It was just the shock of the horse running at us, and His Grace going after it like that. I am over it now."

It was the almost-true story that Andrew had told Aunt and Lady Gardwell, with Millicent's firm corroboration, as they handed Helen into her guardian's tender care. Thankfully, neither of the older ladies had seen the actual incident, but Aunt had immediately decided to take Helen home. One could not be too careful about a shock to the nerves. Helen had stifled her protestations and tried to smile her thanks to her brother, but he would not meet her eyes as he bowed and took his leave. He did not even offer to escort them home. She had never seen him so furious, and she still felt almost as ill from that as from her own stupidity. What *had* she been thinking? A lady did not run after a horse. The Duke must think her an absolute hoyden.

Aunt pursed her lips. "Yes, indeed. It was very brave of the Duke to do such a thing."

"Quite," Helen said, ignoring the note of inquiry in her aunt's voice.

No doubt if Selburn even looked at her again, Aunt would have them married in her mind, with a parcel of children for good measure. It was plain to Helen, however, that in her case he was simply being kind to his best friend's sister. It was a little mortifying, but she still liked him for his kindness—a virtue that seemed in short supply these days.

On that, her thoughts inevitably turned to Lord Carlston: the epitome of a man who did not know the meaning of kindness. She shivered, remembering that last look of cold appraisal he had given her at the park. What was it that he knew? She had to find out.

"Are you cold, my dear?" Aunt asked.

"A little," Helen said, and the Earl was pushed from her mind in the subsequent flurry of rearranged rugs and heated foot bricks.

They soon drew up to the portico of the Howard house. Philip handed her out of the carriage, then had to run to catch her silk shawl as a gust of wind blew it from her grasp onto the gravel drive. "Good Lord, we will be blown away," Aunt said as they hurried up the marble steps. "Helen, is my ostrich feather still upright?"

They gained the safety of the large foyer without further incident, and Helen quickly located the cloakroom, calling a maid over to anchor the large blue plume more firmly in her aunt's turban. With repairs complete, they ascended the staircase to greet their host and hostess, and then made their way through the crowded rooms, nodding to acquaintances. Although the party had been touted as an informal soirée, it seemed most of London was in attendance.

The chatter in the overflowing salon was strangely muted.

Helen quickly saw the reason why. A suite of pink sofas and chairs had been pulled into a loose semicircle around a dark-haired gentleman who was talking with an eye-catching intensity. Every seat was taken by a young woman, and every one of them was leaning toward him, silently rapt. A number of young men stood behind the ladies, equally intent upon the speaker. Helen could not hear what he was saying—the low level of conversation around the room was enough to mask his voice—but he held his audience enthralled.

"Lord Byron is holding court," Aunt whispered. "Go, see what all the fuss is about—Ah! Lord Alvanley, it must be a se'nnight since we last met."

As her aunt moved into a circle of conversation, Helen edged into a space between the murmuring groups, finding a better view of the dark-haired gentleman.

So this was the famous Lord Byron. She had read his poetic masterpiece, *Childe Harold's Pilgrimage*, and savored the glorious, heartbreaking grandeur of its tragedy. Like the rest of society, she had wondered if the author of the book matched the tortured, disaffected hero within its pages.

In contour and form, Lord Byron's face was quite beautiful: a broad brow with black hair curling across it, luminous skin, sensuous lips, a firm chin with a cleft in the center, and large, expressive eyes the color of coffee. Yet even such attractive modeling of muscle and flesh could not explain the mesmerizing draw of the man. Every woman in the circle had her fingers curled at the base of her throat, or touching her hair, or pressed against her mouth. Helen recognized a few, but the most obviously enthralled was Lady Caroline Lamb. She sat beside Byron on the sofa—the queen to his king—clad in white, her hand almost touching his on the pink silk. If Lord Byron was dark, cool sensuality, then Lady Caroline was bright, hot fervency. Helen frowned. Caro Lamb had always been frail and delicate, but in the month since Helen had last seen her at a ball, she seemed to have burned down to bone. Beneath the signature cropped blonde hair bound by pearls, her small white face was all points and angles. Everything was pale upon pale except for the shifting green and brown of her overbright eyes, and the dark blue shadows beneath them.

She and Lord Byron were lovers. Helen repeated the word in her mind, tasting its scandalous heat. Lovers. It was known by everyone, and it was easy to see why. Lady Caroline made no effort to hide her feelings: she was caressing his hand, her fingertips tracing the line of his knuckles. Helen had heard that even Caroline's mother-in-law, Lady Melbourne—a woman notorious for her own discreet string of lovers—had been moved to remonstrate about such public displays. Discretion was everything, but Lady Caroline did not try to disguise her affair from anyone, least of all her poor husband. Was Sir William in attendance and seeing this? Helen hoped not. At least, there was no sign of him in the crowded salon.

She turned back to her study of Lord Byron. He was beautiful, without a doubt, and quite possibly a genius, but what else was there about him that made so many women, and, it seemed, some men, prostrate themselves? It did not take long to find out. He paused midsentence, his long index finger resting for a moment on the fullness of his lower lip, and took in his audience from under his brow. It was a look with so much vice in its dark sweep that Helen felt heat rise to her face and her body sway. His every movement seemed to bring with it the sensation of fingertips sliding across skin, lips brushing against hair, soft breath hot against the nape of a neck. He made her think of that obscene card, the man bent over the woman, and she had to look away to find her footing again.

"You appear quite flushed, cousin," a deep voice said.

Lord Carlston. Standing close behind her. She'd had no expectation of seeing him, yet here he was, the sound of his voice sending a rise of shock across her skin. "Is it Lord Byron's poetry that moves you to such high color, or something else?" he asked.

She turned to face him. His mouth, just as full as Byron's, was curved into a knowing smile. She found herself staring at it and forced her eyes upward. More heat crawled across her scalp and settled in her cheeks as she met the abominable amusement in his eyes.

"It must be the warmth of the room," she said, curtsying.

His evening dress was impeccable, tailored to make the most of his height and muscular breadth. His hair had been cut since the afternoon, shorter than the current fashion for tousled curls and waves. Nevertheless, Helen admitted, its close modeling suited the strong, tanned planes of his face far more than the elaborate Windswept style or the Brutus that was so prevalent amongst the men in the room. It also showed the pale jag of an old scar that ran from his right temple down into his sideburn. Whatever weapon had made the injury, its leaving had been brutal. He was not a soldier, but it looked as though he had been in battle.

"Have you fully recovered from this afternoon's excitement?" he asked. "His Grace, the Duke of Selburn, was most heroic, was he not?" Although it was said blandly, he was watching for her response. But then, he was *always* watching.

"Indeed," she said, keeping her expression just as dispassionate. "I feared for his safety."

"Really? I was rather hoping the horse would trample him."

Helen fought back a surprised laugh, but she could not let him mock the Duke. "He acted most nobly and at great risk to himself," she said crisply, "while others, just as near, sat on their horses and did nothing."

Carlston tilted his head, his mouth lifting to one side as if her jibe had been weighed and found wanting. "You and I both know that he was never in any danger. We both saw it all play out well before it ended, did we not?"

The words roared in her ears, the chatter and perfumed glitter of the room suddenly gone from her consciousness. All that remained was Lord Carlston, standing before her, calmly acknowledging that her strange certainty had been right. Not only that: he was also acknowledging that he had the answers she so desperately needed. "What do you mean, *play out*?"

"I mean exactly what I said. You saw, as I did, that the horse had lost its impetus ten feet away from the fence and would not have jumped." A passing gentleman bowed and murmured a greeting, jolting Helen back into the busy room. Carlston nodded to him, a salute and dismissal in one, then returned his gaze to her own. "Perhaps you did not realize as early as I, but you knew that there was no danger. I did, however, enjoy your attempt to vault the fence."

Helen's skin heated again. "You knew too? Then tell me, how was I so certain?" she whispered. "How did I know?" Her hand closed around her fan, trying to hold back the flood of terrifying questions. Mad questions. Could she see into the future? Or did she make things happen with her mind? She felt as though she might scream with the need for answers.

Carlston must have seen it in her eyes, for he gave a small shake of his head—*Not now, not here*—and said, "Allow me to find you a seat, cousin."

He cupped her elbow in his gloved hand and steered her past the clusters of talking guests to a pair of elegant gilt chairs beside one of the windows. They had been arranged opposite each other, ready for a private *tête-à-tête,* but he shifted one to an angle that was almost intimate. Helen hesitated. Her aunt would take a fit if she found her sitting in such a way with Carlston. It looked so *particular*.

"Your aunt cannot see us from her current position, cousin." He pointedly looked down at the chair.

Helen sat—she could do nothing else. She had to know, even if it set tongues wagging. He took the other chair, long legs stretched before him.

She leaned forward, closing the distance, knowing that it was a little too close for strict propriety. But surely everyone's attention was on Byron. "Tell me, please."

"Not yet."

"I beg your pardon?"

He lifted his hand, holding back her outrage. "You need to cultivate patience." He glanced around the room, but it was no casual study. Helen could see the intense scrutiny behind it. He fixed on someone for a moment—an older gentleman in a canary-colored waistcoat and tight crimson jacket who was making his way toward the circle around Lord Byron. Helen recognized him: Sir Matthew Ballantyne, one of the more eccentric fops. She had danced with him at the Hertfords'—a most amiable gentleman, despite his dubious taste in fashion. The Earl, however, did not seem pleased to see him.

He turned from his study of the man. "I believe your household has recently, and suddenly, lost a member of staff," he said. "Is that correct?"

She stared at him, nonplused at the sudden change of subject. "How do you know that?"

"Am I correct?"

Helen hesitated, trying to collect her thoughts. Would he ask such a thing if he had himself abducted Berta? It seemed unlikely, but perhaps it was a way to muddy the waters. "One of our housemaids went missing six days ago," she said, watching him carefully. "Why do you wish to know?"

There was no flicker of foreknowledge in his eyes. But then, he was a master at hiding his expression.

"And does your aunt plan to replace her?'

"Yes, she has already sought recommendations and written to the registry office."

"Which one?"

"Mrs. Barnaby's, in King Street." She clasped her hands together, trying to contain her frustration. "Lord Carlston, you fire these questions at me, but you do not answer mine. Tell me how I knew about the horse."

He did not answer, his attention on Sir Matthew again. The man had joined the circle around Lord Byron and was edging his way closer to the poet. Carlston watched his progress for a few moments, then said, "No doubt you are aware that Lord Byron and Lady Caroline are lovers."

Helen frowned. Was he introducing this untoward subject to divert her from her own questions? "I don't know what you can possibly mean," she said primly.

He gave that half smile again. "You know exactly what I mean, Lady Helen. I want you to tell me what is in the hearts of our new literary genius and his paramour. I want you to read them."

So he knew she could read faces too. A sudden realization squeezed all the breath from her chest. "This is all some kind of test, isn't it? What is it all about? Tell me now."

The light from the candle sconce beside them shone across his eyes and lit their flat darkness with flecks of deep gold. He dropped his voice, making her lean closer. "Do you want answers?"

She nodded.

"Then do as I ask."

She drew back at the cold command in his voice. "Why?"

His eyes flicked back to Sir Matthew, then to another man—stocky, with a prominent jaw that gave him a pugnacious air—who lounged against the wall and seemed just as interested in the fop. "I cannot stay at your side for the whole evening, madam," Carlston said. "Is it yes or no?"

She sucked in a furious breath. Yet if she wanted an explanation, she would have to do as he asked. She gave one stiff-necked nod.

"I thought so," he said.

Insufferable man. She made a small show of turning away to study the pair on the sofa. Lady Caroline had leaned back against the cushions to watch Lord Byron in a sidelong glance that made heat rush back into Helen's cheeks. It felt as if she was peeking into the woman's boudoir.

"She is infatuated."

"Anyone can see that," Carlston said. "What is in her heart?"

Helen narrowed her eyes at his sarcasm but turned her attention back to Lady Caroline. She concentrated on the small vivid face, pushing deeper into the tiny flickers of emotion that played behind the surface. "Oh dear," she whispered.

"Well?"

"Lady Caroline is—" Helen stopped, trying to find a way to explain what she saw. "I believe Lady Caroline has abandoned herself to him. Does that make sense?"

"Go on."

"Everything is Lord Byron, and when she is not with him, I think she cannot find the core of who she is. There is so much bright energy in her, so much creative force, but it is being funneled into this all-consuming heat."

She looked back at the Earl and found herself pinned by the weight of his scrutiny. "You are correct," he said, "but you can go deeper than that."

Could she? Or more to the point, did she *want* to probe into such a maelstrom of pain and love? She did not often push beyond a person's immediate emotional truth into their secrets. It was so much harder to do, taking immense concentration and a level of calm, and it seemed unfair to unearth a person's darker desires without their knowledge. She focused on the heart-shaped face again, on the tightness beneath the adoration, and the pulsing need embedded in the languorous gaze.

Helen looked away again. There were some things that were too private. "I fear she is close to some kind of mania."

"Yes, very close," Carlston said. "Caroline is a sad caution against uncontrolled feeling. What about him?"

Helen watched the poet smile at his love. Before, she had not caught the slight cynicism and disdain within that smile curling the lip and clouding the eyes. But there was no missing the truth now. "He is unafraid of vice, of abandon, but he is afraid of love. He is already tiring of her. Poor, poor lady—she does not know it." She leaned forward. "Ah, he does not know it yet either. Even so, he is withdrawing from her intensity. He is one of those who must pursue if he is to think himself in love, but she lays herself before him like an offering. In doing so, she drives him from her."

She stepped away, suddenly aware of the unseemliness of saying such things to a man who was little more than a stranger. "Perhaps I am seeing more than there is."

"No, you are right," Carlston said. "Now look upon Sir Matthew Ballantyne. What do you see in his heart?"

There was a strange note in his voice: not quite urgency, but a sharpness that told her this reading was his real interest. What could be so important about old Sir Matthew?

She focused on the fop's lined face and watched the flickers of expression. All very easy to read. "He is enraptured by Lord Byron's words, like all the others."

"Don't waste my time, Lady Helen. We have already ascertained that you can go deeper than that."

Helen fought down the unladylike desire to tell him to *go to the devil,* and concentrated on Sir Matthew again. Amidst the hum of conversation in the room, she gradually found the inner quiet she needed. Yet there was nothing else in the old gentleman's face. "I cannot find any—" Something flashed across his features. "Wait! There is—oh," Helen stopped, confused. "Desire," she whispered.

"And?" Carlston prompted.

It took a minute or so of intense scrutiny, but Helen finally caught a glimpse of what lay deep within the man. She recoiled, struggling to find a description of the fleeting moment of truth. "It is like a cold, ravenous hunger, all aimed at Lord Byron."

"Yes," Carlston said. That smile of satisfaction—the one she had seen in the park—was back on his face.

"But what is it?" Helen demanded, still shocked by what she had seen. "It is so . . . so rapacious. I think Lord Byron is in danger from Sir Matthew."

Carlston leaned forward, his expression intent. "What kind of danger?"

"I don't know. I saw it only for a moment, and it was so odd," Helen admitted. She saw a flash of disappointment cross his face. "But it is there," she insisted. "A malevolent intent toward Lord Byron. Surely, we must warn him!"

"And what do you propose to say? 'Forgive the intrusion, Lord Byron, but I have looked into Sir Matthew's heart and seen a violent and dangerous hunger for your person'?" Carlston shook his head. "He would think you mad or depraved. You and I may be able to see these things, but acting upon them is another matter entirely."

"I cannot ignore it," Helen declared, then belatedly realized what he had said. "You can read expressions as I can?"

He inclined his head. "Yes."

"And you knew the horse would pull up. Please, you must tell me how we know these things. *Why* we know these things. I have done what you asked. I deserve an answer."

"This is not the place to give those answers. It will make more sense if I show you the truth."

After all this, he was still not going to tell her anything? At the corner of her eye, she saw Sir Matthew notice the stocky man's attention, and stiffen with alarm. He quickly made a bow to those around him, backed out of the circle, and retreated through the doorway into the next salon. The stocky man straightened and looked Carlston's way. Helen saw the Earl give a slight nod—a signal—for the man immediately headed through the doorway too.

"Show me what?" she asked sharply. "Is it something to do with Sir Matthew? Will Lord Byron be safe? You must—"

"For now, Sir Matthew and Lord Byron are not your concern, Lady Helen," he said. "I believe you are attending Vauxhall Gardens on Tuesday, are you not?"

"Yes, but you promised to tell me—"

"I promised nothing," he said. "I will show you what you are at the Gardens. You must wait until then. Did you manage to open your mother's miniature?"

She stared at him. What did he mean by *what you are*? He could not say that and move on as if it were nothing.

"Did you open your mother's miniature?" he repeated.

"Yes," she snapped, her sense of ill-use peaking fast. "But what do you mean—"

"Good. Bring it with you on Tuesday."

He rose to leave.

"No!" She grabbed his forearm, then froze, aghast at her awful breach of propriety and the sudden violence that sprang into his eyes. Reflex had instantly clenched his hand into a fist, the muscles beneath her grasp coiling, ready to strike. She snatched her own hand away. "I beg your pardon, Lord Carlston."

He had paled beneath his tan. Drawing in a long breath, he uncurled his fist and bowed. "It is I who must beg your pardon, Lady Helen. I have been too long out of decent society."

He turned and walked toward the door, his hand held stiffly at his side, fingers spread wide as if to stretch away the bunched savagery within.

Ten

Monday, 4 May 1812

THE NEXT MORNING, Helen sat at her dressing table and stared into the mirror, her fingers pressed into the edges of her eye sockets as if she could feel the truth through her skin and bone.

I will show you what you are.

She had woken with that simple seven-word phrase crouched in her mind like a toad. And now, as Darby dressed her hair for prayers and breakfast, it crawled across her thoughts, leaving a poisonous trail of dread.

What was she?

And what had she seen in Sir Matthew?

The cloying mix of sweet lavender and fat in her hair pomade turned her stomach. Across her crown, she felt the gentle march of Darby's fingers as she threaded a navy-blue riband through the construction of topknot and curls.

"Your ladyship looks awful worried," Darby ventured.

"I saw Lord Carlston at the Howards' last night." Helen dragged her fingertips across her cheekbones and dug them into the widest point. The pressure seemed to hold back her unease. She met

Darby's anxious eyes in the mirror. "He has admitted to knowing something about my *abilities*."

Darby sent a swift glance across to the hallway door—it was firmly shut; Helen had already checked—then leaned closer. "What did he say?"

"Not much. He is going to show me something at Vauxhall Gardens. Something about myself."

"Oh, my lady, are you really going to follow him into this strangeness? Do you trust him now?"

"No, of course I don't."

Darby paused in the positioning of a pearl hairpin. "But you must trust him a little to have discussed it so openly with him." She pushed the pin into the topknot, as if to punctuate her point, then bent to rummage through the box for another.

Helen sat back, startled. Darby was right. She had already placed a great deal of trust in Lord Carlston. Not only that, but his acknowledgment of her abilities—and the confession of his own—had made her start thinking of him as an ally. Sweet heaven, she should be more wary than that.

She turned from the mirror. "Darby, he seemed to know we had lost a housemaid."

Darby's attention snapped up from the pin box. "He mentioned Berta?"

"Not specifically. He just asked if we'd had a sudden change in our household."

"It is very strange that he brought up that very subject, don't you think?" Darby said.

Helen had to agree. "Still, I got no sense that he knew anything particular about Berta. In fact, it was the opposite."

Darby gave her a long searching look. "My lady, this is the man who faced society and denied he had killed his wife, then fled the country. It is obvious that he can dissemble with the best of them. I think he is *very* dangerous."

Helen remembered the violence she had seen in his eyes. "And yet he has abilities similar to mine. What does that say about me?"

Her maid's mouth pressed into a thin tight line. Helen nodded. Darby was right again: that question was unanswerable.

~

"YOUR UNCLE WISHES to see you, my dear," Aunt said as Helen entered the breakfast room. "He is in the library."

Helen stopped short, her hand still on the door handle. Aunt's face was tense, and her shoulders, under her green silk shawl, were high and hunched. Uncle had not seemed especially displeased at morning prayers; something must have happened since then. She sucked in a breath. Could he have heard that she'd sat alone with Lord Carlston last night? She had thought it had gone unnoticed, overshadowed by the scandalous behavior of Lord Byron and Lady Caroline. She searched her mind for any other possible misdemeanor. Perhaps the broken lockbox had been discovered—

"Go to him now, Helen," Aunt said. "And, my dear, do not gainsay him. His joints are needling him again, and he is in one of his moods." There was something else she wanted to say, but Helen could see she dared not. With a tight smile, Aunt turned back to *The Times*, her shoulders hunched even higher.

Helen's unease built with each step down to the ground floor. The library door was closed. She stopped before it and smoothed the cream bodice of her morning gown. At least it was a style with a high, modest neckline. One deep, steadying breath, and she knocked.

"Come." His voice held the sharp tone of pain. Setting her face into pleasant inquiry, she entered and closed the door.

"Good morning, Uncle." She curtsied. "You wished to see me?"

He sat at his desk in the corner, writing a letter. The scritch of the quill continued, his attention on the paper before him. She stood, waiting. His charcoal kerseymere coat was cut with a high-turned collar, and its height hid his neck, making him look even more bullish and wide-set than usual. Finally he returned the pen to its gilt holder and sprinkled sand across the page, shaking it off with three taps on the mahogany desktop.

"You have received a letter." Although she had been waiting for him to speak, the clipped announcement made her jump. He picked up a sheaf of folded pages at his elbow, the sealing wafer already broken. "I have read its contents."

"You have read my letter?"

"Do not give me that defiant eye, girl. I will read any letter that comes into my house, if I so wish." He unfolded the pages. "It is from that Cransdon slut. I understand from its framing that you wrote to her after her disgraceful behavior came to light."

Helen drew back her shoulders. "I did."

"And that your aunt condoned this action."

Helen pressed her lips together. She would not give up Aunt.

"I will not be tricked into franking letters to degenerates," he said. "Your aunt understands that now. Do you?"

"Yes, Uncle."

"From this moment, you will not have any more communication with that girl. Neither letter nor visit. Do you understand?"

Helen hesitated for only a moment, but it was enough.

"Do you understand?" he roared, rising from his chair in one violent motion.

She stepped back. "Yes, Uncle."

He picked up his red-bound Bible and strode toward her. "Swear it on God's word." He grabbed her wrist, forcing her palm down flat on the stippled leather cover. "Look at me when you make that vow. I want to see the sincerity in your eyes."

She fixed on his yellowed squint, the crush of his dry fingers sending a pulse of pain up her arm. "I swear on God's word that I will not write to nor see Delia again."

"Good." He lowered the Bible and let go of her hand. She snatched it back, cradling her burning wrist. "I am doing this for your own benefit, Helen. The Cransdon girl is obviously unbalanced." He lifted the letter, waving it at her in a crackle of condemnation. "My first thought was to immediately burn this piece of iniquity. I was not going to allow you to read it. But I have reconsidered. You should witness with your own eyes and understanding your friend's sad decline. She is raving. It will be a valuable lesson for you to see the sickness that is created in a young girl's mind when she engages in licentious and disobedient behavior."

Helen took the letter from his hand, locking her pained wrist to stop the pages from shaking. At least she would have a chance to read Delia's own words. It took her a moment to focus past the blur in her eyes.

"'My dear friend,'" she read.

I cannot tell you how much your letter comforted me on its receipt. I am painfully aware that you must have written in defiance of your uncle's wishes, and so it is doubly precious, as is your assurance of friendship and support. Although your fine sense of courtesy did not allow you to write any question about that day, I feel I must explain to you how this terrible situation occurred, and why.

I fell in love, dear Helen. It is as simple and as complicated as that. Mr. Trent was a revelation to me—a man who thought me all that was good and admirable. A man who found my shyness a mark of modesty, and beauty hidden within my plain looks. You know I am not one for self-deception, but here, I think, I allowed the veil of flattery, and perhaps desperation, to cloud my eyes. How I wanted to be the woman that Mr. Trent saw, and how I wanted him to be the respectable, honorable man that his actions seemed to show him to be. My father, however, did not have the same illusions—Mr. Trent had no connections, no money, and, apparently, no prospects. Thus, when he applied for my hand, he was rejected.

And so, when Mr. Trent suggested we flee to the border and marry, I agreed. Pray, do not be too disgusted. It was a grievously hard decision to make, and my heart was heavy as we boarded the post chaise. Nevertheless, I was a fool in love, and thought, once we had been united under God's eye, all would be well. It transpires I was just a fool—I did not note our direction until too late. We were not headed for Scotland and marriage, but instead a mean inn in the middle country.

This is where my account becomes a little strange. My memory of the events is, perhaps, affected by the horror of what occurred, but I swear upon my soul that this is my true recollection.

Mr. Trent led me inside the inn—with what intention I do not even wish to contemplate—

and as we crossed the doorway, he looked back and swore at the sight of four men arriving on horseback. At first I thought it was Papa come to retrieve me, but I saw the faces of the men and did not recognize any of them, although it was plain by their garb and horses that they were gentlemen. Mr. Trent hurried us up a narrow staircase and into a squalid bedchamber, shutting the door and locking it. You can imagine my bewilderment and growing horror. In less time than it took for Mr. Trent to push me upon the bed, a terrible banging shook the door. "Let her go, you fiend!" a man yelled. And that is when Mr. Trent pulled a pistol from his travel bag. I thought for a terrible moment that he was going to shoot me. As the door was broken open by the men, Mr. Trent placed the gun against his temple and pulled the trigger.

I will not dwell on the physical effect of such an action—you, who have always had such a lively imagination, will need no prompting on that score. But even your mind cannot conjure up the bright flash of light that I saw as well. It was as if Mr. Trent had caught fire, his whole body alight from within. It was gone in an instant, but I swear I saw it. And I swear the men saw it too. He fell to the ground, dead by his own hand, with blistered skin upon his palms. I have dwelled long on this sight—it has been my only subject of thought in those rare hours when I am left alone—and I am convinced that it was the gate of Hell opening to take his soul. A flash of hellfire as his immortal self was dragged below. The men denied seeing such a phenomenon—the blisters, they said, were from the gun. So, I am left clinging to my truth, abandoned by any fellow witness other than a groom who claims he saw it through the second-story window. It is his word and mine—a disgraced woman—against the word of four gentlemen: we must all know the outcome of that contest.

Although Mr. Trent has injured me grievously, I still mourn for his dark descent into eternal damnation, and I pray for him.

Do you think me mad, dear Helen? Do you perhaps imagine that I have turned my horror and grief into fantasy? It is what Mamma and Papa think, and they have called in the doctor to bleed me, and they talk of sanitariums in low voices that I am not meant to hear. Perhaps I am mad, for my grief is like a wall I cannot break through, and I sometimes wonder if it is better that I do not try. What will be on the other side?

I will never mention the events of that day again, in case the world thinks me ready for the asylum. I give you the keeping of my story. It eases me a little to know that someone else in the world has heard my truth, and I know that you will face it with your customary reason and good sense.

I am fully aware that we will not be able to meet again in any foreseeable future. Yet

I hope that such a happy event is not beyond imagination or, one day, reality.

Your friend,
Delia

Helen kept her eyes on the final page. If she looked up, she knew her uncle would take the letter and burn it, and she needed a moment to digest its startling contents. Poor Delia. Her suffering rose from the page, clear and immediate, as if she had walked into the room and spoken the words. Not only her suffering, but also her fear. Once again, Helen read through the paragraph that told of the strange flash of light within Mr. Trent.

Perhaps Delia *was* mad.

No. Delia had always been truthful, and Helen could not see why she would suddenly start lying about something so wild that it could lead to her own incarceration. Aunt, too, had mentioned the groom's account of a strange light, yet the four gentlemen denied it. What possible reason would they have to lie? And Delia's conclusion that Mr. Trent's soul had been dragged down into Hell seemed so Gothic and overly dramatic.

She frowned. Who were these other gentlemen? And why were they chasing Mr. Trent, if not to reclaim Delia from his clutches?

There were no answers to be had in the letter.

She finally looked up from the page. "Uncle, I beg you, please allow me to answer my friend. This one time only. Please."

"Did you not just swear you would have no more contact with the girl?"

"But she is suffering, Uncle."

"And so she should." He snatched the letter from her fingers and strode to the hearth. A flick of his hand and it was in the fire, pulled into its bright orange heart by the leap of a high flame.

The paper flared, raged, then curled into blackened ash. "You have made me your promise, Helen, and if you do not hold to it, I shall cut short your Season and begin marriage negotiations with Sir Reginald. He may be contrary to your aunt's ambitions for you, but I will not harbor a girl who bears false witness on God's own book or will not obey the basic proprieties of society. Do you finally understand me?"

"Yes, Uncle."

"Your father's will has placed you in my care until you are twenty-five, or until another man is willing to take on the burden of your well-being. If you are to become a wife, you must learn that obedience is the cornerstone of femininity." He tilted his head toward the door. "Go."

Helen curtsied and walked from the room, her wrist still aching from the grind of his grip.

Eleven

Tuesday, 5 May 1812

Aunt Leonore wrapped her shawl more firmly over the bodice of her cherry-striped gown and held its edges tightly together in a death grip against the cold evening wind.

"I swear I would not be here if it were anyone other than Lady Jersey," she whispered to Helen. "I hope we are not forced to wander too much longer amongst the trees before we go to our supper box."

A little way ahead, the elegant figure of their hostess and her plump companion, Mr. Saltwell, led the way along the Grand Walk of Vauxhall Pleasure Gardens. Helen glanced over her shoulder at the other pair in their party, Lady Margaret Ridgewell and her brother, Mr. Hammond. Both wore dark colors—the lady stylish navy-blue silk, the gentleman gray—and strolled arm in arm with all appearance of relaxed pleasure. Helen, however, sensed tension in them both, especially Lady Margaret.

On their introduction at the entrance gate, Helen had recognized her as the small, fine-boned woman who had watched her aunt so closely at St. James's Court. Yet Lady Margaret had given no indication of that previous encounter, merely curtsying with delicate grace and murmuring her delight at meeting them. Up close, Helen had been struck by her vivid coloring: black hair against pale, pale skin, and eyes that were almost the same navy as her gown. According to Lady Jersey's whispered intelligence en route to the Gardens, she was a wealthy widow—very rich pickings—and was being escorted around town by her unmarried brother, who had his own respectable fortune of two thousand a year. Mr. Hammond was almost as fine-boned as his sister, with a wiry quickness about him that hinted at some kind of training—fencing, perhaps, for there was precision to his movements. He had bowed to Helen with a charming affability that was belied by the sharp interest in his paler blue eyes.

"Do not despair," Helen said, turning back to her aunt. "I'm sure we will be heading to our supper box soon. Then we will be warm again."

She rubbed her own gloved hands together, hoping she was right. The vigorous chafing set her reticule jiggling on the end of its silk drawstring. She pulled it closer, reassuring herself that it was firmly anchored around her wrist. The small purse held a precious cargo: her mother's miniature, brought in obedience to Lord Carlston's ill-mannered command. Now all she needed was for the Earl to appear and finally give her the answers she craved. The thought of that moment brought a clench of dread. Like poor Delia, Helen was not sure she could cope with whatever lay on the other side of such knowledge.

What was she?

A loud whistle cut through the air. The crowd, primed for the famous lighting of the Vauxhall lamps, paused in their activities. Even the orchestra stopped playing. From every direction came the sound of running feet and the flit of dark figures: dozens of lamplighters taking their positions throughout the Gardens. Helen held her breath. She had seen this once before, but that did not lessen her anticipation. All around, the darkly clad shapes of men waited, each at the start of a line of linked oil lamps, a lit taper cupped in hand to shield it from the wind. Another whistle sounded; the men stepped forward and touched flame to fuse. At once, hundreds of lights flared into life along the Grand Walk, the galleries, and the gardens, bringing a moment of dazzled blindness. Helen gasped. The illumination was so sudden and so glorious, it was as if a divine hand had driven out the descending night in a blaze of holy radiance.

Entranced, she clapped alongside Aunt and the rest of the crowd. The Grand Walk was now so bright, it was almost like a sunlit day—darkness vanquished by the ingenuity and imagination of man. Her aunt sniffed. "These lamps may be pretty, but they certainly stink."

Helen nodded, having just caught the distinctive acrid odor of whale oil mixed with wine. In the brand-new light, she scanned the groups of people that strolled past or stood contemplating the artwork, but found no sign of Lord Carlston. With such cold weather, the Gardens were thin of company, so it would not be too hard to spot him—if, indeed, he was actually in attendance. Helen studied a gathering of gentlemen who stood admiring the elaborate molded frontage of the Chinese Temple, but none of them was his lordship. What if he did not come at all?

"Are you looking for someone?" Aunt asked.

"No." Helen quickly brought her attention back to her aunt. "I am just delighted by all the additions since last season."

Aunt grunted. "I would be more delighted if we found the addition of our supper box."

But that was not yet to be. Lady Jersey and Mr. Saltwell led them along the covered walkways that ran beside the grassy expanse of the Grove, home to the three-story Gothic orchestra building. Its tower was now lit by hundreds of lamps, and the musicians within the gallery were playing a pastoral that soared over the rattling breeze in the trees and the conversations nearby.

They paused for a moment, listening, then Lady Jersey veered away from the Grove and led them across the wide avenue toward a row of supper boxes. As they passed the plainly appointed booths, Aunt peered hopefully into the dimly lit interiors. "Do you think one of those is ours?"

It was early in the evening, so only a few were populated. Each had a large painting decorating the back wall and a country-style table set with linen, glassware, and crockery. At the entrance gate, Lady Jersey had ordered a full menu to be brought to their box: wafer-thin ham, cold chicken, salads, cheesecakes, and, she'd added with a guilty laugh, "a bowl of that terrible rack punch" to wash it all down. Apparently, their hostess was of the mind that one must have the entire Vauxhall experience, including a sore head the following day.

"I think we must be close," Helen said. "Look, Lady Jersey has stopped, and waits for us."

At her wave, they quickened their pace, joining her in front of a supper box a minute or so before Lady Margaret and Mr. Hammond arrived. There was an air of serious purpose about the brother and sister at odds with the frivolity of their surroundings. It was intensified by Lady Margaret's sudden intent regard of Helen.

"Do forgive me, Lady Jersey," Mr. Hammond said, "but my sister is of a mind to take a turn around the Handel Piazza before we go to supper. We would not wish to disrupt any of your kind plans for our entertainment, but if that is possible . . . ?"

"But of course you must," Lady Jersey said. "This is our box here, but our supper will not arrive for an hour yet. Plenty of time for a stroll to take in the art and music."

Lady Margaret exchanged a glance with her brother. "Perhaps Lady Helen would like to accompany us?"

Helen studied the woman's earnest face: beneath its expression of polite inquiry was a held breath, a communication of conspiracy, an urging for an affirmative response. This was no ordinary request. Helen could scarcely believe her own obtuseness: Lady Margaret and her brother were, of course, Lord Carlston's emissaries. He was already in the Gardens, and this proposed walk was the pretext for meeting him.

"A walk would be most pleasant," Helen said, annoyed to hear a slight quaver within her voice. She steadied herself. "Thank you."

"Yes, yes, a wonderful idea," Lady Jersey agreed. Helen had another startling thought: since this was Lady Jersey's party, she must also be at Lord Carlston's service. His reach, it seemed, knew no bounds. "You young people go and enjoy the Gardens," their hostess continued. "We older folk will take our ease in the supper box. After all, that is the point of the exercise, is it not? Enjoyment and pleasure according to one's inclinations." She turned to Aunt. "Unless, of course, you have an objection, my dear. But I can assure you, Lady Margaret will take the most tender care of your niece."

"No, I have no objection," Aunt said, obviously relieved to be finally heading into the box. "But do stay under the covered walks as much as possible, Helen. The chill is coming in with the night."

"We will make sure of it," Lady Margaret said. "Come, take my arm, Lady Helen."

Before she could answer, Helen found herself linked to Lady Margaret. With Mr. Hammond walking with perfect propriety beside his sister, they strolled back past the orchestra that was now accompanying a rather dumpy but sweet-voiced soprano in the midst of a throbbing ballad. To any onlooker, the three of them were all ease and enjoyment, but Helen could now *feel* the tension in Lady Margaret's arm and see Mr. Hammond's tight grip on his cane.

As they left the melancholy song behind, Helen could no longer remain silent. "We go to meet Lord Carlston, don't we?"

Lady Margaret waited until a pair of ladies passed by, then said, "His lordship said you were keen-witted." Her sidelong glance held a distinct moment of reestimation. Clearly, she had not shared that opinion. "We are here to take you to him. He is waiting in the Dark Walk."

Helen drew in a startled breath. The Dark Walk had a bad reputation. On her previous visit, she had insisted that Andrew escort her along it, and both of them had been shocked by the licentious behavior alongside the gloomy, underlit path—men and women pissing in the bushes, drunk gentlemen grabbing at girls, and some couples even engaged in kissing. "Why are we to meet in the Dark Walk?"

"Because that is where the low prostitutes ply their trade," Lady Margaret said, her tone clipped with distaste.

Prostitutes? The raw, shocking word silenced Helen.

They headed toward the ghostly white columns of the Temple of Apollo. A party of well-dressed ladies and gentlemen, hunched against the chilly wind, stood listening to one of the strolling bands play a popular sea shanty. Helen and her two companions skirted them, the jaunty tune bringing a grimace to Lady Margaret's face. Ahead, one of the Vauxhall constables, the Gardens' own peace-keeping force, strolled on his rounds, hunkered into the warmth of his distinctive light-blue greatcoat.

Mr. Hammond took out a gold fob watch and flicked it open. "We need to hurry, Margaret."

With a nod, his sister picked up her pace, pulling Helen into a small skip to keep up. They turned again, heading along the South Walk, the gardens on either side bordered by low trellis fences.

There were fewer people here—the avenue's position made it a disagreeable channel for the wind. Helen felt her bonnet lift under the cold current, and grabbed the brim, her breath coming harder.

"Careful," Mr. Hammond said. "We are attracting attention."

A few people admiring a grotto had turned to look at their brisk progress.

"Make up your mind, Michael," Lady Margaret snapped, but she slowed to a more decorous pace.

"What are we going toward?" Helen demanded. She stopped, resisting the pull of Lady Margaret's arm. "What is in there that I must see? I will go no further until you tell me."

Lady Margaret's mouth tightened at the delay. "Lady Helen, you know what you are going toward." She leaned closer, her voice a hard whisper. "Lord Carlston is going to give you the answers you crave, and that involves something near the Dark Walk. You want answers, do you not?"

"I did not think it involved . . ." Helen gestured to the end of the avenue, where the gloomy junction of the Dark Walk was visible. "I am not a simpleton, Lady Margaret. I will not walk into a place of disrepute with people I barely call acquaintances, let alone allies. Not to mention Lord Carlston and *his* reputation."

Lady Margaret glanced at her brother again, this time, it seemed, for support.

"Upon my honor, Lady Helen, we are your allies, and Lord Carlston is worthy of your good opinion," Mr. Hammond said. He pressed his gray-gloved hands together; almost a supplication. "I understand your natural caution, but I beg you to restrain it a while longer, and you will soon discover the reason for our secretiveness."

"Lord Carlston is quite the bravest man I have ever met," Lady Margaret added. "I would trust him with my life and, on occasion, I have."

The full light of a nearby lamp fell on her pale oval face, and within her level gaze Helen saw the woman's secret: she loved Carlston with as much heat as Lady Caroline loved Byron. No wonder she believed him so worthy of trust.

"And yet he is accused of murdering his wife," Helen said. "Was that a false accusation?"

She had not meant her inquiry to sound quite so blunt. Lady Margaret glanced at her brother, and Helen saw the warning in his eyes: the subject was not to be discussed. Lady Margaret, however, had other ideas.

She lifted her chin and said, "Yes, I believe it was."

Mr. Hammond stepped forward. "Lady Helen, if we are to meet Lord Carlston, we must continue. I ask you, do we go on? Or do we go back?"

The pair looked at her steadily, but she could see that each of them held their breaths.

With her arm still tucked into Lady Margaret's firm hold, Helen felt a strange sense of inevitability, as if everything in her life had been leading to this journey into the darkest reaches of the Gardens. A ridiculously Gothic notion, she told herself, but she could not shake it.

"We will go on," she said, although alarm drummed within her like another heartbeat.

They resumed walking, leaving behind the sparse company on the path until only a deserted stretch of gravel lay between them and the ill-lit junction. Lady Margaret slowed, peering into the somber woods on either side. Helen flinched as a large figure detached itself from the shadows beside a gnarled tree: a huge man, with even more breadth to his shoulders than Lord Carlston. He had pulled the brim of his beaver hat low, but the broad contours of his face were familiar, as was the olive-gold cast to his skin. She had seen him before, loitering outside Half Moon Street:

Lord Carlston's man. Taking off his hat, he dipped his close-shaven head in a bow, the light from a nearby lamp catching thick black horizontal lines across his high cheekbones and broad forehead. Helen recoiled from the sudden ferocity of his countenance, then realized it was a tribal tattoo: she had seen such markings in her uncle's magazines. The man must be from the Indies or Africa. Yet he did not look to be from either place.

"Quinn." Mr. Hammond nodded to him, his own slight stature accentuated by the man's size. "Is Bales here?"

"Aye, sir." Another man emerged from the bushes on the other side of the avenue. He was thickset, his collar up against the cold. Helen glimpsed meaty lips and the flattened bridge of a pugilist's nose.

"Is everyone in place?" Mr. Hammond asked.

"Aye, sir." Quinn's deep voice lilted in a way that was unfamiliar to Helen's ear. He pressed his hat back onto his head, smoothing the curve of the brim between thumb and forefinger before he pulled it low over his brow. It was an oddly elegant action for such a big man.

"And Lord Carlston?" Mr. Hammond inquired.

"Near the obelisk, sir."

"Why are you not with him?" demanded Lady Margaret.

"His lordship wishes me to check the perimeters first, my lady." Helen heard a note of forced patience. "He be waiting for you now, ma'am."

Plainly, Mr. Quinn knew how to shift Lady Margaret from her sharp questioning. Helen felt a tug on her elbow, the woman drawing her onward again, renewed urgency in her step. Her brother had paused, giving a low-voiced instruction to Mr. Bales. Helen glanced back at the South Walk. None of the other visitors had followed—it was as if they sensed something was amiss.

"Why are those men standing guard?" Helen asked.

"His lordship does not want to be interrupted," Lady Margaret said. "Nor would it do you any good to be seen alone in his company on the Dark Walk."

Alone? The prospect sent cold unease down Helen's spine. Apart from Andrew, she had never been alone with a young gentleman. She pulled her shawl tighter.

They paused at the junction, Lady Margaret waiting for her brother to catch up.

"We go left," Mr. Hammond said.

And so they turned into the deeper shadows of the Dark Walk.

Twelve

HELEN'S UNEASE MOUNTED as she surveyed the gloomy, deserted avenue that stretched before them. The oil lamps were set further apart than on the other walks, casting small pools of yellow light across the wide graveled path and into the dense woods on either side. The trees had been allowed to grow unhindered, and their canopy blocked almost all of the weak glow from the quarter moon. Although the wind was not as strong as it had been on the South Walk, the darkness seemed to make it feel colder. Beneath the crunch of their feet on the gravel, Helen could still hear the shanty, its carefree tune at odds with the threatening vista.

Another man stepped out from the undergrowth. This time, Helen recognized the tall lean figure. Lord Carlston. He waited for them to approach, arms folded across the front capes of his greatcoat. He did not wear a hat, and the light from the lamp above him carved the bold planes of his face into hard angles and silvered the scar at his temple. If she had only one word to describe him, Helen decided as she drew closer, it would be *commanding.* Or *enigmatic.* Or *disturbing.* Which, of course, was three words. Lord Carlston was not a man to be contained, even in adjectives. Lady Margaret quickened her pace, pulling Helen with her until they stood before him.

He bowed to them both, but his attention stayed on Helen. The weight of his gaze searched her face, and she knew he was delving deeper. Well, he would find her wary, which was hardly surprising. But she hoped he would not see her fear.

She curtsied. "I have come for my answers, Lord Carlston." She looked pointedly around the gloomy surroundings, gathering her bravado. "Although this meeting place seems unnecessarily dramatic."

"I assure you," he said, "we are here for a very specific purpose." She opened her mouth to question him further, but he had already turned to address Mr. Hammond and Lady Margaret. "Benchley is on his way. One of my sources has confirmed it."

"What?" Lady Margaret looked wildly around the empty pathway, as if the man named were about to jump from the bushes. "No, surely not. He is in Manchester, containing the riots."

Mr. Hammond laid a reassuring hand upon his sister's shoulder, although his own features were marked with trepidation. "What does he want, sir?"

Carlston scanned the archway of trees thoughtfully. "My support, I would say."

"He cannot expect it," Lady Margaret said sharply. "This time I think there is truth in the rumors." She licked her lips, glancing again into the undergrowth.

Helen found herself studying the shadows too; Lady Margaret's unease was contagious. Whoever this Mr. Benchley was, he prompted a great deal of anxiety.

Carlston rubbed the nape of his neck. "I have heard nothing that convinces me he is guilty of such acts. Anyway, he gave me his word after—" He stopped. Helen felt his sudden silence gather into a mutual, uneasy meaning between her three companions.

Lady Margaret pressed a gloved hand to her throat. "Maybe so, but you have not seen him in years. He is much worse."

"I know the man," the Earl said firmly. "Even he would not do such a thing."

From the dubious glance between brother and sister, they did not share his lordship's confidence.

"Come, or we will miss the opportunity to finish our business," Carlston said. He motioned to Mr. Hammond. "Please escort your sister farther along the path and wait there until I call you back."

With a bow, Mr. Hammond offered his arm to Lady Margaret and led her away. Helen saw her glance back at Lord Carlston, but he was already busy withdrawing a fob watch from the pocket in the waistband of his breeches. Only Helen saw the longing in the woman's face, and the remnants of her fear.

"Who is Mr. Benchley?" Helen asked.

Carlston looked up from detaching the black fob riband from the watch. "He was my mentor. Just as I am yours." He returned to his task.

Lord Carlston saw himself as her mentor? Helen turned over the startling idea, finding only more questions and a strange thrill that she quickly quelled.

"There is much I must explain to you," he said, "but we will start here at the very foundation of it all."

He extended his hand, the timepiece flat on his gloved palm. The round case was slightly larger than a normal fob watch, with an unusual cover of rich blue enamel. In the lamplight, Helen caught the glint of large diamonds set around the edge, a stone at each hour mark. In the center was a diamond-encrusted arrow. A touch watch: she had seen one in the window of Rundell's. It enabled the time to be reckoned in darkness as easily as during daylight, just by touch. All one had to do was find the position of the arrow—affixed to the inner workings—in relation to the circle of diamonds.

"It is very beautiful," Helen offered. In truth, it was magnificent, but surely not what she had been brought here to see.

"Beautiful, indeed," Carlston agreed. "But like so much in this world, its true worth is hidden inside."

Ah. Helen leaned closer as he pressed a button at the top, and the blue cover flipped open. His fingers found a place at the bottom of the inner face, and a twist of some unseen lever shifted the whole casing. The frame of the watch swung out on its axis. He held it up in invitation, and Helen peered inside. A small metal mechanism nestled in the shallow concave space, each part etched with elaborate scrollwork. Exquisite. He pressed the edge, and three small gold-mounted circles of glass rose up on hinged arms.

"These are based on Newton's light prisms." With a tap of his finger, he fitted them together, the arms lining up and each prism locking into place with a soft click to form a single lens. He pointed to the first. "This one is glass." His fingertip slid to the next. "This one in the center is Iceland spar. And the third is glass again."

"What does it do?" Helen asked.

"Here." He passed it across. "Hold it up to your eye and look through it at Lady Margaret and Mr. Hammond."

Helen tentatively took the instrument, her kid glove making it difficult to get a firm grasp on its fine edge. The brother and sister stood about fifteen yards away. Helen raised the three-part lens to her eye. Blue light, stark against the inky darkness of the walk, surrounded their bodies. She gasped: it was the same pale blue shimmer that she had seen around Darby. So it had not been fatigue, after all. She looked at Carlston. He shimmered too—a slightly darker blue.

"You see the glow?" he asked.

"What is it?"

"The Orientals call it chi. The Hindu, prana. It is the life-force: the energy that exists in every living thing."

"It exists in everything?" She swung around, sweeping the lens past the undergrowth. All was dark. "But the trees and bushes do not have it."

"The prisms are calibrated to certain energies. What you see is the pale blue life-force of mankind."

Good Lord. She lowered the lens, the shimmers dropping away. "I have seen this before. Around my maid."

"What?" The word was sharp, but the surprise in his face was gone in a second. "So you discovered the use of the mirror in your mother's miniature?"

"No," Helen said. "I saw the glow without any instrument."

He rubbed his forehead. "That's not possible. A lens must always be used. You must be mistaken."

"I think I would remember if I had used an instrument," she said tartly.

She held up the touch watch again. The tiny interlocking circles of glass were nothing like the mirror in her mother's miniature. Yet he had implied that it was a lens too.

"What were you doing when you saw the life-force?" he asked.

Helen cast her mind back. If she recalled rightly, she had been standing at her writing desk and had just decided to hide the miniature in her dressing room. "I was holding my mother's portrait. Could that be it?"

"I don't see how," Carlston said. "Just holding it would do nothing. Did you bring the miniature as I requested?"

With a nod, she raised her reticule. The silk purse swung with the portrait's small weight.

"Then let us put it to the test. Hold it in your hand and see if the life-forces reappear."

An experiment—here was something she could understand. She passed the touch watch back to him and cupped her reticule in her hand. The strings had drawn tight from so much swinging, and it took a moment for her to open it, her fingers clumsy with anticipation. She wiggled her fore and middle fingers inside and, holding her breath, scooped out the miniature.

"Well?" he asked.

"No," she said, strangely deflated. "There is no shimmer."

He cocked his head. "Remove your glove."

It was a decidedly untoward request, especially in that high-handed tone. Still, the mystery had its own impetus. Ignoring the rise of heat to her cheeks, Helen fumbled with her glove's riband tie. She finally pulled it apart, then yanked at the fingers until the kid leather slid free. The chill in the air bit at her fingertips. She glanced up at his face—all of his being seemed fixed upon her bare hand. A strangely intimate sensation. With heart beating harder, she pressed the miniature into her cupped palm. As the cool gold touched her skin, the blue shimmer sprang up around him.

"There it is!"

Carlston pulled off his own glove and held out his hand. "Give it to me. Please."

She dropped it into his palm. The blue glow disappeared. She blinked, dizzy from the shift in color and light.

He shook his head. "I see nothing."

"Is that bad?" Helen asked. "Am I doing something wrong?" How could she know what was right or wrong in this new, fantastical world?

"I have never come across this before." He looked beyond her, calculation narrowing his eyes.

Helen pushed her glove into her reticule for safekeeping, eager to test the miniature on her bare skin again, but Carlston was clearly not ready to return it. He turned the portrait over. "Do you know whose hair is woven here, at the back?"

"My mother's and father's." She looked down at the little red-and-gold checkerboard. "Would that help me see the life-forces?"

"It should not." He passed back the miniature. She closed her hand around it, and the blue shimmer enveloped his tall figure again.

"Why is it important to see this energy?" she asked. The blue was beginning to press in behind her eyes. She shifted the miniature to her gloved hand, feeling a wonderful release as the shimmer dropped away. "Why do I have these abilities, Lord Carlston?" Helen braced herself. "You said you would show me what I am."

Just saying the words brought a dread so deep that it was like a physical ache at her core.

He observed her for a long moment, as if weighing her ability to cope. She raised her chin. Had she not proven herself already?

Apparently, she had, for he said, "You already know that I have similar abilities, Lady Helen." He smiled: a wry acknowledgment of a shared burden. "We are very rare, you and I. There are only eight of us in this country; about two hundred of us spread across the world. Usually, it is impossible to predict when one of our kind will be born. We spring up unbidden, sometimes in the lowest slums, sometimes in the highest houses. A *lusus naturae*. The term means—"

"I know what it means," she said a shade too sharply. "'A whim of nature.'"

"You have Latin?"

"A little," she said, brushing aside the hours she'd spent secretly studying her brother's books. Most men found learning ridiculous in a female, and for some reason, she did not want to see derision in his lordship's eyes. A glance found him still staring, but with that look of calculation again. At least it was not disgust. "You are saying that these talents are a freakish occurrence?"

"Usually, yes. In you, however, they are not." He paused. There seemed to be a great deal of weight on that statement. "You inherited them directly from your mother."

For a moment his face hazed out of focus as Helen fought for air, her chest aching with a locked-breath battle between acceptance and refusal. So this was the mystery of her mother. Or at least part of it. She finally managed to breathe, and gave a shake of her head, trying to loosen some memory, some vague recollection of her mother using such talents. Nothing came. Yet it made sense, didn't it? She raised her eyes to the night sky, fixing on the pale quarter moon as she felt her way through the tumult of emotions. The link that she had suspected—no, dreaded—between her own restlessness and her mother's maligned nature was real. What did that mean about her own nature?

"These abilities, they have something to do with my mother's disgrace, don't they?" She leaned closer to him. "Do you know why she was called a traitor? Do you know what really happened?"

He shook his head. "I do not." He started to add something else, then fell silent.

"You do know something. I can read it in your face."

"You are very good at that, aren't you?" It did not sound like a compliment.

"Yes," she said boldly. "What do you know about my mother?"

"As far as I know, only two people hold the truth of the story."

"Well?" Helen demanded.

"The names will get you no further."

She clenched her gloved hand around the miniature. "Lord Carlston," she said, careful to keep the irritation from her tone, "please tell me their names."

"As you wish. The first is Queen Charlotte." One slanted dark brow lifted: *I told you so.* The fact that he was right—there could be no more information from *that* source—was almost as infuriating as his manner. It did, however, explain the Queen's comment at her presentation.

"And the other?"

"Mr. Benchley."

"Your mentor? He knew my mother?"

"He was her mentor as well. But I warn you, he does not look kindly upon the memory. I doubt he will help her daughter."

Helen bowed her head—not in defeat, but to hide her defiance. A lady did not scowl at a gentleman. Not to his face, anyway. If this Mr. Benchley made an appearance, as his lordship seemed to think he would, then she would ask him. Most *insistently.* She forced her mind back to the reason she was standing there. "If these talents are not usually inherited, then how could you possibly know I would have them?" She crossed her arms, drawing her shawl closer around her body. "How did you know in the first place? You have been testing me these last few days."

"Your mother saw that you could read the truth in faces even as a child. No one believed her, of course. It was an impossibility. Yet we could not afford to discount it entirely. At least, I felt we could not."

Helen looked past him to the shadowy outlines of the trees. If her mother had seen it so early, why hadn't she said anything? Prepared her in some way? Even a child could understand difference and the need for secrecy.

"I had to test you to make sure that you do, indeed, have the gifts." He tapped long forefinger against forefinger, counting off talents. "Acute senses, faster reflexes, quicker healing, extra strength—"

"No," Helen interrupted. "I don't have quicker healing nor extra strength."

"You will. The strength is often the last to come. But I have seen enough to be sure. You caught that portrait with extraordinary dexterity, and you were able to calculate the elements around the horse and react with great speed."

"Calculate?" Helen felt an enormous sense of relief. "I thought I was seeing into the future."

He gave a sharp laugh. "No, we are not clairvoyant." His head tilted as he considered the idea. "A pity, though. We could use it. Did you feel a rush of energy when you realized the danger of the horse?"

She nodded, remembering the exhilaration.

"That rush enables us to see, in our minds, the possibilities of action. It is like an enhanced calculation of what is most likely to occur." He hesitated. "There is another talent that is, perhaps, harder to believe."

"Harder? Than all this?"

"We are able to reach inside a person's soul and remove darkness."

"What?" She shook her head, the absurdity of it breaking into a small laugh that fluttered in her chest. "That is not possible." Yet he had such a look of truth in his dark eyes.

"Nor is reading people's hearts, calculating the future, and grabbing impossibly fast missiles from the air," he said gently. "You need only look to your own gifts to know it is all possible."

Helen swallowed. The world was slipping further from its safe bearings. "What is the purpose of these gifts?" she demanded. "You have not yet told me." At that moment they did not feel like gifts—more like the hallmarks of a freak. She remembered Darby's simple faith in her goodness. Perhaps she was not a freak, but the agent of God her maid had proposed. A terrifying thought, but better than being a freak. "Do we remove sin? Are we some kind of"—she sought the proper Godly instrument—"angels?" Just voicing it made her wince at the arrogance of such a thought.

"Angels?" His laugh this time held no mirth. "I assure you, I have not seen any evidence of such a creature on this earth, and especially not in London. No, you are not an angel, Lady Helen. You are a Reclaimer."

Reclaimer? Helen stilled, hazy memories finally rising from her childhood. Whispered conversations between her parents, the dim shape of a word like *Reclaimer* within them. She remembered other whispers too, echoes of Lord Carlston's words: *souls* and *darkness*. And one that she had heard over and over again: *loss*. If what his lordship said was true—and she was not ready to concede completely to such wild claims—her mother and father must have kept so much from her and Andrew. So many secrets. But why?

"What is a Reclaimer?"

He shifted his shoulders, taking in a deeper breath. "You are no doubt aware of the Bow Street Runners?"

She frowned. The city's small force of detectives was the last thing she had expected him to invoke. "Of course. They are famous."

"Are you aware that they were formed more than sixty years ago by Mr. Fielding, the novelist?"

"The author of *Tom Jones*?" One of her favorite books.

He nodded at her surprise. "He was also Chief Magistrate of Westminster. A prescient man: he saw how many people were pouring into London every year, looking for a better life and failing to find it. He realized that this despair and steady overcrowding of our city would result in more and more criminal activity. So he devised the Runners to create some order amongst the chaos. More impressively, he managed to obtain the sponsorship of the Home Office." His voice took on a sardonic edge. "Not an easy task, since the idea of a police force is an abomination to a right-minded Englishman, being as it is a French idea. As a consequence, there are not nearly enough Runners to make a real difference to the lawlessness on our streets, but at least it is a start."

"So, is a Reclaimer some kind of Runner?" She laughed at a sudden ridiculous thought. "Am I set to be a thief-taker, Lord Carlston? Shall I drag a few ruffians to the gallows?"

He smiled. "No, Lady Helen, not a thief-taker exactly."

She had been funning; of course no woman could do such a thing. "What do you mean, 'exactly'?"

"Mr. Fielding created a brother organization alongside the Runners. A clandestine group he called the Dark Days Club."

"What kind of name is that?"

"An ironic name bestowed by a very worried man," Lord Carlston said. "Mr. Fielding was aware that not all the evil within his city was caused by human agency."

Helen drew back, sure she had not heard him correctly. "I beg your pardon?"

"I know it is hard to accept, but there are agencies *other than human* in our cities, and they require certain special abilities to contain. *Our* abilities. For centuries Reclaimers had worked alone, but Mr. Fielding drew our kind into one group: the Dark Days Club. We are also under the aegis of the Home Office, but unlike the Runners, not officially on the ledger. We do not officially exist."

Helen stared down at the gravel path, trying to absorb what she had just heard. She lifted her head. "What kind of *agencies*?"

"That is what I am about to show you." He gestured to the undergrowth. "Within these gardens is a creature that preys upon mankind, and we are here to stop it. As soon as the fireworks begin and all attention is upon the display, we will go in and you will see the proof for yourself."

Helen peered into the bushes. The flickering lamplight created shadows amongst the foliage, the shapes within them alive with sudden menace. What on earth was he about to show her? Some kind of ghost or ghoul? Five minutes earlier, she would have ridiculed such an idea, but now she was not so sure. He had finally kept his promise—she was getting her answers—but they were steeped in a world far beyond the fantastical. Glowing people, strange gifts, and now nonhuman *creatures*. Helen closed her eyes, feeling everything she had known shift into a new and frightening order.

She opened her eyes to see Lord Carlston beckon to Lady Margaret and Mr. Hammond, who immediately started back toward them. "Are they Reclaimers too?" she asked.

"They are part of the Dark Days Club, as are Lady Jersey and Mr. Brummell, but they are not Reclaimers. Their role is to gather intelligence and assist us," Carlston said, working his glove back onto his hand. "As I said, there are only eight Reclaimers in this country, and that includes you, the only female amongst us. Obviously, eight is not nearly enough for what we must do, so people such as Mr. Hammond and Lady Margaret are essential to our efforts."

He turned to greet the brother and sister, but they had stopped a few feet away, transfixed by the rapid approach of two men: one at front, the other behind in the attitude of a bodyguard. The leader was tall, each long stride kicking up gravel, the dig of his cane into the path adding a thud to the crunch of their progress. As he passed under a lamp, Helen glimpsed a grim mouth and thin nose beneath the shadow of his wide hat brim.

"Benchley," Mr. Hammond said. He looked back at Carlston. "You were right, sir. What should we do?"

Helen heard Lord Carlston curse fluently under his breath in something akin to Italian. Spanish, perhaps. "How long do we have until the fireworks start, Hammond?" he asked.

"Less than ten minutes."

"He certainly chooses his moment," his lordship said. "I will give him five minutes. I suppose I owe him that."

Surreptitiously, Helen passed the miniature from gloved hand to bare palm. The blue glow flared up around the approaching pair: a darker blue around the leader, Mr. Benchley—the same color that surrounded Lord Carlston—and a paler hue around his man. So a Reclaimer definitely displayed a darker life-force than other people, whatever that meant. At least it was something she had determined for herself. She returned the miniature to her gloved hand and blinked as the shimmers fell away, leaving only two dim figures stalking down the path toward them.

Thirteen

HELEN OBSERVED HER companions: all three had braced for Benchley's arrival as if he were a lion out of its cage. Although she had never met Lord Carlston's mentor, even she felt her body coil into watchful readiness. There was something about his arrogant walk and the thud of his cane that spoke of a relentless nature.

"That is not Parker with him," his lordship remarked.

"No. Parker is dead," Mr. Hammond said. "This is a new one, by the name of Lowry."

"Parker was a good man." Carlston's voice held a note of mourning. "He served Benchley well. Quinn will be saddened by the news."

"From all I hear, this Lowry is a very low sort."

"Lady Helen, please stand behind me," Carlston said quietly. "You too, Lady Margaret. Mr. Hammond, by my side."

Helen responded as much to the sudden tension in the Earl's body as to his words, quickly moving back. A moment later Lady Margaret was beside her, the waft of her heavy rose perfume out of place in the cold night air.

She clutched Helen's arm. "It will be quite all right," she whispered, the reassuring words somewhat undermined by the tightness of her grip.

Carlston glanced over his shoulder at them, the message clear: *Keep quiet and stay behind me.*

Benchley stopped a yard or so away: feet spread apart, arms

loose at his sides, his spare body rocked back upon booted heels. His eyes swept over them. For just an instant Helen found herself looking into his pale gray gaze. A jolt of alarm tightened her scalp and, although she stood still, she felt something primeval within herself backing away from his unsettling stare.

The other man, Lowry, had positioned himself at Benchley's shoulder. He pushed back his battered hat and surveyed Lord Carlston and Mr. Hammond belligerently. *A man who revels in violence,* Helen thought, with the kind of veined, pulpy face that spoke of too much hard liquor. He wore a knife, too, pushed into the waistband of his breeches.

"William, my boy," Benchley said, his grim mouth lifting into a smile that creased his hollow cheeks into ridges. He took off his hat, exposing a curled brown wig, and sketched a shallow bow. "Back at last, I see."

He was clearly a middling sort—the quality of his sober clothes and flat-crowned hat attested to it—yet he called an Earl by his Christian name. The two were close, then. Or, Helen amended as she saw his lordship's hand clench at his side, they had once been close.

"What are you doing here, Samuel?" his lordship said. "I thought you to be in Manchester, containing the riots. Bow Street said you have been ordered away from London."

"Read said that, did he?" Benchley's eyes hooded for a moment. Helen placed the name: Mr. Read, one of the magistrates at Bow Street and head of the Runners. "Well, devil take him. I could not miss welcoming back my dear friend, my best student, my compatriot in arms."

"I am honored"—Carlston inclined his head—"but you should not be in London. Not while you are *persona non grata* at Bow Street."

Benchley made a low sound of exasperation. "Good God,

that whole Ratcliffe business is five months past now. There was no evidence pointing to me, and I was in the clear as soon as Williams hanged himself in his cell." He shot Carlston a jovial look. "A stroke of good luck."

Helen stiffened. *John Williams.* The man who had brutally slaughtered the two families in their homes along Ratcliffe Highway. The Home Office had closed the case, and his suicide in jail had confirmed his guilt. Bow Street had even paraded his corpse through the streets to prove that the murderer had been found. Yet this man Benchley spoke as if he himself was the killer.

"Are you saying you actually slaughtered the Marr family and the King's Arms people?" Carlston said, echoing her thought. From her vantage point, Helen could see only his profile, but it was enough to show his disgust. "God's blood, man, they were innocents!"

Benchley held up an indignant hand. "You didn't know? I thought Read had told you."

"Read only told me he had sent you to Manchester for the riots. The rest was rumor." Carlston's voice flattened. "But now you have confirmed it."

"Ah, well played, my boy." Benchley eyed Carlston, wariness behind his congratulatory smile.

"You killed *innocents,* Samuel. What were you thinking?"

"Get off your high horse, William. Not all of them were innocents. There were at least two creatures in the mix. I am not that far gone."

For a moment, there was a terrible silence. Helen saw Mr. Hammond glance back at his sister, their eyes meeting in dismay. Carlston stood motionless, but the muscles of his jaw were knotted.

"No, on the contrary, I would say you are very far gone," his lordship finally said. His voice was hollow. "You gave me your word, Samuel. Your word! You said it was time to stop."

Stop what? Helen wondered. *Killing innocent people?* Beside her,

Lady Margaret reached toward his lordship's rigid back. Helen caught her wrist, meeting the woman's stricken eyes with a shake of her head. A presumption on their short acquaintance, but it was obvious that this was not the time for solace, or distraction.

Benchley shrugged. "It was a misjudgment. An overzealous moment. You know they happen." He smiled, a gleam of yellow-toothed complicity. "It is no good dwelling on these mistakes, William. You should know that by now. *Mea culpa* is a waste of time."

"For Christ's sake, Samuel, you cut the throat of a baby!"

Helen flinched, not only at the savage blasphemy, but at the image that his lordship had conjured, made lurid by the newspaper reports she had read. What kind of monster did such a thing?

"A *baby*, Samuel!" his lordship said again. "You could have saved the child."

"Saved it?" Benchley's voice rose into rasping fury. "Not you too, William? I thought you would understand, of all people. You'll be where I am soon enough. Then I guarantee even you'll start thinking twice about reclaiming some draper's puling infant." He viciously stabbed his cane into the path. Once, twice, the dull thuds resounding through Helen's head. The thud of a maul against a tiny skull. "I did what was best. They were all tainted."

"Tainted?" Helen repeated, aghast. His lordship turned, his eyes warning her to stop. But she could not. "How could an infant be tainted?"

Benchley's head snapped up. "Ah, and here is the reason you have returned to us." His pale gaze fixed upon her again, and this time she did step back. She could not help it. For one terrifying second she thought he was going to lunge across the small space between them. Her mind projected the rise of the cane, the cut of it through the air, the impact—

Carlston stepped forward. *"Samuel!"*

Benchley rocked back, a look of madness sliding whip-tailed from his eyes. He blinked, licked his lips—one flick of a white-coated tongue—and smiled.

Dear God, the man was deranged.

"Will you not introduce me, William?" he asked silkily. "I am most eager to meet our little savior." He waved a hand at Carlston. "Yes, yes, I have heard all about your grand Continental theories. Direct inheritor, sign of a Grand Deceiver. All very portentous."

"You have no business with Lady Helen," Carlston said coldly. "The Home Office has placed her in my purview. That is official. Do you understand?"

Helen cast a startled glance at Carlston: The Home Office knew about her too?

"I am not here to poach, William. Merely to observe." Benchley showed a flash of pale palms. He cocked his head, smiling at Helen. "Allow me to introduce myself, my lady, since Lord Carlston's manners have deserted him. I am Samuel Benchley." He bowed, his eyes never leaving her face. "You have the look of your mother, my dear. Do you have her traitorous nature, too?"

Helen sucked in a breath. She felt Lady Margaret's hand tighten around her arm. No wonder his lordship had said she would get no information from the man.

"Samuel, leave now," Carlston said, his voice hard. "Bow Street may know what you have done, but I will take this up with the Home Secretary. Mr. Ryder will not tolerate it. You are finished." He jabbed his finger toward the path. "Go."

Benchley leaned both hands upon his cane and gave his lordship a long pitying look. "Dear boy, do you really think Ryder and Pyke at the Home Office do not know what happened? Of course they do. How else would a manacled and well-guarded man like Williams hang himself in his cell?"

Carlston stared at him, his skin the color of ash. "Ryder and Pyke covered for you?"

Benchley gave one slow nod. "Of course."

The fast crunching sound of footsteps broke the tension. A large man approached from the far end of the path, long coat flapping behind, hat in his hand. He passed beneath a lamp, the brief flare of light catching the black lines across his cheekbones. Mr. Quinn. For all his bulk, the big man moved with great speed.

"Ah, I see Quinn is still alive and as protective as ever," Benchley remarked. "I now have Lowry." He indicated the man behind him. "Parker is dead. The poor fellow got too old and too slow."

"That is a poor eulogy for a Terrene who served you so well," his lordship said.

Terrene? Helen knew the word meant *of the earth*. A strange thing to call a man.

"The fool got himself killed," Benchley said. "Lowry here is no Parker, of course, but he has other talents, and some interesting predilections." Behind him, Lowry grinned.

"Samuel, go!" Carlston rasped. "Or I will forget you have the protection of the Home Office."

"Of course, my boy. But before I take my leave, say you will dine with me on Thursday night. At the old place."

Helen saw Carlston's hands bunch into fists. "I will not eat with you, Samuel."

"Come now, don't be like that. There is something of import we must discuss." Benchley stepped closer, his voice flattening into hard urgency. "For both of us."

"I have nothing to discuss with you."

"On the contrary." Benchley's eyes flicked to Helen and back again. "It is about your young harbinger of evil and what she brings to us."

Helen frowned. *Harbinger of evil?* She met Lady Margaret's sidelong glance, startled to see fear in the woman's face.

Carlston hissed out a breath.

"Yes, I thought so," Benchley said, satisfied. "Thursday?"

His lordship gave a stiff-necked nod.

Benchley bowed. "At seven, then. Pigeon pie, I think. And maybe some suckling pig." He turned, his cane digging into the path again. "And a good claret to wash it all down," he threw back over his shoulder. "Come, Lowry."

His man swept one last belligerent glance over them all, then pivoted on his heel and followed.

Quinn drew up beside Carlston, his breath short.

"Tell Dunne and Reynolds to make sure those two leave the Gardens," his lordship ordered in a low voice. "Then return. We must still finish tonight's work."

Quinn ducked his head. "Aye, my lord." He set off, and in a moment Helen heard Benchley greet him, all affability.

Hammond pulled out his watch and flicked it open, angling its face to the lamplight. "By my reckoning, sir, the fireworks are set to start in less than two minutes."

"Yes," Carlston said, still watching the departing figures. He gave himself a small shake as if to rid himself of Benchley's presence. Or perhaps his own fury.

"That man is not in his right mind, is he?" Helen said.

Carlston pressed the heels of his hands into his eyes. "He has been reclaiming too long. It has taken its toll."

Lady Margaret made a sound of contradiction deep in her throat. Carlston lowered his hands and stared at her, his face forbidding.

Helen, however, was not deterred. "He should be answering for the Ratcliffe murders." She looked from Carlston to Hammond, finding no accord in either. "He admitted to them."

"You heard why he is not," Hammond said. "The Home Office has covered it up. He is too valuable to them." He tapped his temple. "Lots of information."

"But that is not right," Helen said.

"Enough talk of Benchley," Carlston said abruptly. "We have work to do. Lady Helen, I want you to wear my coat." He removed it, revealing the close-fitting black tailcoat beneath. "Your white gown is not the best color for moving unnoticed through the undergrowth."

He draped the heavy garment over her shoulders. Helen clutched at the front capes to stop it slipping, and smelled the scent of him in the woolen folds: a mix of woodsmoke and soap, with a tang of male exertion. She, however, was not finished with Mr. Benchley. "What did he mean when he said I was a harbinger of evil?"

Carlston hesitated. For a moment she thought he would not answer.

"There are old texts that suggest a direct inheritor, like yourself, is a sign of something worse arriving in our world."

"But that is ridiculous. Surely you cannot think that of me?"

His lips pressed together in mute apology. "I cannot discount it." He motioned to the path ahead. "You wanted to know what you are, Lady Helen. You are a Reclaimer. Now I am going to show you *why* you are. Keep a firm hold on that miniature, and try to see past your natural shock and disgust. Do you understand?"

Helen wondered if she had the wherewithal to be shocked again, but she nodded and quickly transferred the portrait to her bare hand. The dark blue shimmer surrounded Lord Carlston's body.

He gave her one last measuring look, then turned and led the way along the gravel path.

Fourteen

WRAPPED IN THE shield of his greatcoat, Helen followed Lord Carlston further into the darkness. Questions whirled through her mind, but only one found an anchor in the tumult of emotions that rocked her between bewilderment and fear. Could she really be a harbinger of evil? It was a ludicrous idea. It *had* to be ludicrous, because if it was not, that meant . . . She gulped for breath. She had no clear idea *what* it meant, but the thought crushed the air from her chest.

Before long, Carlston stopped in a stretch between two lamps, his shimmering blue arm pointing to a break in the bushes. He pulled the touch watch from his pocket and deftly assembled the three-part lens. A loud bell rang. Helen recognized it: the call to the start of the fireworks at the other end of the Gardens. Everyone would be streaming toward the display, leaving the Dark Walk and its surroundings deserted.

"Stay behind me," Carlston whispered.

They entered the dark cavern of undergrowth, both stooping under the overhanging trees. The narrow, flattened path smelled of crushed leaves and the sap of broken branches. *Newly forged,* Helen thought, then felt absurdly pleased at the logical deduction. There was comfort in logic: it brought order and sanity, unlike this brutal Reclaimer world that had the likes of Mr. Benchley in it.

She glanced back to see the paler blue figures of Lady Margaret and Mr. Hammond still at the start of the path. She was to be alone, then, with his lordship. The prospect should have been alarming, but her idea of danger had shifted somewhat in the last half hour. She tightened her hand around the hard oval of the miniature.

Behind them, a large popping explosion made her duck her head even lower, shoulders tensing. Above, a staccato run of high-pitched whistles threw whizzing red and green wheels past the treetops. The fireworks had begun.

Carlston held a large branch out of her way. "The display will keep the area clear, but we must hurry. The show does not last long."

She edged past the straining branch, ignoring the dig and scrape of smaller twigs against the woolen coat. They stepped into a compact clearing, an expanse of night sky visible again, lit with a showering bloom of pink stars. Combustive cracks boomed through the air, bringing an orange comet arcing through the slow fall of pink. The spectacle held Helen still for a moment, her neck craned back. But she was not here for childish wonder. Turning from the fireworks, she found his lordship already by a clump of pale, ghostly trees across the clearing, his lens lifted to study another kind of light: an ominous blue glow about thirty yards away, near the boundary wall. Even at that distance, Helen could see it was brighter than the blue shimmer around Carlston. A virulent ultramarine.

He beckoned. "Come. Meet one of our adversaries."

Adversaries. The word tolled through her. She crossed to his side and squinted into the deep blue light, the edges of the miniature biting into her clenched hand. What she saw did not make sense: a jumble of arms and legs and long trails of energy that pulsed in her sight. Then her skin tensed with cold understanding. It was two people up against a wall, enveloped in the violent, throbbing ultramarine: a woman, garish pink skirts up around her waist, exposing a pale thigh and ragged stockings, and a man in a greatcoat pressing her against the bricks, holding her pinned with the length of his body. But this was no normal man: two long tentacles of energy protruded from his back, whip-thin and bright with brilliant blue charge. Another tentacle, as thick as an arm and the blue-black color of a new bruise, wove through the air above the woman like an obscene, oversized leech, then plunged into her chest. She convulsed, her head hitting the bricks as it impaled her body, the tentacle shivering with an influx of pale energy. The man slammed up against her, the sound of his grunt carrying across a lull in the crack and whir of the fireworks.

Helen stepped back. "Holy God, what is he doing to her?"

"He is fornicating with her, and at the same time harvesting her life-force," Carlston said calmly, lowering his lens. "That is a Deceiver. He and his like are why you have your gifts."

She felt her blood rush in her ears, her breath hard as if she had run for miles. *Fornicating.* She had seen the carnal act illustrated on Berta's card, and that had been shocking enough. But to see it enacted before her, by some kind of heinous creature, was truly terrifying. "Is it a demon?" she finally gasped. No, demons were metaphors for the evil in man, not monsters made of flesh and blue energy that walked Vauxhall Gardens. They could not be real. Yet here was the proof, pulsing before her eyes.

"They have been called many things," Carlston said. "Evil spirits, hellions, lamia. Whatever they are called, they have been among us for centuries. Creatures that thrive upon human lust."

Even with the horror before her, Helen could not help flinching at such language. *Fornication. Lust.*

"Forgive me," Carlston said quickly. "I use the word in its broader sense: overwhelming appetite. These creatures feed upon human yearning and desire. They seek to foment it among us, according to their needs. This one is a Pavor: a particularly foul creature that feeds on physical and mental suffering and our most primal desire to stay alive."

"Will he kill her?" She could barely form the question.

"He will, but not yet. The energy within her fear is what he feeds upon." Carlston's face was grim. "This type of Deceiver is one of the worst, but there are others: the Cruors, which feed on bloodlust and dominance; the Luxures, which seek out the climactic energy of se—" He stopped, visibly correcting himself. "The physical expression of love; and the Hedons, which seek to sustain themselves from the energy of art and creativity."

Helen motioned to the man. "But it looks human."

"Yes. You start to perceive our difficulty. They colonize human bodies and live at all levels of society, wherever their particular taste will be best satisfied. These Pavors are more often found in the lower and middling orders. You will always find Luxures in the demimonde, the Cruors are often drawn to the military, and the Hedons are generally among our own social sphere."

The Pavor's bruise-black tentacle was writhing through the woman, her back thudding against the bricks. The light of the fireworks flashed across her face, bringing detail to the pale, drained features. Helen recoiled. Under her revulsion, she felt a sickened outrage gathering in her body. "He must be stopped!"

"Yes, and he will be. But I must wait for Quinn. You see those two energy whips that come from his back, on either side of that feeding tentacle?" Helen nodded, transfixed by the awful flexing of the appendages. "They are very effective weapons. This is not his first victim tonight. He is in a glut—feeding to his fill—and close to forming a third whip from the energy he has gathered. Do you see how the feeder penetrates her chest?" Helen nodded again. "He is draining her life-force through her heart. The first rule: always protect your heart." He tapped his chest. "This is what they aim for.

It is difficult to fight two whips and still stay clear of a feeder tentacle, but fighting against three whips is almost impossible for one Reclaimer." He shot a glance at her. "One *trained* Reclaimer."

"Is that what you do? Fight them?"

"It is what *we* do."

Helen stared at him. She could not fight anything, let alone one of these creatures. A large explosion of green sparks lit the sky. The Pavor looked up, his face clear for a moment in the sickly light. It was a normal man's face, but his lips were drawn back in a loathsome smile of lust that seemed horribly stretched beyond the mouth it was fixed upon.

She turned her head, unable to keep watching. "Where did they come from?"

"Some have said Hell; others say they were born from our own hatreds and base natures." Lord Carlston lifted his shoulder: the shrug of a practical man. "Whatever the truth, it is the duty of the Dark Days Club to keep them in check."

Them. Helen stared into the darkness, seeing leering faces in every shadow. "Are there more here now?"

"If there are, they will stay clear. Deceivers are territorial and do not gather together. Collaboration is not in their nature. From our standpoint, a most fortunate trait; it would be disastrous if they did."

At the corner of her eye, Helen caught something moving across the clearing. She spun around.

Lord Carlston laid his hand fleetingly on her shoulder. "Be easy. It is Mr. Hammond."

"All clear," Hammond reported. Helen's face must have worn her horror, for he swiftly stepped to her side and said, "Do you need to sit down?"

"Lady Helen is coping well," Carlston said, peering through the lens again.

He thought she was coping well? She felt as if her whole world had been torn apart.

"Here is bad news, though," he added. "The creature has two whips."

"Two?" Hammond's attention turned fully to his leader. "Already?"

"Almost three." Carlston closed the touch watch with a snap. "He is in another glut. Bow Street has already found six bodies in Cheapside—no wonder they want him stopped. If the deaths are linked to one perpetrator, it will be another mass panic." He stared at the Pavor again. In the hard, clean lines of his profile, Helen thought she discerned a fleeting weariness. "And as we now know," he said softly, almost to himself, "the Home Office will go to any length to avoid a panic like Ratcliffe again."

Hammond frowned at the violent scene in the distance. "What if he builds the third whip? You cannot take a full complement."

"I know, I know, but we cannot leave him killing at his leisure in Vauxhall Gardens." He gestured back toward the path. "Get Quinn. He should be back by now."

"I must protest, sir. You cannot take three whips."

"Well, he does not *have* three yet, does he?" his lordship said dryly. "But if you keep standing there instead of finding Quinn, he will have the third by the time I get to him."

"Yes, sir." Hammond disappeared into the undergrowth.

Helen peered into the bushes and heard a moment of low-pitched, fast conversation, and then the rustle of movement. Lady Margaret burst into the small clearing, her gown gathered scandalously high above her ankles.

"You must not take three whips," she said, stopping in front of Carlston. "Not for a whore."

Helen stepped back from her vehemence.

"Calm yourself; he has only two at present," Carlston repeated.

He pulled off his tailcoat, the close tailoring taking some force to remove from the width of his shoulders. "This has to be done. The poor unfortunate out there is just his latest victim. Bow Street wants him curtailed." He tossed the coat to the ground. "And I can think of no better way to show Lady Helen the role of a Reclaimer."

Lady Margaret drew herself up—a small but furious height. "Bow Street be damned." Although her eyes cut to Helen, she refrained from damning her as well. She jabbed her finger at the sky. "It is only a quarter moon. Everything is against this, my lord. Please, we have only just got you back."

Helen looked up at the slim crescent in the sky, a band of cloud crossing its pale light. What did the moon have to do with it?

"Lady Margaret, this kind of foul attack is one of the reasons why I have come back," Carlston said reprovingly. His eye lit upon Helen, and she knew that she was the other reason. "I have been too long gone from my duty."

He tugged at his cravat, unraveling its intricate folds and pulling it free. The waistcoat was next, thrown to the ground with no regard for the ivory silk. He stood clad in only boots, buckskin breeches, and white shirt, the lower part of each sleeve covered by a thick black armguard laced from wrist to elbow. Heat rose to Helen's cheeks: she could almost see the skin of his chest through the fine linen. He pulled on the end of one leather glove, working it well over the edge of the guard. The sound of approach made him turn. Hammond and the huge shape of Quinn emerged from the undergrowth.

"Two whips," Carlston said in way of greeting to his man. "On his way to three, but there should be enough time to stop him. We cannot kill him yet—he still has progeny—so I will only disarm the whips."

Quinn nodded, his eyes flicking across to Helen. He reached inside his greatcoat and pulled out a long knife. It had a smooth, pale handle—ivory, perhaps, or bone—but the blade was not steel. It was transparent. Helen leaned closer. It was made of glass, and easily her handspan in width. His lordship rolled his shoulders. "Ready?"

"Aye, sir." Quinn straightened, his coat falling back around a scabbard strapped to his leg.

Carlston held out the touch watch to Helen. "Keep this safe for me."

The drop of its small weight into her hand felt like a finality. She had a sudden image of him lifeless on the ground. "But don't you need it?"

"Here is your second rule," he said. "We must absorb a certain amount of a Deceiver's whip energy to defeat it, but metal acts as a conduit for their power and concentrates it into a lethal blast. Never carry metal when you face a creature that has glutted and built whips. If you do, you will be dead in the time it takes to blink. That means no normal knives, swords, or pistols."

Quinn passed him the glass knife. Helen could not take her eyes from the blade. Its broad length was etched with a swirling design around a phrase: DEUS IN VITRO EST. God is in the glass.

Carlston hefted the weapon in his hand. "Use that miniature, Lady Helen. Watch carefully. This is what you are. A Reclaimer built to fight Deceivers." He paused. "Perhaps to fight something even worse."

She stepped back. No, she was not built for battle. Nor was she some harbinger of evil. She was just a girl.

Lady Margaret picked up Lord Carlston's jacket, holding it against her body. "Do not take on three. Please."

He gave a nod and strode from the clearing, Quinn following like a huge shadow.

"What does he mean, 'use the miniature'?" Hammond demanded.

Helen showed the portrait in her ungloved hand. "When I hold this, I can see the energy around everyone. Around that creature."

"Without a lens?" Lady Margaret asked, clearly astonished. She crossed to Helen, her voice urgent. "We are not Reclaimers; we cannot see the energy, *ever.* All we see are two men fighting. You must tell me what is happening with the whips. Please!"

The force of Lady Margaret's fear gathered Helen to the edge of the clearing. Mr. Hammond took up a position on her left side, his sister on the right. Perhaps to stop her from fleeing. No, a mad thought, born from her own fear.

Carlston walked directly toward the Pavor. The creature was still intent upon the woman, its feeder buried in her slumped body, the two bright blue whips curved over its back. But Quinn no longer followed his lordship. Helen scanned the trees and finally found him moving stealthily into a position near the wall.

"Does Quinn fight the Pavor too?" she whispered.

"No," Hammond said. "He is not a Reclaimer. He is Lord Carlston's Terrene."

"Like Parker was for Mr. Benchley," Helen said, recalling the reference to Benchley's servant. Hammond glanced at her in surprise. Did he think she could not put two simple pieces of information together? "What does a Terrene do?"

"When his lordship takes the energy from those whips, it will stay within his body. He must be in contact—the whole length of his body—with bare earth in less than twenty seconds to discharge it, or it will render him insane. It—"

"Or kill him, if it is three whips," Lady Margaret cut in. "If it was a full or new moon, he would have a better chance, but it is a waning quarter." She chewed on her lower lip, her eyes fixed upon the figure of his lordship moving cautiously through the undergrowth.

"The gifts of a Reclaimer are linked to the energies within the earth, and those energies are at their peak during the new and full moons," her brother explained.

"But what if the creature is indoors, or his lordship is too far from bare earth?" Helen asked. "How would he discharge the energy then?"

A grim smile flitted across Mr. Hammond's face. "In the words of the Bard: *The better part of valor is discretion.* His lordship would not fight a creature without a clear path to earth. The risk is too great. Quinn does not fight because he must be ready to get Lord Carlston onto the ground straight after the battle. He must hold his lordship there until he releases the Deceiver energy into the earth."

"He must hold him?"

"Yes, his lordship will fight to keep it."

"Why?"

Hammond shook his head. "He has never explained why."

"If Quinn cannot help him, then why don't you, Mr. Hammond?" Helen asked. "Why is he fighting this creature alone?"

It was as if the air contracted between them. Hammond rounded on her, his voice tight. "Do you think I want to just stand here and watch like some Goddamned coward?"

Lady Margaret's attention snapped to her brother. *"Michael!"*

He bowed his head for a moment, his hands balled into fists, then took a deep breath. "Forgive me, Lady Helen. His lordship has forbidden anyone to approach. You will see why once they start. He and the Pavor will move faster than anything you have ever seen—too fast for a normal man to keep up. Too fast even for a Terrene like Quinn. His lordship says if anyone tried to help, it would just distract him and put him in more danger." He looked back at the unfolding scene at the wall. "I would be a liability."

Lady Margaret reached over and covered one of her brother's fists with a gentle hand. "You would help if you could."

He nodded, but frustration pulsed from him.

Lord Carlston stopped two yards away from the creature and its victim, the glass knife catching a flash of light from the fireworks. He must have called a challenge, for the Pavor suddenly ripped his feeder from the prostitute and spun to face him, the obscene blue-black length retracting somehow into his back. The woman's body slid down the brick wall and slumped to the ground. Was she still alive? Helen could not tell.

"Has it built a third whip?" Lady Margaret asked.

Helen tightened her grip on the miniature, as if more pressure might give her a clearer view in the shifting light. "No, I can see only two. What are they?"

"Weapons made from the creature's true energy form. If those whips penetrate a human body, they can lock a man into convulsions, or stab and slice like a rapier. They burn flesh, too," Mr. Hammond said. "That is why his lordship is wearing gloves and armguards."

"For all the use they are," Lady Margaret said under her breath.

The Pavor advanced upon Carlston, whips curling back into striking position above his shoulders, like two scorpion stingers. The primeval curves sent a shudder through Helen. Although the man was shorter than Carlston and more heavyset, it did not seem to hinder his speed. He punched a whip at Carlston's chest, the other swinging into a savage slash at his neck. Helen gasped, hearing the crack of energy as Carlston spun to the left and ducked away from the first lash, grabbing for the second as it sliced above his head. His gloved hand grazed it but did not connect. Hammond was right: they were both moving with abnormal speed. Carlston's grace and agility thrummed through Helen's body, as if she, too, were spinning and ducking and grabbing for the Pavor's whip. She looked down at the touch watch in her other hand. "How does he see the whips without the lens?"

"He doesn't," Lady Margaret said tightly. "He is using his other senses to locate them. He says he can hear their shapes in the air, feel their movements, even smell them."

"What?" Helen croaked, her mouth dry. "He is trying to grab those whips without seeing them?"

"Yes," Hammond said, eyes fixed on the fight. "He must wrap both whips around his forearm and hold them so that he can cut off the creature's weapons with the glass blade. Only then can he absorb the energy and discharge it into the earth."

The Pavor lunged at Carlston. For a second the Earl did not move—*why wasn't he moving?*—then Helen realized he was listening for the creature's next attack. Suddenly he launched himself to the left, dropping into a roll, the end of a whip biting into the earth inches from his head. So close! He clawed at the energy, but it was already snapping back. The Pavor ran forward again, both whips curved high above his head. The left one snaked toward Carlston's chest, the right massing into a ball of power that swung horizontally through the air, like a mace. His lordship dived to the right and then launched himself at the flicking end of the left appendage. Helen heard his gasp of pain as his glove closed around the pulsing blue power—her fear leaping at the sound—but he did not hesitate, circling his wrist to wrap the lash around the armguard.

"He has caught one!" she said. The danger of it throbbed in her blood.

"Thank God," Lady Margaret said breathlessly.

The Pavor wrenched at Carlston's hold, pulling him off-balance. His lordship hit the ground as the other whip slammed down. He rolled, the blue shaft of power plunging into the earth next to his head, sending up an explosion of dirt and grass that merged with the cracking roll of fireworks. Carlston staggered to his feet, shaking his head, blinded by the shower of dirt, but still holding the end of the first whip. The other snapped from the ground and came at him, too fast to duck. He turned, taking it across his back, waistcoat and shirt slicing open into a bloom of blood. Helen flinched.

Lady Margaret gasped. "No!"

"He is still holding the first whip," Helen said.

Carlston staggered then recovered, pulling himself up with the writhing energy whip. The Pavor, seeing his advantage, kicked at Carlston's shoulder, trying to free himself. The other lash curved back for another attack, the dark length of the Pavor's feeding tentacle flicking out behind it. Carlston dropped his knife and grabbed the man's foot, twisting. The Pavor fell facedown onto the ground, his free whip rising up, striking at Carlston's head. But this time Carlston was too fast. He caught it, forcing it down, the effort baring his teeth.

"He has the second," Helen cried.

Carlston wrapped the writhing end around his wrist alongside its mate, and snatched up the knife. A slash high across the pulsing energy severed the whips near the man's shoulder blades, just missing the feeder as it retracted into his back. Helen heard a scream, but could not tell if it was the Pavor's agony or Carlston's as he lifted the captured whips and slammed their blue energy into his own chest. The force of it dropped him to his knees. The Pavor kicked at him, the weak blow making no impact on Carlston's arched, rigid body. Then the creature hauled himself to his feet, panting, the glow around him reduced to the same pale blue that shimmered around Lady Margaret and Mr. Hammond. Helen blinked at the bright corona around his lordship, an intense, burning ultramarine light that throbbed with power. Through the blue haze she saw him throw back his head and smile up at the Pavor, the glass knife still in his hand. Helen had never seen such a smile. It was beyond joy; an ecstasy of total abandon. Of madness. There was no boundary left within him, and it was terrifying. The Pavor staggered back, then turned and ran.

"Does his lordship have the Pavor energy?" Lady Margaret demanded.

"He is—he is surrounded by bright blue light," Helen stammered. She followed the Pavor's retreat through the trees. "But the creature looks as if he only has human energy now."

"Unless they are glutted, their life-force looks the same as ours," Hammond said. "That is why they are so hard to find amongst us." He searched the dark wood. "Quinn should be on his way. What is holding him up?"

Lady Margaret peered intently into the undergrowth. "Why does he not come?" She clutched Helen's arm, fingers digging through the layers of clothing. "Lady Helen, prepare to run to Lord Carlston. In an emergency, one Reclaimer can absorb a share of whip energy from another. You can share the load. It will save his life."

Helen tried to pull her arm free. She did not want any part of that mad energy.

"Margaret, no!" Hammond said. "She cannot. She does not have her Reclaimer strength."

"But Quinn is not coming. Why is he not coming?"

As if conjured by her despair, Quinn emerged from his hiding place at a dead run, dodging trees and leaping over bushes with astounding speed and agility. He tackled Carlston just as the Earl rose to his feet. The brutal impact sent both men sprawling to the ground. Quinn recovered first and launched himself at the Earl's prone body, straddling his chest. He grabbed Carlston's wrist and forced it back until the glass knife dropped into the grass, then slammed his knee across Carlston's arm, pinning it against the ground. He groped at the scabbard strapped to his leg, but the momentary slackening of his grip let Carlston free his other fist. He drove it into the big man's jaw, the vicious blow rocking Quinn backward. Carlston tried to throw him off, but Quinn hammered his elbow into the Earl's face and grabbed his flailing arm, forcing it back down. He threw himself over Carlston's body again, pressing him into the ground. The Earl strained against him, bucking under the fierce hold of his Terrene as he tried to wrench himself free.

"Let it go, sir!" Quinn's desperate voice reached Helen. "Let it go. Or I must use the spike!"

Lady Margaret pressed her fingertips to her mouth as if she could not bear to ask the question. "Is he releasing the energy?"

"No."

"It must be near twenty seconds. He is running out of time," Hammond said.

Quinn had come to the same conclusion. In one fluid movement he pulled a spike from the scabbard and raised it high. Helen gasped as he drove it straight through Carlston's left hand, pinning it to the earth. The Earl screamed, writhing as the bright blue energy roiled around them, the sound melding with the booming finale of the fireworks. Quinn's head jerked back, his teeth bared in pain as he grimly held on to the spike. The pulsing ultramarine power imploded. This time the Earl's scream was a howl of loss as the brilliant blue light collapsed through his body and drained away into the earth under the two agonized men. Above, a final explosion of green and red and white stars burst over the gardens, the clap and rumble fading into distant cheers and applause.

"He stabbed him!" Helen cried.

"But is the energy gone?" Lady Margaret clutched Helen's arm. "Is it gone?"

"Yes." Helen watched, horrified, as Quinn wrenched the spike from Carlston's hand and rolled off him, huge chest heaving with effort.

The Earl clutched his wounded hand, the last of the Pavor energy flickering from his body into the earth. He rolled onto his side, curling around his hand.

Hammond exhaled. "Thank God."

"He stabbed him," Helen said again.

"It is not always the case," Hammond said quickly. "Sometimes his lordship keeps enough of himself to let the energy go."

"I think he has got worse since we last saw him," Lady Margaret said softly, searching her brother's face for confirmation.

He gave a short nod. "Three years of fighting on the Continent has taken its toll."

Helen drew in a sharp breath. Did he realize Carlston had used the same words about Benchley?

Hammond touched his sister's shoulder. "We must help get him back on his feet and out of here, then return to the supper box." He led them swiftly through the bushes.

"Will he be all right?" Helen asked, as she kept pace with Lady Margaret.

"Yes. Now that he has released the energy."

Helen nodded, trying to maintain her calm, but the shock of what she had seen could not be contained. "His lordship seems to think this is what I am meant to do. How could I ever fight such creatures? I cannot do what he does. His own man stabbed him!" She stopped, her sudden halt bringing Lady Margaret to a standstill. The dark shapes of the garden tipped into a dizzying whirl. "It is impossible." She flung her hand out, trying to push it all away.

Lady Margaret grabbed her arm. "There is no choice, Lady Helen. His lordship has shown you this hidden world because you are a Reclaimer, and we are desperate for your talents."

Carlston was on his feet again, his injured hand cradled in the other. He turned to give an order to Quinn, and for a moment Helen saw his back through the wreck of his shirt. A long, bloody slash stretched from the muscles of his shoulder to the base of his spine, crisscrossing a half-healed older wound. She looked away from the shock of his bare skin. And the awful damage.

Quinn passed them, intent on the woman slumped against the wall. He kneeled beside her, his hand hovering at her mouth for a moment. "She still breathes, my lord," he said. "She may survive." He gathered her into his arms and, in one mighty hoist, lifted her up.

Carlston flexed his injured hand, hissing as the wound stretched. A cut across his forehead oozed blood through the lift of his eyebrows.

"This is what you had to see, Lady Helen," he said, wiping blood from his eye. "Welcome to the Dark Days Club."

Fifteen

Wednesday, 6 May 1812

Aunt Leonore looked up from her tambour frame, the thin hook she was plying momentarily suspended in the air.

"You are quiet, Helen," she said for the third time that morning. "Did you take some of that dreadful rack punch last night?"

Helen raised her eyes from the linen cravat she was hemming. Or failing to hem, as it happened. She could not focus on stitching when all she could see were snaking blue whips, plunging spikes, and that terrible moment of madness in Lord Carlston's face. Everything else seemed frivolous and inconsequential. It was ridiculous to be poring over dance invitations and hemming a cravat when foul creatures walked upon the streets, hidden as humans. Yet what else could she do? She had, at least, taken the precaution of holding her mother's miniature during morning prayers to study the life-forces of everyone in the household. They had all been a reassuring pale blue. Although, Helen reminded herself, Mr. Hammond had said Deceivers' energy looked the same as humans' unless they were in a glut. So maybe it was not so reassuring after all.

"No, I didn't drink any punch," she said. "I am just a little tired."

Her aunt pushed the hook into the linen she was embroidering and tugged at the length of silk thread. "Yes, it was a long night. But that Mr. Hammond was a pleasant young gentleman, was he not? So attentive to you."

Mr. Hammond had, indeed, been attentive when they had returned to the supper box. Under the guise of procuring her a glass of orgeat, he had slipped her a startling measure of brandy, and then engaged her in conversation that had been a one-sided description of his new bay hunter while she recovered her composure. Although she burned to question him about the Dark Days Club, he had forestalled her with a grave warning in his sympathetic blue eyes and a smile that never faltered. "You will see his lordship at Almack's," he had whispered as they vacated the box at the end of the evening, and Helen had almost laughed. Apparently, Lord Carlston went from battling Deceivers in the Dark Walk to dancing a cotillion at Almack's, all in twenty-four hours. It seemed as incongruous as the idea of her fighting demons.

He had said she was a Reclaimer. She tasted the word again. *Reclaimer.* No, it was too absurd. She placed a stitch in the cravat, somewhat crooked, and tried to suppress the rise of the other epithet that had been placed upon her: *harbinger of evil.* She shivered, as much from the idea as from its source: Mr. Benchley. She had, in truth, encountered two monsters in Vauxhall last night.

"Yes," Aunt mused, intent upon her embroidery, "I liked Mr. Hammond a great deal. A good family and some land in Gloucestershire." She looked at Helen over the frame, clearly trying to judge if her approval was having any effect. Helen placed another distracted stitch. Her aunt pressed on. "Did you like him, perchance?"

"Well enough," Helen said shortly.

Her aunt knew the end of a subject when she heard one, and offered another. "Lady Jersey was so generous last night. I truly think she has settled on you as her favorite this Season. It is most gratifying. When I told her of our missing housemaid, she was very sympathetic. She has even offered us one of her own maids."

That caught Helen's attention. "One of her own housemaids?"

Since Lady Jersey had colluded with Lord Carlston to get her to Vauxhall Gardens, this had the touch of his lordship upon it too. Yet why would he want to place a maid in her home? She could think of only two possibilities: protection or spying. The latter brought an ugly notion in its wake. Did he remove Berta, after all, to make way for his own spy? It seemed farfetched, but she did not know enough about this clandestine world to even guess at his motivation. He seemed ruthless enough. In fact, all of the Dark Days Club seemed ruthless, right to the very top at the Home Office. Helen stared sightlessly at the linen in her hands, overwhelmed by the enormity of such high-placed corruption. The government had hushed up Mr. Benchley's involvement in the Ratcliffe Highway murders, and there was no getting away from the fact that his lordship was complicit—not only by his silence, but by his tolerance of such a madman. Her brother always said that a man could be judged by the company he kept. If that was the case, then Lord Carlston could not be trusted. Yet he had been appalled by Mr. Benchley's confession. And even with all the horror, one had to admit it had been a stirring spectacle to watch him battle the Pavor so bravely.

For a moment, all Helen could see were those two bright blue whips curved in the air and the disgusting feeder buried in that poor woman's chest. She pressed the back of her hand to her mouth, swallowing the rise of terror. Her whole world had shifted beneath her feet. What had once been solid ground was now a chasm of endless questions and fear.

"I do hope Lady Jersey's girl is suitable," Aunt said. "Although even if she is not, I shall have to give her the position. We cannot offend a patroness. It is just too bad of Berta to have run off like that before your ball. It has put me in such a difficult position."

"What if she did not run off, Aunt?" Helen ventured. "What if she was taken?"

"You have such a vivid imagination. If she had been taken, I'm sure someone would have seen something. We are in the middle of Mayfair, for heaven's sake."

Helen put down the cravat. Someone *had* seen something: the Holyoakes' page. He had reported a gentleman's coach to Philip. Maybe he had seen more. Here, at least, was something she could do, instead of tormenting herself with unanswerable questions. "I think I need some air, Aunt. May I take Darby and walk a little?"

"I thought you were tired." Aunt clicked her tongue. "You would do better to go upstairs and rest. You do not want to fail in the last dances tonight."

Helen shook her head. "No. It is not rest I need. It is air. Please, Aunt."

"Just for a short while, then. I have engaged Mr. Templeton from midday to refresh your steps."

Helen nodded, although she was in no state of mind for dance instruction.

"And wear your warm pelisse," her aunt added, peering out of the window at the sunlit street. "It may look pleasant, but I think the day is quite cold." She turned back to her tambour frame. "The last thing we need is for you to get a chill before your first appearance at Almack's."

~

TWENTY MINUTES LATER Helen and Darby could attest to how cold it was outside. A frigid wind cut through Helen's red wool pelisse and blew Darby's straw bonnet askew as they walked along

Curzon Street toward Berkeley Square, where the Holyoakes lived.

"Do you see any of the creatures, my lady?" Darby whispered. She righted her bonnet and deftly retied the yellow ribands under her chin, her eyes fixed upon a plump matron in a salmon-pink mantle walking along the pavement. "Is she one?"

Helen shook her head, feeling a little dizzy. Before they had left, she had tucked the miniature under the buttoned wrist of her left glove, tight against her skin, and consequently, a pale blue shimmer surrounded every person on the busy street. While that was reassuring, the effect had produced a heavy, dragging ache behind her eyes, as if something was being wrenched from her head.

Darby sniffed. "It seems unfair that people are going about their business not knowing these creatures are among them." She lifted her shoulders as if the idea had crawled across her nape.

Helen waited until a red-coated army officer walked past, then said, "Just think what would happen if everyone did know about them. It would be like the witch hunts in history." She glanced at a young gentleman coming out of a shoe shop, his portly body bathed in pale blue. "The creatures look no different from us, Darby, so anyone could be a Deceiver—a husband, a wife, a brother, a friend. People would turn on one another. Mobs would attack anyone who did not fit. It could even bring on a Terror, like in France." Helen wet her lips. The grim conclusion had been another weight upon her: she could not share the fact of the Deceivers with anyone. At least, no one but Darby. "We must keep silent about them. You do understand, don't you?"

"Of course, madam." Darby rubbed her forehead. "I just don't see why you are the one to fight them. Forgive me, but what kind of people expect a young lady to fight demons?"

"Desperate people, I think. Lord Carlston says there are only eight Reclaimers in the whole country."

"Well, it is not right. Demons are the work of the church, not a girl of eighteen."

Helen gripped her maid's arm. "You are very good to believe me so readily."

Darby fleetingly placed her hand over Helen's. "My mam says there's much more around us than our eyes can see. You've never lied to me, my lady, and I've seen what you can do: catching that box and reading the expressions of those around you." She shook her head. "Still, it's fair mad to think you can fight like a man. If I was you, my lady, I would stay away from Lord Carlston and his like."

"It is not as easy as that," Helen said. "Although I wish it were." She could not forget what she had seen, nor the hope that had been placed upon her abilities.

They walked on. Helen wriggled her right forefinger into the opening of her other glove, easing the tight fit of the red kid. Perhaps it was the overfirm press of the portrait against her skin that was causing the headache. Or maybe its use had a time limit upon it: fifteen minutes and then it brought a sickening migraine.

A flicker of something dark and sinuous caught the edge of her vision. She turned, feeling the pain in her head sharpen into tiny daggers. Across the street, a middle-aged man with high color in his cheeks had stepped out of a house in the company of two friends, his life-force a few shades brighter than their pale blue glows. A livid purple-black tentacle of energy extended from his back through his fashionable green tailcoat and undulated across the shoulder of one of his companions. A feeder.

Helen stopped, her body thudding with alarm as the groping, tubular end of the foul extrusion sucked at the younger man's life-force, drawing up a thin, pale thread of his energy as if into a pulsing mouth. Yet there was nothing in the young man's demeanor that spoke of pain or weakness. Quite the contrary: he was frowning, vigorously arguing a point. Clearly, the creature beside him was not in a glut like the one at Vauxhall, but it was still drawing energy from oblivious victims, like a fly supping on spilled honey. All three men descended the steps to the street, the tentacle still constricting and relaxing in an obscene sucking motion. The Deceiver stood between his friends as a servant girl approached, errand basket in hand. Without even seeming to notice her, he reached his tentacle outward, sliding it across her bodice and caressing the curve of her bosom as she passed. He smiled.

Helen felt her gorge rise. Beneath her horror, she could feel something else. Another beat within her that whispered, *Do something, do something, do something.* She stepped back. There was nothing she could do.

"Lordy, you've seen one, haven't you, my lady?" Darby whispered.

"The man over there, in the center."

"But he's a gentleman," Darby said.

"I told you it could be anyone."

The Deceiver suddenly looked over at Helen, a frown on his reddened face, as if he had sensed she could see his true form. Gasping, Helen turned her face and grabbed Darby's arm, pulling her into a quick walk. She dug at the miniature inside her glove. Finally it slid free. She folded her gloved hand around its hard edges. Instantaneously, all the shimmering blue outlines dropped away, and with them the vicious ache in her head. She closed her eyes for a moment, sighing into the sudden release of pressure and pain.

They reached the bend in Curzon Street that veered toward Berkeley Square. Helen risked looking over her shoulder. The Deceiver had turned back to his oblivious friends, and they were strolling in the other direction, pausing to let an elderly gentleman pass. Did she dare take one last horrifying look? With heart pounding, she pressed the portrait to her skin and off again, leaving a loathsome image in her mind of a bruise-black tentacle reaching for the pale glow of the old man.

~

BEFORE LONG, HELEN and Darby stood opposite the Holyoakes' house in Berkeley Square.

"Are you sure you don't want to return home, my lady?" Darby asked anxiously. "You look awful peaky."

Helen shook her head, although she still felt unnerved by the encounter with the Deceiver. It was one thing to witness Carlston's battle with the Pavor in the Gardens, but another entirely to see one of the creatures on the street, passing as human and feeding on those around him.

"We are here now," she said, forcing some steady practicality into her voice. "We may as well try to speak to the page."

Behind them, the large fenced garden in the center of the square was busy with people who had dared the chill for a chance to stroll in the weak sunshine. Helen glanced over her shoulder. Nurserymaids called warnings to well-swaddled children, ladies strolled arm in arm under the plane trees, their heads bent together in conversation, and a young girl in an ill-fitting dress sang a sweet love ballad, offering song sheets for sale to a small group of onlookers. Beyond her, Helen glimpsed Gunter's Tea Shop at the opposite corner of the square. Two men lounged against the rails outside, spooning up the famous ice cream.

Any of them—male or female—could be a Deceiver.

She turned from the unsettling thought, ignoring the small voice that told her to fish the miniature out of her reticule and check everyone's life-forces. One encounter was enough. Besides, what could she do if she found another Deceiver?

She rubbed her gloved hands together and frowned at the

Holyoakes' firmly closed door. "Perhaps I should just go and ask for the boy. We will freeze to death if we wait for him to come out."

"No, my lady. What will it look like, you asking for a page at the front door?"

It was true. She was not acquainted with the Holyoake family, and such outlandish behavior would be rightly refused. She could, of course, offer her card and explain her quest. Still highly unusual, but it was possible she would be invited within and allowed to talk to the boy. She did not, however, want to do so with his employer or a senior servant present; that was a sure way of finding out nothing. Nevertheless, waiting for the page to emerge from the house was a fool's errand.

Darby adjusted her bonnet. "Let me ask at the kitchen."

"But you know no one in the household either."

"It is worth a try, don't you think, my lady?"

Although dubious, Helen nodded her agreement, and they crossed the road.

The stone steps that led down into the basement courtyard were guarded by an iron gate and a small white-and-tan terrier sitting on the second step. The dog stood as they approached, tan tail poised, waiting for final identification of friend or foe.

"Hello," Helen said. "Hello, boy."

The dog's tail gave a doubtful wag. It looked too big and alert to be a turnspit dog: those poor, overworked animals had to be small enough to fit inside the wheel that turned the meat spit over the fire. This must be a pet then, or perhaps kept for the rats.

"He seems friendly," Helen said. "I think he will let you pass."

Darby walked up to the gate. "I don't know, my lady. These small ones can give a nasty bite."

"Don't show him your fear," Helen said, but it was too late. The dog had made his judgment. His small body bounced with each shrill bark, front legs stiff with the outrage of Darby's hand on the latch. She snatched it back.

"Perhaps you would like to go past him first, my lady," she said pointedly.

"Rufus, be quiet!" A woman's voice cut through the barking, but did not stop it. "Rufus, you mangy cur! Hold your tongue."

Rufus subsided and, with a last glowering look at Darby, trotted down the steps, his job done. A woman's face, plump and heat-reddened, peered up from the basement courtyard, her thick gray hair tucked back into a clean cook's scarf. "Oh, I didna know someone was there. I thought the little beggar was just making noise again." She took in Helen's person and then gave a quick bobbing curtsy. "Are ye lost, madam?"

"No, I would like to speak to the Holyoakes' page."

"Thomas, ma'am? Has the little scoundrel done summat wrong?"

"No, not at all."

The woman twisted a cloth in her hand. "Do ye wish to go to the front door, Madam . . . ?"

"No, I am quite happy to wait here for him."

With another bob, the woman disappeared through the basement door.

"You are shivering, my lady," Darby said. She moved to shield Helen from the wind, then leaned closer, her voice lowering into secrecy. "Do you really think this Dark Days Club has taken Berta?"

"I don't know, but after what I saw last night, I think the removal of a maid would not bring them any anxiety."

Movement in the courtyard stopped their conversation. They both peered down. A fair-headed boy of about ten years, clad in smart blue livery, had come into the courtyard, escorted by Rufus.

"Stay," he told the dog, then took the steps two at a time. They moved back as he opened the gate and came through, then bowed to Helen in a marvel of pretty dignity. "You wished to see me, my lady?"

"You know who I am?"

"Lady Helen Wrexhall. From over on Half Moon Street." He smiled, its sweet hesitancy shifting into a smothered grin. "I've seen you in Hatchards, my lady, reading the natural philosophy books. While I've been waiting for Lady Holyoake."

Helen bit her lip. She often perused a book of science hidden inside one of the poetry folios at the bookshop. "You won't tell, will you, Thomas?"

The grin blossomed. "No, my lady."

"Thomas, you probably know why I am here."

He nodded gravely. "Your maid."

"That's right. I know my footman Philip has already spoken to you, but I was hoping you might have remembered something else."

Thomas looked down at the ground. "I don't know, my lady. Perhaps."

Darby clicked her tongue. "I know a guilty rascal when I see one, my lady. You've known something all along, haven't you, boy?"

Thomas raised his eyes, fair skin flushed. Guilty, indeed. Helen felt a rise of excitement.

Darby crossed her arms. "You should have told Philip everything you saw, boy. Poor Berta's been gone over a week now."

"It's all right, Darby." Helen crouched down in front of Thomas. "Philip is a very large man, isn't he, and a bit impatient."

"He was all pushy and grabby, my lady. Gave me the creepies," Thomas muttered, giving a theatrical shiver. Darby snorted. "He did an' all," the boy added defiantly.

"Likely you gave him too much cheek," Darby said. "Philip's got no patience for cocky little whelps." She leaned forward. "Nor does her ladyship."

"Darby, please," Helen said. She smiled reassuringly at the young page. "So, you told him about the carriage?"

"Yes, my lady, but he said he'd give me a hiding if I was giving him hum. I didn't like the look in his eye, so I took off."

"But you saw something else, didn't you?"

"And make it straight. No pitching the gammon," Darby said.

Helen glanced up at her maid. Wherever had she picked up such language?

Thomas gave Darby a haughty glare. "I ain't no liar."

"Then tell her ladyship the truth, before I get old and die."

He narrowed his eyes, then turned back to Helen. "There is not much to tell, my lady. The coach pulled up on Berkeley Street just as your girl was walking by—"

"She was on an errand, my lady, for Mrs. Grant," Darby murmured.

"Yes, I know." Helen motioned for Thomas to continue.

"The whole underside of it was covered in mud like it had come far. I couldn't see who was in it, and it didn't have any markings on it, but I saw traveling trunks strapped to the back. One of them had a coat of arms."

"Do you know whose?"

He shook his head. "Sorry, my lady."

"Can you describe it?"

"The shield had blue and yellow chevrons"—his fingers traced triangles in the air—"and two unicorns at the sides." He curled his hands and raised them into rearing hooves.

Helen did not know it either, but the two supports meant it belonged to a peer. It would be listed in her uncle's copy of *Debrett's*. Finally a fact amongst all the conjecture.

"And then what happened?"

"What do you mean, my lady?

"Did you see Berta after that, or did someone get out? Did she approach the carriage?"

He shook his head. "I was picking up a parcel from the stationery man along there, and I went into his shop. When I came out, the coach was gone. And I didn't see your girl, neither."

"And she never came back to the house after that, my lady," Darby added. "I asked all the other staff, and not a soul can remember seeing her after Monday morn."

Below, Rufus barked. They all peered down.

"Get away, you silly hound," the cook said, sweeping her way clear of the circling terrier with an impatient foot. She looked up the stairwell. "Thomas, her ladyship wants yer."

"Begging your pardon, my lady, but I must go," Thomas said, bowing, his hand on the latch.

"Wait." Helen opened her reticule and reached inside for a coin. Her fingertips touched the frame of her mother's miniature, and pale blue glows leaped around the boy's slight body and Darby's ample figure. She blinked away the sudden spike of pain and hurriedly withdrew a coin. "Thank you, Thomas." She pressed the farthing into his hand. "You've been very helpful."

He looked down at the coin for a moment, then passed it back. "No, thank you, my lady. I don't want to profit from a girl gone missing. That ain't right."

With another little bow, he was through the gate and down the steps, Rufus announcing his return with shrill barks and tight twirls of delight.

THE WALK BACK to Half Moon Street was brisk and silent. Darby seemed lost in her own thoughts, and Helen was intent upon retrieving her uncle's copy of *Debrett's Complete Peerage*. The book contained color plates that illustrated every coat of arms in the country. It would soon tell them who owned the luggage.

Was it Carlston? The thought made Helen quicken her step, as much from a sudden desire to exonerate him as from the need to know the truth. So far, she had met only two other Reclaimers—his lordship and Mr. Benchley—and neither of them had exhibited much in the way of morality. Yet she now realized she had been clinging to the hope, the belief, that Lord Carlston, unlike his former mentor, still had some conscience. If she found that he had, in fact, taken Berta—removed her to make way for his own instrument—then it seemed that a Reclaimer was truly a creature without a moral center. And she did not want to become such a creature.

Back at the house, Helen found her goal thoroughly thwarted. Her uncle had decided to spend the afternoon in his library, addressing overdue paperwork, and Mr. Templeton was already waiting in the drawing room to refresh her memory of the Almack's dance repertoire. An hour into that instruction, Helen saw her uncle leave for his club. It was another hour, however, before Mr. Templeton pronounced her ready for the evening, and departed with one last admonition to refrain from anticipating the dance leader's call. She was finally free to creep down to the library.

She found *Debrett's* tucked away on the bottom shelf of the wall-length cabinet. Settling onto her knees, she opened the leather cover. An 1802 edition—out of date—but it was a fair guess that the owner of the luggage was not a new peer. She flicked to the color plates, running her finger past the coats of arms of the Dukes. None matched Thomas's description. The same with the Marquesses. With a sense of foreboding, she turned to the first plate of Earls' arms. Her fingertip passed over Shrewsbury, Derby, Suffolk, Pembroke. She turned the page. Cholmondeley, Ferrers, Tankerville. Her finger stopped. Carlston. Blue and yellow chevrons with two unicorn supports.

Helen turned the page, as if there might be another blue-and-yellow shield borne by unicorns. She leafed through the remaining

Earls, passing her own family's red-and-gold display, and continued through the Viscounts and Barons. But, of course, there was only one coat of arms with that particular blue-and-yellow configuration. She turned back. Carlston's family motto was emblazoned on a scroll at the bottom: *En suivant la vérité.* In following truth.

Helen exhaled a long breath. Truth, indeed. It had been his carriage in Berkeley Street after all, and that was too much of a coincidence. Of course, she had always suspected he had been involved—unreasonably, at first, and then with some cause—but now that it was certain, she felt as if she had lost something. She slowly closed the book and slotted it back into the cabinet.

Sixteen

"IT IS NOT overly grand, is it?" Millicent whispered in Helen's ear as they walked into the hallowed ballroom at Almack's.

Helen took in the large, crowded room. It was, indeed, chastely decorated: only two huge mirrors, three chandeliers, classic medallion molds along the walls, and a plain wooden floor. Through the shift of people, Helen glimpsed the supper and card rooms. They looked to be in the same Spartan state. At least the orchestra was a good size. It was seated high on a gallery supported by gilt columns, and in the midst of playing a lively rendition of "Juliana."

"It needs some new paint," Helen whispered back. "And a few more handsome men."

Millicent gave a soft snort of laughter that held as much nervous excitement as it did amusement.

Helen understood the excitement. There was a thrum of energy in the room that quickened her heart and pushed her onto the balls of her feet. Perhaps it was the beat of the music or the abandon of the dancers as they held hands and swung each other around. She scanned those who had gathered to watch. Twice her gaze was snagged by a tall dark-haired man, but neither was Lord Carlston.

She had not yet settled on what she was going to say to his lordship, but she had at least resolved to confront him about Berta as soon as she had the chance. It was the right thing to do. Even so, she could not shake a tiny desire to forget she had ever seen his coat of arms in *Debrett's*.

"We cannot stay in the doorway, girls," Aunt said behind them. "In. In." She flapped her hands, ushering them toward a small space that had opened up alongside the wall. "This will do for the moment, until we can find a better position."

They gathered at their new vantage point, Lady Gardwell already resorting to her fan against the heat. Helen took the opportunity to search the crowd again, this time finding the lanky figure of the Duke of Selburn. No Andrew at his side, of course; her brother had made it clear that Almack's was very poor sport. She had seen neither since Hyde Park, and it was quite possible that the Duke would not acknowledge her after such a show of improper conduct. A most depressing thought. He was in conversation with a poised young lady in pale yellow: Caro Lamb's cousin, Annabella Milbanke. Rather pretty, in a reserved, muted kind of way.

Resolutely, Helen continued her search. No sign of Carlston. Either he had not yet arrived, or he was in the card room. Her plan was simple: to ask him if he had taken Berta, and, as he answered no—for the answer would surely be the same if he was innocent or guilty—she would try to penetrate his masterful concealment of his inner self. Of course, what would happen then was a little less certain, especially if she discovered guilt. At least the public nature of the assembly would provide some safety.

Stealthily, she withdrew the miniature from her silk evening reticule and pressed it to the bare skin at the top of her glove. A pale blue shimmer sprang up around every figure in the room, the effect quite astounding. But nothing out of the ordinary. She gave a small dry laugh. When had seeing the life-forces of others become ordinary? She slipped the miniature back into her reticule, letting the tiny purse drop from its green silk riband to hang from her wrist.

"Girls, I see Lady Jersey. We must give her our compliments," Aunt said, urging them forward again.

They passed the dancers: a long row of couples who stood watching as the first lady in line—a flushed brunette with a knowing smile—skipped across to the second gentleman and, clasping his hands, swung with him in a full circle. The dance was a single-figure Juliana, Helen noted, pleased with her quick identification. Mr. Templeton would be most gratified.

"Single-figure Juliana," Millicent whispered a moment later. "And we have missed it."

Helen nodded her own disappointment and followed Aunt and Lady Gardwell through the throng. All the gentlemen wore the dark coats and pale satin or black breeches demanded by the club, so it was only the ladies who added color to the proceedings. At least the older ladies did, in rich vibrant silks. Most of the younger ladies favored diaphanous cream or white, with only a few, like Helen, daring a stronger color. She glanced down at her pale green gown, still pleased with the choice. Aunt had felt that it did not do enough for her décolletage, and had even ventured the idea of slipping in some wax frontage to bulk out the elegantly pleated bodice. Helen had refused. At an overheated assembly a month ago, she had seen the outcome of such subterfuge: a vigorous country-dance had induced slippage in one girl, and another had edged too close to the fire, resulting in an unbecoming stain. She would rather be thought meager than have her bosom melt.

As they crossed the floor, a strong smell of soapy lavender brought a sting to Helen's eyes. She had been resolutely ignoring the clash of different perfumes—sickly jasmine, artificial rose, heavy sandalwood—but the lavender was particularly offensive. She had never noticed such powerful scents before. Was this another Reclaimer talent? If so, it was quite horrible. She located the source of the stink: a nearby matron on one of the bench chairs arranged around the walls. These prized positions were mostly taken by hopeful mammas keenly watching the proceedings and exchanging comments. Helen felt their sharp eyes following her progress. A whisper rose as she passed—*Forty thousand pounds*—and her new Reclaimer hearing caught the acid rejoinder: *That will wipe away any stain.*

Helen drew a sharp breath. With all that had been happening, her mother's disgrace had been overwhelmed by the discovery that Lady Catherine had been a Reclaimer. Although the revelation had not explained her infamy, it had at least offered a possibility other than espionage. And one that, perhaps, was not grounded in ignobility. It had been a comforting thought in the long, wakeful hours of the previous night. As had been another thought that offered a morsel of hope about his lordship's character: perhaps the Countess, his wife, had been a Deceiver, thus necessitating her demise. It would explain the silence around her disappearance, and Lady Margaret's conviction that he was innocent. Yet the only person who could possibly confirm either premise was Lord Carlston, the man she was about to accuse of abduction.

Lady Jersey saw them coming, and graciously turned from her conversation to accept their curtsies.

"How lovely to see you again," she said to Aunt and Helen. "Vauxhall was so invigorating, was it not?" Her eyes rested for a moment on Helen, a smile of conspiracy within their restless depths, and then turned her attention to Millicent and her mother. "Lady Gardwell and Miss Gardwell. You are most welcome." She glanced around the room, searching the assembly. "Ah, now I know two charming young gentlemen who would be most eager to make the acquaintance of Lady Helen Wrexhall and Miss Gardwell. Allow me to call them over and introduce them to you."

And so started two hours of seamless dancing. Both Helen and Millicent had a number of sets secured by eager young men who knew how to dance—a most gratifying situation. Helen let Lord Carlston and his brutal world fade as she grasped firm male hands, skipped into breathless laughter, and chased a gentleman around a clapping circle, only to be chased back. She caught Millicent's eye as they weaved past each other in a ladies' chain, and returned her friend's grin of delight. This was all so straightforward. She knew the steps in this world. She knew what she was meant to do and who she was meant to be. No dark mysteries. No violent savagery. It was as if she had stepped into the light again.

Of course, such perfection could not last. In the third set, Helen was partnered with Mr. Carrigan, a stubby, flat-featured gentleman who had obviously padded the shoulders of his coat and could not seem to manage even the simplest steps of Butter'd Pease. In the end, she was forced to grab his flying hands and maneuver him into position for the promenade. The mortification made her skin crawl and itch; most uncomfortable, since she could hardly scratch in the middle of a dance. As she steered him down the middle of the couples, she saw Selburn, his sympathetic smile bringing a moment of solace. He was still willing to be her friend, even after her behavior at the park. She smiled back but then had to correct her panicking partner's swing corner. When she looked up again, Selburn had moved away.

It was a relief when the set ended and Mr. Carrigan returned her to Aunt with a jerky bow.

"How do these types get in?" Aunt said as he hastily withdrew. Her mouth pursed even smaller. "Oh no, look who has arrived. How on earth did he get a voucher?"

Lord Carlston was making his way toward them. The mandatory dark coat and satin breeches suited his physique well; no need for padded shoulders or sawdust calves. Helen averted her face in case she betrayed her keen attention, and found her eyes on the Duke again. He was making no secret of watching Carlston, his patent hostility causing Lady Melbourne, by his side, to stare at the man herself. At her obvious query, the Duke shook his head and turned away, but it was clear that he did so with reluctance.

"Lady Pennworth," Carlston said to Aunt, bowing to her curtsy. "How well you look tonight."

Helen glanced down at his hand. The white silk glove was tight and smooth—no indication of a bandage.

"Lord Carlston, I had not expected to see you here," Aunt said.

"It seems they will let in anyone these days," he said pleasantly. He turned to Helen as she curtsied. "And my young cousin. Your first time at Almack's, I believe. Perhaps you would do me the honor of standing up with me for the two sixth?"

Helen met the purpose in his eyes: the two sixth were the last pair of dances before supper. As her partner, he would be expected to escort her into the supper room and converse with her during the break. A neat strategy that sidestepped the problem of particularity, and would give them time to speak of last night and the fate of Berta. Helen bit down on her apprehension. "I believe I am free," she said. "Thank you."

His eyes narrowed; he had seen her disquiet. "I await them with pleasure," he said, and bowed, gracefully making way for the gentleman who had secured her for the cotillion.

"Now we will have to take supper with him," Aunt whispered sourly in her ear. "What a waste. I was hoping Selburn would ask you."

Helen made a noncommittal sound and took her new partner's hand, making her escape. Her enjoyment of the next two sets, however, was muted by the prospect of the last.

Inevitably, they were finally called. She watched Carlston take his leave of Lady Jersey and cross the room, his height and notoriety parting a way with relative ease.

"Come to me as soon as supper is called," Aunt instructed as he approached. "Perhaps we can arrange the seating so that you have a more congenial partner on your other side."

Helen nodded, but all her focus was on his lordship. Should she immediately demand an explanation about his presence in Berkeley Street? No, a dance was hardly the time to accuse a man of abduction and try to read his inner truth. She would have to wait until supper, and hope she could find a moment of privacy.

He bowed, taking her hand. The smell of him—soap again, but mixed with some kind of green, woody scent—was a welcome respite from her aunt's pungent jasmine. "You seem ill at ease, cousin," he murmured as he led her to the center of the room. "Are the events of Vauxhall weighing upon your spirits?"

"I would be made of stone if they did not." She leaned a little closer. "The woman. Did she survive?"

He gave a small shake of his head. "I am sorry. She did not last the night."

For an instant an image of the convulsing, dying woman seemed to suck all the light from the ballroom. Helen blinked, forcing the dark horror away. Such a terrible way to lose one's life.

"The creature had taken too much from her." His lordship flexed his injured hand. "I particularly dislike Pavors."

"I hope you are healing well," Helen said. "I am surprised you can even move it."

"Mr. Quinn has had a lot of practice. He knows exactly where to aim for maximum effect and minimum injury. It is no mean talent."

"Quite," she said dryly. Despite his matter-of-fact manner now, he had been in agony.

"It is usable again," he said. "One of the advantages of our calling."

"It is the need for such an advantage that alarms me," Helen said flatly.

They took their places opposite one another for the Triumph.

Their rank brought everyone in behind them, which meant that Lord Carlston, as first gentleman, would start the dance with the second lady. Helen smiled politely at the girl beside her in the second couple, a lush blonde in cream silk. One of the Talleyrands, if she remembered rightly. The girl smiled back hesitantly, then looked across at Lord Carlston. It clearly took a moment for her to realize with whom she was about to dance. She gasped, but Helen was not deceived: the sound held as much delight as trepidation. No wonder, Helen thought, as she observed the girl's partner: a short, ginger-haired man with patchy sideburns who was glaring at his lordship. There wasn't any wonder to his reaction either. No man of small stature would want to be placed beside his lordship's commanding height and elegance.

The orchestra struck up the introduction. With a quizzical glance at Helen, Carlston crossed the floor and took Miss Talleyrand's hand. She blushed and, smiling insipidly, allowed him to lead her down between the two rows. Her partner hurried down the outside of the ladies' row to meet them at the end, his gait stiff with belligerence. The dance then called for the two men to make the triumphal arch over the lady's head, but the ginger-haired man could barely bring himself to grasp Carlston's hand. Nor did he do himself any favors on the return to the top of the two rows, his heavy steps and lack of poise in sharp contrast to the Earl's athletic carriage.

Helen watched the other ladies eye Carlston as he passed. He did move with extraordinary authority. For a dizzying moment she was back in the Gardens watching him lunge at the Deceiver, twisting and ducking, grabbing those deadly whips, taking that brutal lash across his back.

"My lady?"

Helen stared at the ginger gentleman's hand, thrust out and waiting.

"Yes, of course." She laid her fingers over the plump knobs of his gloved knuckles. For a moment he stared at her, then shook his head and led her into the skipping walk down past the other couples.

"It is an excellent assembly tonight," he said politely over the music, but his eyes were following the Earl as he made his way along the outside of the ladies' row.

"It is indeed," she answered.

At the edge of her vision, she saw some of the bolder ladies turning to observe his lordship. He ignored them, his gaze fixed upon her and her partner. They met at the bottom, the ginger gentleman dwarfed by Carlston. His lordship took her left hand in an oddly protective grasp.

"Our fellow dancer is a Deceiver," he said softly in her ear. "A Hedon."

She stiffened, eyes cutting to the little man at her side. What was she to do? She did not want to touch him again.

"Keep going," Carlston added, his voice little more than a breath. "Do not let him see you off-balance."

The man took her right hand. Gritting her teeth behind a smile, Helen fought the instinct to snatch it away. To run.

He glared up at the Earl. "So you are back," he said.

"It would appear so," Carlston said. "I give you fair warning, Mr. Jessup. Leave the assembly after this dance."

He knew the creature's name? The two men arched their arms over Helen's head, Mr. Jessup's meager height making the triumphal arch somewhat lopsided. She glanced up as their hands locked above her in a crushing grip, straining ridges of tendon visible beneath the thin white silk of their gloves. Her eyes were suddenly drawn down to his lordship's other hand: he had pulled the touch watch from his breeches pocket. He pressed upon the diamond arrow. From the fierce look on his face, this was no check of the time. Mr. Jessup's arm jerked, his breath drawing into a pained hiss. "Do you call that fair warning?" he demanded.

Helen stared down at the touch watch again. What had it done to him?

"I do," Carlston said. "Mr. Benchley would give you none."

"Benchley!" By his tone, Jessup would have spat on the ground had he not been at Almack's. "Do you still blindly follow your old master?"

"I follow no man," Carlston said coldly.

That was not completely true, Helen thought. He might not follow any man, but he bowed to the authority of the Home Secretary.

The music shifted into the procession, and they started the return to the top of the row, the obvious tension bringing a murmur of interest from their fellow dancers.

Jessup eyed Carlston speculatively. "Then you must know he is not holding to the Compact, my lord." Helen saw Carlston blink at the sudden deferential use of his title. "He is hunting without cause," the creature added. "You know where that leads."

"Do you speak for your kind now, Jessup?"

"You know I do not." He glanced at Helen. "Perhaps we should continue this later."

"Did I not make myself clear?" his lordship said. "You will not be staying after this set. Say what is on your mind."

"I speak from a sense of self-preservation," Jessup said through his teeth. "If anything will gather those of us who thrive on pain and death into a force, it is Benchley."

Helen felt a whisper rising through her blood. A call to battle.

Mr. Jessup switched his narrowed gaze back to her, surprise flicking into his eyes. "I thought I sensed something. You are one as well." He looked back at Carlston, something else dawning on his face. "Holy God, she is Lady Catherine's daughter. A direct inheritor."

His words closed around Helen, crushing out her breath. How did he know she was a Reclaimer?

The Earl's hand tightened around her own as they continued up the center of the two rows. She must not show her fear to the creature nor to his lordship. She forced herself to look into Mr. Jessup's disturbing interest.

"I am," she said. It came out as more of a challenge than she had expected.

The Earl looked at her with an odd smile. "Already spoiling for a mill, madam?"

She had heard Andrew use the same cant phrase, and dug for an answer. A show of bravado. "He's a real rum 'un," she tried.

"I beg your pardon," Mr. Jessup said, straightening into offended dignity.

Carlston laughed. Soft and deep. "And you, my lady, are bang up to the mark."

Helen managed a smile.

At that moment the three of them arrived at the top of the column, the two men bowing as they delivered Helen back to her position. Carlston's hand tightened briefly around her own again before relinquishing it: *Well done.* Mr. Jessup strode back to his own place, his bristling gaze shifting between her and Carlston.

From then on, Helen could hardly concentrate. She was the third point in a triangle of smiling animosity. Nothing more was said, but the atmosphere was so charged that it affected everyone in the dance, creating small flurries of wrong turns and missed cues. It was a relief when the set finished and she made her final curtsy to Carlston's bow. He crossed the floor and took her hand just as the refreshment hour was announced.

"Let us wait a moment here before we repair to the supper room," he said. "I would be certain that our friend takes my advice and leaves the assembly."

Helen felt caught between the demands of propriety—his lordship should really be leading her straight back to Aunt—and the desire to make sure Mr. Jessup was out of the building and far away. She searched the crowd and found her aunt and Lady Gardwell heading into the supper room, caught up in the implacable force that was Lady Jersey. A moment's grace then, until she was missed. Across the room, Mr. Jessup was leading the Talleyrand girl back to her mother.

"I cannot believe I danced with one of them," she said. "He looks so normal."

"You have, in fact, danced with two this evening," Carlston said, flashing her a smile. "Mr. Carrigan, the gentleman who kept standing on your toes, is also a Hedon. They seek out the energy of pleasure and creativity. You may have already guessed this, but Sir Matthew Ballantyne is one as well. He was circling Lord Byron the other night, trying to feed on his artistic energy, until the Dark Days Club stepped in."

"So that is what I saw in him?"

"Yes. While they are not as immediately dangerous as some of the others, like the Pavor you saw last night, they can still harm humans. Did you feel your skin itch when you danced with Mr. Carrigan?"

"I did!" She rubbed her arm at the memory. "What was that?"

"He had recently fed. We can feel the energy that they have consumed on our skin. Even normal people can sometimes feel it."

Fed. Helen shuddered, unable to stop the image of the woman impaled on that thick pulsing tentacle, and the red-faced man caressing the bosom of the passing maid. Across the room, Mr. Jessup bowed to Miss Talleyrand and her mother. By the sour looks on the women's faces, he was taking his leave rather than escorting them to supper. They did not know how lucky they were.

"You knew each other by name," Helen said. "I did not expect that."

"To all outward appearance, they are human and live human lives. I know quite a few of them who move in polite society." His sidelong glance acknowledged the irony. "The Dark Days Club and the Home Office have a strange pact with these creatures. We do not want the world to know that they exist—imagine the panic—and they do not want to be discovered. There are too many of them for us to kill outright, and we could not do so without serious repercussions: a number of them are in very high positions. So, if they stay hidden and"—he paused, clearly picking through a number of phrasings—"minimize their supernatural activities, we leave them in peace. But if any of them act in ways that could bring their kind to the notice of the public, then we are sent in to stop them."

"Stop them? You mean kill them?"

He inclined his head. "Sometimes we kill them. It depends upon a number of factors."

"How many Deceivers are there?"

"Approximately ten thousand in England alone." He lifted his brows: *Now you understand.*

"That many?" The number seemed terrifyingly—and insurmountably—huge.

Carlston nodded. "And there are only eight of *us* in this country, spread throughout the strata of society. So, you see, it is not feasible to think we can eradicate them. Thus, we have the Compact: a toleration of lesser evil to avoid an even greater evil."

"What greater evil?" Helen asked.

"The possibility of the Deceivers gathering into a force against us. The Compact may not be noble, but it is practical."

"Yet Mr. Benchley is hunting them."

"And without cause, if Mr. Jessup is to be believed."

"Like the Ratcliffe murders."

Lord Carlston did not answer. All of his attention was upon Mr. Jessup as the man strode to the doors that led to the foyer. The Deceiver looked back at them, his gaze coming to rest on Helen for a long uncomfortable moment before he walked out.

She twitched her shoulders, trying to throw off the press of malevolence. "How did he know about me?"

"You have seen how our life force surrounds our bodies. If they come into contact with it, they can recognize our energy."

Helen looked up at his stern profile. There was an undeniable sense of threat about him, always present, but even so, it was not the only reason the Deceiver had left so readily at his command. "You did something to him, didn't you? To make him leave."

Carlston lifted his other hand. The touch watch still lay in it, the blue enamel more brilliant and glossy than she remembered. "This is not only a lens. It is a weapon, able to debilitate the Deceiver for a short time."

"How does it work?"

"I don't think you would understand."

"Please, I would like to know." She hesitated, then took the chance and admitted, "I read quite widely."

He gave a small, dismissive shrug, as if to say that her impending female confusion was not his fault. "If I press upon the diamond arrow on the outside, it deforms the Iceland spar within and creates a spark of energy—a mechanical generation of a charge. That spark passes through my body and is amplified by my Reclaimer biology and the silk in my glove. When I clasped Mr. Jessup's hand, it made a circuit." Helen nodded: it was not so hard to understand. "The mechanical charge is not to Deceiver taste, shall we say," he continued, "and has an effect like a small dose of poison. Not lethal, but it sickens them and blocks their capacity to feed for a short time." He closed his hand around the watch. "You will find that the crystal in your mother's miniature has the same effect when the outer frame is compressed. Mr. Brewster, a brilliant Scot, developed them for us."

Helen knew the name from her reading: Mr. David Brewster, a specialist in optics and properties of crystal. She cupped her reticule, feeling the weight of the miniature—now a weapon too—and suddenly made the connection. "I see. You are using natural philosophy against them. Knowledge about the world against creatures who are of the netherworld."

He looked up from pocketing the watch, startled. "Yes, you understand. I believe natural philosophy is where our advantage lies." She could hear the vehemence in his voice: he had been forced to defend this opinion before. "If we understand the way the universe works, then with that knowledge, we can control these creatures." He gave a slight shake of his head. Not in disapproval—that was clear—but in a kind of bemused realignment of her in his mind. "I had not thought to find a fellow rationalist in you, Lady Helen."

Perhaps it was the pulse that still whispered through her blood, or the unexpected warmth in his manner, but she found herself saying, "I rather think, Lord Carlston, that you had not thought to find any thought in me at all."

He stared at her for a moment, then threw back his head and laughed. The sound resonated around the room, almost an echo. Helen looked around, suddenly aware that they were nearly alone. Only a few older ladies were still in the corner, collecting their shawls and rising stiffly from their chairs. She felt the *frisson* of another kind of malevolence: the eyes of busy matrons. "Lord Carlston, we cannot stand here by ourselves. My aunt will be uneasy."

"Then let us make our appearance at supper." He bowed and

offered his arm, his laughter still in his face. "Your aunt's distress would, of course, be my own."

She stifled a smile at the blatant lie.

THE SMALL SUPPER orchestra was already well into a sweet Haydn piece when they entered. The high molded ceiling and velvet drapes seemed to soak up some of the sound, smoothing the soaring music and chatter into a heavy hum. Even so, Helen flinched at the assault on her enhanced Reclaimer hearing.

Most people were already seated at the long white-clothed tables set with platters of the famously sparse dry cake and buttered bread supper. Helen found her aunt and the Gardwells at Lady Jersey's table, an honor that had Lady Gardwell sitting bolt upright. There were, however, no vacant chairs. Aunt was craning her neck, searching the melee for their arrival. She located Helen and waved vigorously. Helen started toward them, spotting Millicent further along the table and watching the doorway, no doubt ready to offer silent sympathy for the misfortune of being escorted by Lord Carlston.

Helen felt a sharp moment of guilt. Millicent still thought everything was the same: parties and dances and whispering the latest *on-dit*. She still shared every secret. How Helen missed being able to do the same. She could not share anything about recent events, and had even kept back most of the information in Delia's letter, only reporting the bare bones of its sad intelligence. Millicent did not need to know about Mr. Trent and his strange inner light, especially since it had occurred to Helen—after Vauxhall—that the man might have been a Deceiver, and the four gentlemen associated with the Dark Days Club. More questions for Lord Carlston.

"My dear," Lady Jersey called, motioning them over, "there are no places here—I have told Mr. Macall over and over again that these tables are not large enough—but you and Lord Carlston may sit at this table behind, with some young friends of mine. It is overly small, I know, but I am sure the four of you will make a merry party." She indicated the table, set back slightly in an alcove. "Allow me to introduce Miss Tarkwell and Mr. McDonald."

The lady and gentleman in question made their bows, politely returned by Helen and the Earl. This particular lack of space was no chance occurrence.

"How many are in this club of yours, Lord Carlston?" Helen asked softly. "You seem to have very powerful friends."

"There are not many of us," he said, taking the seat next to her. "But as you have noted, some are very well placed."

Across the expanse of the two tables, Helen met Millicent's sympathy with a smile, trying to allay her friend's concern. Aunt peered over, clearly vexed at the seating arrangement. Helen gave her a small shrug. *What could I do?* Aunt heaved an irritated sigh—*Nothing, I suppose.*

Carlston removed his gloves below the table, angling his hand to show the site of his injury. "See," he said with a small smile, "it is all but healed." Only a red mark between finger and thumb gave any evidence that Quinn had driven a spike through the flesh. Did his lordship think that was reassuring?

He gathered his gloves and settled them on his satin-clad thigh. "I fear one cannot find much in the way of edible food and drink here," he said. "Still, may I arrange some refreshment?"

"Lemonade, please." Helen pushed the length of her own right glove down her wrist and began to work it from her fingers, glad of a task that took her from considering parts of his body.

"I imagine you have questions about last night." He picked up a glass jug of lemonade from the center of the table and snagged two tumblers, each etched with an elaborate facing of scrolls and lozenges. "Do not fear that we will be overheard," he said, his voice just above a whisper. "This tone is for our acute ears only, and, thanks to Lady Jersey, we are sufficiently set back to add another level of safety. Nor should you be perturbed by our new friends here. They are with us to gaily talk over our own conversation." He smiled. "So you see, we are well secured."

She glanced across the table at Miss Tarkwell and Mr. McDonald, who, as if on cue, began to converse intensely about fox hunting. They were both of substantial size, and the congenial angle of their conversation blocked much of the room's view of herself and his lordship. He had gone to quite some trouble to arrange as much privacy as possible: no doubt he was expecting an avalanche of questions. But only one mattered. None of the others could be asked until she knew the truth about Berta and Berkeley Street. But how to ask such a question, especially now?

She pulled off her glove and laid it on her lap, starting work on the other. She should not have danced with him: his natural grace could excite nothing but admiration, and their confrontation with Mr. Jessup had awakened a very ill-advised sense of camaraderie. When she had imagined this moment of interrogation, he had always been cold and overbearing, not amusing and personable. The former was much easier to accuse.

At her silence, Carlston looked up from the glasses. "You may ask me any question you like, but you should be swift about it." He began to pour the cloudy lemonade, the sharp citrus smell a pleasant buffer from the room's fug of overheated, perfumed humanity. "No doubt your aunt will soon send a deputy to rescue you from my discomfiting clutches."

He was being personable again. Helen pulled off her left glove and laid it with its mate in her lap, using the time to gather her courage. It was not the question she dreaded now, but the answer.

"There is one thing I must know," she said, modulating her voice to match his own careful pitch. "Were you at Berkeley Street on Monday morning before last? In your carriage?"

He stopped pouring, the jug poised over the glass, his eyes on her own. "Berkeley Street?"

For an instant she was certain she saw wariness. Perhaps she did have a chance of reading the truth.

"Were you there?" she repeated.

He finished pouring, set the jug back onto the table, and placed the filled glass before her, every move deliberate. "What is this about?"

She leaned closer. "It is about my missing maid. I have spoken to a witness who says your carriage was in the same place at the time she disappeared."

"I see." He crossed his arms, his face impenetrable again. "Your witness is correct. I was in Berkeley Street on that day."

"Did you take Berta, Lord Carlston?"

"For what reason would I want your maid, Lady Helen?" He frowned, the diabolic angle of his brows even more pronounced. "My pleasure? Is that what you think? Or did I step off my yacht in Southampton that morning with the sudden need to murder a young woman?"

She drew back. Well, she'd got her wish: the cold and overbearing Lord Carlston had returned. "So I am to believe that it was mere coincidence that you were so near my home at the very time my maid went missing?"

He sat very still, watching her with narrow calculation. She shifted under his scrutiny. A scrap of Miss Tarkwell's nearby conversation rose through the throng: "A most *thrilling* story, Mr. McDonald."

"It was no coincidence," he said, finally. "I had ordered a man to watch your house. He was delivering his report to me."

He was having her watched?

"But what about Berta?"

He shook his head. "I didn't see your girl that morning."

Did she believe him? It was hard to make a judgment when he was so adept at masking his expression.

"Read me," he said, obviously seeing her mistrust. "I will not stop you." He sat back, arms still crossed. The offer was as much challenge as it was invitation.

She took a deep breath, trying to see past the overwhelming physicality of him to the tiny signs that would tell her the truth. The fact of his eyes upon her made it near impossible to find the calm she needed to read so deeply. A phrase from a poem came to mind, by a little-known poet named Blake: *fearful symmetry*. An apt description for his lordship's countenance. Before her was the classic correspondence of strong chin, angled cheekbone, and sensuous curve of lip that she had seen so often in Roman sculpture. Yet within that masculine grace something chilled her blood. Perhaps that was not so surprising: he dealt in destruction. She slowly took in the shapes and textures of him, seeing both the parts and the whole of his face as an ever-changing map of emotion.

"Did you take Berta?" she asked again.

There were the quicksilver markers of distrust, apprehension, concern, but no sign of guilt. At least no guilt around Berta. She felt an odd lift of gladness: it was almost certain he had not harmed the girl. *Yet something was harming him.* The intuition settled into certainty. She drew in another steadying breath, testing the unconscious knowledge. Yes, on her search for the truth she had also recognized the shapes of a puzzle within his face—dark and subterranean. Gathered together, the separate pieces formed a shadowy picture of suffering. Old and never-ending and, for the most part, masterfully concealed. Helen hesitated—she had her answer about Berta—but the temptation was too great. Pushing deeper, she followed the secret path of pain through the hard, unforgiving lines of his face, the traitorous shift of jaw and mouth, the strain around his dark, watchful eyes. She had never seen anything like it before. Something vital within him was fighting for survival: years of struggle etched into every breath he took, every blink, every tiny flick of muscle. And he was losing the battle.

She saw him tense, heard a startled, indrawn breath. "That is enough," he said, ending her inspection by the simple expedient of turning his face.

Wrenched out of her narrow focus, Helen blinked, eyes aching and dry. Still, she had not missed the flare of the finely modeled nostrils—resentment—or the astonished widening of his eyes. He had not thought her able to go so deep. Nor had she. Her elation lasted only a moment, swept away by shame.

"How did you do that? It was as if you were looking straight into my—" He stopped.

Soul, Helen finished silently. She closed her eyes and pressed her lids lightly with her fingertips. A retreat from the room, from him, from her own deplorable behavior. Yet she could see him still, clear in her mind. Was that what it was: his soul, battling for survival? Against what? Perhaps the death of his wife after all. The burden of murder. Yet she did not want to believe such a thing. Had she fallen prey to a handsome face, just like Lady Margaret?

Helen opened her eyes. That face was pointedly turned from her; perhaps his own retreat. She cleared her throat. "Why can we read at such depth? What use does it have?" A safer subject than his soul.

"The Deceivers have been living in human bodies for centuries, but they are not creatures of flesh. They do not feel emotions as we do. Nevertheless, most of them are now masters at simulating the right response." He finally looked squarely at her again, his face once more under tight guard. "Occasionally, in moments of high or sudden emotion, it is possible for us to see a false note, a slip so tiny that it would not be discernible to normal eyes. It is a way we can determine who is a Deceiver and who is not."

"And a way for us to see if humans are telling the truth," Helen said.

He observed her for a long, chilly moment. "Quite. And so, have you determined if I am telling the truth about your maidservant?"

Helen met his cool stare with her own. "Yes, you are telling the truth." He tilted his head in sardonic gratitude. "But if you did not take her, who did?"

"How can you be sure she was taken? Perhaps she met with an accident or ran away."

"She was on an errand nearby," she said. "An accident would have brought her back to us. And we still have her lockbox."

"Granted, that could be suspicious. Or indicative of haste." He drummed his fingers on the table. "There is another explanation, of course. She is a Deceiver."

"What?" Her voice broke out of the careful tone.

"For God's sake, keep your voice down," he hissed, his eyes raking the room.

It had hardly been a shout. Even her aunt had not noticed: she was deep in conversation with Selburn.

"It is *possible* she is a Deceiver," Carlston amended. "Did you notice anything different about her?"

A black-ink man and woman flashed through her mind. She blinked away the awful image. That was definitely something different, but how could she tell his lordship? To even admit to seeing such obscene illustrations would be an acknowledgment of depravity. She did not want him to think she was a degenerate. Helen took a sip of lemonade, wincing at its watery sourness. *Come now,* she chided herself, *does his lordship's opinion matter so much?* A glance at him—dark head tilted to one side, his attention sending heat through her—put a sharp end to that self-delusion. His good opinion did matter. Admitting that she had seen and understood those foul images could produce nothing but disgust in him, yet they might give her a clue about Berta's disappearance. And she had promised Darby.

"I opened Berta's lockbox," she said, choosing her words carefully. "Hidden within it were cards of a dubious nature."

"Playing cards?"

Helen shook her head. "Illustrations. Obscene illustrations," she whispered, forcing the words out. "One of them was by Rowlandson."

"Ah." He sat back. It seemed he was acquainted with that side of Rowlandson's work. She risked a glance: he was frowning, but not from disgust. "It is not conclusive, but it does support the idea that she may be a Deceiver. Specifically, a Luxure."

Helen shook her head. Surely not. "How?"

"As you have seen, a Deceiver inhabits a human body and lives a human life. In order to do that, it needs to maintain a higher level of energy than ours for the body to survive. Last night you saw one way in which they meet that need—the feeding glut. As you also saw, a glut not only nourishes the creature; it can also provide enough energy for them to build whips. Most do not feed in that manner: it is generally fatal to the human and against the Compact. There is, however, another less destructive way that they feed."

"Yes, I think I saw it today, on the street." She described the man reaching out with his foul tentacle and caressing those around him.

Carlston nodded. "We call it skimming: they gather life-forces from a group of people, taking a little from every person. Mr. Carrigan was skimming in the cardroom until I put a stop to it."

Helen wrinkled her nose. "That is despicable. What does it do to the people they steal from?"

"It can heighten aggression. The skim pulls a person's violent tendencies to the forefront—most dangerous if more than one Deceiver is skimming in a large crowd. As we have so often seen lately, a crowd can quickly turn into a mob. Even though the creatures do not work together, they sometimes gather at the same event to feed, and the effect can be catastrophic. That is when we must defuse the situation."

"I see." Good God, she was expected to defuse mobs, too?

"Three of our number are in Nottingham monitoring the Luddite riots. As you can imagine, with all the unrest around the country, our resources are stretched. Right now I should be in Liverpool."

Helen saw the shift of his jaw. "But you are detained here because of me?"

He nodded. "At the moment the priority is to prepare you for duty. We are desperate for another of our kind."

"I see," Helen said again.

"Do you?" He gave a soft sound of disbelief.

"I am trying to," she said tightly.

"Yes, I suppose you are." He wrapped his hand around the lemonade glass and dragged his thumbnail across the etched design. Helen shifted in her chair, but he still did not look up. He seemed strangely discomposed. "There is a third way in which some of them feed. It could explain the illustrations in your maid's possession and place her as a Luxure." He paused, the moment lengthening into awkwardness. "When the possibility of a glut or a skim is not available to a Luxure, they are able to use the body they inhabit to generate enough energy to survive. They use the body's own appetites." He searched her face. "Do you understand?"

She frowned. "No, I don't. In what way?"

It seemed it was his turn to choose his words carefully. "By way of self-pleasure."

She stared at him blankly. Did he mean what she thought he meant?

"Mon Dieu," he muttered. He leaned closer, his voice even softer. "Perhaps you will recognize the Latin: *masturbari.*"

Helen froze. Yes, he did mean that.

He leaned back. "It is not an activity confined to Deceivers, so it is hardly conclusive."

"But would a woman—"

"It is not confined to men, either, Lady Helen."

"Oh." She wet her lips. Her whole mouth was suddenly dry. "And the cards?"

"Could be used for titillation."

She sat very still, the lurid information too unsteady in her mind for any movement. Or any comment. Finally she focused on the main fact and managed to say, "So, Berta may indeed be a Deceiver."

"It is possible, although it would be strange for a Luxure to take on the role of a housemaid." He looked up, his own skin slightly flushed. "A Luxure would not willingly limit her opportunities for sexual energy in such a way, nor for so long."

Helen studied the white tablecloth for a breathless moment, until the shock of such plain speaking passed. "But if the creature did take such a role, why would she do so?" Her body tensed with foreboding. "To kill me?"

"If that were the case, you would have been dead long ago."

"Most reassuring," she said dryly.

"Perhaps it was to spy," his lordship continued, as if thinking out loud. "But then why suddenly leave in such strange circumstances? No, it seems more probable that Berta is human and has been removed to make room for a Deceiver replacement, or is just a maid who has left suddenly for her own reasons." He raised his glass and took a sip of lemonade, brow still furrowed in thought.

"Do you think there could be another Deceiver in my home?"

"I doubt it. Nevertheless, to be safe I have made certain that your new housemaid is someone from our own camp." Helen nodded: another suspicion allayed. "And we will make a concerted effort to locate your missing girl, or her trail."

"That is what I have been attempting to do."

"And it led you to me." He raised his eyebrows. A congratulation. Or perhaps he was being facetious, since she had been wrong. "I will take over now. I have the resources within those areas of London where she may have gone."

Through her flash of annoyance, she felt relief: she was no longer alone in the search. "I will keep looking too," she said firmly. "I gave my word."

"As you wish." He set the glass down on the table with a small snap of decision. "We will start your training tomorrow. The sooner you start, the better for all of us."

He seemed to think she would follow him into this dangerous world without question, but she had not even consented to being part of the Dark Days Club, let alone starting some kind of training schedule.

"You will have to learn to fight at some point, but not yet," he continued. "That must wait until you have your full strength. For now, you will study the more esoteric parts of our duty; most importantly, some alchemy that is essential to our work. I will show you tomorrow."

"Alchemy?" Helen drew back. That was the realm of charlatans: turning lead into gold, and false elixirs of youth.

He gave a small grimace, clearly seeing her derision. "It did not sit well with me at first either. I think we would both prefer to trust in the laws of natural philosophy. However, some of the pathways that a Reclaimer must tread are very old indeed, and come from a tradition that has its foundation in ancient wisdom. You will be surprised at how often the territories of alchemy and natural philosophy overlap." He swept a glance around the room, lowering his voice even further. "I think the woven hair within your mother's miniature has alchemical properties. I am not sure what its purpose is yet, but I believe it may be quite powerful. Do not let it out of your sight."

Helen looked down at the reticule looped around her wrist, the small weight within it no longer a comfort. Deceivers, fighting, and now alchemy?

"I do not want to study alchemy, Lord Carlston," she hissed. "It is heretical nonsense. Nor do I want to fight. All you have shown me is a world of danger and threat, and yet you expect me to step into it without even asking me if I wish to do so." He opened his mouth as if to argue, but she held up her hand, forestalling him. "I am no warrior, sir, nor do I aspire to be. I have been taught to sew and sing and dance, and my duty is to marry, not fight demons. Look at me: I am an Earl's daughter, not a man versed in swords and fisticuffs."

He leaned closer, the raw sincerity in his face more frightening than any cold mask. "Lady Helen, I assure you, I would much rather have a grown man fighting beside me. But you are a Reclaimer, and as such you are part of the Dark Days Club, whether you want to be or not. I urge you to take on the responsibility of your gifts, as your mother did. Right now we need every Reclaimer we can get and, frankly, you cannot afford to be a defenseless female in this world."

"You seem to be saying that I have only one choice: to be a Reclaimer," Helen said, sitting straighter. "I do not see why that must be so. I may have these abilities, but I do not have to *use* them. Surely, I can just step away and live a normal life."

"And how do you propose to inform the Deceivers that you will never use your gifts against them? An advertisement in *The Times*?" Carlston asked acidly. "No. Once the Deceivers are aware that you exist, you will be a target. Even if you do not use your power, you will still be a threat to them. There will always be a few who do not hold to the Compact and see only the benefit of destroying a Reclaimer. You must learn to defend yourself as soon as your strength arrives. Until that happens, you will be protected. You saw Mr. Jessup's interest. I am not the only one who thinks you may be a sign of something coming. Something that will change the game for Reclaimers and Deceivers alike."

Helen bowed her head, fingers picking at the top of the reticule, unwilling to let him see how hard his words had struck. "What exactly am I supposed to be a sign of, Lord Carlston?" she asked tightly.

"The rise of a Grand Deceiver in England."

Helen jerked her head up, aghast. "Do you mean the Devil?"

"No, not the *Great* Deceiver," he said quickly. "A *Grand* Deceiver. Still one of these creatures, but more cunning and ruthless, possessed of great personal charm and even harder to detect. They usually rise from a lowly beginning to a position of great power, often military, in one human lifetime, bringing war and destruction and thriving on the chaos." He raised his brows. "Does that sound at all familiar?"

She stared at him. "Are you saying Bonaparte is one of them?"

"He fits the description. Our fear is that one of these creatures is now set to rise in England, too. It is thought that a direct inheritor is not only a sign of a Grand Deceiver coming into our midst, but is also the creature's antithesis, as if the universe is trying to create some balance."

"Did a French direct inheritor arrive alongside Bonaparte?" she asked sharply.

Carlston acknowledged her challenge. "There was a direct inheritor, but he did not survive to adulthood. He and his entire family were guillotined during the Terror."

Still, Helen thought stubbornly, that was no proof that she herself was a harbinger of one of these creatures. Or its antithesis.

"Where does this so-called 'knowledge' come from?" she asked.

"Old texts. From the Babylonians. They were the first to record the existence of the Deceivers."

"It sounds like superstitious nonsense to me," she said.

"Perhaps. But direct inheritors like yourself are rare, and I would rather be prepared for the possibility of a Grand Deceiver than leave us open to a Terror."

Helen shook her head. She knew that many, like her uncle, still feared the specter of a Terror, but surely such a thing could not happen in England. "I am hardly some kind of balance in the universe, Lord Carlston. And even if I agreed to your training, I cannot conceive how you would propose to manage it. My aunt will never allow me to be in your company alone. I doubt she would even allow me to ride out with you in the company of one of our own grooms."

He gave a grim smile. "I am well aware of that. Do you go to Hatchards bookshop tomorrow, as usual?"

He knew her habits? Of course; he was having her watched. "Yes."

He looked up, his mouth compressing into a thin line. "Ah, you are about to be saved."

Helen saw the tall figure of the Duke of Selburn approaching. His long-boned face was set into pleasant neutrality.

Carlston's voice quickened. "Lady Margaret will drive past on

Piccadilly and offer you a place in her carriage. Take it. And wear your plainest dress." He looked at her urgently. "Will you do so?"

Reluctantly, Helen nodded just as the Duke arrived. He had obviously been sent by her aunt, and although his company was always welcome, she felt a *frisson* of frustration. Her "rescue" had come far too soon. She had only begun to get the answers she craved.

His lordship stood and faced Selburn. The men were near equal in height and, as they eyed each other, there was a sense of two dogs circling.

Carlston gave a slight bow. "Your Grace." It was half a sneer away from insult. Helen held her breath, but the Duke's face remained tranquil.

"Lord Carlston. Three years, is it not, since we last saw you? I am surprised that you have returned so soon." He paused. "Very surprised."

"Three years," Carlston agreed. "Much has changed."

"Much has stayed the same." The Duke smiled, and Helen could see the bared teeth within it. "You can be quite certain of that." He turned to Helen. "Your aunt would like you to return to the ballroom with her, Lady Helen. May I escort you to her side?"

"I am quite able to return Lady Helen to her aunt, Duke," Carlston said. "I think you interfere where there is no need."

Selburn observed him through narrowed eyes. "Lady Pennworth has specifically asked me to escort her niece."

Helen gathered her gloves from her lap and stood up into the middle of the rising antagonism. "If my aunt requires me, of course I shall come." She took Selburn's offered arm and dipped into a curtsy to the Earl. "Thank you for escorting me to supper, Lord Carlston."

As she had hoped, it broke the tension, her implacable momentum forcing Selburn to move away from the table. Although she longed to look over her shoulder, she did not. Yet she fancied she could feel Carlston's eyes on her back like the warm press of a hand.

"I hope he did not upset you," Selburn said.

"No, not at all. He was most moderate in his conversation." She smiled through the lie.

"I do not like to see you in his company. He is the worst kind of corruptor. Insidious. He brings destruction to everything he touches."

His vehemence was startling. "You refer to his wife, Lady Elise?" Helen asked.

"I do. It is strange, but you remind me of her. Not in your person—you are not similar in appearance at all—but in your spirit. You have the same quickness of understanding and intelligence as Elise, and a similar sense of curiosity about the world. I think you would have enjoyed her sense of irony. I know she would have enjoyed your wit." Helen felt heat rise into her cheeks: she was not immune to the implied compliment. The Duke's face softened. "You would have been good friends. Elise was so full of grace."

"You paint a lovely picture," Helen said. She looked away from the intimacy within his voice: the lady's name used without title, and said with such tenderness.

"If you remind me of Elise, then I am certain you remind Carlston of her too," Selburn said. "I fear he may be wishing to relive the past. Do not be fooled by him, Lady Helen. His looks may be noble, but his heart is far from it."

"I am not fooled by him," Helen said, keenly aware that only minutes before she had been giving herself the same warning.

"Good. Then let us leave his lordship behind and think of more pleasant subjects. Such as dancing. Would you do me the honor of promising me the next?"

"I would be delighted," Helen said, and she meant it. The Duke was a fine dancer, and she needed to step back into the light, away from Lord Carlston and his shadowy world.

However, as the Duke delivered her to her aunt, and they returned to the ballroom, a rather subduing thought crossed her mind. Perhaps it was Selburn, and not Lord Carlston, who was wishing to relive the past.

Seventeen

Thursday, 7 May 1812

HELEN WENT DOWN to family prayers the next morning in her plainest dress—a brown muslin—with the miniature tucked inside her stays, and a reminder for Aunt that she had plans to spend the whole morning at Hatchards bookshop. Her aunt, however, was still abed with a headache and did not descend for the devotions, nor did she join Helen in the drawing room afterward to await the breakfast hour. Helen made her way to the morning room with a sense of guilty relief: Thursday was her uncle's day to breakfast at his club, and so, with Aunt upstairs, she would have the luxury of dining alone, and an easy path to her rendezvous with Lord Carlston.

On opening the door, however, she found her uncle at the table, already started upon a pasty and a mound of beef that sent an overpowering smell of charred flesh into the air. But it was too late to back away. He had already looked up from *The Times*.

Smiling through her dismay, she curtsied. "Good morning, Uncle. You are not at your club this morning."

He finished his mouthful. "Try not to state the obvious, Helen."

She closed the door, breathing as shallowly as possible. Surely, there had to be some way of regulating the sudden intensities of her Reclaimer senses. Another thing to ask Lord Carlston. The anticipation of that meeting quickened her step to her chair.

She sat as her uncle grunted at something in the newspaper. Helen readied herself, but he merely shook the pages and squinted more closely at the print. It seemed he had no desire for conversation. A blessing.

She unfolded her linen napkin and considered the morning ahead. *Alchemy*: just the word brought unease. She had woken with a sharp sense of regret that she had agreed to take part in something so irreligious, yet she had to admit to an equally sharp sense of curiosity. The previous night's avalanche of information was still making her head whirl with amazement and disquiet.

"Just a sweet roll, please, Barnett," she said to the butler's inquiring bow. "And some coffee."

These were quickly supplied, only the sound of pouring liquid, the ticking of the mantel clock and Barnett's soft tread across the carpet breaking the silence. From the corner of her eye, Helen watched him take his position by the servery. Could he possibly be a Deceiver—dear old Barnett? Lord Carlston had said it was unlikely that one was within the household, but that was no guarantee. Perhaps Mrs. Grant was a Deceiver. Or Tilly, the housemaid—no, surely not sweet little Tilly. It was impossible to know. Yet if one had insinuated itself into the house, what was it doing? Helen's shoulders twitched as if the creature's eyes were upon her. She shot another glance at Barnett. Perhaps they were.

She could use the miniature to check his life-force. She looked down at her bodice, suddenly realizing the rather severe limitations of her hiding place. One could hardly fish something out of one's stays in polite company. Although, Helen thought with a smile, it would be funny to see Uncle's face if she tried to do so at the breakfast table. She bit into the roll. Barnett's life-force had been pale blue when she had last checked. No doubt it still was.

"They've brought fourteen hundred militia into Manchester," Uncle suddenly announced, rattling *The Times* in approval. "That should keep those Luddite fiends quiet."

Helen looked up. *Fiends.* Was it possible that the Luddites—those desperate men attacking their own employers—had been infiltrated by Deceivers? The thought dried her mouth around her bite of bread. No, Carlston had said the creatures did not work together; she was seeing Deceivers in everyone and everything. Still, the Luddite mobs did attract the creatures, eager to skim all that angry energy: it was why the other Reclaimers had been posted to the troubled cities, ready to defuse any violence. Could she do such a duty? It seemed impossible to even contemplate.

She swallowed and cleared her throat. "Are they expecting more riots, Uncle?"

"Most likely," he said, noting her interest with surprise. "They have discovered a written Luddite oath in the pocket of one of those unholy dogs. Apparently, there are thousands who have sworn to it. Listen to this abomination." He read from the paper:

> "I, A. B., of my own voluntary will, declare and swear never to disclose the names of the persons who compose the Secret Committee, or by describing, either by word or sign, their persons, features, clothes, connections, &c. cause them to be discovered, under the penalty of being put out of the world by the first brother who may meet me, and of having my name and character ever held in abhorrence."

He looked up. "It even goes on to declare that he would commit murder to keep this foul pact. Outrageous, I say!"

Helen nodded, although her mind turned to another secret

pact, between the Dark Days Club and the Deceivers. It was a strange thing to know something so important and dangerous when her uncle did not.

The door opened to admit Aunt. She faltered for a moment, then entered the room. "Good morning, Pennworth. You are not at your club: what a pleasant surprise." She smiled wanly at Helen.

"Perceval has his head on right about these Luddites," Uncle said as she took her seat. "He is showing true leadership in this dangerous situation. True leadership."

"Quite," Aunt said with careful tranquility. She paused as Barnett poured her tea, and then added, "Although the Tory cabinet is in disarray about the American matter, is it not? You said so yourself."

Uncle grunted his agreement. "Cursed scoundrels." Helen was not sure if it was Prime Minister Perceval's cabinet or the Americans who were the scoundrels. Probably both. "We'll be at war with 'em before long, mark my words." Uncle shook the newspaper again to punctuate his prophecy.

"Are you feeling better, Aunt?" Helen asked.

"Yes, I took one of Dr. Roberts's powders and feel much restored." Aunt took the top invitation from the pile on the silver salver, eyed it dismissively, and put it aside. She squinted across at Helen. "Why are you wearing that gown, my dear? I thought you were going to give it to Darby. The color was a mistake for you from the beginning." Aunt shook her head. "Do change before we go out."

Helen straightened. "Out?"

"We have an appointment with Madame Hortense this morning. She sent a note yesterday to say your ball gown is ready for a final fitting. I thought we might visit Mr. Duray, too, and order your new riding habit. Last night the Duke was most interested in your riding prowess. I believe he will soon invite you to accompany him along the Row. You must have a new habit." Aunt's smile was congratulatory.

"I see," Helen said, torn between the gratification of Selburn's interest and frustration at the disruption of her morning's plan. "Are you sure you are well enough?"

"Of course."

Uncle sucked at his teeth thoughtfully. "Duke? Which Duke?"

"Selburn," Aunt said triumphantly. "He danced with her too, at Almack's. And was most obliging to me."

"But, Aunt, I was going to walk to Hatchards this morning."

"Not today. Your books can wait. And for goodness' sake, don't let Selburn know how much you read."

"But if you are not feeling well—"

"Helen, I assure you I am at the peak of good health. Besides, don't you want to see your ball gown finished? I certainly do."

Helen dug her fingernail into the soft center of her roll. She knew that look: nothing would persuade Aunt from the mantua-maker and tailor. There would be no alchemy today.

Somehow she would have to get a note to Lord Carlston as soon as possible. Not via one of the footmen—Darby must take it, and wait for an answer. Helen ground a piece of bread into the white porcelain of her plate. Now that the meeting had been torn from her grasp, she realized just how much she had wanted to keep it. For all her misgivings, there was something tantalizing about the idea of being trained by his lordship. He knew how to navigate this frightening underworld, and seemed to face its unnatural dangers with calm courage. If there was any place safe now, it was most likely by his side. Or, Helen thought wryly, standing a little way behind him.

"Selburn is a Whig," Uncle said heavily.

"That may be so, Pennworth, but he is a Duke first," Aunt said. "And he is Andrew's dear friend. It would be a most fitting match."

"Being Andrew's friend is no recommendation," Uncle said from behind the paper.

"You are running ahead of yourself, Aunt," Helen said.

"You are not set against him, are you?" Aunt demanded.

"No, I like him very much." Helen clenched her hands in her lap, arrested by a sudden thought. How could she ever marry if she stepped into the life of a Reclaimer? No man would allow his wife—the potential mother of his heirs—to fight demons. In fact, the very idea that a woman could even do so was absurd. And yet, her father had allowed her mother to face such danger. Why? The reason was so obvious that Helen almost groaned. Not only must he have known about the Dark Days Club, he must have been one of them before his marriage to Lady Catherine. It was even possible that he had become her mother's Terrene. A rare match indeed. "It is just that the Duke and I hardly know one another," she finished lamely.

Aunt waved away that foolish consideration. "That will come. You know, he has not shown any particular interest in a girl since Elise de Vraine married Carlston. Poor, poor girl. I think the Duke may finally be over that sad incident and ready to marry."

"Regrettable business, all that," Uncle said to Aunt. "Well, if he makes an offer for Helen, she must take him. No one would slander Selburn's Duchess, and it will get her out of harm's way and in proper hands." On that pronouncement, he folded the paper and hauled himself from his chair. He looked back at Helen as Barnett opened the door for him. "Duke of Selburn, hey? Better than I thought you'd get." He laughed, the rasp of it breaking into a wheezing cough as he left the room.

HELEN LEFT THE breakfast room not long after, ostensibly to change her gown, but actually intent upon writing to Lord Carlston in the privacy of her bedchamber.

The note was surprisingly difficult to formulate. Helen started it twice, burning the first attempt because it read far too stiffly, and the second because it seemed to witter on in no direction at all. The third draft still did not capture the tone she wanted—something between regret and carefree courtesy—but Philip arrived with a request from Aunt to prepare for the carriage, and so it became the final version.

Half Moon Street. 7 May 1812

Dear Lord Carlston,

I hope you will forgive the brevity of this discourse. Circumstances have prevented me from visiting Hatchards bookshop today. My apologies for any inconvenience caused to you or to Lady Margaret.

Saturday morning will be the first opportunity I have to take another walk along Piccadilly.

Yrs, etc,
Helen Wrexhall

She sealed it with a wafer and pressed the packet into Darby's hand. "He resides in St. James's Square, although I do not know the number."

"It is eighteen, my lady," Darby said, with a smug smile.

Helen returned the smile; not much escaped her maid. "Wait for an answer."

"Yes, my lady."

"And if he asks any questions—" She stopped. She had no idea what kind of questions he would ask a servant.

"Yes, my lady?"

She gripped Darby's hand for a moment. "Say what you think is best."

Not long after, Aunt ordered the carriage to be brought around, and Helen was soon sitting beside her as they drove along New Bond Street, listening to a list of tasks that still needed to be addressed for her upcoming ball. Three hundred or so six-hour candles had to be ordered, her aunt noted, as did the champagne and the desserts from Gunter's. Aunt was also set upon having white soup, and that necessitated at least five geese. Or was it five ducks? She could not quite remember.

After the appointments with Madame Hortense and Mr. Duray, Aunt decided that they might as well call on her milliner to order a riding hat to match Helen's new habit. At the finish of that lengthy consultation, Aunt conceived the desire for luncheon, so they stopped at Farrance's for soup and one of the famous tarts. They then continued on to a number of other shops to buy various little necessities: silk stockings, Asiatic soap, and Ceylon Tooth Powder. Helen endured each foray with a smile, although she longed to return to Half Moon Street and read Lord Carlston's response. Finally Aunt directed their driver home, sighing with satisfaction at a day well spent. Helen's sigh was one of relief.

Darby had carefully kept his lordship's return note tucked within the long sleeve of her gown. She handed it over in the privacy of Helen's dressing room.

"He sent this, too," she said, rummaging in the workbox. "I hid it, just in case." She pulled out a brown-paper-wrapped parcel, unmistakably a book from Hatchards, and handed it to Helen.

"He said for you to start reading, and that you would probably not understand most of it, but to read it anyway."

Helen bristled. "Does he think me a dull-wit?"

She motioned for Darby to bring scissors. A quick snip of the string, and the paper came away to reveal a book with a red leather cover and a gold title: *The Magus, or Celestial Intelligencer; being a complete system of occult philosophy by Francis Barrett, F.R.C.*

"Occult, my lady?" Darby said, eyes widening with shock.

"Apparently, there is an alchemical aspect to being a Reclaimer," Helen said shortly. She put the book down on her dressing table, as if it might explode, and broke the blue wax seal on the letter.

St. James's Square. 7 May 1812

Lady Helen,

Until Saturday.

Yrs etc.,

Carlston

Helen stared down at the thick parchment. Was that all? His writing style was even more abrasively curt than his conversation.

"Did he say anything else to you, Darby?"

"He did, my lady. He asked me a lot of questions."

"About me?"

"No, about me." Darby's pink cheeks deepened into blotched crimson. "He is quite disconcerting, isn't he? Those eyes, looking at you. And he knew that I knew about you-know-what."

"What did he ask you?"

"All sorts of things, like whether I thought myself 'a strong woman, in mind and body.' But really, I think he wanted to make sure I would not expose you in any way. He asked me to swear upon my soul that I would not. On the Bible."

"Upon your soul on the Bible?" Helen repeated, startled. That seemed alarmingly official. And why was he asking a maid such strange questions?

Darby smiled anxiously. "I swore, my lady, most willingly. After all, who would believe me?"

Strong in mind and body? An image of Mr. Quinn rose into Helen's mind. Did his lordship think Darby could be her Terrene? It was true—the girl *was* strongly built and sensible. Helen shook her head. No, she could not allow Darby to take on such a role; it was far too dangerous. Who then? Helen frowned, not at the problem, but at the sudden realization of what she was doing: weighing up potential Terrenes as if she was already part of the Dark Days Club. She paused, and searched her heart. No, she had not truly decided to join them: there were still too many unknown elements. Only a fool would blindly believe everything she was told—particularly by someone as dubious as Lord Carlston—and there were still so many unanswered questions. Yet, now that she knew about the Deceivers, about the threat to herself and humanity, could she claim to have a choice? Surely, there was an obligation, a duty beyond her own safety, to help.

"You are very good to have sworn so," Helen said, touching her maid's arm in thanks. She looked down at the letter and book again, hiding her unease. *Until Saturday.* "So he asked nothing about me?"

"No, my lady."

Helen nodded and tossed the note into the fire, newly stoked to warm the room for her afternoon toilette. She watched in silence as the paper flared and curled into black.

THAT NIGHT IN bed, by the light of a single candle, Helen started *The Magus*. She was glad to find that the author was not a pagan or a heathen, but less delighted to read about the highly questionable "magic" of plague amulets made from worm-ridden toads, and the use of a live duck, applied to the belly, to relieve colic. As his lordship had irritatingly predicted, there were chapters that made little sense, seemingly encoded with strange references to ancient gods and the like. Nevertheless, Helen's interest was caught by the idea that words had magical properties when combined with strong intent, and she reread, three times, an interesting passage about talismans that referred to the use of hair. Was that what his lordship had meant about her mother's miniature having alchemical properties? She caught up the tiny portrait hanging from a riband around her neck—a new safekeeping precaution for the night—and studied it. Was it a talisman of some kind? It seemed likely that the red-and-gold checkerboard was the reason she could see human and Deceiver life-forces. Perhaps the miniature also provided some kind of protection. That was the role of a talisman after all. She let it fall back against the linen bodice of her nightgown. *Protection from what?* she wondered. *Deceivers, or something even worse?*

Eighteen

Saturday, 9 May 1812

HELEN WAS WAKENED by the clunk of the shutters being drawn back from the far window, the patch of sky visible through it oppressively gray. She blinked into the gloomy reaches of her room, the blurred sense of the day ahead sharpening into purpose: Lord Carlston.

"Good morning, my lady," Darby said. She slid a tray onto the bedside table, the porcelain cup jumping against its saucer in a ringing clatter.

The smell of her morning chocolate—bitter sweetness arriving on a curl of steamy warmth—prompted a pang of hunger. Helen raised herself to her elbows, waiting as Darby arranged the pillows behind her, then settled back against them. The new position brought a crouching figure into view: a maid sweeping out the hearth. Not Beth: too round in shape. And far too broad for Tilly. "Darby, who is this?"

The new maid looked up. She was older than Darby, with a square, competent face that was saved from manliness by a fine nose. She immediately clambered to her feet, ash brush still in hand, and curtsied.

Darby carefully passed Helen the cup and saucer. "This is Lily, my lady. Come new to us, yesterday. From *Lady Jersey*."

"Hello, Lily," Helen said, studying the new girl's face.

"Morning, my lady." Shrewd eyes surveyed her with respectful curiosity: she was being studied in return.

Here was Lord Carlston's replacement housemaid. Was she protection or spy? Perhaps both. Helen took a sip of her chocolate. Should she acknowledge the hidden agenda?

"I believe you have worked for Lord Carlston too?" she tried. That seemed suitably oblique.

"More or less, my lady. His lordship said to tell you that, yes, I will be reporting back to him." She cast Darby a deferential glance. "I'm to help Miss Darby here, to keep you safe."

"Oh," Helen said, setting the cup back into the saucer. Lily was not one for obliqueness then. "And everything is all right?"

"Nothing unusual to report, my lady." She bobbed another curtsy and returned to the hearth. "I'll let you know if something comes up."

"Good," Helen said briskly. "Excellent." She turned to Darby. "Is my hot water ready?"

"Yes, my lady."

She chose not to see the amusement on her maid's face.

By midmorning, when Helen set off for Hatchards escorted by Darby, the threat of rain hung heavy in the clouds. The London smoke haze had descended lower than usual, stinging Helen's eyes and leaving a taste of ash in her mouth. As she led the way down Half Moon Street, she could barely see the expanse of Green Park opposite.

At the corner, Helen paused and looked skyward, considering the chance of rain. She wore her second-plainest gown, a coral-red walking dress, but had chanced a favorite cream silk spencer that would be ruined by a wetting. Beside her, Darby was clad in the dress reviled by Aunt. She had received the cast-off with delight, and quickly altered it to fit her broader lines, the soft chestnut suiting her rosier complexion. When she had appeared for the excursion to the bookshop—or wherever they were truly bound—Helen had smiled at the slight jauntiness in her maid's step, knowing it came from the joy of a newly acquired gown. It had been a moment of lightness within the uneasy anticipation of the day ahead.

She peered up Piccadilly. It was at least a twenty-minute walk to Hatchards, and there was definitely a taste of water in the air. "I think we may get wet, Darby."

"Perhaps we should fetch an umbrella, my lady. It won't take more than a few minutes."

With a sigh, Helen consigned the spencer to Darby's wardrobe or the ragman if it rained. "No, if we go back, my aunt may find something *far more important* for me to do. I don't want to risk missing Lady Margaret."

She motioned Darby around the corner, sidestepping an apple boy who had set up his basket at the prime position.

"Apple, m'lady?" he called. "Green and hard. Only a halfpenny."

"Be off with you," Darby said. "My lady don't eat apples on the street like a hoyden."

"What about you?" The youth grinned, all dimples and startling good teeth, and deftly juggled two of his shiny green offerings.

"Who are you calling hoyden?" Darby said, but she smiled over her shoulder as they left him behind. "Cheeky monkey."

Helen looked back too. Could the boy be a Deceiver? She shook her head. He had not done anything to point to it. If she panicked at every how-do-you-do or bow, she would go mad. She could not imagine how Lord Carlston managed to move through the world with such calm.

She scanned the wide road, already busy with hackneys, carriages, and carts. The pavements, on the other hand, were still relatively free of activity. Ahead, a lady walked on the arm of an officer in red, a few gentlemen strode toward important business, and a peddler with his goods box on a strap around his neck hurried to the next servants' entrance.

"Do you know when Lady Margaret will drive past?" Darby asked.

Helen shook her head. "It could be that she will wait until after we have visited Hatchards."

They walked up Piccadilly in silence. As they approached the corner of Stratton Street, Darby cast a swift glance across the main thoroughfare at the soft blur that was Green Park. "My lady, I do not wish to alarm you, but I think that gentleman over the way is keeping pace with us."

Helen looked across the road. The gentleman—very well dressed in a navy-blue greatcoat and a smart, high-crowned black beaver—did seem to be keeping abreast of them. She squinted through the haze, but could not see the details of his face. He seemed familiar. Heavens, it wasn't Mr. Benchley, was it? The last thing she wanted was to meet that madman. For a moment the gentleman was hidden by the rumbling passage of two coaches and a hay cart, then she saw him again, matching their pace, his blurred face turned toward them. No. Whoever this was, he was not tall enough to be Mr. Benchley.

"Do you think he is one of Lord Carlston's men, keeping watch?" Darby asked.

"Perhaps." Helen risked a longer look. There was something about the way he stared at them: a purpose in his gaze that did not have an air of protection about it. "No, I don't believe so."

"You think he may be one of the creatures?"

Helen wrenched off her tan glove. "Hold this, Darby, while I get the miniature. Maybe he has been feeding, and I will be able to tell."

Darby took the glove, watching the man as they walked. "He is still with us. It seems to me, my lady, that it ain't very sporting that you must use instruments to discover these creatures, but they don't need them to find you."

"No, not sporting at all." Helen dug inside her silk reticule and grasped the portrait. A pale blue shimmer jumped into being around Darby and everyone on the street, including the gentleman. "Well, he has a normal blue life-force."

"That don't mean he's not one of them," Darby said darkly as they passed the magnificent Palladian frontage of Devonshire House. She handed back the glove.

"No, it doesn't," Helen agreed, finding a fleeting moment of amusement at her maid's quick assimilation of the Deceiver world. She seemed to have taken it all in her stride. "I think we should err on the side of caution."

"Good idea, my lady."

They stopped at the corner of Berkeley Street, waiting for a barouche to slowly make its turn from Piccadilly. "He has stopped too," Darby reported.

Helen pulled on her glove. "Come, let us walk more swiftly."

"Sweep, yer ladyship?" a young voice singsonged. "Cost a farthin'." A boy in a filthy cotton smock darted in front of them, brushing the road free of dung with an old besom, his vigor sending up a cloud of dust. Helen dug into her reticule again, found the hard edge of a coin, and followed the boy across the cleared clay road, Darby a step behind. She tossed him the coin, taking the moment to check the other side of Piccadilly. Their well-dressed shadow had started walking again, keeping pace. She scanned further along the street behind him, hoping to see a Dark Days Club man following too, keeping watch. No one, however, was acting like a guard. If Lord Carlston's man was out there amongst the growing numbers on the pavement, he was well hidden.

"Come on, Darby." Helen quickened her stride, glad she had chosen to wear her stout half boots instead of a pair of kid slippers.

"What are we to do if he approaches?" her maid asked as they crossed Dover Street.

"I don't know."

An elderly lady, trailed by a footman, shook her head in disapproval as they strode past. It was true they were walking far too fast for propriety, but Helen was not going to slow down and let a possible Deceiver catch them. She had no idea what he could possibly do on a busy street like Piccadilly, but she did not want to find out.

"Perhaps we should have brought Hugo or Philip with us," Darby said, beginning to pant.

"And how would we explain if something happened?"

"Something *is* happening, my lady."

True. Helen chewed on the inside of her mouth, unsure of what to do. They were still a little way from Hatchards, but she could not turn back and risk missing Lady Margaret.

"Oh no, I think he is coming toward us," Darby said.

The man had indeed stepped out onto the road, only to be forced back onto the pavement as a gig tore recklessly around the St. James's Street corner. Helen grabbed Darby's elbow. If they could reach the bookshop, they might meet an acquaintance who could provide the shield of his company. She could feel her heart pounding in her chest, hard against the constriction of her stays. Beside her, Darby's face had reddened, her breaths coming in small gulps.

"You are doing well, Darby," Helen said. "We will be there soon."

"He is crossing again!" Darby gasped.

The man stepped off the pavement. Helen saw the next five seconds play out in her mind: he would intersect their path at the corner of Albemarle Street. Even if they slowed, he would be able to adjust. She looked around and fixed on a young gallant swaggering toward them, ogling every passing lady with an air of self-satisfied masculinity. If she screamed, he would respond; it would at least deflect the man for the moment.

Helen gathered herself. In three seconds, then.

"Lady Helen!" a woman's voice called.

She spun around. A small town coach, plain, and on the more worn side of well used, rumbled up beside them, the two bay horses coming to a stamping standstill. Lady Margaret looked out from the window, her vivid face topped by a plain chip hat. "Lady Helen, well met. Do you walk down Piccadilly?" She looked up at the threatening sky. "I think it may rain. May my brother and I offer you a seat in our carriage?"

"Thank the Lord," Darby murmured.

Mr. Hammond, seated beside his sister, leaned forward into view. "Good morning, Lady Helen," he called. Helen dipped her head in greeting, but her eyes were fixed on the window on the other side of the dim cabin and its prospect of the road beyond. The well-dressed man had returned to the pavement. For a moment he watched the coach; then he turned and was gone from sight. "There is plenty of room," Mr. Hammond added.

Helen steadied her breath. "I would be most glad of the seat, thank you."

Lady Margaret leaned further out of the window, motioning to the footman sitting in the rumble seat at the back of the carriage. "Geoffrey, open the door for Lady Helen, then help her maid up beside you."

Both brother and sister drew back inside the cabin as their man nimbly descended and opened the coach door, flipping the steps down. "My lady," he said, offering his hand. He was tall, like all footmen, but he also had a burly breadth of shoulder and a direct gaze. More than a footman, Helen decided.

She took his hand and climbed into the coach. Mr. Hammond had courteously moved across to the opposite seat, his back to the driver. Bending to accommodate her height, Helen took the few awkward steps across the cabin and sat next to Lady Margaret. "I must tell you," she said, peering out the window, "that I was followed here by a man."

"What?" Mr. Hammond leaned across to the other window, his face intent. "Is he still there? Which one?"

Helen studied the figures on the opposite pavement. "I cannot see him anymore. An older gentleman in a navy-blue greatcoat and black beaver." She looked back at the brother and sister. "He was there, truly."

"We do not doubt you, Lady Helen," Lady Margaret said. "One of our men has been following you for your protection, but he does not fit that description. No doubt he will have seen this older gentleman and will be tracking him even now."

Mr. Hammond nodded his own reassurance. "We will know soon enough if he is a threat." He knocked his cane against the wooden front of the cabin. "Drive on."

Helen sat back, relieved, as the carriage lurched into motion. "Where do we go?"

"To the Devil's Acre," Mr. Hammond said. "Behind Westminster Abbey."

She let the information sink into her sketchy knowledge of the city beyond Mayfair. The Devil's Acre was notorious: surely he was joking. "But, sir, that is a rookery, is it not?"

"One of the worst hellholes in London."

Helen looked across at Lady Margaret. She did not seem concerned at the thought of entering such a squalid, vice-ridden neighborhood. In fact, she was struggling to contain her excitement: her gloved fingers were woven tightly together in her lap, and her dark blue eyes were almost black with anticipation.

"Why do we go to such a dangerous place?" Helen asked.

"It is where Lord Carlston wants us," Lady Margaret said. "Do not worry. He will be there. It will be safe with his lordship."

Safe? Wherever his lordship went, danger was bound to be present. Nevertheless, Helen smiled an agreement, using the moment of connection to probe deeper into Lady Margaret's over-bright excitement. Sweet heaven, it was the burn of true belief. The lady not only loved Lord Carlston, she believed in him with an almost religious intensity. Helen quickly turned to look out the window. She barely noted the half-timbered shops and dwellings of Shaftesbury Avenue as she tried to think through the discovery. Such fevered belief created fairy tales in the mind, particularly about the virtues of the beloved. To Lady Margaret, Lord Carlston was no doubt a paragon of virtue. Even her conviction that he was innocent of murder was probably based on nothing more than her own devotion. To be fair, Helen could hardly criticize her: after all, she had told herself the same story. How much had her own "instinct" about his innocence been the physical effect of the man? Yet all of this musing could be answered by a simple question. Helen gathered herself: it was time to put aside her own reticence and ask what had been playing upon her mind.

"Tell me," she said, "was Lord Carlston's wife discovered to be a Deceiver? Is that why she disappeared?"

For a moment it seemed she had not been heard. Mr. Hammond stared at the silver handle of his cane, and Lady Margaret continued to look out of the carriage window.

Finally Mr. Hammond met her eyes. "The Countess of Carlston was not a Deceiver," he said. "She was human. We do not know what happened to her, and his lordship and Mr. Benchley have made it clear that she is not to be discussed."

Helen wet her lips. The subject of her mother and now Lady Elise, both taboo. It seemed the Dark Days Club held as many secrets from its members as it did from the outside world. "Do you think his lordship killed her, Mr. Hammond?"

He opened his mouth to answer.

"Michael," Lady Margaret warned. She turned to Helen. "It does not matter what we think. This is not a game with written rules, Lady Helen. There are uncertainties and ambiguities all around us and in everything we do. You must come to terms with that."

"That is true," Mr. Hammond said more gently. "All of us engaged in this calling are guilty of blurring the lines of morality. It is the price of dealing with these creatures." His eyes met hers for a moment, and behind their sympathy was an immense sadness.

Their response had in no way relieved her unease—quite the contrary. Must she be content with a leap of faith about his lordship's innocence? It did not sit well at all to be on the same level as a lovelorn lady. For a moment she had the wild thought to ask Lord Carlston for the truth, straight and bold, just as she had done regarding Berta. *Did you kill your wife?* Helen's shoulders tightened. No, of course she could not do it. Besides, even if he did answer—which was unlikely—it would be near impossible to read him accurately. Now that he knew her level of skill, she had no doubt he could hide anything from her if he so wished.

Lady Margaret motioned to her brother to pass over a bundle of clothes that lay beside him. She removed a faded gray pelisse. "When we go into the Devil's Acre, you must wear this over your dress and change your bonnet for a cap. I have similar to wear."

"We must also refrain from using titles," Mr. Hammond added. "Use only *brother* and *sister*, with our Christian names. Like the Quakers."

"Christian names?" Helen echoed. One did not use bare Christian names for anyone but family, and possibly a close friend. "Even Lord Carlston?'

"*Especially* his lordship," Mr. Hammond said firmly. "His name is William. And, please, call me Brother Michael."

Lady Margaret handed Helen the cap and pelisse. The odor of unwashed bodies and sour spills wrinkled Helen's nose.

"That is nothing compared to the smell of the rookery," Lady Margaret said. "The stink of the place will announce itself well before we arrive."

Helen loosened the cream silk bow under her chin. "What can his lordship wish to show me in a place like the Devil's Acre? Is it more Deceivers?"

"No, something quite different," Mr. Hammond said. "Deceiver progeny."

"They have children?" Helen had not even considered if they could procreate.

"Not in the way that we think of children," Lady Margaret said. "From what we know, their natural form is pure energy. Here, however, on this earthly plane, they cannot exist outside flesh. They do not seem to have our limited lifespan, so they do not produce children to continue their bloodline. Rather, the same Deceiver passes from generation to generation by stealing a new human body when the old one dies."

"And not just any human body," Mr. Hammond added. "The only bodies they can steal are those of their own progeny: children made with a human. Every time a Deceiver sires or gives birth, it embeds a vestige of its own energy in that child's soul. When its body dies, the Deceiver passes into the body of its nearest progeny—pulled from dying flesh into living flesh by that vestige of energy—and so survives to live its next life. It does not even need to be in the same country to transfer to the new body."

Helen smoothed her bonnet ribands, trying to make sense of the Deceivers. Such creatures were against the basic law of nature: that all was in motion, moving toward improvement. "What happens to its child?" she asked. "The one already inhabiting the body?"

"Its human soul is obliterated by the arrival of its Deceiver parent. All that is left is a human husk, ready to be filled by the Deceiver."

"It kills the soul of its own child? But that is heinous."

Mr. Hammond nodded. "Indeed."

Helen paused in removing her bonnet, appalled. "Does that mean the souls of ten thousand English children are annihilated every generation?"

"Yes, although by the time the Deceiver leaves its old body, the progeny it enters may have reached adulthood," Mr. Hammond said, his narrow face grim. "Every Deceiver is centuries old, and they are wily—consummate actors playing the part of humans. Of course, their lack of true reproduction means there is a finite number of them. A blessing of some sort, I suppose." He looked across at his sister. "Margaret, you may not think it is proper for me to explain their habits, but I think she needs to know them."

Lady Margaret nodded her permission, but her mouth was pinched with distaste.

Mr. Hammond leaned forward to counter the sudden loud crunch of the wheels on a grittier part of the road. "By now, in this century, most Deceivers have maneuvered themselves into male bodies in order to beget as many children as they can upon as many women as possible. Of course, they try to have legitimate offspring, but they also spawn by-blows in case all their legitimate issue die." He cleared his throat. "It is why we find so many progeny amongst the demimonde, the lower orders, and women in the rookeries."

"If you are going to tell her, you may as well be plain about it," Lady Margaret interjected. "He means among kept whores, servant girls, and gypsies but is too missish to say so."

Mr. Hammond's hand tightened around the handle of his cane, but he did not respond to his sister's derision. "Once we are sure of the identity of a Deceiver, Sir Jonathan Beech locates its progeny, legitimate or otherwise. Sir Jonathan is our senior Tracer. He tracks them through records and rumor and other such ways. You will meet him today."

"As you can imagine," Lady Margaret said, "it is not an easy task to find all the progeny of one Deceiver."

"Sometimes it feels almost impossible," her brother said. "However, when we do find tainted offspring, a Reclaimer removes the vestige and returns them to full humanity. We may not be able to eradicate the Deceivers from our midst, but at least we can claim the victory of saving human souls."

"Is that what his lordship meant when he said we remove darkness from the soul?" asked Helen.

Mr. Hammond smiled. "Yes. And when all of the progeny have been found and their souls cleansed, then a Reclaimer can deliver *Mors Ultima* to the Deceiver sire or dam."

Final death. "I assume that means exactly what it intimates," Helen said.

"Yes," Mr. Hammond said. "It is quite a show: a flash of fiery light as if the creature is lit from within."

A flash of light as if lit from within? The same phenomenon that Delia had reported in her letter. Mr. Trent had indeed been a Deceiver. Delia thought she had been debased, but in fact she'd had a lucky escape.

"It is a most satisfying moment to see," Mr. Hammond added.

Lady Margaret nodded her agreement. "It is very satisfying. But what we will see today—a reclaiming—is far more glorious." That burning belief was once again in her eyes. "You will see why the risks we take are worth it."

Nineteen

LADY MARGARET WAS right: it was the stink of the Devil's Acre that came first. Even with the windows closed, Helen almost gagged as the coach inched its way along Duck Lane and turned into Old Pye Street, the thick of the rookery. She tried to breathe through her mouth, but the stench of human and animal excrement, rotting food, fetid bodies, and greasy smoke overwhelmed her newly acquired Reclaimer sense of smell. Even Lady Margaret and Mr. Hammond were suffering, both of them pressing their hands over nose and mouth.

"It gets worse every time we come here," Lady Margaret said. She wore a linen cap also pulled from the bundle, the yellowed cloth draining her skin of any color. Or perhaps it was the dreadful stink that blanched her face.

"We are almost there," Mr. Hammond said. He had changed his smart beaver and superfine coat for a dusty tricorne and stained broadcloth jacket. "It will be a little better once we go inside." He rapped his cane on the wooden front again. "The house beside the Red Lion," he called to the driver.

Helen doubted the man had heard him through the cacophony. Shrieks of children, calls of street vendors, dogs yelping, people shouting, and all through it the bells of Westminster tolling, every sound resonating through her ears into her very bones. To distract herself, she tried to focus on the task ahead.

Since Deceivers did not look any different from humans, their progeny must look the same as normal children too. The difference, of course, was within, and it would be fascinating to see his lordship remove the vestige: the spark of Deceiver energy. It was hard to imagine how he could reach inside a soul to do so, and yet she was supposed to be able to do it as well. Maybe he would ask her to help. Dear God, could she? Should she?

Helen watched the filthy children running alongside them, this time trying to distract herself from her own fear.

The coach drew to a stop. Mr. Hammond opened the door and climbed out. "Off with you," he growled at the huddle of gawking children, sending them scattering. "Sister Margaret, if you will."

Gathering her threadbare blue pelisse, Lady Margaret took her brother's hand for the step down to the road. They both turned to receive Helen. She slid across the worn leather seat and leaned into Mr. Hammond's strong grip as she stepped down onto a wooden board laid across the wet ground. It sank a little under her weight, stinking mud oozing up around the edges. Murmuring her thanks, she looked up at Darby in the high rumble seat at the back; her maid's begrimed face was tight with disgust, and she was brushing futilely at the dust and mud spatters on her refashioned gown.

"Brother William has instructed us to bring your maid inside," Mr. Hammond said quietly.

"Has he so?" Helen replied, affronted by his lordship's high-handedness. Still, she did want Darby inside, so she allowed Mr. Hammond to call the girl down.

He led the way to a three-story dwelling whose upper floor leaned perilously over its stone foundations. The short trip to the front door was a slippery, smelly business. Helen clutched Darby's arm for support as they tentatively placed their feet on the wooden planks already slimed by previous pedestrians. Two filthy, emaciated little girls ran across the road toward them, bare feet deep in the sludge and hands cupped for alms. Mr. Hammond chased them off before Helen could withdraw a coin from the reticule hidden beneath the musty folds of her borrowed pelisse.

"My lady, why are we here?" Darby asked as they made the hazardous step from one board to the next.

Helen steadied herself then leaned closer. "His lordship is going to show me how to reclaim a soul," she whispered.

"Only one?" Darby muttered, glancing at the sly, lounging men watching them pass by, and the blowsy women outside a gin shop. "I'd say there's a thousand here who need saving."

"You must not call me my lady while we are here," Helen instructed. "Call me Sister Helen."

Darby shook her head firmly. "I can't do that, my lady. That's not right."

"Please, it is what his lordship wants. I presume you are to be Sister Jen."

Her maid gave a soft snort. "Sister Jen? God preserve us."

The peeling front door was wide open. Helen followed Mr. Hammond and Lady Margaret inside, the bare boards of the entryway creaking under their feet. The pungent smell of mold, beef-tallow wax, and urine was almost a relief from the putrid air outside. Helen peered into the gloom, making out a staircase at the very end of the corridor and the shadowy shape of another person descending the steps. A man, but too short and round to be Lord Carlston.

"Brother Jonathan?" Lady Margaret said. "Is that you?"

"Yes, it is I," the shadow answered, bowing. "Wait one moment, and I will arrange a taper for the climb."

He was gone, a series of creaks marking his progress up the staircase. A minute or so later another set of creaks and the approaching glow of soft light announced his return. The man—

doubtless Sir Jonathan Beech, the Tracer—hurried down the hallway to meet them, the taper casting his face and rotund body into sharp relief. He smiled up at Helen, his cheeks rounded under a shrewd gaze. A luxurious set of gray sideburns fluffed from temple to jaw, perhaps compensation for the wispy fringe of hair that circled his crown. "Ah, you must be Lad— *Sister* Helen," he corrected, his smile turning into a quick grimace of self-censure. "What an honor it is to meet you. Such an honor. I am Brother Jonathan." He bowed again, the taper light dipping across the wall, showing plaster covered with a black creep of mold that had bloomed into spidery circles. "My apologies for the lack of formal introduction."

Helen smiled back. Sir Jonathan's civilized manner was as welcome as the light he carried. "I understand, considering the circumstances."

"Yes, yes indeed." He glanced along the hallway, greeting the rest of the party with another nod of his head. "Well, shall we? They await us upstairs." Holding the taper high, he led the way to the staircase. Helen grasped the banister. Something wet seeped through her glove; she snatched her hand back. On the first floor they passed open doorways dimly lit by half-boarded windows. One small room held a family of at least twelve: a mother nursing on a stool, children hunched over piecework, and a wasted man on a mattress, spitting into a tin bowl. In another, men crouched around a dice game, the raucous sounds of loss and gain punctuated by laughing and the clink of bottles. A brown dog, all legs and rib cage, slunk past them on the second-floor landing, stopping to urinate in a corner where a man lolled beside a befouled night bucket. Helen looked back at Darby, seeing her own shock mirrored in her maid's face. How could people live like this?

They climbed the last set of steps. A door and wall had been added, closing the third-floor landing from common access. It was obviously a later addition, the makeshift wall built from raw deal and the door from a single piece of stouter wood with a lock under the handle.

"Here we are," Sir Jonathan announced.

He opened the door and entered, standing to the side as they gathered on the shallow, whitewashed landing within. Two doors led off it: one open, one closed. Helen peered through the open doorway. Four plain bentwood chairs had been drawn up to a scrubbed wooden table. On it was a loaf of bread in a clean blue cloth, an earthenware pitcher beaded with moisture, and two matching cups. The corner of an iron grate was visible, and on its painted mantel a candle stub stood in a tin holder. It was all scrupulously clean. Someone had created a private suite of rooms. Someone with means.

Sir Jonathan knocked on the other door. Through the narrow gap left by its ill-fitted hinges, Helen glimpsed a sliver of bedpost and the red-striped bodice of a woman's gown.

"Yes, come." A male voice that she didn't recognize.

Sir Jonathan pushed on the handle, the catch sticking for a moment before the door opened. He stepped back and bowed Helen into the room. The occupants, clustered around a low bed, all turned toward her: Lord Carlston, Mr. Quinn, a young priest, and the woman in the gaudy red dress. "I am glad you have come, Sister Helen," Lord Carlston said.

He also wore old clothes: a rough shirt and breeches with a carelessly tied blue belcher at his neck. Even so, his natural authority was obvious. It was absurd to think that he could be mistaken for anything other than a man of great rank. Her skepticism must have shown, for his eyes met hers, the warning in them clear. *No titles.*

Helen licked her lips. The room was intensely hot, the closed window holding in the heat from a small fire in another iron grate.

Mr. Quinn dipped his head and stepped back against the wall, clearing a pathway to the bed. Helen, however, was transfixed by the sight of the boy upon it: about twelve, fragile, and tied to the frame at wrists and ankles. His hands were twisting the crumpled gray under-sheet and his blond head moved restlessly upon a dingy pillow. Why was the poor child restrained?

She looked back over her shoulder. Sir Jonathan stood in the doorway, but Darby, Lady Margaret, and Mr. Hammond had retreated into the room across the landing. Apparently Lady Margaret would not be seeing a soul reclaimed today after all.

"Allow me to introduce Reverend Pellham," Carlston said.

The priest—young, with the hollow-cheeked asceticism that seemed to be a badge of the lesser clergy—bowed with a murmured "How do you do." He gestured to the woman and the boy. "This is Mrs. Coates and her son, Jeremiah, who is in need of your help."

The woman bobbed into a curtsy. She must have been pretty once, but fatigue and fear had worn deep lines into her face and dragged her mouth into a thin arc of suffering. "Thank you, Sister, thank you for comin' today. You and Brother William are my last hope. No one knows what's wrong with my boy. They say he's mad. But I think he's possessed."

"Young Jeremiah has been overcome by something of a nature unknown," the priest said delicately. "When I saw the state he was in, I knew immediately that it was a case for Brother William."

Helen shot a glance at Carlston. *Is the Reverend one of the Dark Days Club too?*

His lordship inclined his head. *Yes.*

She resolved to ask, very soon, how many the Club actually numbered.

"It is time to start," Carlston said. "We will rid your son of this evil spirit, madam, but it is too dangerous for you to be present. I must ask you to leave the room with the Reverend." He bowed, the courtesy prompting a teary murmuring of thanks from the frightened mother.

Helen had not thought him capable of such a gentle tone, let alone of bowing to a woman so far beneath him. Perhaps there was kindness in him after all. Deep down, and hidden most of the time, but still present.

The Reverend ushered Mrs. Coates gently toward the door. "Come, we will leave Jeremiah in their care. You can trust them."

As they walked past, the woman reached for Helen's hand and clasped it tightly for a moment. The fervent gratitude in her eyes forced a smile of reassurance from Helen. The woman had such faith in them; hopefully it was deserved.

"Do not just stand there, Brother Jonathan," Carlston said as the Reverend urged his charge across the landing. "Come in."

Sir Jonathan edged into the room. The bonhomie that had marked his greeting was gone. Helen watched him press himself against the far wall, his eyes never quite landing on Lord Carlston. Was he frightened of his lordship? Perhaps there was some fear, but there was something else, too—guilt, perhaps, or shame. What had happened between the two men to prompt such unease?

"Is Darby with you?" Carlston asked, pulling Helen from her examination. At her nod, he motioned to Quinn. "Get her."

"You want Darby to be my Terrene, don't you?" Helen said after Quinn had closed the door behind him.

Carlston paced around the bed, watching the boy strain against the soft cloth ties. "I do," he said, not raising his eyes. "We had someone ready to be your personal maid and Terrene, but you thwarted that plan when you gave the maid's position to Darby. Still, I think you chose well." He finally looked up. "Perhaps your blood chose for you."

Her blood had chosen? Helen hurried past the startling thought. "You had someone ready to be my Terrene?"

"Yes. But Quinn can train your girl just as easily, once she is bound to you."

"Bound to me?"

His lordship regarded her thoughtfully. "You saw Quinn tackle me at Vauxhall?" At her nod, he crossed to Sir Jonathan. "Would you mind if I used your person to demonstrate something, Brother Jonathan?"

"Not—not at all," the Tracer stammered. "Not at all. Glad to be of service."

With astounding speed, Carlston grabbed the front of the plump man's coat and lifted him, one-handed, high against the wall, with no apparent effort. Sir Jonathan stared down at him, eyes bulging with surprise, and a little awe.

"Obviously, a normal man could never tackle and hold down a Reclaimer," his lordship said to Helen. "I have bound Quinn to me, and so he shares some of my strength and speed, and also that curious ability to calculate probability. Likewise, when your strength comes, you will bind your Terrene to your power so that she can ensure your survival."

He lowered Sir Jonathan to the floor and released him with a small bow. "Thank you, Brother Jonathan."

"My pleasure, of course." The man tugged his coat back into place, adjusting his neckcloth with a trembling hand.

Helen was silent for a moment. Was it possible that she would soon be able to pick up a man with such ease? The idea of it was strangely thrilling. And a little frightening.

"You mean it is some kind of magical binding?" she asked. "Like that described in *The Magus*?" Even if such a thing was possible, she could not imagine Darby agreeing to it.

"You have read some of the book then?"

She remembered her manners. "Yes, thank you for sending it to me. It is"—she paused—"*interesting*."

"Very *interesting*," he agreed with a smile. "I know some of it is nonsense, but there are other parts that still hold a good deal of truth." He waved her over. "Come, take a look at the boy."

Helen crossed to the bed. "I do not want to put Darby in any danger."

His sidelong glance was narrow. "We each have our calling, Sister Helen."

"I would normally agree," she said tartly, "except you seem to think that *you* are the caller, Brother William." Her voice wavered on the intimacy of his name, taking the bite from her words.

She saw his mouth lift into the irritating half smile. "I have good reason," he said. "Did Brother Michael explain to you about Deceiver progeny? About the vestige within each of them?"

A soft knock interrupted, the door opening to admit Darby and Quinn. Carlston looked at his man, a silent exchange completed in the fleeting glance. Helen caught only Quinn's side: a resigned acknowledgment of something expected. The big man closed the door behind them and ushered Darby to stand by the wall, next to the rotund Tracer.

"Brother Jonathan, how many people live in Britain at the moment?" Carlston asked.

Sir Jonathan cleared his throat. "In the census of last year, our population numbered over twelve and a half million."

"And, Lady Helen, do you remember how many Deceivers I told you are in England alone?"

How could she forget the terrifying number? "Over ten thousand."

Carlston fixed his attention upon Darby. "That means that in every twelve hundred people or so, one will be a Deceiver. And there are only eight of us capable of destroying them, one of whom is your mistress. Do you understand the importance of her now?"

Darby nodded. "I always did, my lord."

Helen frowned; what was he doing?

"Good. Since you are aware of her significance, I am sure you will want to help her in her duty."

Darby nodded again, as if mesmerized.

"Lord Carlston," Helen said sharply.

"We are not using titles, Sister Helen," he said mildly.

She glared at him. How dare he try to press-gang her maid.

His lordship seemed singularly unrepentant. He turned back to his study of the boy. "This child is the progeny of the Pavor at Vauxhall Gardens."

Helen drew in a startled breath, her anger doused.

He leaned down and pressed his palm across the pale damp forehead, clearly testing for fever. The boy wrenched away from his touch. "Brother Jonathan is certain this boy is the Pavor's last living progeny." He looked across at the Tracer. "You *are* sure, aren't you, Brother Jonathan?" There was a caustic edge to Carlston's voice.

"Yes. Well, as sure as I can be," the Tracer said. He readjusted his neckcloth. "You know it is a difficult thing to determine."

"Yes," his lordship said. "I am quite aware how difficult it is."

"No, I am completely certain." The man drew himself up. "Positive."

Carlston returned to his examination. "So, this child's body is the Pavor's last avenue of survival. If that is gone, then when the Pavor's body dies"—he looked up at Helen—"or is *killed*, his energy will have no place to go. It will die too."

"Mors Ultima." Helen said.

"You did listen closely to Brother Michael," his lordship said. "Yes. Final death."

Darby lurched forward. "What are you going to do to the boy?"

she demanded, her audacity bleaching the color from her face. "I won't let you harm him."

Quinn caught her by the shoulder. "Now, miss, no harm is going to come to the lad," he said. "They are going to remove the demon energy from within his soul and reclaim it. It is his father—one of the foul creatures—that we hunt."

Darby looked suspiciously up at him. "Is that true?"

The big man nodded. "I'd have no part in killing children, miss. You can be sure of that. They are going to help the boy."

"What Quinn says is true," Carlston said. He glanced back at Helen. "You may have wondered why I did not kill the Pavor at Vauxhall. If I had, he would have shifted into Jeremiah's body, and the boy's soul would be lost. We must reclaim Jeremiah first, and then kill his sire."

"All right then," Darby said. She stepped back against the wall, crossing her arms over her chest. "All right."

"I am glad we have your approval," Carlston murmured.

Darby flushed. "I'm sorry, sir."

He eyed her, and Helen saw the calculation in his face. "If you wish to help save this boy, Darby, there *is* something important you can do."

She ducked her head under his attention. "Anything, sir."

Helen glared at Carlston. "Brother William," she warned.

"If I tell you to take your mistress from the room," he continued, regardless, "will you do so? In any way you can? It will keep her safe."

Safe from what? And he was still pressuring Darby into his service. "You don't have to do anything he asks," Helen said. "In fact, you are under no obligation even to stay."

Darby chewed on her lip. "But I want to help you, madam. Is it all right if I do?"

Helen sighed. She was definitely losing this battle. "Yes, of course."

"Brother Jonathan, you may go," Carlston said. "You have done your part. Thank you."

At the dismissal, the older man's face seemed to fold in upon itself. Clearly, he had wanted to stay. He bowed. "Of course."

As soon as the door closed behind him, Carlston sat beside Jeremiah, motioning Helen to the boy's other side. She hesitated; to sit on a bed with a man was far beyond impropriety.

"I can assure you that your person is quite safe," Carlston said impatiently. "We are, after all, securely chaperoned."

Somewhat mortified, Helen sat, the straw mattress hard and ungiving. The boy smelled of sweat, and the bedclothes were damp under her hand. His chemise had come untied, and his narrow breastbone was sharp under his thin pale skin.

Carlston took hold of the boy's chin, halting the ceaseless rocking of the blond head against the pillow. "Most of the time a Deceiver's vestige has only a small effect upon its progeny. It heightens the appetite for pleasure and sensation, but not usually so much that it is noticed." He peered into the boy's wide, unseeing eyes. "But, on occasion, it has a devastating effect. It may manifest as extreme violence or promiscuity, but in some cases the effect is to the mind." He cupped the boy's chin for a moment with a tenderness that Helen had not known he possessed.

"Is he mad?" she asked.

"Well on his way," Carlston said.

"Will taking the vestige from his soul save his mind?" It suddenly seemed immeasurably important to rescue the boy from the insanity thrust upon him by his Deceiver father.

"Perhaps." Carlston did not sound convinced. "All we can do is try."

"Am I to help you reclaim him?"

"This first time, you may help me call the soul, but I will do the actual reclaiming. Your duty is to watch and learn."

Helen had the sudden uneasy knowledge that she, too, was being masterfully manipulated. If she helped Carlston save the child, it would be an irreversible step—an implied acceptance of this violent, dangerous life. Yet how could she possibly live in such a way? Even walking up Piccadilly had been fraught with danger. On the other hand, she could not refuse to help, either. Not with the boy in such clear distress. For the moment, that had to be her guide: saving a child's sanity and soul. The implications of it would have to come later.

Carlston took a small silver bowl, the kind often used for leeching, from the side table. "I will need a piece of your hair, Sister Helen." He reached for a knife.

Her hand flew to her head. "Whatever for?" Even as she said it, she realized why. "Oh, for the alchemy."

"Yes, it is the way Reclaimers have traveled the pathway to the soul for centuries. We blend together a small amount of hair from the Deceiver parent, the progeny, and the Reclaimer, purify it, and ingest the leavings." He made a moue of distaste. "Quite revolting. But it bonds us with the essence of the boy and the vestige within him."

Helen wrinkled her nose. "Why hair?"

"It is made up of the body's materials, and one of its most indestructible parts." He pinched his fingers into the bowl and held up a length of pale blond hair. From the color and texture, it was the boy's. "It is also the most easily obtained."

From behind them, Quinn snorted. "Easy?"

Carlston flashed his man a sympathetic smile. "Easier than other parts of the body," he amended, and dropped the hair back into the bowl. He hefted the knife. "May I?"

Helen hesitated for a second, then leaned closer to the knife, turning to offer the curls at the side of her nape. She felt his warm, bare fingers touch her skin as he lifted her hair, the sensation sliding down her spine, and then the slight drag as the blade sliced a curl clean.

"There," he said.

She pulled back, face hot, her hand going to the place where his touch had been. She had never known that such a public place on her body could feel so private.

He placed the ringlet in the bowl and then lifted the knife to his own hair. Three quick saws and a short dark length came away. He angled the bowl so she could see the mix of his black hair, her brown curl, the boy's blond lock, and a dull brownish hank—the last, no doubt, from the Pavor sire.

"Quinn, a taper," his lordship ordered.

The man quickly lit a long thin candle from the fire and passed it to his master. Carlston glanced at Helen. "I apologize in advance for the stink." He touched the flame to the hair in the bowl. A small hiss sounded, an eruption of flame, then the strong smell of sulfur wrinkled Helen's nose. Behind her, Darby coughed.

"You can understand why this part of the process is called Casting out the Devil," Carlston said, waving away the pungent smoke. He peered into the bowl, angling it again to show Helen. "As you see, it is ash. We now mix that with a solution of seawater and milk to symbolize the ocean of milk from which the nectar of immortal life is drawn."

He lifted a pitcher from the side table and poured in a small amount of the diluted milk, then swirled the mixture in the bowl. "The Elixir of the Soul." With a pointed glance in her direction, he raised it to his mouth and took a large swig, shaking his head as he swallowed, as if to force the stuff down his throat. "Disgusting," he said, offering the bowl to Helen. "One large mouthful will be enough. I suggest you hold your nose."

Helen took the bowl, doubtfully eyeing the pale liquid within. His lordship had obviously taken the first draught to show her it was harmless, but still, the idea of drinking other people's burned hair was nauseating. Nor did she like the idea of swallowing some kind of so-called magic potion.

A soft moan from Jeremiah made up her mind: if their actions had a chance of helping him, she must do it. Taking his lordship's advice, she clamped her nose between gloved forefinger and thumb and tipped the bowl. The liquid was salty, with a strong taste of bad eggs and sour milk. Foul. Her stomach lurched. Stoically, she swallowed once more, then passed the bowl back to his lordship.

Swirling the elixir again, he caught Jeremiah's chin and deftly poured some of it into the boy's gaping mouth, closing his hand around the narrow jaw as the child swallowed and coughed.

"Well," Carlston said, replacing the bowl on the side table, "that is the easy part." He held out his hand. "For the next part, we will need to forge a connection." His gaze dropped to her hands in her lap. "Without gloves."

She peeled them off and then reached for Carlston's hand across the boy's chest. The weight of her reticule dragged at her wrist. "Wait," she said, "let me take this off too."

Two twists, and the drawstring was unwound from itself. As she slid it over her hand, the reticule swung before Jeremiah's face: a rose silk pendulum. His eyes fixed upon it and he screamed, pushing himself away, hard, against the iron bar at the head of the bed. "Dead!" he sobbed. "Dead, dead, dead, dead."

Helen jerked her hand back, clasping the reticule to her chest. Immediately the boy quieted, collapsing back against the pillow, his thin chest heaving under his worn chemise.

"What did I do?" she gasped.

From outside the room, they heard Mr. Hammond say, "No, madam. You must not go in."

Carlston twisted around, gesturing Quinn to the door. He was there in a moment, blocking any possible ingress.

"But my little boy . . ." Mrs. Coates's voice, pleading. Poor lady.

"You must trust Brother William. Please, sit back down."

The voices retreated. Quinn tilted his head, listening, then nodded to his master. "They are back in the other room."

His lordship took the reticule from Helen and swung it before Jeremiah's face again. The boy's eyes followed the arc. Carlston's frown deepened.

He handed the reticule back to Helen. "Try it again."

The scream was like a spike through her head. Carlston winced too. She pulled the bag away, and the shrieks stopped.

"He does not seem fond of you or your reticule," Carlston said dryly. "What is in it?"

There could only be one thing that could affect the child of a Deceiver. "My mother's miniature," Helen whispered.

"Ah, I see. Let us put that to the test. Show it to him."

"But it scares him."

"Yes, and I would like to know why."

Helen dug the miniature from the reticule and held it tightly as the life-forces in the room blossomed into blue shimmering outlines.

"Do you see Deceiver energy?" his lordship asked.

"He is just pale blue, as normal."

"Perhaps in his eyes?"

She studied Jeremiah's face. His head rocked from side to side again, the restless rhythm sending a shiver down Helen's back. She followed his eyes, slate gray and staring, but there was nothing unusual about them. "No."

"Press the miniature against his skin."

"But it will—"

"No doubt," Carlston said.

With misgiving, Helen gently pressed the woven-hair side to Jeremiah's bare arm.

He shrieked. "Dead, dead, dead!" His staring eyes swung across to Helen, pinning her in their mad depths. "All gone. All gone."

Carlston grabbed her wrist and held it down, keeping the miniature against the boy's bare skin. His lordship's face was almost touching her own. She felt the heat of his breath against her cheek, the fierceness of his focus.

"What do you mean, boy?" he demanded. "What's all gone? The Deceivers?"

"Dead, dead, dead!" Jeremiah bucked under the pressure, the words trailing off into a howl.

"Let me go," Helen demanded, but it was as if his lordship did not hear her voice. All his attention was fixed upon the boy's reaction. Helen raised her voice over the screams. "You are hurting him! You are hurting me!"

Carlston blinked, his eyes sharpening back into the moment. He released her wrist. "I beg your pardon."

Helen clutched her wrist to her chest. The boy's shrieks had ceased.

"Are you all right, my lady?" Darby asked, pushing past Quinn.

"I am unharmed." She opened her hand, the portrait flat upon her palm. "It must be my mother's and father's hair that makes him scream so. Do you not agree?"

"I think it is the most probable explanation," Carlston said. "Some alchemy has definitely been woven into the hair. But I do not know its purpose."

Helen looked down at the boy, who was once again rocking from side to side. "What does he mean when he says, 'All gone'? Does he mean us or the Deceivers or himself?"

"I wish I knew," Carlston said, "but I think he is past making any sense." He held out his hand again. "Put the miniature aside and let us reclaim him now, before we cannot bring him back at all."

"Darby, keep these for me," Helen said. She passed the miniature and reticule to her maid—the shimmers dropping away—then laid her hand in Carlston's grasp.

"Put your hand on his breastbone, beside his heart," he said. "This is the gateway to the soul. In Eastern practices, it is where the spiritual energy is centered."

He pressed her palm against the boy's chest, his hand covering her own with warm weight. She felt the quick thud of Jeremiah's heart through her flesh, into her bones. Carlston caged one side of the boy's head in the span of his other hand, holding it still.

"Take the other side," he ordered.

She obeyed, her fingers cradling the curve of Jeremiah's skull through his matted hair. His nostrils flared, eyes widening until the whites showed, like an animal's. He tried to pull away, a low moan rising into a sob.

"There now," Helen said, in the tone she used for gentling her mare, Circe, stroking his head with her thumb. "It will be all right." The boy looked up at her, calming under her touch.

Out of the corner of her eye, she saw Carlston nod his approval. "We must find the soul, break the hold of the vestige, and rip it from the child's energy."

"How do you find a soul?" Helen asked, still stroking the matted head. "Though prayer?"

"Through compassion," Carlston said. "And we find that through meditation. Are you familiar with the term?"

"*Lectio, meditatio, oratio,* and *contemplatio,*" Helen recited. "The *Lectio Divina,* but that is a Catholic practice, Brother William. I am not a Papist."

"I was referring more to the Eastern tradition," he said. "A deep internal awareness achieved through the control of breath. We must seek our own compassion in order to find the boy's soul. To find his light."

"His light?"

He nodded. "It is no accident that all the great artists paint the soul as pure light. A vestige is like a small dark mass within that bright grace. Once we find it, we can pull it out and restore him to full humanity."

"How?"

"You will see. Come, breathe with me. I will help you."

He drew in a breath, nodding as Helen matched it. She could feel his pulse in the hand over her own. The slow measure of his exhalation drew hers with it, a long release. They breathed in and out, in and out, again and again until the boy's ragged breath slowed to meet their steady rhythm, his eyes hazing.

"Close your eyes. Open them when you feel your heart open," Carlston said.

Although Helen did not know what he meant, she closed her eyes, her pulse blending with his, with Jeremiah's, the unified beat drawing her deeper and deeper into each breath. She felt the rise and fall of Jeremiah's chest beneath their bare hands, the warmth of his lordship's skin against her own, the gentle pull of an inner rhythm that ebbed and flowed beyond the limits of flesh . . .

Distantly, she sensed time passing, bound into every draw of air and throb of pulse. She heard a low sound, repeated over and over again, seep into her mind. Building and building into a sweet pressure. And then she felt something spring open, bringing a breath so deep and so full of harmony that it must have come from her soul. Or from her heart.

Now she knew what he meant.

She opened her eyes. Jeremiah's body lay upon the bed, surrounded by a pale, sickly yellow light. Carlston leaned over the boy, his hand held above Jeremiah's crown. He was surrounded by light, too, but it was brighter and had a denseness to it. It was not, however, as bright or dense as the light that surrounded herself. She held out her other hand, squinting at the intensity. Lud, was she looking at her own soul? She looked across at his lordship again. Something did not feel right. Her eyes were drawn to a deep vein of darkness that threaded through the illumination around his arm and reached into his body. Was that the vestige already leaving Jeremiah? No, that would have to be pulled from the boy's soul. This was a darkness within the man. An old darkness. She reached toward it, following an impulse to pull it from his body.

"No," Carlston said. The shock of his voice broke the union of their breath and sent a shiver across her skin. "Stay back. Watch the boy."

She breathed in, finding the rhythm again, and turned her attention to Jeremiah. Set into the light at the boy's crown was a nugget of darkness no larger than a walnut, with tentacles that had rooted themselves deep. Here was the vestige. Dear God, how she wanted to reach across and rip it out. Carlston dug his fingers into the light, forcing a way between the tentacles that seemed to heave against his touch. He hooked two fingers around the vestige. Helen felt its resistance, like a backwash of sourness, as his lordship tightened his hold. A heartbeat of hanging silence, a deep-drawn breath of bright compassion—and then he wrenched the dark damage from Jeremiah's soul. Something screamed. Was it Jeremiah, or the vestige as it ripped free?

Helen watched the sweet light of the boy's soul brighten into incandescence. She laughed from the sheer joy of the sight.

"Help me undo him," Carlston said, pulling at a tie around the boy's wrist.

She blinked, the sudden wrench back into the room like a tearing of something deep within herself. She looked across at Carlston. His hand was shaking so much, he had dropped the end of the binding. "What is wrong?" she asked.

"It is nothing." He clenched his hand, then opened it again, the shaking gone. "Quinn, undo his ankles."

Uneasy, Helen bent to the task of unpicking the knot around the boy's other wrist. It was obvious that something was awry: sweat dampened his lordship's hair, and his mouth was tight with pain.

With Darby and Quinn to help, Jeremiah was soon free. He sat up, rubbing his wrists, his dazed eyes searching the tiny room. "Where is Mamma?" he whimpered. "Please, sir, where is my mamma?"

Carlston pushed the boy's damp hand into Helen's. "Take him to the other room. To his mother."

"Should we not fetch her to him, and let the poor child rest?"

"No, take him out. Now." Carlston swallowed hard. He was clearly making an effort to speak and move normally, but beneath the rigid control something was wrong.

"You are not well, Lord Carlston," Helen said. She looked for Quinn. Surely the Terrene could do something to stop his master's distress, as he had at the Gardens. But Quinn had already crossed to the doorway. "What is wrong with him?" she demanded.

"I just need to rest," his lordship said before his man could answer. He motioned to Darby. "Now is the time to take your mistress out. And the boy, too."

"My lady, we must go, like his lordship says."

"Darby!" Helen said, taken aback by her maid's firmness.

"Come along, boy." Darby swung Jeremiah's thin legs across the rumpled sheet and pulled him to his feet. He buckled, his weakness stifling any more protest from Helen. She took his other arm. Together they helped him across the room.

"Will his lordship be all right?" Helen whispered to Quinn as he opened the door.

Carlston sat on the bed, his head bowed, fists clenched. A tremor passed through his body.

"He just needs to rest," Quinn said stolidly, and ushered them over the threshold with worrying haste.

Mrs. Coates stood on the landing, anxiously watching. She gave a sobbing cry as Helen and Darby brought Jeremiah from the room, and rushed forward to receive her boy.

"God's love is great and wondrous," the Reverend said.

Beyond him, Lady Margaret's eyes were fixed upon the bedchamber. Helen looked back. The door was closed. And Quinn was not behind her—he had stayed in the room.

Mrs. Coates held her son at arm's length, peering into his face. "Are you all right, my love?" He nodded and was drawn into a tight embrace. "Oh, thank the Lord!" She smiled over his thin shoulder at Helen. "Thank you, thank you, Sister." Her attention shifted to the closed door. "Where is Brother William? I want to thank him, too. You have wrought a miracle."

"He needs to rest," Helen said. She urged Darby forward. "Help Mrs. Coates take Jeremiah into the other room, Sister," she ordered, then looked pointedly across the landing at Lady Margaret. "I am sure the boy could do with some food and drink."

"Of course," Lady Margaret said, leading the joyous mother and dazed son through the doorway. With a worried backward glance, Darby followed.

Alone, Helen contemplated the closed door of the bedchamber. If his lordship was resting, she should not intrude. Yet there had been something in his eyes that had been most alarming, as if he had been sorely hurt.

With a soft step, she returned to the door, hand poised to knock. She heard a soft moan, so soft, she knew it would be inaudible to other ears. Courtesy warred with curiosity. And concern. With a prickle of shame, Helen stepped closer and peered through the gap in the frame.

She caught her breath. Carlston was no longer on the bed but curled on the floor, his head and shoulders cradled in Quinn's lap. He shook as if he had the ague, his hair and forehead wet with sweat. Quinn's arms were locked around his master's chest, bracing him against the convulsions that rocked his body. She made out the shape of a chair wedged under the door handle: Quinn had made sure no one could enter the room.

"Holy God," Carlston swore as a harder spasm curled him even tighter upon himself.

Helen winced. She had seen him in pain before, but nothing like this. The agony seemed to come from somewhere very deep indeed.

Quinn grabbed his master's forehead, holding him still. "You shielded her." The accusation was pitched for privacy, but no guard against her Reclaimer hearing.

"Of course I did," Carlston gasped.

Helen pressed her cheek against the rough wood, angling for a better view. Of course his lordship had shielded her from the vestige; that had been the plan. He would reclaim the soul, and she would watch. Did Quinn mean he had shielded her from something else?

The big man hissed out a breath. "I do not like to say it, my lord, but perhaps Mr. Benchley is right."

Carlston panted as another spasm shuddered through his body. "Benchley can go to Hell."

Quinn gave a grim smile. "Too late—he's already there." He tightened his grip around another violent convulsion. "Benchley is right about one thing, my lord," he continued after the spasm had passed. "It is madness to think she can fight. Did you even consider what he said?"

Carlston gave a rasping laugh. "Right now it is *all* I can think about." He looked up at his Terrene, frowning with the effort of speaking through the pain. "She does not even have her strength yet. Until then, no one can do anything."

"Sister Helen? Are you coming?"

Helen spun away from the door to face Lady Margaret, heat rising to her cheeks. "Yes."

"Mrs. Coates would like to offer you some refreshment." Lady Margaret stared at the gap in the door, then back at Helen. She licked her lips: a prelude to a question.

"Of course. I will come directly," Helen said, moving toward the happy gathering in the other room. If she was quick enough, perhaps she could avoid the exchange. Lady Margaret, however, held her ground.

"Is he all right?" she whispered.

"Yes," Helen said. "Just resting."

Lady Margaret nodded, her relief flickering into a smile. Helen smiled back, not really knowing why she had lied.

Twenty

Monday, 11 May 1812

TO HELEN'S DISCOMFORT, lying to everyone around her was becoming a habit. Or perhaps not a habit, she amended, but a terrible necessity. Aunt had wondered why she had not returned with any books from such a long visit to Hatchards. She had blithely answered that none had taken her fancy and, instead, she had taken an extended walk along Piccadilly with Darby. And now, in the drawing room of Lord and Lady Farrington, the Duke of Selburn was standing before her and asking if she had been bothered by Lord Carlston recently.

"No, not at all," she said, smiling up into his grave inquiry.

She took refuge from his scrutiny by taking a sip of coffee, hardly tasting it. She and the Duke had not been table companions—Annabella Milbanke had been the recipient of that pleasure—but he had made his way directly to her side when the gentlemen had finally rejoined the ladies in the drawing room. A situation that had been most flattering and pleasurable until a moment ago, when she had been forced to lie again.

"Carlston?" her aunt exclaimed from beside her on the sofa. "Helen has not seen him since Almack's. Have you, my dear?"

"No. As I just said."

"You were most kind to have rescued my niece from his attentions on that evening," Aunt added.

"It was my pleasure, madam." Selburn bowed. "I am at her service."

"It grieves me that he seeks to use my family as an entrée back into society. Although, of course, up until this sixth Earl, the Standfields were unimpeachable."

"Quite," Selburn said. "I do not agree with those who think that the sins of one family member must always blacken the reputation of the others."

Aunt cast a fleeting look of triumph at Helen and then smiled up at him. "I see that you take my own view, Duke." She sent a searching glance around the room. "Ah, Lady Farrington wishes to speak to me. You will excuse me, won't you?"

She rose and made her way to Lady Farrington, who, Helen noticed, was deep in conversation and appeared quite surprised to have Lady Pennworth arrive at her elbow.

"May I sit with you?" Selburn asked.

Helen nodded. "Please do."

He flicked back his coattails and sat with some grace considering the fact that the shallow sofa offered neither of them much in the way of comfort for their long legs. Helen shifted to allow him more room, meeting his smile of sympathy with her own.

"I was hoping to see you at the promenade yesterday," he said. "You usually attend on Sunday, do you not?"

"Usually, but I was indisposed," she replied.

Another lie. She had claimed a headache during Sunday luncheon, and spent the whole afternoon in her chamber trying to make sense of what had happened at the Devil's Acre, and studying the woven hair at the back of the miniature. There could be little doubt that it had caused Jeremiah's violent reaction; nothing else about the portrait could have prompted such a fit. Something alchemical—she could not bring herself to allow it to be magic—must have been worked into the tight, smooth pattern, as his lordship had said. Still, he did not know what, and that was most unsettling. It was almost as unsettling as what she had seen through the gap in the door.

Even now, here with Selburn, she could not shake the haunting image of Lord Carlston convulsed in agony. He had told her that he would shield her during the reclaiming of Jeremiah's soul. Yet from his gasped conversation with Quinn, the agony seemed to be something more—and he had shielded her from that, too. A noble act, but what had caused such torment? And what had Mr. Benchley said that Quinn was urging his master to consider? Perhaps it was irrational, but Helen could not help thinking that anything to do with Benchley held some kind of threat toward herself. There was something about the man that drove hard fear into her heart. Whatever it was that he and Carlston had discussed, it all appeared to rest upon her attainment of her Reclaimer strength: an event that apparently brought far more than just the ability to lift a man with one hand. They seemed certain that it would happen to her, yet it seemed so unlikely that a woman could manifest such strength. Her skepticism brought a strange mix of relief and regret. What would it be like to be so strong?

"I hope you are now recovered," Selburn said, bringing her full attention back to the drawing room.

"Oh yes, it was a trifling matter." She cast about for another subject, unwilling to lie again. "Do you plan to view the Society's watercolors this month, Your Grace?"

"I do, although I must admit my taste lies more with the oils. I am hoping that Mr. Turner will be exhibiting next month at the Royal Academy."

"You are also an admirer of Mr. Turner?" Helen leaned forward, one of her enthusiasms sparked. "I know he is not to everyone's taste, but I find him brilliant. There is such excitement to be found in the wildness of his brushstrokes, and yet there is so much control of the medium."

Selburn leaned forward too. "Indeed, his use of light is remarkable—"

The door suddenly sprang open. The two footmen in attendance stepped back, startled. A gentleman, not attired in evening dress but in crumpled breeches and jacket, strode to the middle of the room with such an air of import that it silenced all conversation.

"Why, Mr. Collison, we had given up on you," Lady Farrington said.

"Forgive me, my lady, for my late arrival and disheveled appearance," the man said. "But I bring terrible, melancholy news."

Those gentlemen who had been sitting stood almost as one. Bad news, it seemed, must always be received standing, and in the last month there had been too many grim reports from the war against Bonaparte: the bloody cost of the victory at Badajoz and, in its aftermath, the shameful slaughter of its citizens by British troops. Were there more atrocities to come? Helen looked up at the Duke. His countenance was fixed, as if braced against Mr. Collison's next words. He must have felt her gaze, for he glanced down and gave a small smile of reassurance.

"I have come from Parliament," Mr. Collison announced heavily. "Lord Perceval has been assassinated. Shot dead in the lobby of the House of Commons."

Helen drew in a short, shocked breath. The Prime Minister, murdered? She looked at the stunned faces around the room: like herself, they had expected war news, not something so close to home and so terrible—a direct attack upon the sanctity of government. One of the young Miss Cecils gave a loud moan and fell back in her chair, her breath coming in shrill sobbing cries, pale hands beating the air. Such a dramatic onset of vapors broke everyone's shocked thrall. The ladies rushed over to her, fanning and calling for salts. The men, including Selburn, surged toward Mr. Collison, demanding more information. By rights, Helen should have been clustered around Miss Cecil with the other ladies, but she stayed on the sofa, listening to Mr. Collison's report.

The details were few but painted a vivid picture. A man had approached Lord Perceval in the lobby of the House of Commons and, at close range, fired a gun. The bullet had pierced him though the heart. The Prime Minister had cried, "Murder, murder!" staggered, and then fallen to the ground. The perpetrator was found sitting nearby with the gun still in his hand. By all accounts, he was not an enemy of the state, but a respectable merchant by the name of Bellingham—an Englishman, by Jove!—with a grievance against his government. He had been taken into custody.

Amongst the exclamations of horror and outrage, Helen heard a few quiet comments. Who would replace Perceval as Prime Minister: Lord Liverpool or Melbourne? Or was this the Whigs' chance to secure power? Politics, it seemed, did not stop to mourn.

Naturally, the party broke up soon after. The Duke left at the same time as Helen and her aunt, and stayed with them until their coach was brought around to the front door, handing both ladies into the cabin.

"Well, now," Aunt said, settling back against the silk cushions as they pulled away. "The Duke has been most attentive, has he not?"

Helen looked back at Selburn standing on the gravel drive. He lifted his hand in farewell, his face solemn with the recent events. Helen raised her own hand. She could not help but admire him: he was a man who obviously felt deeply about the world but showed just the right amount of sensibility. Lord Carlston would have looked coldly upon the matter and made some caustic remark. No, that was not fair, Helen chided herself. She had seen his humanity all too clearly in that room in the Devil's Acre. The Duke and his lordship were both men of deep feeling. She moved away from the window, breaking the strange pairing in her mind. Neither would be flattered to be in the other's company.

"It is too bad that the party ended so soon, don't you think?" Aunt asked, pulling the fur carriage rug higher over their laps.

"It could hardly continue, Aunt."

"Yes, I know. This business with poor Perceval is terrible. I must say, though, I am glad we sent out the invitations to your ball this morning. One really cannot send out invitations the day after the Prime Minister is murdered."

It seemed that Aunt did not stop to mourn either.

⁓

OVER THE NEXT few days, the horror of the assassination and the subsequent political unrest was the only topic of conversation at the assemblies and parties that Helen attended with her aunt. Even as they shopped for the ball, ordering bouquets and new glassware, the subject was overheard amongst the shopkeepers and lower orders. The sentiments expressed by those citizens, however, were not always dismayed or sorrowing. Sometimes they held a disturbing note of satisfaction.

"Mark my words, this could bring the Tories down," Uncle said at breakfast on Thursday, the day before Bellingham's trial. "With the King still indisposed, the Prince Regent will slide in his Whiggish friends before you can say, 'God rest Perceval's soul.'" He looked across his plate of gammon at Aunt. "You will not believe what I heard outside one of the low tap houses yesterday. Men were drinking to Bellingham. Toasting the blackguard as though he were some kind of folk hero! And the hatred for Perceval and his government—it was terrifying. I fear a mob is building."

At the word *mob,* Helen paused in slicing a wedge from the breakfast seed cake. Was it possible that the Deceivers had orchestrated the Prime Minister's murder to create a civil uprising? Lord Carlston said there were certain Deceivers that thrived on violence and the high emotions of a mob, but also that the creatures did not work together. Could there be another Deceiver motivation? It was a question only Lord Carlston could answer, but she had not seen nor heard from him since they had reclaimed Jeremiah's soul. She resumed sawing through the sugar crust. For all her misgivings about his lordship and the Dark Days Club, this sudden silence was even more disquieting. Perhaps he had not recovered from the reclaiming agony. Then again, perhaps he was just busy defusing the dangerous emotions that had been aroused amongst the people. If that were the case, would he ask for her help? Part of her fervently hoped not, but she had to admit that another part wanted to be called into action. A shocking admission. She put the knife down and looked sourly at the wedge of cake. Too much self-knowledge did nothing for one's appetite.

As was her usual Thursday practice, she and Darby visited Hatchards after breakfast, both keeping a sharp lookout for any reappearance of the shadow gentleman or Mr. Hammond's carriage. There was, however, no sign of either, and they walked to the bookshop and back to Half Moon Street without any mishap or communication from the Dark Days Club. Helen could not shake her sense of unease. She considered sending a note to Lord Carlston via Darby—to the point of unlocking her writing desk and sharpening a pen—but decided against it. A letter would give the impression that she wanted to be involved.

Friday brought Bellingham's trial. Its outcome was discussed at the dinner party that Helen and her aunt and uncle attended that evening, but the information passed around by the men at the table was largely secondhand and obscured by bombastic opinion. The later discussion in the drawing room between the ladies—waiting for the men to rejoin them after port—was far more interesting. One of them, Mrs. Forbes, had actually attended the trial, the excitement still evident in the quick flutterings of her red silk fan as she related the details.

"Mr. Bellingham pleaded not guilty," she said to the ladies clustered around her chair, "although he had already confessed to the murder at the scene. His defense tried to argue insanity, but he would have none of it. He said that his government had failed him when he was wrongly imprisoned in Russia, and then refused to make him any reparation. It was enough for any man to take the law into his own hands, he said. The jury, of course, did not agree. They took only an hour to find him guilty."

"I am surprised it took that long," Lady Beck said.

Although everyone had already heard Mr. Bellingham's sentence—death by hanging, with his body to be delivered for dissection—Mrs. Forbes announced it again with the death knell in her voice. A shiver of horrified delight ran through the women. The public execution had been set for the following Monday morning at eight o'clock outside Newgate Prison. *A rather quick dispensation of justice,* Helen thought: Mr. Bellingham had been tried and would hang within just one week.

"My husband and I have decided to attend," Mrs. Forbes said. "I do like a hanging, and this one will be especially momentous."

A murmur rose around the room, some scandalized at the intention, others expressing similar enthusiasm for such a spectacle.

"But surely you remember what happened five years ago," Aunt said. "Haggerty and Holloway."

A few of the older ladies in the room nodded gravely at her invocation of those two names. Messrs. Haggerty and Holloway had been found guilty of murdering a man on Hounslow Heath during a robbery, and the much-followed case had prompted forty thousand people to attend the execution. An incident in the huge crowd caused sudden, widespread panic, and thirty unlucky souls had been crushed to death, some of them women and children.

"Well, I am not intending to stand on the ground with the Great Unwashed," Mrs. Forbes said briskly. "We will hire a room overlooking the gallows, have a spot of breakfast, and be as safe as you like."

"Yes, yes, a wise decision," Lady Beck said, the purple feather in her turban waving vigorously with each nod. "But you had best hurry for a room. I'll warrant all the good ones will be gone by tomorrow."

At eight o'clock on Saturday morning, the Right Honorable Spencer Perceval was interred. Kneeling in prayer in the library, Helen heard the bells of Westminster Abbey and St. Margaret's Church toll as the funeral procession made its way from Downing Street. Under Uncle's direction, the household had gathered for a solid hour of intercession for the Prime Minister's soul. Lord Pennworth had wanted to follow the funeral procession as an official mourner and staunch Tory man, but the bereaved family had written back that attendance at the burial was to be a private affair. Uncle's subsequent prayers were—to Helen's ear—edged with a rather sulky pique.

After breakfast, Helen and Aunt had just taken their usual places on sofa and chair respectively in the drawing room when the doorbell rang.

"Are we expecting anyone, Helen?"

"No."

They both watched the double doors. Finally footsteps were heard, and the doors opened to admit Barnett, a folded packet on his silver salver. "This was just delivered by footman for you, madam," he said, bowing. "From the Lady Margaret Ridgewell."

"Lady Margaret?" Aunt said, after Barnett had withdrawn. She turned the letter over in her hands. "Why does she write to me?"

"I don't know," Helen said. She clasped her hands together to hold back her impatience. Lord Carlston was finally making contact again.

Aunt slid her finger under the wafer and opened out the page. "Ah, she has written to me to request your company this afternoon. She proposes a drive with her and her brother to Richmond Park to take your minds off this melancholy day." She looked up. "It is a little unusual. We have only just made their acquaintance."

"True, but they are very pleasant, are they not?" Helen said, trying to keep her voice even. This was no excursion to Richmond Park. If she had to wager on a reason for the hurried invitation, it would be Bellingham's hanging on Monday. Perhaps Lord Carlston wanted her to be part of his plans after all. "And they have Lady Jersey's friendship and support," she added, hoping that the reminder of the patroness's endorsement would be enough to overcome the small irregularity of the invitation.

"Yes, they are very pleasant. Mr. Hammond, especially." Aunt returned to the letter for a moment, then looked up again, a strange hesitancy in her manner. Helen read her aunt's face: embarrassment. "My dear, what I am about to say may seem a little inelegant, but I think that you are mature enough to understand the realities of the world." She cleared her throat. "Selburn seems to have an interest in you, and I know we both have high hopes in that area. Nevertheless, Mr. Hammond is a very genteel young man from a good family with solid property. Building a friendship with him and his sister would be most appropriate. Just in case."

Helen nodded gravely, although the idea of Mr. Hammond as a husband seemed somewhat ludicrous. He *was* a pleasant man, of course, and worthy, but he suffered from comparison to more—

she searched for the appropriate word—*effective* men. He was a follower, and Helen had to admit that she admired those who led.

Her aunt smiled. "Yes, I think you may go today. And we will send Mr. Hammond and his sister a card for your ball, too."

"Thank you, Aunt." Helen paused, wondering how to best handle her next question. She wanted Darby to accompany her, but it was not strictly necessary since Lady Margaret would be chaperone enough. She decided on the contrary course. "I will not need to take Darby, will I?"

Her aunt considered the implications. "I think it would be best if you did, my dear. After all, we do not know them very well."

"Of course," Helen said meekly.

"Now, what to wear," Aunt mused. "Perhaps your burgundy silk would do well for the occasion—appropriately somber, but still with some color. Public mourning is so hard to manage in spring."

Unable to help herself, Helen said, "More so in summer, don't you think?"

"Yes, yes," Aunt agreed. "One never feels inclined to grieve in summer."

~

"Do YOU THINK we will come up against any Deceivers this afternoon?" Darby asked as she buttoned the back of the carriage gown. "I hope not. Neither of us is really prepared, are we? Mr. Quinn says I will need to be trained before I can take on the duties of your Terrene. But I am ready for it, my lady. Ready and willing."

Helen twisted around to meet her maid's eagerness. "Let us not get ahead of ourselves. Lord Carlston may want you to be my Terrene, but I have not even agreed to be a Reclaimer yet."

Darby paused in her fastening. "Really, my lady? Forgive me for saying so, but you are acting as if you are part of the Dark Days Club already."

"What do you mean?"

Darby gently turned Helen back around and resumed her buttoning. "Well, I have not seen you retreat from anything Lord Carlston has asked you to do. You even helped him save Jeremiah, and that was real Reclaimer work, wasn't it?"

Helen opened her mouth to protest and then closed it again. Darby had a point.

"What you and Lord Carlston did for that boy was marvelous, my lady."

Helen craned around again. "Tell me, what did you actually see and hear? Did his lordship sing?"

"Sing?" Darby shook her head. "No, my lady, but he was chanting some kind of foreign words. You were too." She tugged on the top of the sleeves, rearranging the gathers. "Did you not know you were doing it?"

"No." Helen felt as if her heart had seized for a moment. She could not remember saying any words at all. "Did you see anything?"

"I did, my lady. There was a moment when his lordship said something that sounded final, like the end of a prayer, and I saw the boy *lighten*." She shrugged. "I don't know how else to put it. Then a calm came across him, and I knew his mind was whole again. It was God's work, plain and simple."

"Is that why you would be my Terrene?" Helen asked. "Because it is God's work?" She wished she had Darby's steadfast belief in the sanctity of her gifts.

Darby brushed down the back of the bodice, then walked around to face Helen. "Mr. Quinn told me that your Reclaimer blood chose me to be your Terrene. It is a big thing to be chosen."

"It is," Helen said. "But I did not know I was choosing you for something so dangerous when I raised you to lady's maid."

Darby turned to the dressing table and picked up a pair of small garnet drop earrings. She held one up for Helen's inspection. At her nod, Darby gently pushed the earring hook through the piercing. "I've been in service since I was fourteen, my lady. Until a month ago, I knew what was before me: keeping your ladyship's wardrobe and keeping your ladyship well." She flapped a hand, denying any discontent. "I'm blessed to be in such a position. But now I've been chosen to do something more. Something that is in service to the *whole* of mankind. Me! Jen Darby." She inserted the second earring. "I don't know why I've been chosen, but if the Lord wants me to help you, I can't walk away." She smiled, a rare impishness making her seem far younger than her twenty years. "And, in truth, being your Terrene is not too far from what I'm doing now, is it? I'm to keep you well and safe, and maybe stab you in the hand now and then."

Helen laughed. "Darby!" She shook her head. "Truly, though, it is no joking matter. The Deceivers are deadly. Do you even know what you would have to do as my Terrene? Did Mr. Quinn tell you that I would have to bind you to me? Through alchemy?"

Darby sobered. "I do know. Mr. Quinn told me all about the binding and the duties and the dangers. He didn't hold back, neither."

"That may be so, but you have not seen these creatures," Helen said. "They are so vicious and powerful. And you have not seen the effect they have on a Reclaimer. The madness that came over Lord Carlston . . ." She hugged her arms around her chest at the memory of his lordship's brutal attack on his own man. He had lost himself within that bright blue glow of power. "It was terrifying to see him so, Darby. To be that untethered from one's sense and intelligence—no, I cannot face that kind of horror."

"But I will be there to stop it, my lady," Darby said. "That is what you have chosen me to do. I'll help you get rid of the energy, and you'll be all right."

Helen felt Darby's hand cover her own: a small warmth against the chill that seemed to have spread through her whole body. "I am not sure I can do it," she whispered. "I don't want to get hurt or go mad."

She bowed her head, shamed by the confession. Her mother had faced such peril. Her father, too. Perhaps she was just not as brave as her parents. Surely it would have been better for everyone if Andrew had been the direct inheritor.

Darby patted her hand. "I know you, my lady. How would you live with yourself if you did not do your duty or act upon your conscience?"

Helen raised her head. "But is it my duty?" she asked. "Does an accident of birth compel me to put you and myself in such danger?"

"I do not believe it is an accident that you've been gifted in this way," Darby said softly.

"I think you put too much upon me," Helen said. She looked into the mirror and saw the tight lines of fear in her face. "Just as his lordship does," she added, and turned away from her reflection.

Twenty-One

AT TWO IN the afternoon, Lady Margaret and Mr. Hammond drew up in a smart blue barouche drawn by four bays, its rear hood raised to counter the threat of the dark clouds overhead. Helen was handed up into the carriage by Philip, who settled her next to Lady Margaret and, with a small flourish, placed a mohair rug across her knees to guard against the possible chill of driving in an open vehicle. Mr. Hammond sat opposite, all smiles and enquiries about her comfort, but Helen saw the strain beneath his bright gallantry. In fact, brother and sister were both tense. Lady Margaret was pleating her skirt between her fingers, the nervous action creating ugly creases in the bronze silk. She saw Helen note it and stopped, pressing her hands together in her lap.

With Darby seated beside the driver, and a few final courtesies to Aunt, who watched from the town house steps, they set off. Helen listened to Mr. Hammond's comments upon the weather and the state of the road and the crowds drawn by the funeral of Lord Perceval, waiting for the truth of their destination to emerge.

Finally, as they reached the corner and turned into the noise and bustle of Piccadilly, Mr. Hammond leaned forward, all pretense of lightness gone. "We think we have found your housemaid."

Helen felt every nerve in her body tighten: this was the last thing she had expected. "Where? Is she all right?"

Lady Margaret shook her head. "The girl is dead."

"Dead?" Helen echoed. She looked up at Darby's solid back. All that hope and prayer for Berta's safe recovery had come to nothing. "Was she murdered?"

"We don't know," Mr. Hammond said. "Possibly."

Had poor Berta been innocent after all, a victim rather than a Deceiver? Mr. Hammond leaned closer. "His lordship received word this morning that a corpse matching your maid's description had been found in a derelict building near the Leadenhall Skin Market. He has ordered it removed to a tavern opposite. That is where we go now. To meet him and view it."

"View her?" Helen drew back. "I am not sure I can do that."

"You must," Lady Margaret said with a grimace of sympathy. "Only you can determine if it is your girl."

Helen rubbed her hands together, needing some kind of movement to relieve her agitation. She had, of course, seen dead animals—foxes from the hunt, dogs in gutters, sheep on the estate farm—some of them weeks old and foul in their decay. But she had never seen a dead person, and this one, when alive, had walked in her rooms and curtsied to her every day. The dread of the duty prickled across her skin, made worse by the knowledge that she now had to inform Darby that they were probably driving toward her friend's corpse. Nearly three weeks ago she had promised she would find Berta. Well, Berta was found, with the worst possible outcome. She looked up at her maid laughing with the driver. She would wait until they arrived to tell her the grim news. Let Darby enjoy the ride.

Mr. Hammond leaned closer again. "I have no definitive information about that gentleman who was following you on Piccadilly. Our man tracked him for a while, but lost him near the Privy Gardens in Whitehall. Does that have any meaning to you?"

"The Privy Gardens?" Helen echoed. "No, not at all."

"Then all we can do is keep watch for him again." Mr. Hammond sat back.

Leadenhall Skin Market was in Cheapside, another dubious area of London. The stench of the nearby tanneries and slaughterhouses was even worse than the Devil's Acre. Helen swallowed hard, fighting back nausea. They passed the narrow three-story building that formed the corner of the market, the outer stalls busy with butchers in aprons, poulterers with live and dead birds, and the vegetable men calling their wares. The progress of their barouche caused some stir, especially when their way became stalled by the slow progress of a long cart edging into the market courtyard. Helen looked past the gawping men to glimpse stacks of cattle skins, the pale horns still attached. Buyers picked through them as workmen dragged huge pallets onto drays, their shouted instructions almost indistinguishable from the clamor of squabbling geese in a nearby stall.

They finally made their way through the maelstrom to the Lamb Tavern. It was a large-windowed establishment with a hanging sign duly painted with its woolly namesake, all sweet black face and knobby knees. Mr. Hammond alighted first, then offered his hand to Helen. At least there was pavement here, and not boards laid across mud and sewage. Still, the strong smell of waste in the gutter quickly sent her to the front door of the tavern to await the others.

"His lordship said he would be inside," Mr. Hammond said as the driver handed Darby down. "Allow me to go first. This is a tavern frequented by those in the skin trade."

He led the way, Helen following Lady Margaret into the dim foyer, Darby at the rear. The narrow space was hung with smoke-darkened paintings of dead game, and the steamy air brought the taste of broiled meat—beef, Helen decided. The muted rumble of male conversation and the ring of cutlery on plates came from within.

Reluctantly, Helen turned, stopping Darby's progress. "I have very bad news," she said quietly. "His lordship thinks he has found Berta. Dead. We are here to see if it is her, or another poor girl."

"Oh, my lady."

"I know."

Darby's top teeth bit hard into her lip, holding back her shock. Always so brave. Helen touched her arm, drawing her forward again. Mr. Hammond and Lady Margaret were already at the end of the corridor.

They were met at the stairwell by a short, portly gentleman in a neat jacket and vibrant scarlet waistcoat.

"Would you be Mr. Hammond and party, perchance?" he asked, dipping his head. A rather grizzled, gray powdered wig covered his dark hair.

"Yes."

"I'm the owner of this establishment. Mr. Pardy, at your service, sir." His worried eyes took in Helen and Lady Margaret. He gave another bow and motioned toward the staircase, lit by oil lamps set into the wall. "Lord Carlston is waiting for you below. This way, please."

He led them down wooden steps worn into creaking curves from thousands of journeys to and from the cellar. Helen smelled a sickening decay building in the air as they descended: no doubt the corpse. The strength of the stink did not bode well for the state of the body. She covered her nose with her gloved hand, breathing through the soft, sweet leather. As they neared the bottom of the steps, her companions became aware of the stench too.

"Good Lord," Mr. Hammond murmured.

"Yes," Mr. Pardy agreed. "I've begged his lordship to get rid of it afore that reek gets up into my dining hall. It'll drive out all my customers." He crossed himself. "God rest her soul."

Lady Margaret pressed a lace handkerchief to her nose. "Quite."

"His lordship's in the cool room." He pointed down a stone

corridor to a rectangle of yellow lamplight that spilled onto the stone flags. "If you don't mind, I'll not be going in there again. I want to keep me dinner." He mounted the stairs, but clearly bethought himself of something else and turned back. "Are you sure you want the ladies to see it, sir? Not the thing for delicate females. I've a private room upstairs where they could wait." He smiled encouragingly at Lady Margaret. "A nice drop of ratafia, too, my lady. Peach flavored. Or if you'd prefer, cherry."

"We will not be needing your private room nor your liquor, my good man," she said.

"Are you sure, Margaret?" Mr. Hammond asked. "There is no need for you to see this. Let me escort you upstairs."

"Thank you, brother, but I am not perturbed." She gave him a challenging stare, then strode down the passage and into the cool room. For a moment there was silence, and then the harsh sound of retching echoed against the stone walls.

"Mr. Hammond?" It was Lord Carlston's voice. "Your sister is not well."

Mr. Pardy cleared his throat. "Well, the private room is available if you need it." With a bow, he ascended the steps.

Mr. Hammond sketched a bow to Helen and hurried after his sister, disappearing through the doorway. "Margaret, can I—Holy God."

Helen took a shallow breath of the putrid air, trying to steady her nerves but not turn her stomach. "Are you ready, Darby?"

Her maid retreated a step. "I'm not sure I can, my lady."

"I am not sure I can either, but we have to, for Berta." She held out her hand. "Come."

Darby drew herself up. "Yes, my lady."

Helen felt Darby's cold hand lock into her own. She gave it a small squeeze of encouragement, then led her down the corridor.

"Where is Lady Helen?" she heard Lord Carlston ask.

"I am here." She let go of Darby's hand and entered the narrow doorway.

The stink of new vomit rose through the noxious decay of flesh, bringing a retch into her throat. She jammed her hand over her mouth, transfixed by a bulging eye that stared up at her from the long table, the pale arc of the socket visible underneath blackened, burst skin and oozing tissue. Good God, was this thing Berta? She swayed and groped for the support of the wall. At the back of the room, Mr. Hammond held up Lady Margaret, her face turned into his shoulder. Mr. Quinn stood near them, his gold skin bleached to a sickly yellow. Behind, Darby gave a small moan and clutched the doorframe.

"What has happened to her?" Helen whispered.

"About three weeks of decomposition," Lord Carlston said at her side.

He gently took her arm, breaking her thrall. She looked up into his face, a blessedly still anchor in the pitch and roll of the room. She noted the small sympathetic smile that curved his mouth, and the gold flecks in his dark eyes, and he was saying something, but it was all so far away. Far, far away, and blurring. Was she going to faint?

"Head down, Lady Helen."

She felt his hand cupping the back of her head, pushing her into a most inelegant stoop. For a moment she thought she might topple over, but his grip held her firm. She looked blankly at the blurry stone floor, his lordship's mud-caked Hessian boots, her own burgundy hem, and then the world burst back into full sight and sound and foul smell.

"My lord, what are you doing?" Darby was asking. "My lady needs salts!"

"Gently," he said. "Come up slowly." The pressure on the back of her head eased. He helped her upright and looked into her eyes: a keen examination that was far too close for propriety. She drew back.

"I am quite well," she said, but her voice felt as light as her head. Darby had bravely entered the room and was at her side, face turned away from the table.

"Are you well enough to see if this girl was your missing maid?" his lordship asked. "The sooner we can determine that, the sooner we can all go upstairs into fresher air."

Stepping closer to that ghastly form on the table was the last thing Helen wished to do. But it had to be done. "I am ready," she said. She stroked Darby's arm. "I am so sorry. She was your friend, I know. But you knew her best. Will you help?"

Darby grimaced, the tendons on her neck fanning with horror, but she nodded.

The least distressing way to look at the corpse, Helen decided, was in quick snatches. A purple-black hand, fingernail sliding off. A bloated arm. The folds of a cotton tucker, wet with brown matter. Pale sinew showing through a gaping throat. And the face: swollen tongue forced between teeth, tight cheeks, protruding eyes. All topped by thick, matted black hair. Yet, with all the horrific disfigurement, there was a sad familiarity.

"I think it is Berta," Helen said. "I can see her face in there. And the hair is the same."

"Yes, it is Berta," Darby said, her voice heavy with certainty. She pointed to a hairpin caught in the mass of dark hair. A small metal flower, painted blue. "She always wore it." She blinked rapidly and swallowed. "May I retrieve it, my lady? As a memorial, for her mother."

"I'll get it, miss," Quinn said. "You don't want to be touching the remains." He leaned over and pulled out the pin, then wiped it on his sleeve. With a dip of his head, he passed it to Darby. She received it with a wan smile.

"How did Berta die?" Helen asked.

Carlston leaned over and examined the corpse. "She cut her own throat. There are marks here that speak of hesitation. And she was found with a knife near her hand."

"Self-murder," Mr. Hammond said. "God pity her soul."

Darby crossed herself.

"No, not suicide," Carlston said. "This was a Deceiver leaving its body for its next vessel."

Helen stared down at the grotesque, bloated form. "How can you be sure?"

"This girl, or should I say the Luxure in her body, crossed my path a few years ago. In Prussia." He turned away. "Come, let us remove ourselves from this sight and stench."

He ushered everyone out of the room to the bottom of the staircase.

"Now that we are certain this is your maid, Lady Helen," he resumed, "I think I know what happened. She must have seen me that day on Berkeley Street. She might even have noticed my man stationed outside your house, seen him talking to me and made the connection. Whatever the case, she would have realized I was there for you and that I would recognize her as a Deceiver. I believe she saw me, panicked, and left to avoid discovery, with the intention of killing this body to move into the next."

Helen pressed her hand to her forehead, feeling very ill indeed at this intelligence. "So there was a Deceiver in my house after all. For over a year." She looked up at his lordship. "But why?"

He shook his head. "That, I cannot rightly fathom."

—

IN THE END, they did avail themselves of Mr. Pardy's private room. Lord Carlston, however, refused the peach ratafia and ordered brandy for everyone instead.

"Thank you, Mr. Pardy," he said as the publican slid the tray, set with decanter and glasses, onto the small dining table. "You may go."

Mr. Pardy bowed and backed out of the room, closing the oak door with another bobbing bow. *Like a little robin,* Helen thought, *bippidy-hop-hop-hop.*

She shook her head. There was a buzzing at the base of her skull that would not go away. It was probably just the shock of discovering that a Deceiver had been living in her home. She had even given the creature an old muslin tucker—most likely the one still on the corpse. She lifted her shoulders, trying to shake off the grisly image of the stained material. The smell was still in her nostrils. Perhaps it would never go. She had chosen to sit at the small writing desk by the open window—feeling the need for space around her and some fresher air—but she still felt too closed in.

His lordship lifted the brandy decanter and poured generous measures into the glasses. He passed one each to Lady Margaret and Mr. Hammond at the table, then another to Darby, who hunched on a low sofa along the wall. She took it with an awkward, embarrassed nod. Finally he picked up the last two measures and walked over to Helen.

"Drink this." He held out a glass.

"I don't like spirits."

"Today you do. I have found that taking brandy in one draught washes away the hold of the dead."

She took the glass by the short stem, the fumes of the alcohol prickling high in her nose.

He lifted his own measure. "Come, down it in one. With me."

Obediently, she swallowed the whole in a large gulp alongside his lordship. For a moment there was just the rich oaky taste, then a terrible burning engulfed her mouth and throat and chest and even her nose. She coughed, the room blurring behind tears. He was right: the brandy did sear away that terrible stink.

"Are you all right, my lady?" Darby asked, preparing to rise.

"Stay where you are." Helen waved her back. "Drink your brandy. It will help."

Darby took a timid sip and then cleared her throat. "May I ask a question, my lord?"

"Of course."

"Could Berta—I mean, the Deceiver that was Berta—have passed into another person in our household?"

"That would not be possible," his lordship said with a reassuring smile. "She can only pass into the body of one of her own progeny. It was obvious, even in that terrible state, that the girl downstairs was not old enough to have an adult child who could have infiltrated your household alongside her and now be the vessel for that Deceiver."

"That's true, my lord, Berta was only"—Darby corrected herself again, with a hard swallow—"that body was only eighteen."

"So where is the creature now?" Helen asked.

"Probably in one of the German states," Carlston said. "Most likely in a child's body. That is one of their great fears: to be consigned to the body of an infant and have to survive childhood yet again."

"Well, let us hope that is her fate," Mr. Hammond said. He held up his glass to his sister, who touched it with her own in a chime of crystal.

Helen watched the toast, irritated. "You say Berta could not have passed into another body in our household, but could there be another Deceiver still in my home?" she asked his lordship.

"I think it unlikely, but Lily is there now, so be easy. She has a keen eye, and will look out for anything that might point to a Deceiver."

She nodded, the idea bringing a little relief. But only a little. The corpse downstairs was too real for any sense of ease. There had once been a girl in that flesh—the same age as herself—destroyed to make way for a Deceiver. The unfairness of it brought a wave of rage.

Carlston walked back to the decanter again and poured a smaller measure, then tilted it toward Helen: an invitation for another. She shook her head. She had enough of an irritating buzz in her head without adding more heavy spirits to it. Every joint in her body seemed to ache with the need to move. She flexed her hands and lifted her feet in her half boots.

A knock sounded on the door, which opened almost immediately to admit Mr. Quinn. For a moment the big man filled the whole doorway, then he stepped in and bowed to his master.

"It is all arranged, my lord." He closed the door.

"What is arranged?" Helen demanded.

Mr. Quinn cast a questioning look at his lordship. At Carlston's nod, he said, "The disposal of the creature's human remains, my lady. By fire."

"Should she not be buried at crossroads with a stake through her heart, my lord?" Darby asked. "It was a suicide."

"I can assure you that the corpse does not have a soul that may rise again," Carlston said. "The Deceiver destroyed that girl's soul when it took over her body."

"Oh." Darby took another nervous sip of her brandy.

His lordship waved Quinn to the last glass on the tray, then crossed to the marble mantel, where a fire burned in the grate. He stood for a moment staring into the flames. An unnecessarily theatrical pose, Helen thought peevishly, then realized he was drawing a line through the discovery and disposal of Berta. It was done, and now there was something else on his mind. This world of his moved with brutal speed—it was unreasonable. She placed the brandy glass on the writing desk with a loud thud. For a moment she was overcome with a mad impulse to smash it. She snatched her hand away.

"We have a potential problem on Monday," Carlston said. "Bellingham's execution."

Helen sat up straighter. Was he going to ask her to attend a public hanging? Surely he must know she could not. She rubbed the base of her skull, trying to dislodge the buzz.

"I have received a communication from the Home Office," his lordship continued. "The Luddites are stirred up even more by Bellingham's trial. None of the other Reclaimers can be spared from the North to assist with the crowd at Newgate."

"That's bad," Mr. Hammond said. "They are predicting a crowd as big as that which attended the Haggerty and Holloway execution."

His sister shook her head. "I think it will not be as large. *The Times* is already urging people to stay away."

Helen wiped her mouth with her fingertips. Her tongue felt so dry, and through the lingering woodiness of the brandy, she could taste metal.

"It will be large enough for the Deceivers to attend, whatever the case," Carlston said. He looked at Helen, and she knew what he was going to say. It was as clear as his stupid, self-important pose. She felt a surge of resentment.

"I suppose you want me to go to the execution and help defuse the mob," she snapped. "And how am I to do that? There is no possible way I can attend a public hanging. Particularly in your company. I may as well march over to Covent Garden and set up for business."

She halted, aghast. What was she saying? She looked around the room. Lady Margaret stared at her in horror. Darby's mouth was agape. Mr. Hammond, intent upon a sip of brandy, snorted, his amusement amplified by his near-empty glass.

His lordship crossed his arms. "Are you quite finished?"

"I beg your pardon," Helen said, feeling heat washing through her body. The buzzing was in her spine now, and every limb. She shifted her legs, jiggling one of them in a fast rhythm. It seemed to release some of the unbearable energy that was building behind the infernal hum.

"I do not expect you to go into the crowd with me," Carlston said. "I have secured a room overlooking the square. I want you to view the crowd from the window with your miniature in hand, and direct me to those Deceivers you can see feeding. In that way I can curtail their activities and . . ."

Although he had not moved from the hearth, his voice sounded far away. Helen gritted her teeth, feeling a wave of energy rock her body. What was happening to her?

His lordship's voice suddenly stopped. She looked up to find him squatting at her side. "Are you quite well, Lady Helen?"

She dug her fingernails into the arms of the chair, feeling them sink into the wood. "No. I am not very well at all."

"Look at me." She forced her eyes up again. "Are you feeling an excess of energy in your body?"

She nodded, clenching her hands into tight balls. "Everything is humming. I can taste metal." The compulsion to slam her fist into his face was overwhelming. She groaned with the effort of holding back the mad desire to strike. It was as if some savage, wild part of herself was taking over.

Carlston rose to his feet. "Quinn, get everyone out. *Now!*"

His man sprang into action, pulling Darby from the sofa. Lady Margaret and Mr. Hammond stood, bemused, their glasses still clutched in their hands. Quinn herded them toward the door.

"What's happening?" Helen gasped. Uncontrollable waves of energy surged through her, shaking her whole body.

"I cannot leave my lady alone," Darby cried, then she was out on the landing with the others.

Quinn firmly shut the door on them and spun around, staring at Helen. "What's wrong, my lord?"

"Her strength is coming."

"But that's meant to come slow, with the training."

"I know." His lordship shoved the tray at his man. "This looks like it's coming over her all at once. Get rid of the brandy and the glasses. Anything that could be a weapon." He whirled in a quick circle, eyeing the sparsely decorated room. "Those candlesticks over there." He pointed to a heavy pair on the mantel. "And that pitcher. Then go!"

Quinn snatched up the glasses and candlesticks, piled them on the tray, then hooked the gaudy jug by its handle. "Let me stay, my lord."

"You know you won't be able to keep up. You'll just get hurt. Whatever you hear, don't let anyone in."

Quinn opened the door. "Aye, my lord." He hurriedly maneuvered the tray through the door and closed it.

Helen grabbed the arms of the chair, as if it could anchor her into sanity. "Am I going mad?" Her terror rose into a shriek. *"Am I going mad?"* She closed her eyes, gasping for breath.

"Look at me."

She opened her eyes, panting. Carlston leaned over her, a hand on each arm of the chair. "Look at my face. You are not going mad. This is your Reclaimer strength. You must let it come."

She did not want to follow this dizzying descent into savagery. The darkness was waiting like a huge maw. "I cannot! I cannot!"

"It is going to come—you cannot stop it. I will not let you lose yourself." He grabbed her forearms; the promise made physical. In reflex, she pulled back, gritting her teeth, hot blood pounding in her temples with the effort. No, it was more than effort. Her blood was hammering a battle call, beating through her veins, her muscles, her sinews, bringing a sudden burst of power. For a moment she fought it, then it crashed over her, sweeping away any coherent thought. She was nothing but combat and instinct. Savage power held down by an enemy. With a scream of rage, she wrenched both hands up against his grip, locking them into a stalemate of brute force that shook their arms.

"That's it, that's it," he said through his teeth, his breath shortening under the sudden strain.

Gathering her strength in her legs, she surged up, driving the crown of her head into his jaw. *Kill him, kill him.* The impact brought a moment of streaming color across her eyes. She felt herself jerk up out of the chair as he reeled back, his hands still locked around her forearms. She staggered forward, dragged by his momentum. A shake of her head and the blinding colors cleared into opportunity—a flash of what-would-be. She propelled herself into his body with her whole weight. They crashed to the floor, sending a small side table cannoning into the wall. Her head hit his shoulder bone, the crack bringing a few moments of sickening gray. Beneath her, he gasped for breath. *A chance.* She yanked her arm free and aimed for the damage already done to his jaw. It was a wild strike from her weaker side. *Too slow.* He blocked: a raised forearm. It was like hitting stone. Pain burst through her hand, but it barely registered. She punched again, aiming for his eye, this time feeling the skin split, the heat of blood against her knuckles.

He grabbed her shoulders, thrusting her off with a groan of effort. She was in the air, then hit the floor, breath forced out of her, rolling across the thin carpet. Her back slammed into the stone hearth, the hem of her gown catching around her ankles. Distant pain throbbed along her spine. Panting, she drew up her legs and wrenched the material free, her attention suddenly riveted by the sight of metal inside the grate. An iron poker. *Weapon.* She snatched it up as the man groped for the edge of a chair and hauled himself into a crouch.

"Ah," he said, wiping blood from a gash in his forehead. "Didn't see that."

She smiled: a snarl of animal delight. The length of iron felt good in her hand. Power sang through her blood, her muscles readying for the next attack. She felt fluid, fast, deadly. She felt right. The man stood, watching her warily. She tightened her grip, ready to swing. *Not yet, not yet.* It would be in his eyes: the right moment. He moved. She was across the short space in a heartbeat, iron slicing through the air at his head. It connected—but there was a cracking explosion of wood instead. A chair lifted into a shield. She swung again, the metal smashing through the seat.

"Stop!" he yelled.

She raised the poker. Swung and smashed, demolishing the chair. Large splinters of wood spun up into the air. A tearing pain dug through her shoulder.

"Lady Helen!"

This time the poker found its target, slamming into the man's right side. He gasped, absorbing the impact, then lunged for the end of the weapon. She yanked it back, but it was too late. He had it in his grip.

"Helen!" he yelled in her face.

For a moment she hung suspended in the harsh sound of her bare name. Then, with a moan, she crashed back into herself, a slamming of savagery and sense into one screaming unity, all her breath forced into a long howl that sang her new strength, sang her power. It was terrifying, and it was glorious.

Finally she ran out of air. She gasped, gulped, blinked. Lord Carlston stood before her, panting, face bloodied, grimly holding the end of a poker. She looked down: her hand had the other end in a death grip. She let it go, her chest suddenly flaming with pain. A sizeable splinter of oak chair was lodged under her collarbone, blood seeping into her burgundy silk bodice. She touched the jagged end of the wood, snatching her hand back as the small pressure sent a spike of agony through her body. "What is that doing there?"

"It is part of the chair you demolished," Lord Carlston said. "Here, let me see how deep it is."

He tossed the poker to the carpet, the motion drawing a soft hiss of pain, and closed the short distance between them. He bent to study the wood embedded in her flesh, his breathing pained and shallow. Over his shoulder, she saw pieces of chair littering the carpet. A small table in two pieces, a chunk of plaster missing from the wall above it. And of course, his bloodied face. The evidence coalesced into sudden shocking images of the last few minutes. Attacking him. She closed her eyes. She had slammed a poker into his side; she could still feel the force of it in her hands.

"I hit you. With the poker."

He grunted. "Broke my ribs, I'd say. I wasn't quite expecting that much force. Reclaimer strength does not usually come all at once like that."

"Why did it, then?"

He looked up from his examination. "I don't know." He smiled, wincing slightly. "It was very impressive, though."

"No!" She shook her head, appalled. To raise her hand against another. To be so unrestrained. So wild. It went against everything that was womanly. "I was not in my right mind. I was like an animal."

"That won't always be the case. With training, you will control the power—not the other way around." He turned his attention back to her wound. "This is not deep. Brace yourself." She felt the splinter twist in her flesh, pain radiating through her shoulder, and buckled, feeling his strong hands catch and hold her up. "It is out," he said. "You won't feel it in a minute or so. One of our most useful gifts."

"That was not much time to brace myself," she said through her teeth.

Yet he was right: the pain was already receding. Enough for

her to realize the scandalous proximity of his body. He was holding her elbows, his chest almost against her own, the heat of him blending into the soft howl that still sang through her blood. Something leaped within her: a remnant of that savagery. She moved. It should have been away from him, but it was not. The shift brought his eyes to her own. He stood still, wary, like a wolf caught in the open. The smell of him—soap and sweat and brandy—drew her even closer. She slowly reached up, shocked by her boldness, her shaking fingertip brushing the damage she had wreaked upon his jaw. A realization stilled her hand.

"You did not fight back," she whispered.

She saw the answering leap in his eyes. His head tilted to follow her mouth, the warmth of his answer on her cheek. "No, I did not."

She turned toward his words, her mouth now so close that she felt the soft quickening of his breaths as if they were her own. "Why? I could have killed you."

He bent closer. Her vision filled with him—the cleft of his chin, the curve of his lower lip, a smear of blood. If she swayed forward, she would feel his mouth on her own.

"No," he said. "I could have killed you."

"My lady?" Darby's voice came from the landing outside the door, shrill with concern. "Are you safe? Are you safe?"

Carlston gave a soft laugh. Regret. Or was it resignation? "You are safe, my lady."

Helen felt his hand fleetingly touch her cheek, just before he stepped away. Just before the door opened and the civilized world came clamoring back into the room.

~

WITH A CLICK of her tongue, Darby pressed a pad of cloth against the wound under Helen's collarbone.

"Your bodice is quite ruined." She glared at Lord Carlston.

"It is not his fault," Helen said. "The piece of wood flew from the chair." She looked pointedly at her maid. "Which *I* broke."

Darby shook her head, still amazed at such strength, and returned to dabbing the wound. Helen glanced at his lordship, standing at the door and talking reparation to a stoical Mr. Pardy. It seemed that the publican had witnessed far worse than a mere gouged wall and broken furniture. She averted her eyes from Carlston, remembering the caress of his hand, his warm breath on her skin. Sweet Heaven, she had stepped closer to him and touched him. Her own wantonness brought a flush of humiliation. Yet, she had to admit, the urge to touch him was still shamefully insistent.

Darby withdrew the pad again and peered at the gash. "You're right, my lady: I think it is already beginning to close. Fancy that!" She dabbed one last time. "Your shawl will hide it for the journey home. Once we are safe in your room, I'll fashion something to cover it." She studied Helen's face. "Are you sure you are well?"

"I have never felt better, Darby," Helen whispered. "It is remarkable. I feel so . . . strong." She could not contain a smile of wonderment; *strong* did not even begin to describe the sense of power that still thrummed through her body.

Across the room, Mr. Quinn picked up one half of the split table and tidily placed it next to its mate, while Mr. Hammond helped himself to another brandy from a new-brought tray. Lady Margaret sat on the far sofa, watching Helen with a strange intensity. Her narrowed eyes flicked to his lordship, then back to Helen again, lower lip caught between her small white teeth. Had she guessed what had happened? Helen pressed her knuckles against her cheeks, feeling the heat in her skin. Perhaps the lasciviousness was marked upon her face.

A low bow from Mr. Pardy signaled the end of the negotiations, and he withdrew. His lordship took the glass of brandy Mr. Hammond held out, then crossed to Helen, his arm held protectively over the ribs on his right side.

"Have you recovered?" he asked.

She looked up at him, forcing herself to see past the memory of his lips almost upon her own. "Yes, completely. I feel very well." She gave a small, self-conscious laugh. "Almost too well, I think."

He smiled. "Yes, I remember that feeling."

"Your poor ribs," she said. "I am so very sorry." Such inadequate words for what she had done.

He waved away the consideration. "I should have been quicker."

Helen lowered her voice. "How much strength do I have?"

"Probably the equivalent of two men."

She squeezed her hands together, trying to control the heady marvel of it. "Well, then," she said a little breathlessly, "perhaps now I will be able to drive a team-and-six, as I have always wanted."

Carlston laughed. "When your strength is properly trained and under control, I promise you may drive my own team."

"That is no small offer," Hammond said. "His team of matched grays is legendary."

"You will let me drive them?" Helen looked up at his lordship, astounded. "Truly?"

"Truly," he promised gravely. He turned and swept a glance around the room. "The afternoon is almost gone, and Lady Helen will be expected back by her aunt before long. Let us finalize Monday morning."

He paced to the fireplace. "The hanging is set for eight, but the crowd will start to gather at dawn. It is my wish that we persuade the Deceivers in attendance to leave before the actual event. If too many start skimming the crowd at once, they may provoke high aggression and, with it, a fatal crush like five years ago." He looked across at Helen. "I know that you are dubious about attending a public execution, and I understand your hesitation, but your assistance would be invaluable. I ask you to help me protect the crowd from the effects of the Deceivers. Will you?"

Helen felt her spine straighten. She had her strength. He needed her help. She was invaluable. And he was smiling at her, one Reclaimer to another. From the corner of her eye, she saw Lady Margaret lean forward.

"Yes, I will," she said, and immediately felt sick with the decision. If she were discovered at the hanging, even with her maid, her reputation would be sullied. And if she were found at such an event in the company of Lord Carlston, in a hired house, she would be ruined.

"Thank you," Lord Carlston said. His smile stayed upon her for a moment longer. Did she see a new tenderness within it? Her skin warmed. "Make your way to the house on the corner of Giltspur and Newgate by seven. I have a room reserved that overlooks the gallows and the crossroad square."

"My own way?" Helen repeated, all the warmth replaced by cold alarm. She was expected to arrange her own transport?

"Yes. I have another task for Mr. Hammond and Lady Margaret that prevents them from taking you to the hanging, but they will be able to return you home," his lordship said. "Take a hackney. Go through the bottom of Smithfield and into Green Dragon Lane. Quinn will meet you and lead you to the house."

"Of course," Helen said, although she had never hired a public hackney in her life, and Smithfield was another place of very low repute.

"Once there, you will direct me to Deceivers in the crowd, using your miniature. I will create a signaling system which you can learn on the morning."

Helen took a steadying breath, anxiety lodging in her chest. Hundreds of lives potentially rested upon her skills. Perhaps even thousands. Never before had such expectation been placed upon her, nor such an assumption of competence. It seemed that Reclaimer strength brought more than just this wild sense of power. But what if she failed? She could already foresee a problem: how was she to leave the house in the morning without raising an alarm? Yet his lordship had faith in her ingenuity. So, by the grace of God, she would find a way. She blinked, overwhelmed by a flash of remembered sensation: the tang of sweat and blood and the warmth of his body so near her own.

"Are you sure that you feel able to attend, Lady Helen?" he asked, breaking her moment of thrall. "If you have any doubts that you can do so, you must voice them now."

She felt Lady Margaret's eyes upon her, and realized she had pressed her hands to her face again. She lowered them into her lap.

"No, I will attend," she said, forcing confidence into her voice. "You have my word."

She was rewarded with Lord Carlston's smile, and Lady Margaret's gaze dropping from her own.

Twenty-Two

THAT EVENING, HELEN sat in the town carriage with Aunt and Andrew, absently plucking at the beaded fringe on her reticule as she pondered two questions. First: How was she to attend the hanging on Monday morning without alerting her aunt and uncle? And second: What on earth had happened between her and Lord Carlston at the tavern?

The carriage turned into Conduit Street, passing a row of handsome town houses. Helen stared out unseeingly as the pale stone facades flashed by, her mind fully occupied with that dizzying moment when his lordship's lips had been so close to her own. She hunched her shoulders, once again appalled by the knowledge that she had swayed toward him. That sudden, wanton moment of desire had been a consequence of her Reclaimer strength—a symptom of the violence and wild pounding within her blood. Yet, if she was not mistaken, he had felt it too, although he had gallantly stepped away. He must think her a trollop.

She tugged the edge of her shawl over her collarbone. After much deliberation, she had chosen an evening gown with a filled décolletage, and Darby had wrought a marvel of discreet bandaging. Even so, she could not shake the fear that her healing wound would somehow be divined by all and sundry through the layers of white spotted muslin. She saw a sudden image of herself slamming the poker into his lordship's side. Her Reclaimer strength: the notion was still a tumult of wonder and fear.

Andrew yawned, the accompanying sound pulling Helen from her reverie. A heavy sigh followed the yawn. She met her brother's bored eyes and frowned. It was true that Aunt had cornered him into escorting them to the Handel concert, but his bad grace was wearing thin. Still, it was the first time she had seen him since the Hyde Park incident and, while he did not seem inclined to make any comment on that day, it was best not to poke a sleeping bear.

Aunt turned from peering out of the window. "Andrew, my dear, do you know if the Duke of Selburn will be attending tonight?" Her tone was a study in casual inquiry.

Andrew flashed a knowing glance at Helen before answering. "I believe he is escorting his great-aunt Isolde and her family."

"Ah, I thought so." Aunt dabbed at her lips with a fingertip. "Has the Duke, perchance, said anything about Helen to you?"

"Aunt!" Helen protested. "He would hardly discuss me with my own brother."

"Actually, sis, he can't seem to stop talking about you," Andrew said. "Mighty tedious it is too."

She frowned at him again. "Very amusing, Drew."

"No, I swear, he seems quite taken with you. Apparently he likes a girl with some spirit. I'd hazard a guess, though, that too much spirit would turn him sour." He looked at Helen pointedly, the message clear: *You are lucky I stopped you at the promenade.*

The bear, it seemed, was awake, although there was no real rancor in his face. Perhaps he had forgiven her after all.

"Well, an overabundance of spirit would disgust anyone," Aunt said. She leaned forward, hand tight around her fan. "How taken is he, do you think?"

Andrew shrugged. "You want to know if he'll offer, but I haven't a notion. He has mentioned setting up house, so that could mean something."

Aunt dropped back against the silk cushions with a grunt of satisfaction. She patted Helen's arm. "Well, then, we must manage some more time for you with His Grace, the Duke."

Helen looked out of the window again. Such machinations seemed so far removed from her world now.

They drew up into the queue outside the concert hall. As they waited to alight, Aunt pointed out Viscount Cartwell with two ladies of the demimonde upon his aged arm: fashionably plump women in fine muslin that clung to their figures in shocking detail. "He keeps both of them, you know," she commented.

Andrew leaned across from his seat, a touch to Helen's arm calling her attention from the Viscount and his companions.

"I must say, sprite," he murmured, "I wouldn't mind calling Selburn brother. Or you Duchess, for that matter. Do you hold him in any esteem?"

"I do," she said sincerely, the memory of the wit and warmth of their encounters making her smile. "He is admirable, and all amiability." Even so, it was impossible for her to think of marriage with the Duke. She could not expose an unsuspecting man to the dangers of the Deceiver world, especially one as worthy as His Grace. As much as it pained her to do so, she had to steer herself—and her brother—away from such thoughts. "But, Andrew," she added softly, "you know I do not wish to marry yet."

"Is that so?" her brother said, and sat back, a disbelieving smile upon his face.

By the time they had made their way through the foyer and into their seats at the center of the hall, the concert was about to start. Helen drew her shawl more securely around her shoulders and turned her face politely toward the orchestra as it struck up the overture to *Saul*. Yet she hardly heard a note of the opening allegro. Her mind was set upon her two problems to the exclusion of everything else, even Mr. Handel's exquisite music.

The question of the hanging was far less confusing than her thoughts about Lord Carlston. At least with the hanging, there was a chance of her finding a solution: a feasible excuse to leave the house at such an early hour with only Darby for company. But that excuse remained stubbornly out of reach, perhaps because an image of his lordship's lips kept intruding upon her thoughts.

The music gathered intensity. Beside her, Aunt's eyes were closed. Dozing already. Helen looked around the room. How many Deceivers were in attendance? The hall could seat near one thousand people, and it was full. That meant there would be at least one of them. The possibility brought a small shiver along her spine.

A strange restiveness in the first few rows caught her attention. People were shifting in their chairs as if none of them could find any comfort for their bones; perhaps a sign that a skimming Deceiver sat in their midst.

Helen worked her fingers into her reticule and pulled out the portrait, tucking it into the top of her glove. The room blossomed into the shimmering blue of humanity. And the brighter blue corona of *two* Deceivers. She had been right: one of them *was* seated in the second row. A woman with a pretty band of diamonds in her carefully curled brown hair. The other, an older man with a beard, stood at the very back of the hall. Both were skimming from the unsuspecting people around them. Helen watched the woman draw back her blue-black feeding tentacle, sending it out in another direction, the caressing appendage sliding over a young man's shoulder and into his lap. He scratched at his neck. Helen looked away, wishing she could stop such an obscene, insidious attack.

The allegro finished, the swell of applause jolting Aunt upright and into a vigorous clap. Helen joined in, keeping her hands close together to stop the miniature from slipping out of her glove. At the corner of her eye, she saw the female Deceiver suddenly turn and stare straight at her, neat features twisted into a look of cold malevolence. Holy God, had the thing recognized her as a Reclaimer? Helen looked back over her shoulder. The other one was staring at her too. Neither was close enough to sense her Reclaimer energy. She searched her mind for any contact: a casual brush in the foyer? No, not that she could recollect. And if one had touched her, it would not have communicated with the other anyway. Perhaps the miniature had drawn their attention. The memory of Jeremiah's screaming face brought certainty. She flicked the portrait out of her glove into her lap, covering it with the end of her shawl. The room plunged back into the dull yellow light of the oil lamps. She took a deep breath, and another, trying to calm her heart.

"Are you all right?" Aunt whispered.

"Yes. Just trying to stop a sneeze."

The clapping eased into silence. The female Deceiver turned to face the orchestra again as lilting strings began the overture's larghetto. Helen studied the woman's tensely held head and rigid shoulders. Rationally, she knew the creature would not attack. Not in the middle of a public concert. But she could feel her blood pulsing with the possibility.

"My dear, look over there." Aunt indicated seats closer to the stage. "The Duke." Helen obediently peered past the ostrich feathers of the ladies seated in front of them and quickly found a set of broad shoulders, neatly cut blond hair, and the unmistakable height that could only be the Duke of Selburn. Mercifully, he was nowhere near the Deceiver and her foul tentacle.

As if suddenly aware of Helen's gaze, the Duke turned in his seat, catching her eye before she could look away. How humiliating. Yet he smiled warmly and bowed his head. She smiled and nodded back.

"Ah, he has seen you," Aunt whispered with satisfaction. "He will seek you out at the interval, mark my words."

Those words turned out to be prescient. In the foyer, during the short interval, he made his way through the crowd and bowed. "I hope I find you well," he said. "But then I see you are both in sparkling form."

"How kind," Aunt said, rising from her curtsy.

"And how are you, Hayden?" he asked Andrew.

"I must say I am champing at the bit for Monday."

"Monday?" Helen asked.

"Selburn and I go to the hanging," Andrew said, grinning at his friend. "Should be famous sport."

"The hanging?" Helen's mouth dried around the words.

"Do you have a room hired, Duke?" Aunt asked.

"No. By the time we had resolved to go, all had been taken. But Byron has invited us to join his party, and I believe he has a room directly opposite the gallows."

Helen closed her eyes. Dear God, no, that had to be in the same row of houses as Lord Carlston's room.

"I fancy being on the ground," Andrew said. "Right in the thick of it."

"I rather thought you would," Selburn said. "We can—"

"No," Helen blurted. "You must not go."

All three pairs of eyes turned to her, startled.

"Helen," Aunt said. "That is not for you to say. Apologize to the Duke."

Selburn brushed it aside with an elegant hand. "There is no need. I am sure Lady Helen is merely voicing her concern for her brother's safety." He smiled at Helen, and the easy warmth of it drew her own smile again. "Please, do not worry. I promise I will not allow any harm to come to this young scapegrace of yours." He turned a mock-stern look upon Andrew. "You have heard your sister, Hayden. We will take up Byron's offer."

Helen saw the twitch of irritation in Andrew's face—he did not appreciate her interference—but Aunt nodded approvingly. "That is very kind of you to take such care of my niece's concern, sir."

"It is my honor, Lady Pennworth." He gave a small bow, turning the end of it toward Helen. "Perhaps your niece would consider riding with me along the Row during the Monday promenade so that I can reassure her that all is well?"

From the corner of her eye, Helen saw Aunt's chest rise with jubilation. "She would be delighted, Duke." Aunt beamed at Helen. "Wouldn't you, my dear?"

Helen curtsied. "That is very kind of you, sir."

"Until Monday then. I must return to my party before the bell is rung."

With a pang of guilt, Helen watched him make his way through the crowd. She truly liked the Duke, yet she could not, in all decency, encourage him now. For a moment she played out the possibility of marrying him. He would, of course, have to be told about the Dark Days Club and the Deceivers, and that would mean he would have no choice but to be drawn into their dangerous struggle, whether he wished to join it or not. And even if he could accept that she was a Reclaimer and had a duty to use her strange talents, he would hardly allow her to train and associate with Lord Carlston, the man who had brutally horsewhipped him and had, by all accounts, murdered the woman he had loved. No, it was completely untenable.

"We must have your new habit by Monday morning, Helen," Aunt said, her own eyes following the Duke. "I pray your hat will be ready, too. You must look your absolute best."

For all the impossibilities of such a union, the idea of them riding together still brought a tantalizing image to mind: their horses walking side by side, Selburn talking to her of art and books, and laughing with her at the latest intrigue. A glimpse of the life she was meant to lead. A life without Deceivers: safe and happy and normal. And yet, that life would also be without Lord Carlston. There was loss wherever she looked, even in the world of her imagination.

"Shall I start calling you Duchess now?" Andrew whispered in her ear. "Selburn's not usually one for riding Rotten Row with women."

Rotten Row. Helen drew in a sharp breath at a sudden idea, feeling the click of old knowledge into new need. Every morning at dawn, the Row was reserved for grooms employed by the Quality to exercise the horses under their care. The rule against galloping was relaxed, and it was not unusual for gentlemen to join the grooms for that opportunity to ride without restriction. Sometimes, even a few ladies joined them; she had done so herself a number of times in the past year.

The bell rang for the end of interval. As they joined the queue into the hall, Helen bent her head as if listening to her aunt's whispered advice about the ride with Selburn. Yet she heard none of it.

Aunt and Uncle would not think her dawn departure too out of the ordinary. Of course, she would have to take one of the grooms for propriety's sake. If Darby were to accompany them, Helen could send the man and Circe back to the stables after the ride, along with the lie that she planned to walk for a while in the park with her maid. Then she and Darby could take a hackney to Newgate. She gripped her reticule tightly, trying to contain her triumph. She had found her way out of the house.

With everyone seated and the orchestra in place, Helen searched the rows at the front of the hall. Where was the woman

Deceiver? Her eyes found a vacant seat: the creature had left. She glanced over her shoulder; the man had gone too.

Again she closed her hand around her reticule—the miniature safely hidden inside—and felt another kind of triumph. Perhaps she had stopped the two creatures after all.

~

AT CHURCH THE next morning, Helen struggled to sit quietly. She had yet to obtain permission from Uncle to ride out early on Monday, and the whole of her plan rested upon his agreement. She stole a glance at his jowly profile, his thick brows drawn together in a thunderous frown at the homily. In celebration of the impending execution, Reverend Haley had decided upon a special hanging sermon, and its vigor was only outdone by its length. Helen stifled a sigh and weaved her gloved fingers together, channeling all her anxiety into the tight clasp. What if Uncle refused?

Finally the good Reverend finished, and Philip was sent to bring the coach around. The sermonizing, however, had not yet ended. On the journey home, Helen and her aunt received a full account of Reverend Haley's theological failures from her uncle, as well as a scathing account of the fool's Whiggish ways. The tirade finished just as the coach made its slow turn into Half Moon Street.

"Uncle," Helen said, seizing the opportunity, "do you think I could stay with the coach to the stables and walk back with Hugo and Philip? I want to organize an early morning ride on the Row tomorrow."

"An early morning ride? On Bellingham's hanging day?" Uncle wiped the end of his nose. "I don't think that would be wise. The city will be under siege by ruffians of all types."

Helen bunched her toes in her boots. "But surely not at the park, Uncle. The jail is on the other side of the city, is it not?

Circe is underexercised, and I am engaged to ride with the Duke of Selburn tomorrow afternoon. I do not want her too fresh for the outing."

Uncle turned a heavy eye upon Helen. "The Duke, hey?"

"Yes, Pennworth," Aunt said briskly. "Andrew says Selburn is quite taken with her, and he seeks her out at every opportunity. I rather imagine that Helen's request is not only to exercise her horse." Aunt gave her an odd smile of conspiracy. "You want to see the lie of the land too, don't you, my dear? Prepare for the prettiest ride."

It had not even occurred to Helen, but she nodded vigorously. The coach drew up to the house. Her uncle did not look convinced.

"Please, sir," Helen added, bringing out her best argument. "I cannot trust any of the grooms to take off Circe's edge. They do not understand her little tricks, and if she is lamed, I will not be able to ride."

"Heaven forbid," Aunt said. "Pennworth, this ride with the Duke is crucial. It must be perfect."

Uncle sniffed. "Very well then, but you must take one of the senior grooms. I'll not have you escorted at such an early hour, and on such a day, by a mere boy."

"Of course," Helen said meekly, trying to contain her exultation. "As you wish, Uncle."

The carriage door opened, and Hugo bent to let down the steps.

"I will send one of the footmen to Mr. Duray's," Aunt said, gathering her shawl and reticule. "We shall insist he deliver your habit in the morning, or lose our custom. But your hat will prove a problem—millinery does take so much longer." Aunt took Hugo's proffered hand. "We will discuss it when you return." She looked up at the dull gray sky. "Do be quick, my dear. I think it will soon rain."

The coach rocked as Aunt and Uncle descended. Helen settled

back into the silk cushions with a sigh of relief. She had done it. Well, at least some of it. At the coachman's call, the carriage jerked into motion again, the town houses passing by in a brisk series of sashed windows and spiked fences. A dark-clad figure caught her eye—a man stepping off the pavement. She pressed her face to the cold window, but a hackney was close behind and blocked the view. Was it Lord Carlston? The sighting had been too fleeting to settle on any firm identity, but she was left with the startling realization that her first thought had been the Earl.

Two streets along, they arrived at Lambeth Mews and the Pennworth stables. The senior groom, Peter, hurried to her side with reassurances that Circe was as bonny as ever, and was her ladyship taking her out today for the promenade? It took only a few minutes to arrange the ride at dawn the next morning, and Peter did not even blink at her unusual order to take Circe straight to Rotten Row rather than bring her round to the house.

Helen smiled to herself. After that initial scare with Uncle, her plan was coming along very nicely; perhaps she could do this after all.

Stocking up on apples from the barrel, she visited Circe, the chestnut mare huffing with recognition over her stall gate. They played Hunt the Treat, Circe bumping Helen's hands in gentle demand and making short, crunching work of the fruit. With a last pat of the glossy neck and a whispered promise of a good gallop the next day, Helen called Philip and Hugo, and they departed on foot. All she had to do now was keep her impatience in check and continue on through an afternoon visit to the watercolor exhibition at Bond Street, followed by a rout at the Harleys'. And then it would be Monday morning, and she would help keep thousands of people safe. An exhilarating and frightening thought.

It was as they turned into Clarges Street that she saw the man standing on the corner of Curzon. Navy greatcoat and black high-crowned beaver: the man who had followed her and Darby on Piccadilly. Helen stopped, her reticule clutched before her like a shield. He must be a Deceiver. Why else would he be following her? She swallowed, mouth suddenly dry. In her mind, once more, she saw the two wicked blue whips snaking from the back of the Vauxhall Gardens Pavor. What if this man had two whips as well, or even three? She wrenched open her reticule, fingers groping for the miniature.

A pale blue shimmer; at least he did not have whips.

Still, how could she fight a Deceiver on her own? She had the strength—if she could control it—but no training. She tried to recollect the battle moves that Lord Carlston had made in Vauxhall: the lunging and rolling. She could not do that in a dress and pelisse. And what about her jewelry? Lord Carlston had said metal meant certain death. She caught at her left earlobe, feeling the smooth gold oval dangling from it. And her gold cross on its chain. Not to mention the pins that fastened her gown and secured her petticoat. No, now she remembered: metal only killed if the creature had whips.

"Is something amiss, my lady?" Hugo asked at her shoulder.

Both footmen must have sensed her alarm, for they had stepped close behind. Deep within, she could feel the savage whisper in her blood, gathering that exhilarating strength.

The man began to walk toward them. He was intent upon her; she could see it. His features tugged at her memory. She had seen him before, some place other than the predatory walk along Piccadilly. But where?

"We will cross the street," she said, and stepped off the pavement, leading the way swiftly to the other side.

The greatcoated man paused, clearly perturbed. From the alley behind him, another figure emerged. Stocky and dark, barrel chest heaving from exertion. She had seen him before too; he brought an image of night and trees and cold. She frowned. Bales! That was his name: one of his lordship's men. At Vauxhall Gardens. He was a guard. *Her* guard. The realization brought a moment of giddy relief.

Her Reclaimer sight caught a flash of metal and polished wood in Bales's hand. A pistol! Good God, did he intend to shoot the Deceiver? Andrew always said pistols were unreliable. But even a wounding shot would give her a chance.

"What is happening, my lady?" Philip demanded. He was alongside her, large hands clenched, and she could hear the growing excitement in his voice.

She shook her head. What could she say: that a hellish creature in a man's body was about to attack, and a guard from a secret society was going to shoot him? She scanned the street: a solid line of houses with steps up to the front doors and down into the basement yards. There would be no way out except *through* a stranger's home. The man in the greatcoat stepped off the curb. Helen slowed. There was no use rushing to meet him.

"I think we should see what this flash cove wants," Philip murmured to Hugo. "What do you say?"

Hugo nodded, squaring up. "I am with you."

"No, don't approach him," Helen ordered. If the man was a Deceiver, he could rip the footmen apart.

"But, my lady, we—" Philip said.

"No, do as I say." She heard the young footman's huff of frustration.

Helen tensed, the pound of her heart joining the roar of her blood. She had to do something before Philip and Hugo stepped into a danger they could not even imagine. The miniature had shown her that the man had no whips, and surely he would not attack in the middle of Mayfair. Did she dare approach him and demand what he wanted? She had her strength. And she had the miniature. Perhaps it would frighten him away, as it had the two Deceivers at the concert.

She looked over her shoulder. "Stay where you are."

Philip's mouth thinned in mutiny. "My lady, no!"

"I mean it, Philip. Move, and you shall be dismissed."

Hugo caught Philip's arm. "You heard her ladyship."

Gathering her courage, Helen walked forward, hands clenched around her reticule. Five, six, seven paces away from the anxious presence of her footmen.

"You there," she called to the man standing directly across the road. "What do you want?"

He lifted his hand in a wave. "Lady Helen!" He paused, waiting for a curricle to pass, then hurried across the grit and mud. "It is Sir Desmond. May I speak to you?"

Helen drew in a shaking breath. Of course: Sir Desmond, the Palace official at her presentation. Surely he could not be a Deceiver. Could he?

"I am sorry to have alarmed you, my lady," he said, stepping onto the pavement. He lowered his voice until Helen could barely hear it. "I have a message for you from Her Majesty, Queen Charlotte."

"From the Queen?" Helen repeated, suspended between shock and distrust. The pound of her blood pulled her up onto her toes.

"Yes, my lady." He reached into his coat and withdrew a thick packet, shielding it from curious eyes. "I am to deliver this to you on Her Majesty's bidding."

Emblazoned upon the folded parchment was the large red Royal seal. She had seen the same on the summons for her presentation. He really *was* delivering a message from the Queen. She looked wildly beyond him. Mr. Bales had stepped off the curb and was crossing the road, the pistol in his hand.

"No!" she yelled, waving him back.

Sir Desmond recoiled. "But my lady, this is on Her Majesty's order."

Bales halted and gave her a hard stare, but that ominous flash of gray metal and wood was back under his jacket.

"Sir Desmond," Helen said, wrenching her attention back to the bewildered man, "I am sorry. Of course I will accept it." Hastily remembering her manners, she curtsied. "My apologies. You took me by surprise."

"No, no, it is I who must apologize." He bowed. "It has been quite challenging to find an appropriate moment to place this in your hands. I think I alarmed you last week on Piccadilly."

"Yes. Forgive me, I did not recognize you." Helen could not take her eyes from the letter clasped in Sir Desmond's elegantly gloved hand. "What is this message you bring me?"

He looked past her to Hugo and Philip a good distance beyond. "It is a private matter, Lady Helen."

"Private?" It was all becoming more and more extraordinary. She turned to the footmen. They were beyond casual earshot, but Sir Desmond's caution was contagious. "Wait at the corner," she called.

"But my lady—" Hugo protested.

"Go. Now!" Helen said.

What could the Queen possibly want with her?

Sir Desmond waited until the two footmen were well beyond sight or sound. "Lady Helen, the Queen's conditions under which I was to deliver this to you were very specific: you were not to be in the company of family or friends, and it was to be in your hands within a month of your presentation. I was beginning to despair of finding such a moment." He held out the letter. "Her Majesty said to tell you that this is from your mother, Lady Catherine."

Helen stared down at it. "My mother?" She took hold of the thick paper. It was real. "But how?"

"Her Majesty said that Lady Catherine once did a great service for her, and in return was offered a Royal boon. All that the Countess required from Her Majesty was that she keep a letter for you. It was to be delivered after your presentation if both your parents were no longer living." He crossed himself, soft sympathy in his face. "May they rest in peace. I have now discharged my duty. There is only one more message to pass on to you. Directly from Her Majesty. She said to tell you, 'Sometimes there is no good choice.'"

He bowed again, his large brown eyes kind. "I wish you well, my lady. Good day."

Helen curtsied, the letter from her mother pressed hard against her chest.

Twenty-Three

HELEN WATCHED SIR Desmond walk away, every part of her wanting to rip open the letter and read it. She looked down at the thick wax disc of the Royal seal. No, this had to be done in private. With shaking fingers, she undid the top two buttons of her pelisse and shoved the letter against her gown bodice.

A quick glance along the street confirmed that Bales had gone too, or at least had retreated to a less visible vantage point. Helen waved Hugo and Philip to join her again. Had they seen the Royal seal? She hoped not. She pressed her hand to her chest, feeling the stiff parchment. Whatever they had seen, it would be all around the servants before long, and then to the ears of Aunt and Uncle. Accepting a clandestine letter from a man was a serious transgression of propriety. They would demand to read it, and when it was discovered to be from her mother, Uncle would most certainly burn it. Somehow, she had to forestall the gossip. She braced her feet more firmly on the pavement flags, an idea dawning. Perhaps she could direct the inevitable whispers toward a tale that would prompt her aunt to defend her privacy rather than invade it—in the name of matrimonial ambition.

"Are you all right, my lady?" Philip asked.

"Yes, quite," Helen said. "That was a friend of the Duke of Selburn's," she added. Both footmen were straining to hide their interest. "He had a message from His Grace."

"Yes, my lady," Hugo said blandly, but he sent a salacious glance to Philip.

Helen looked away and cleared her throat. The hallmarks, she hoped, of a lover, caught out. "I would not want to bother my aunt or uncle with the thought that the Duke was corresponding with me."

"No, my lady," Philip said quickly. His face, unlike Hugo's, held sympathy. Helen allowed herself a small inner smile of relief. Philip was a romantic; he would defend her secret.

"Or any of the other servants," she continued firmly. "I would be most appreciative of such discretion." She swung her reticule, the movement bringing both footmen's eyes to it.

"I saw nothing out of the ordinary on this walk," Philip said.

"Nor I," Hugo agreed.

Helen nodded her thanks. Hopefully her story and the promise of money would be enough.

—

THE RETURN WALK was swift, the letter like a burning coal against Helen's chest. She was lucky: Aunt was still in her dressing room, and Uncle had already retired to the library, as was his wont before Sunday luncheon. She passed through the foyer and up the stairs with only a nod to Barnett.

Inside her bedchamber, all was quiet. The morning fire in the grate had burned out, so only a dull light from the threatening sky came through the unshuttered windows.

"Darby?" she called.

There was no answer. Fingers fumbling at the buttons of her pelisse, Helen peered into the dressing room. Empty. Either Darby was at a task elsewhere, or still at the servants' dinner. She shut the adjoining door and hurried to the window: it would take too long to light a candle.

She pulled out the packet and turned it over; the front was inscribed with her name in the formal calligraphy of the Court. A letter from her mother: she could barely believe it. A flick of her thumbnail and the wax seal broke with a crack. Inside was another packet, bearing her name in her mother's neat hand and another seal, this time with the Hayden arms. She cracked the wax, her hands shaking as she unfolded the pages. Shaking so much she could not read the writing. With a soft sob of impatience, she anchored the letter between her hands on the recess of the windowsill and, by the dim light, read the first words she had received from her mother in ten years.

Windsor Castle. 10th April 1802

To Helen, my dear daughter,

It is hard to imagine that you are reading this, aged eighteen and a woman, when I know that at this moment you are sleeping in your bed at Deanswood, only eight years old and as smart and mischievous as a monkey. Or perhaps I should say that you should be sleeping in your bed, for I know that you are probably hunched over one of your books, burning a four-hour candle stolen from Mrs. Lockwood's household stores.

Helen smiled through a blur of sudden tears. Her mother had once caught her stealing a six-hour candle, and had solemnly advised her to take only the shorter four-hour candles. "Less likely to be noticed," she'd said. Of course, Helen now knew that a housekeeper as assiduous as Mrs. Lockwood would have noticed even the loss of a pin, but somehow the missing candles had been consistently overlooked. Helen drew a sharp breath. Only her mother and Mrs. Lockwood would have known about the candles. Her mother was using the memory as proof that she had indeed written the letter.

I have rendered a service for Her Majesty, Queen Charlotte—one mother to another. As a reward, she has agreed to deliver this letter to you on the event of your Court Presentation if your dear father and I have already departed this world. Therefore, I write this knowing that if it does come to your hand, you and your brother have been alone for a time, and that our plans to flee did not succeed.

There is, of course, so much I wish to say to you, but the Queen awaits this letter, and so it must be brief.

By now you will be aware that you are different, that you have abilities beyond that of a normal man or woman. Perhaps you have even heard the phrase lusus naturae. I saw these abilities in you early—a shock, since they are not usually inherited, and Andrew showed no sign of them—and, to my everlasting grief, I did not keep the knowledge to myself. I am assuming that you have been approached and tested by others with the same gifts. If they are still alive, it may be Mr. Samuel Benchley, or Sir Dennis Calloway, or the young Earl of Carlston, Mr. Benchley's new acolyte. These are the men I know, all of them lusus naturae *too. All of them Reclaimers.*

Do not trust them, dearest. They are monsters.

Helen stopped. Reread the sentence: *Do not trust them.* She stared unseeingly at the roof of the opposite town house. The shock of the warning proved one thing—she had been lying to herself. For all her protestations to Darby, she did trust Lord Carlston, and now her mother had reached from her grave to name him a monster. Helen shook her head. Ten years had passed, and from what she had seen, he was no longer Benchley's acolyte.

Have they shown you the Deceivers? Told you their history? Impressed your own importance and destiny upon you? Mr. Benchley did the same to me—he was my mentor—and I felt the call of duty, for the threat of the creatures is undeniable. The Dark Days Club—that is their name—will tell you our duty is to contain them, and to rip the vestige from the souls of their progeny to reclaim the children back to full humanity.

They will not have told you what that does to us.

By the time I learned the truth, it was too late: my soul had been compromised.

When a Reclaimer takes the vestige

from a progeny's soul, it cannot be discharged into the earth like the energy from the whips. A vestige stays within the Reclaimer's soul—a darkness that eats away at our very essence. With each reclaiming, a little more darkness is deposited, until eventually it destroys all capacity for compassion, for love, and brings madness. A Reclaimer must stop before such darkness envelops him, or he will become a monster. A mad brute capable only of killing.

Helen raised her eyes from the paper. That was what she had seen in Lord Carlston's soul: the darkness from reclaiming. And perhaps it explained Mr. Benchley.

No doubt you also know that, as women, we are expected to take up much of the burden of reclaiming, as we, of course, do not fight like our male counterparts. I was willing to do my duty, for the descent into darkness takes years and, after all, was I not going to stop reclaiming before it affected me?

Helen frowned. Lord Carlston had made it clear that he wished her to fight. Had that been a lie, or had something fundamental changed? Her mother was right about one thing, though. He had failed to tell her about the terrifying effect of the vestige darkness. Helen pressed her hand under her breast, a small aching pain making it hard to draw breath.

Mr. Benchley, however, discovered an ancient way to rid himself of all the darkness he had already accrued, and so extend his ability to fight and reclaim and hold off the madness. All he needed was a vessel, and what better vessel than a woman? During a reclaiming—without my knowledge or consent—Mr. Benchley poured all the darkness of his own soul into mine. Shared the burden, he said. I could feel love dying within me, my darling daughter. It was agony, and it continues to be so, but I am not totally destroyed. I have a tiny corner of love left for you and Andrew and your father, and I will defend it to the very last.

Helen closed her eyes, unable to keep reading. She had seen what one reclaiming had done to Lord Carlston. What had her poor mother suffered at Benchley's hands, with so much darkness poured into her all at once? The man was beyond a monster. Helen clenched the edge of the windowsill, a sudden rage rocking her on her feet. The wood shifted and creaked under her Reclaimer strength. She snatched her hands away. If she were not careful, she would break the window in her fury. How she wished she could take all her new strength and make Mr. Benchley suffer.

She stared down at her clenched hands, an awful connection clicking into place. Good God, that was what Lord Carlston and Quinn had been talking about in the Devil's Acre: Mr. Benchley had proposed to dump all his darkness into her soul, as he had done to her mother, and invited his lordship to do the same. Helen grabbed the edge of the sill again, this time for support. His lordship had said nothing could be done until she had her Reclaimer strength. Now she had it.

I will defend you to the very last too, my darling. I did not have a true choice, but you do, Helen. It is not only Mr. Benchley who can use ancient alchemy for his own ends.

I have bequeathed to you a miniature of myself painted by Sir Joshua Reynolds. By God's mercy, I hope that you have it.

Helen clutched the reticule still hanging from her wrist.

Set at its back is a disc of woven hair. You will have been told it is made from my own and your father's hair: a love token. It is not. It is made from three sources: my hair, your hair, and a Deceiver's hair, taken at its final death.

A Deceiver's hair? She yanked open the reticule and slid the miniature into her cupped hand. The portrait had of course not changed, but her mother's face seemed more somber now, and the painted blue eyes looked straight at her as if, any moment, they would blink and the image would whisper the words on the page. Unsettled by such vivid imagining, Helen turned it over. Now that she knew, the weave of her mother's auburn hair did seem to hold a slightly darker strand. That must be her own. And the blond hair had belonged to a Deceiver, not her father. This was the reason she could see Deceivers' life-forces. But why did the miniature create such fear within Jeremiah?

The three strands are bound together by ancient alchemy and by God's love. They are woven into a way for your soul to escape destruction. Undo the three strands, purify them with fire to take them back to their elements, and absorb them into yourself, and you will undo your Reclaimer powers. They will be stripped from you. No longer will you be in peril from Deceivers or the Dark Days Club. You will be normal and able to live a life full of love and compassion with your eternal grace safe.

Our gifts are linked to the energies within the earth. We are at our strongest at the full and new moons when those night energies work upon the earth's very structure. You must do this on a full moon, at the peak of its rise—midnight—for it to fully take effect. Burn the three strands, mix them with sanctified water and, on the last stroke of twelve, drink. It will, I am told, be very fast.

There is one other warning I must give you, and which you must consider alongside the danger you face. I do not know how much of our natures are linked to our Reclaimer gifts. It is probable that as they are stripped away, you will also lose some aspects of yourself that you treasure. Some of your quickness, perhaps, and cleverness. Perhaps even your natural curiosity. I cannot be certain, but there will be change to your essential self. It is a sacrifice, I know, but you will have safety and a normal life and a soul without the darkness of the Deceivers upon it. You will be able to love with joy.

Helen stopped, and reread the warning. Lose one's quickness and cleverness—would anyone choose that? She stared through the window at the leaden sky, feeling a terrible sense of foreboding.

There is now a new truce with France, and your father and I have a plan to flee England and the Dark Days Club with you and your brother. We will find a place on the Continent where we can live in some kind of safety. Where I can search for a way to rid myself of Benchley's darkness, or at least save what is left of my eternal grace. I will not lose the ability to love you and Andrew or your dear father, not for any duty. Not even for my country. But then, if you are reading this, it is almost certain that our plan failed. I know that I leave you in danger again, and it makes me heartsick. Yet I gain some comfort in the thought that you may have the miniature and a way to escape what I could not.

Save yourself, Helen.

With my everlasting love,
Your mother,
Catherine Wrexhall

Helen gave a soft moan. Now she knew why her mother had been named a traitor. She had refused the role that the Dark Days Club and the Home Office had forced upon her, and had planned to flee. She had turned her back on her country to save her family. No wonder the Queen had said, *Sometimes there is no good choice.*

~

A KNOCK ON the door lifted Helen's head from a third reading of the letter.

At some point during the second, she had lit a candle and propped herself against the headboard of her bed, knees drawn to her chest, miniature clenched in one hand and the letter held in the other to save it from her tears. Now, staring at the door, she felt frozen in that position, as though she might break if she moved.

"Who is it?" Her voice had dried into a croak, and her pelisse and gown were hopelessly creased. If it was her aunt, she would have to claim the female malady.

"It is Darby."

"Come."

Darby bustled into the room and closed the door. "My lady, Mrs. Grant wishes me to tell you that Cook has made your favorite apple tart for luncheon." She stopped midway between door and bed. "My lady, are you ill? Shall I fetch help?"

"No." Helen motioned her closer. "I have received a letter from my mother, Darby. It came via the Queen." She gave a curt account of its delivery and then held out the sheets of paper. "Read it."

Darby's cheeks reddened. "I am not quick at reading, my lady."

Helen shook her head—it did not matter—and pressed the letter into her maid's hands. She watched as Darby slowly read Lady Catherine's words, their import building into a soft, horrified gasp as she reached the end. "Oh, my lady." Darby looked up from the pages. "His lordship should have told you about the darkness."

"Yes, he should have." Helen reached for the letter, needing her mother's words, her mother's love, back in her hands. "Darby, I overheard a conversation between Lord Carlston and Quinn after we saved Jeremiah. It did not make sense at the time, but now I think Mr. Benchley has proposed a plan to his lordship: to use me in the same manner as he used my mother."

Darby pressed her hands against her chest, as if her heart hurt. "Do you really think his lordship would do such a thing?"

"I don't know."

Darby shook her head. "I cannot believe it, my lady. Not Lord Carlston."

"My mother says he is not to be trusted, and I have seen the darkness in him." Helen rubbed her swollen, burning eyes. "What do we know of him after all? That he is accused of killing his wife. That he was mentored by a monster."

"He saved Jeremiah," Darby said, a soft note of defiance in her voice. "And Mr. Quinn is a good man. He trusts his lordship."

Helen smiled bleakly. "A character reference from a servant who stabs his master in the hand."

"It is his job, my lady, and he is a protector of children and . . ." She sighed—an acknowledgment of her own doubt—and gestured to the miniature. "Will you use it, my lady?"

"I don't know." Helen balanced the portrait on her palm. So

much power in such a tiny gold case. "If I do, Darby, you will not be a Terrene." She rubbed her thumb across the glass that shielded the checkerboard of hair. And what would she, herself, be? A vapid girl with no sense or curiosity, with nothing special about her except forty thousand pounds?

"That does not matter, my lady," Darby said. "You know I will follow you in whatever you do. Whatever decision you make." She paused, her voice dropping to a whisper. "But if you do use it, your mother says it will change you. Forever."

Helen nodded at the echo of her own fear. "I must speak to his lordship," she finally said. "Tomorrow."

"But surely you will not go to the hanging," Darby said vehemently. "Not after this."

"I must," Helen said. "People will be at risk." She looked at her maid's mutinous face. "I gave my word I would be there. And I need to know the truth."

~

LATER, WHEN DARBY left the room to collect heated water for the washbasin, Helen forced her stiff body to move to her writing desk. She unlocked the desk hatch and retrieved her copy of *The Magus* from its position next to her confirmation Bible and the current edition of *Old Moore's Almanack*. A flick through *The Magus* quickly found the required page: "Of Sorceries." Helen slid her mother's letter into its new hiding place and closed the book. She slotted it back on the shelf, her hand hovering before the spine of *Old Moore's*. Her mother had said the alchemy must be used at a full moon. She pulled out the almanack and leafed to the moon pages, running her finger down the phases for May 1812.

Of course, she already knew the answer: the next full moon was on the twenty-sixth. If she was going to use the miniature to strip herself of her Reclaimer abilities, it would have to be at midnight at her own ball. On the anniversary of the news of her parents' death. She replaced the almanack, closed the desk hatch, and turned the lock. A grimly appropriate date, she thought as she pressed the key back into its spring-loaded secret compartment.

Twenty-Four

Monday, 18 May 1812

HELEN SAT FORWARD on the worn seat of the hackney carriage and pressed her fingertips against the side pins that secured her veil. She peered through the fine Mechlin lace at the passing shop fronts, trying to ignore the overwhelming aroma of fresh bread in the cabin; whoever had hired the carriage before her must have been carrying a new-baked loaf.

Across from her, Darby sighed. "Heavens, that smell makes me feel hungry. I should have brought some food for us, my lady."

Helen shook her head. How could Darby even think of eating? So far, the morning had gone as planned, but she still felt sick with anxiety.

They had arrived at Hyde Park Corner at daybreak to find Bernard, one of the senior grooms, waiting with Circe at the start of Rotten Row. Helen had galloped the mare for twenty minutes, with Bernard riding his hack close behind, while Darby watched from the path. She had then handed Circe back to the groom with the instruction to tell Barnett that she would walk for a while before breakfast. All as smooth as silk. Hailing the hackney on Park Lane had been easy too, although the driver had warned her that going anywhere near Newgate Prison that morning would be difficult.

But now they were on their way, and that meant she was getting closer and closer to Lord Carlston. And closer to the truth.

"Darby, are you certain you cannot see my face?" she asked, patting the pins again.

"Yes, my lady. Your features are not clear at all. I anchored the veil hard into your hair. It won't come off."

The veil had been a last-minute addition under her riding hat: a disguise for the walk to Lord Carlston's hired room. It would be a disaster if someone recognized her in the crowd. Helen knitted her fingers together in her lap and prayed: *Lord, please don't let Andrew or the Duke see me today.*

The carriage made its slow way along High Holborn. A remarkable number of people, mainly men, were spilling from the pavements in front of the carriage and walking on the sides of the gravel road toward Newgate, heads hunched into collars against the drizzling rain. Helen heard their driver curse loudly as a group of young bucks cut in front of his horses. They yelled back, their remarks lost in the sound of the wheels and the shouts from a line of oystermen turning a profit from barrels on the corner. A solid wall of people and red-coated soldiers blocked one side of Snow Hill and the mouth of Skinner Street. It was going to take a while to negotiate their way closer to the prison.

Helen sat back again, her hand finding the edge of the riband under the collar of her riding habit; she had hung the miniature around her neck for safekeeping. She would honor her promise today and help his lordship find the Deceivers in the crowd. After that, she did not know what she was going to do. She laid her palm against her chest, feeling the hard oval under the olive wool. Did he still want her to fight at his side, or did he now intend to use her as a vessel for his own darkness? It was the first thing she must find out. And even if he did want her to fight, did she actually want to join the Dark Days Club?

She had a way out now. She pressed harder on the miniature beneath her coat. It was an impossible choice: a safe life with a family of her own, but with part of her essential self destroyed and a duty abandoned; or a life using all of her gifts in the service of mankind, but filled with loneliness, danger, and the prospect of madness. Nor did it make it any easier to know that one life possibly held the Duke of Selburn, and the other Lord Carlston.

"My lady," Darby said, "I am not sure we are going to get through Smithfield. There are already so many people about."

"I know. We will just have to get as close as we can."

Darby pointed out of the window. "Oh, my lady, look!"

A large placard came into view, carried on a pole by a soldier. Helen read the inscription painted in black letters:

**BEWARE OF ENTERING THE CROWD!
REMEMBER, THIRTY PERSONS WERE
CRUSHED TO DEATH BY THE CROWD
WHEN HAGGERTY AND HOLLOWAY
WERE EXECUTED.**

"Well, that is to the point, isn't it?" Helen said.

They turned into Cow Lane, inching behind a line of other coaches. Helen slid along the seat and peered out of the opposite window, her veil softening the colors and shapes of the street and buildings. The first lane through to Giltspur Street was full of chattering, yelling people. No room for a coach even to push its way through. If the next was in the same state, she and Darby would have to get out and make their way on foot.

Hosier Lane was still open: a contingent of soldiers was keeping the road clear. The hackney turned into the narrow lane and ponderously made its way to the other end—Giltspur Street—at the bottom of Smithfield Market.

"We will get out here and walk," Helen said.

Darby twisted around and rapped on the cabin wall. "Stop here," she called.

The carriage drew to a halt.

"Here we go, my lady," Darby said, and, with an anxious smile, opened the door and descended, holding out her hand.

Gathering the long train of her habit over her arm, Helen stepped to the wet ground. The sound hit her first—thousands of voices raised in excitement—and then came the stench, a wet-wool smell of damp humanity mixed with the sickening decay from the nearby cattle and meat market.

A surge of people surrounded the carriage as they headed toward the prison, pushing Helen back against the wet, grimy coach door. A man thrust a handbill at her as he passed, his face a pale blur through her veil, and in reflex she took it. The smeared black print stated:

DO NOT ENTER THE CROWD!

Dropping the paper, she pressed the veil over her nose and, with Darby at her heels, edged her way to the front of the coach to hand up the fare to the driver. He squinted down at her as he took the coins. "Are ye sure ye want to be 'ere, madam?" he yelled.

"Quite sure."

"Good luck to ye then." He touched his hat and then snapped his whip between his horses, the old carriage lurching off toward the market.

"Stay close, Darby." Helen pulled her maid's arm through her own. She had never been in the middle of so many people. "We must not be separated."

"Are there any of the creatures near us, my lady?" Darby asked, scouring the crowd around them. "Should you check, perhaps?"

A good idea. Lord Carlston had warned that just a few skimming Deceivers could cause a deadly crush. The thought of his lordship brought an anxious skip to her heart. She pulled her glove from her hand, hooked the miniature on its riband out from beneath her habit, and scanned the multitude.

A glow of pale blue sprang up around the mass of people. At the corner of her eye, she caught a flick of brighter blue at the bottom of the hill near Newgate Street. Two—no, three—men standing in a tight group, all of them with tentacles reaching out and skimming energy from the people milling around them. It looked as if the creatures were even conversing. Helen shook her head. She must be mistaken: Deceivers did not band together.

She narrowed her eyes, focusing on the three men, and saw them turn, as if one, in her direction. The miniature! They could sense the miniature when she held it, just like the two Deceivers at the concert. She stuffed it back beneath her coat, watching as the three lost their point of focus. Their heads bent together in obvious discussion. What could such collusion mean?

"You saw some, my lady?"

"Yes," Helen said. She smiled reassuringly. "But we are far from them."

Darby regarded her for a moment, clearly sensing her disquiet, but nodded.

Green Dragon Lane, where they were to meet Mr. Quinn, was a good distance past the entrance to St. Bartholomew's Hospital on the opposite side of the street. Helen made for that entrance, pulling Darby into the crowd. Immediately they were caught up in the frightening push toward the prison. Helen felt Darby's arm drag on her own as the girl slipped on the carpet of wet handbills underfoot. Helen pulled her upright, glimpsing Darby's startled eyes at the show of strength. A sudden, astounding realization stopped her in the midst of the maelstrom: if need be, she could force her way out. She had Reclaimer strength. For a moment she felt gloriously invincible, and then sudden, hot pain burst through her exhilaration. Some oaf had stood upon her toes through the thin leather of her boot. An elbow caught her in the ribs. She felt her breath, hot and fast, on her skin, trapped by the screen of her veil.

"Hello, lovely!" a man shouted near her ear, the words reeking of liquor. He grabbed at the veil, but was shoved away by a stout lady using a large basket to gouge her way through the pack of people.

With a tug on Darby's arm, Helen pulled them into the woman's wake, gaining immeasurable ground behind the matron's formidable momentum. They reached the entrance to the hospital, and Helen spied the mouth of Green Dragon Lane less than ten houses away.

"Nearly there, Darby!" she yelled.

"I can see Mr. Quinn," Darby cried. She pointed ahead.

Helen caught sight of him too, his height and hat placing him a good head taller than the crowd. He stood against a wall, scanning the multitude, his tattooed face fierce with concentration. For all the lack of room, people were giving him a wide berth.

He saw Darby and held up his hand.

"Thank goodness," she said.

Helen heard the relief in her maid's voice, and the warmth. She understood it—Mr. Quinn had a sturdy presence that always gave comfort—yet she had to remember that he had also urged his lordship to use her as a vessel. He might be an ally for the moment, but he was not her friend.

The crowd carried them forward. But even as Helen gathered herself, ready to wrench Darby sideways, Mr. Quinn stepped out, grabbed her wrist and Darby's forearm, and yanked them into Green Dragon Lane like a fisherman hooking two salmon.

"My apologies for manhandling you, my lady," he said, abruptly letting them go as they stumbled into the relative quiet of the lane.

"Lordy be, I thought we were going to sail right by," Darby said breathlessly, smiling up at him.

He smiled back. "Nothing to fear, miss. I had you."

Darby covered her mouth, stifling a giggle. "I daresay you have not!"

Shocked, Helen stared at her maid's flushed countenance. "Darby!"

The girl looked demurely at the puddled ground, but the edge of the smile was still in her voice. "I'm sorry, my lady."

Mr. Quinn's skin had darkened to a deep rosy gold. He cleared his throat. "You are late. It is near half seven, and Bellingham hangs on the hour. We must be swift."

He led them past a group of well-dressed men and women also taking refuge in the short lane. Although Helen's veil was still in place, she felt a moment of relief that she knew none of them. "Mr. Quinn," she said.

The big man looked back. "Yes, my lady?"

"I saw something strange in the crowd: three of the creatures, conversing. I am sure they were together."

Mr. Quinn frowned, his tattoos angling into ferocity. "That would be most unusual," he said slowly. "And most unwelcome. Are you sure?"

"Yes."

"Tell his lordship as soon as you see him," Mr. Quinn advised. He stopped at a small gap between two houses. "We cut through here."

Helen peered down the narrow walkway. It looked to be more mud than path, with an overpowering odor of urine and feces in the damp air.

"Pe-ew, that does stink," Darby said, pinching her nostrils together.

"Aye, it does," Mr. Quinn said. "But better a stink than be in that crowd out there."

Helen had no argument with that. She hitched her train more securely over her arm, gathered up her hem, and followed Mr. Quinn into the befouled alley. At each step, her boots sank into the slimy ground, the cold wetness seeping through the leather. Behind her, she heard Darby's soft grunt of disgust. They would both have to throw boots and stockings away after this expedition.

The alley turned a sharp right. Through open gates and tumble-down brick fences, Helen glimpsed the ramshackle backyards of five dwellings before they came to the last house at the end. By her reckoning, it had to be the corner of Giltspur and Newgate Streets, opposite the prison. The alley narrowed to an opening onto Giltspur, barely three bricks wide. Beyond it, all Helen could see was a solid wall of people on the roadway, waiting for the spectacle of death. The last house was apparently their destination, for Mr. Quinn hammered on a stout gate set into its intact high brick fence. He stepped back as it rattled—swollen, wet wood sticking—then sprang open. Mr. Bales peered out, a lethal-looking truncheon in his hand. "You, then," he said.

"Aye," Quinn answered.

Mr. Bales lowered the weapon and stood back. "Morning, my lady," he murmured. "His lordship is upstairs."

The yard was, at least, paved, with a brick privy in the corner, and coal and ash bins set side by side along the wall that bordered Giltspur Street. A large water butt stood beside the back door, collecting rain from the gutters above.

Inside, the house was a pleasant surprise. Helen followed Mr. Quinn through a clean, neat kitchen and felt a moment of regret at leaving such a track of filth on the scrubbed floor. Through the connecting doorway, a gloomy hallway stretched ahead. She could barely see its end through the veil. She stopped, pulling the lace aside. "Darby, can you do something with this, please?"

Darby removed the riding hat and folded the veil back over

Helen's hair, pinning it in place. With deft fingers she tucked back an errant curl, then replaced the hat and nodded her approval. "It looks well, my lady."

"It does not matter how I look."

Darby raised her brows but said nothing.

They entered the long hallway, papered in a stylish red-and-gray stripe. A narrow staircase was set along the right wall. Helen looked through an open doorway to the left and glimpsed a glass-fronted bookcase and a wing-back chair: a library or study. This was the house of a gentleman, or at least a professional man.

"Is the owner here?" she asked as they climbed the stairs.

"Aye. But he and his wife are in their boudoir and will not be paid if they come down while we are here. His lordship has leased the whole house."

He stopped in front of a closed door on the first landing and knocked.

"Come." It was Lord Carlston's voice.

"My lady, his lordship wishes Miss Darby to stay here with me," Mr. Quinn said as he opened the door.

"No!" Darby protested. "I will not leave my lady's side."

"It is all right," Helen soothed. It was a definite step away from propriety, but so was accusing a man of lying and conspiring to destroy a soul. Her soul.

Mr. Quinn stood back and bowed. With a deep breath, Helen walked through the doorway, hearing the latch click shut at her back. She stopped a few steps into the room, held motionless by the bleak view through the front windows: a huge gray brick wall—the prison—with a gallows set on a high platform before it, a noose suspended from the crossarm. She looked away, her gaze ranging across the room to find his lordship, still in his greatcoat, standing before the hearth. And beside him, a yellow silk sofa. With another man seated upon it. Mr. Benchley.

Helen froze.

"Lady Helen," his lordship said, bowing.

Mr. Benchley rose to his feet and bowed. "Your ladyship, how pleasant to see you again." He smiled, the silky falseness of it tightening Helen's scalp. "So soon."

Helen clenched her reticule, wishing it were a knife or sword. This was the man who had almost destroyed her mother's soul. And he wanted to do the same to her, too.

She drew in a ragged breath. "What is he doing here?"

Lord Carlston frowned. "Mr. Benchley is here at my invitation. I want him to see your abilities."

Helen gave a small, pained laugh. *At his invitation?* Her mother was right: they *were* in league together.

His lordship stepped forward, plainly seeing her distrust. "I can assure you, Mr. Benchley is here to assist, Lady Helen." He motioned to a small table with pieces of different cloth laid out upon it. "So far I have seen only ten Deceivers, but let me show you the flag system I have developed."

"Assist?" Her vehemence stopped Carlston. "That man is here to destroy my soul." She took a breath, forcing more measure into her tone. "I know about the vestige darkness that comes from reclaiming, Lord Carlston. I know he wants to unload his own darkness into my soul. Has he invited you to do the same?"

His lordship stiffened. "How do you know about that?"

Helen stepped back. Dear God, she was right.

"Yes, how *do* you know about that?" Benchley asked. He leaned upon his cane, that terrifying smile widening.

"A letter has come into my hands from my mother, written before she died. It explains everything," she said. "How you forced her to take your corruption. She said I cannot trust either of you, and she was right."

"Do not be so dramatic, girl," Benchley said calmly. "It was her duty as a Reclaimer and a woman. As it is yours."

Carlston rounded on Benchley. "You did not tell me you had done a vestige transfer to her mother!"

Benchley shrugged. "It is why I have been able to continue for the last ten years." He cocked his head. An invitation. "So, you see, it does work. You will get another decade, William."

Carlston shook his head. "It is not Lady Helen's duty to take the darkness from your soul, or mine, Samuel. I believe it would be a waste for us even to limit her to reclaiming progeny—she is not like the other female Reclaimers. She must fight like us. I brought you here to see her strength. To show you the miniature and what it can do in her hands. I tell you, she is a direct inheritor, and she is here to fight a Grand Deceiver. We would be stupid to reduce her to a refuse pit for our own use."

Through her fury and fear, Helen felt a surge of relief: his lordship was not planning to destroy her soul. But she continued. "You both stand there discussing me as if I have no say in the matter. Why didn't you tell me about the vestige darkness, Lord Carlston? Why did you lie?"

He straightened as if her words had been the flick of a whip. "Lie? I did not lie. I wanted you to come willingly to the Dark Days Club, Lady Helen, with true conviction. I wanted you to *choose* to fight. This duty of ours is a heavy responsibility, and it must be done with full commitment."

"No woman would choose to fight," Benchley scoffed. "A woman is made to do as men tell her; that is the natural order."

Carlston rounded on him again. "And that worked out well with her mother, didn't it?"

"It worked out well enough for me," Benchley said calmly.

Helen sucked in a breath. "You nearly destroyed her!"

"For the good of England. I was far more valuable than your

mother." He glanced at Carlston. "I am still far more valuable than this chit."

Such callous disdain! Barely holding her rage in check, Helen said to Carlston, "You kept the truth from me so that I would make the choice you wanted me to make."

His lordship looked away, conceding the point. "I was waiting until you had your full strength to tell you. I wanted you to feel the power, to enjoy it, before I explained the negative side of our calling."

"But you didn't tell me when my strength came, did you?" she accused. Silently, she added, *Instead you almost kissed me. Why?* Surely he could see the question within her eyes.

"That was a mistake," he said.

She stared at him. Did he mean failing to tell her, or the almost-kiss? But his face was closed.

Benchley lifted his head, his expression sharp and predatory. "She has her full strength?"

"Do not even think it, Samuel," Carlston said coldly. "Lady Helen, I wanted you to make your own choice, but do you not see that, in the end, there is no choice? You are a Reclaimer."

"You are wrong. I do have a choice," Helen said. She raised her hand to the miniature beneath her coat. "My mother has given me one."

For a moment there was a heavy silence.

"What do you mean?" Carlston said.

Benchley gave a soft laugh. "The miniature. God's blood, your mother made one, didn't she?" He bowed his head, shaking it with incredulity.

"Made what?" Carlston rapped out.

"A *Colligat*," Benchley said.

The word was Latin based, but strange. Helen translated it as best she could: *collect*, perhaps, or *gather*.

Benchley dug his fingers into his forehead as if trying to drive home this new information. He looked up at Carlston. "You said there was some kind of alchemy within this miniature? I would hazard that it does not have two sources of hair in it, but three—one of them a Deceiver—and the ability to strip Reclaimer powers." He turned to Helen. "I can see by your face, girl, that I am right." He narrowed his eyes. "Did your mother also tell you that in the hands of a Deceiver, it can be used as a weapon against all Reclaimers?"

Helen drew in a breath. *All Reclaimers?*

Carlston rubbed his mouth. "I had not even considered a *Colligat*. It is beyond comprehension that *anyone* would risk making such a thing." He looked at Helen. "No wonder it affected Jeremiah in that way. It is extremely dangerous."

"My mother made it for *me*," Helen said. "So I would have a choice."

Benchley shifted his grip on his cane. "You said she would have it with her, William."

Carlston held up his hand. "I will take care of this, Samuel."

Helen stepped back. Good God, they were going to take it from her—she could see it in Benchley's eyes. He was going to take away her only way to escape this nightmare.

Benchley stepped forward as Lord Carlston said, "Lady Helen, you must understand—"

Helen focused on Benchley, the next few moments projected in her mind in bright, horrific detail. She could see him accelerating, cane raised, reaching for her, ripping the miniature from her neck—

She whirled around and wrenched open the door. Beyond it, Mr. Quinn's head was bent to a smiling Darby. He drew back sharply, staring past Helen into the room.

"My lady?" Darby said. "Can I—"

"Stop her!" It was Carlston's voice.

Quinn sprang forward, but Helen blocked him with her shoulder, knocking him against the wall. She ran, stumbling over the train of her habit, her hip hitting the edge of a table in a sharp clip of pain.

She heard Benchley snarl, "Get out of the way."

"Run, my lady!" Darby yelled. "I will—" Her words were stopped by a sickening crack of wood on flesh.

Helen faltered. Looked back. Darby was almost on her knees, clinging to Mr. Benchley's arm, one side of her face red and already swelling. He raised his cane for another blow.

"Run!" Darby screamed.

Helen grabbed the banister and snatched up her train with her other hand, holding it against her body as she ran down the stairs. She heard the fast, pounding footsteps of pursuit.

"Benchley, stop it! Leave this to me!" Carlston's voice was a command.

She took the last three steps in a jump, landing on the carpet and staggering to the side, her shoulder slamming into the wall. Through the front door? No, the crowd: too hard to get through. She spun around and ran, Benchley in the corner of her sight at the bottom of the staircase, Carlston a step behind him.

"Lady Helen, stop!" Carlston yelled. "It is not as you think."

Helen lowered her head and ran faster down the hallway, She would not let them take her miniature, her choice, her chance of a normal life. She burst through the kitchen, past the hearth and benches, the figures of two men in the small courtyard ahead. Bales, but who was the other in the long black coat? She shouldered her way through the door, the collision of bone and wood shuddering through her body. It was Lowry, Benchley's man. He would have bound strength. Both turned at the slam of the door against the outside of the house. Helen saw Bales gape at her speed, but Lowry was ready, pouchy eyes fixed upon her, his muscular body crouched. He grabbed, but his fingers only scraped her arm. She hit out at him, gloved knuckles connecting with his forehead. He reeled back. For a moment she stopped, shocked that she had hit a man. That he was on the ground.

She turned and yanked at the gate. Stuck. A glance back saw Lowry up on his knees, and beyond him, Benchley coming through the back door, Carlston still a few steps behind, yelling for him to stop. She pulled hard. The gate came away from its hinges. Shoving it aside, she burst into the alley, her breath hard and pained. Cover—she needed cover. She turned and headed for the narrow opening that led to Giltspur Street.

"Make way!" she yelled, rebounding off the side of the brick wall in her speed. "Make way!"

The man wedged into the gap turned to look. She saw his eyes widen, the sound of other voices protesting as he stepped back into the crowd, away from her flailing arms. She forced her way through the opening, the bricks catching her hat and scraping it from her head. It fell back into the alley as she felt hands grasp her forearm and pull her through.

"Madam, are you all right?" another man, broad and red-faced, asked.

"Some ruffians are after me," she gasped. "Stop them, I beg you."

She pushed into the crowd, leaving the two men glowering through the narrow gap. A look over her shoulder showed a black-clad arm being beaten back by her protectors. Lowry. Panting, Helen forged through the bodies around her, sharp protests following her progress. Should she work her way up to Hosier Lane again? She rose on the balls of her feet and saw a flurry of motion: Mr. Benchley and Lord Carlston emerging from Green Dragon Lane. Mr. Quinn, too. Her eyes connected with Carlston's, his expression a mix of frustration and fury.

"My lady?" Darby's shrill voice wrenched her around. Her maid had clearly come through the narrow gap—another woman in distress—the men closing ranks after her.

"Darby," she called, and pointed down Giltspur, toward the prison. Away from Green Dragon Lane. Darby nodded and plunged into the crowd.

Helen edged along, trying to find a way through the tightly packed spectators. She looked over her shoulder again. Lord Carlston was gaining on her, his height and obvious rank clearing a path. Darby seemed to be making better headway along the side of the house—more efficient than pushing through people. Helen started threading her way to the wall.

"Three minutes to go, by my watch," a man ahead commented. "Oy, what is all this pushing? You'll have us all down."

"My apologies, sir," Helen gasped.

In the middle of Giltspur Street, three big men were moving up through the crowd, a trail of sharp insults and complaints following their relentless progress. Helen saw the leader focus on her, his blunt, swarthy features narrowing into intent. He quickened his pace, shoving onlookers aside. Helen groped for the miniature around her neck and pressed it against her throat, giving a soft moan of recognition as the bright blue glow flared out. The three Deceivers.

The leader's focus shifted. She followed his gaze and saw four more bright blue life-forces skirting a cart in Newgate Street, packed with people standing upon it. Seven Deceivers circling her, one of them a woman in a scandalously low-cut gown, her black hair dressed with extravagant green ostrich feathers—a member of the demimonde, causing a sensation amongst the men on the cart. The lead Deceiver circled his finger, then pointed to Helen. It was true: the creatures *were* working together. And they were after the miniature too.

The *Colligat*. Her choice. Their weapon.

Fighting back panic, Helen thrust the portrait down the front of her habit and renewed her efforts to reach Darby. The girl still clung to the wall, and there were only four or five people between them. She could slip Darby the miniature and then lead the Deceivers away. She looked back. Lord Carlston was almost as close as the three Deceivers. She saw him lift the touch watch lens to his eye, then jerk it away, horror on his face: he had seen the creatures working together. He searched the crowd again. For her. Their eyes connected, his expression one of raw relief.

Stay. Let me help you.

How could she trust him now?

"My lady," Darby called.

Helen's boot caught on a soft flash of dark fur and pricked ears threading its way underfoot. She stumbled and collided with a woman in a soiled linen cap, earning herself a foul curse that sprayed itself across her face. Wiping the repulsive spittle from her eyes, Helen forced her way past two gentlemen with loosened cravats, reeking of liquor and snuff. She dodged as one of them tried to grab her pinned-back veil, his leering mouth breathing a hot moment of claret across her forehead. Finally she was at the wall beside her maid, panting. Darby's cheekbone was horribly swollen and red, a blue bruise already under the fair skin. The blow from Benchley must have been very hard indeed, but there was no time for consolation. Helen pulled out the miniature and yanked at it, the riband cutting a sharp pain into her skin before it snapped free. She pressed it into Darby's hand. "There is more to this miniature than we thought. Take it and get away from here. Do not let it out of your sight, and trust no one. Not even his lordship. There are Deceivers after it. And Benchley, too."

"I cannot leave you here, my lady."

"Do not be anxious for me." She wrenched her reticule strings from her wrist and crammed the bag into her maid's hand: there was still some coin in it. "Take a hackney. I will meet you at home." She pushed Darby's shoulder, urging her into the crowd. *"Go!"*

With an agonized backward glance, Darby obeyed.

Helen took a few steps after her—a pretense—then stopped as if blocked by the crowd. She turned to the faces ten deep around her, frantically searching for the blunt features of the Deceiver leader. Without the miniature in hand, it was hard to find him and his cohort among the shifting crowd. She gulped a relieved breath—he was not in grabbing distance—and widened her search. Her gaze landed on a familiar face beneath a stylish charcoal gray beaver. A dumbfounded face, staring at her with the same brown eyes as her own.

Andrew.

Good God, no!

And beside him, the Duke of Selburn. She reached for her veil, but, of course, it was too late. The Duke's long-boned face was set into blank shock. Helen could not move, frozen in his blue gaze, waiting for him to recover and realize the terrible impropriety of her presence. Waiting for the disgust. She watched as he blinked, but the contempt did not come. Instead he gave a small smile, something akin to admiration, the fleeting expression shifting almost immediately into concern and determination. He held up his hand, a signal for her to stay at the wall, then bent to Andrew's ear. Her brother nodded, giving a quick clasp of his friend's arm in eloquent thanks. For a moment Helen saw the red fury in Andrew's face before the Duke stepped in front of him, leading the way toward her and her lack of any believable explanation for her scandalous presence.

A murmur rose through the crowd. "Bellingham has been brought out."

The words were like a flame touched to kindling. En masse,

the crowd swarmed toward the gallows, some calling, "God bless you!" and others, "Farewell, poor man!" while still others called, "Silence!" Helen felt herself carried forward, unable to stop the frightening momentum. Hands pushed at her back, pressing her against the side of a large cart full of men watching the raised platform.

She found her gaze drawn inexorably up to the gallows. A bound man stood in a brown greatcoat with a noose around his neck and a black hood over his head, fastened by a white kerchief tied across his nose and mouth. The assassin, John Bellingham. Beside him, a clergyman stood with hands folded and lips moving in prayer. A terrible quiet descended across the crowd, all attention shifting to the executioner as he checked the rope once more, then made his way down the scaffold steps, ready to strike away the supports to the trapdoor.

"He is coming, you know," a woman's voice said softly behind Helen. "He is coming for you."

Helen turned her head and looked into a pair of hard hazel eyes beneath black curls and a sweep of green ostrich feathers. The demimonde Deceiver. The creature smiled, small perfect teeth in a lush mouth.

"What?" Helen gasped.

The prison clock struck the first toll of eight o'clock. Helen and the Deceiver stared at one another. It was as if the pealing bell held them still. On the seventh knell, a crack and clang rang out as the trapdoor supports were struck away and the flap dropped open. Helen looked up to see Bellingham's body plunge down at the end of the rope, his horrifying convulsions locking her gaze through the eighth toll. Her mistake.

The Deceiver reached across and grabbed her throat. "Where is it?" she snarled.

Helen wrenched herself out of the vicious hold. She hit wildly, her hand slamming into the soft cartilage of an ear, but her balance was gone. She slipped, her feet losing purchase on the carpet of slimy paper. Staggering, she groped for the cart. Her hand missed the edge and grabbed air. She felt herself falling. Shouts of alarm came from above her, hands reaching, brushing against her veil, but she kept falling. Her head clipped something hard and sharp, the sickening impact bringing a wash of swirling black nausea and a roaring in her ears that held the frantic thud of her heartbeat and the hissing approach of oblivion.

Twenty-Five

Thursday, 21 May 1812

Helen opened her eyes, head throbbing from the effort, the soft glow from a nearby candle adding to the pain that pulsed in her temple. She closed them again, seeking the soft dark that still hovered at the edge of her consciousness. No, it was too late: her mind was sorting the glimpse into coherent sense.

She was in her bedchamber. On her bed.

Her eyes flew open. The hanging! She lifted her hand from the bedclothes, clumsily finding the soft skin of her throat. The Deceiver with the dark hair . . .

"My lady?" A hazy form leaned over the bed.

"Darby?" she croaked. Her mouth was so dry.

"Oh, my lady. You are awake!"

Helen blinked, bringing her maid's face into focus. A dark bruise discolored one cheekbone, and shadows ringed the girl's anxious eyes. "I will fetch your aunt," Darby said.

"Wait." Helen lifted her hand but had to let it drop. Every movement felt as if she were wading through water. "Are we alone?"

"Yes, my lady."

"The miniature?"

Darby touched her high-necked bodice. "I have it safe, my lady," she whispered.

"What happened? How did I get here?"

"Your brother and the Duke of Selburn brought you back. I was waiting for you here. Your head was bleeding so bad, my lady. We thought"—Darby's voice caught—"we thought you would die."

Helen reached up and felt a bandage around her brow. "The Duke?" she managed.

"Yes." Darby nodded vigorously. "He was very commanding, my lady. He told your uncle that he would stop any stray reports in the papers, and advised them to say that you had taken a fall from your horse. That is what has been put about among your acquaintances. His Grace the Duke has also been past the house six times, inquiring after you." She drew back, pointing to a pair of extravagant bouquets set in vases beside the bed. "Those are from him," she said, then indicated the top of the locked secretaire. "And those other four posies, too. The violets are from Miss Gardwell. You missed her ball, but she was ever so sweet when she brought the flowers. The irises are from Mr. Brummell, and the roses are from Lady Margaret and Mr. Hammond." Darby leaned closer. "Lord Carlston has been past too, but no flowers."

Helen felt a treacherous lift of her heart at his lordship's name. A rush of bitter memory swamped it: Mr. Benchley and her mother's letter. She focused past a sudden, empty ache and reached out to brush her fingers across the soft petals of one of the bouquets. *Six* of them from the Duke?

"How long have I been senseless?"

"Close to four days. It is Thursday night, my lady. Doctor Roberts was so worried. We were all so worried." Darby straightened. "You must be thirsty, my lady." She turned to a pitcher and poured a glass of milky liquid. "The doctor said that if you were to awake, you might have small sips of barley water."

Helen pushed herself up onto her elbows. Darby helped her to sit, a sturdy arm around her back. With the glass held at her lips, she gulped at the tepid cordial, feeling her parched throat ease.

"You may only have a little, my lady," Darby said apologetically. She pulled the glass away and eased Helen down. "I must call your aunt now."

A sudden anxiety lifted Helen onto her elbows again. "Darby, are *you* in trouble?"

"No, my lady. Your aunt assumed you'd sent me home and gone on alone. I didn't say otherwise. Was that right?"

"Yes, well done." She frowned. "Your poor face—what did you say about it?"

Darby cocked her head. "My lady, you know as well as I do that no one is going to interfere in a lady's dealings with her maid."

"They think *I* did it?" Helen was aghast. She had never beaten a servant.

"I'll get your aunt now, and your brother."

Andrew was going to be so angry. Helen slumped back against the pillow and closed her eyes, the tantalizing wrap of soft darkness blocked by the pounding ache within her head.

The click of the door roused her again. Slowly, she opened her eyes.

"Helen?" Aunt's face peered over her, fatigue set into the powdered lines. "How are you feeling?"

Behind her, Andrew smiled, pale and drawn. "Hello, sprite."

"My head hurts," Helen said.

"Yes." Aunt sat down in the chair set beside the bed, smoothing the skirt of her morning gown. "The doctor will be here soon. He has bled you twice already. Such a good man." She leaned across and briefly clasped Helen's arm. "It is such a relief to see you awake, dear girl."

Helen gave a wan smile. "I am sorry," she whispered, her eyes flicking to her brother.

"I don't know what's come over you lately," he said. "Have you any idea what—"

"Andrew!" Aunt said sharply. "Perhaps you should withdraw."

He rubbed the back of his neck. "I'm glad you are recovered," he said gruffly. Helen watched in silence as he left the room.

"He has stayed here the whole time, waiting," Aunt said as the door closed.

"Is Uncle very angry too?" Helen asked.

"Quite furious, my dear. I think he was ready to cast you out, even in your unconscious state. Luckily, the Duke's kind intervention and continued attentions have gone some way to ameliorating his temper." She stood and walked to the secretaire, her back to Helen. "Such beautiful flowers from His Grace, don't you think? Six arrangements, and all of them hothouse. I daresay there will be another two tomorrow."

"Yes, it is very kind," Helen murmured.

Aunt whirled around. "How could you do such a terrible, terrible thing, Helen? Attend a hanging! By yourself!" She clasped her hands together, fingers shaking. "No, I vowed I would not rail at you when you are in such a delicate state." She drew a steadying breath. "Suffice to say, I was sure this shameful behavior had ruined your chances, but it seems His Grace has not been put off at all. You are *very* lucky, my dear. I cannot understand it myself. Perhaps he feels some sort of responsibility for you now. I don't know. It does not matter, does it? As long as he feels it." She smiled: a tight, overwrought flash of teeth.

A knock on the door broke the strained silence.

"Come," Aunt called.

The door opened to admit Dr. Roberts and his apprentice, a stocky young man who protectively clasped the physician's black leather bag to his chest.

"This is a happy sight," the doctor said in his calm, measured way, but Helen saw the relief behind the professional bonhomie. He gave an elegant bow to them both and crossed to the bed, trailed by his apprentice, a genuine smile on his lean, gray-whiskered face. "How do you feel, Lady Helen? I imagine you have a tremendous headache."

"It feels as if someone is dancing a jig in my head, Doctor," she said as he pulled the chair closer to the bed. "But it has already eased a little since I woke."

He gave a pleased, professional grunt. "Let me take a look at you then."

The examination was brief: he measured her pulse with cool fingers pressed to her wrist, checked her eyes and tongue, and, taking a reed from his bag, placed one end against her chest and the other to his ear to listen to the beat of her heart.

"All excellent. I do not think I will need to bleed you again." He passed the reed back to his apprentice, then patted Helen's hand. "A good thing, too. You are remarkably hard to bleed for any length of time."

"Are you sure?" Aunt asked. She was a keen believer in the advantages of a bloodletting, particularly during the month of May.

"Quite sure," the doctor said. "Now let us look at the wound." With careful, practiced fingers, he removed the bandaging and studied the injury just above her hairline. "Ah, now this is *very* pleasing. Will you allow me to show my apprentice, Lady Helen?"

She nodded.

The young man sidled closer.

"Do you see, Mr. Ewell? The gash has all but healed. Remarkable." Dr. Roberts smiled at Helen. "I believe you do not even need a dressing."

"That is an awful quick heal, isn't it, sir?" ventured Mr. Ewell.

Helen held her breath. Mr. Ewell was far too perceptive.

"Lady Helen is a very healthy young woman," Dr. Roberts said. "Never underestimate the body's ability to heal itself."

Especially a Reclaimer body, Helen thought.

The doctor turned to Aunt. "She has made an excellent recovery, Lady Pennworth. The injury was obviously much less severe than we had first feared. I will make up a draught for her to take for the next few days—Mr. Ewell here will bring it round—and I will visit again tomorrow morning. If she continues to improve, she may even exit her bed tomorrow."

"So soon?" Aunt asked. Her surprise held a note of calculation.

"Yes, but gently, and only to a chair." He sent a mock-reproachful glance at Helen. "No rushing around to parties and being a giddy miss for a few days yet."

"I had all but decided to cancel her presentation ball," Aunt said. "Do you mean she may be well enough for it to proceed?"

"When is it?"

"This coming Tuesday."

The doctor gave Helen's hand another reassuring pat. "If she stays quiet and her improvement continues at this pace, then it is very possible."

Aunt smiled, raising her brows at Helen in congratulation. "Well now, that is a relief. 'Tis a good thing, too, that I did not stop Cook from working on the white soup."

Helen smiled back: her own overwrought flash of teeth.

By early next morning, Helen knew that her Reclaimer powers had restored her to full health. No headache, no haziness in her mind, and the wound, when she looked in the dressing-room mirror, was barely visible. She stepped back, eyeing her grim face. If she used the miniature as her mother had instructed, she would lose this amazing ability. She touched the faint scar. What else would she lose?

Another face, burned into her memory, rose before her eyes: a hard hazel gaze, lush mouth, and dark hair. The demimonde Deceiver. She had said, *He is coming for you.* Helen circled her hand protectively around her throat. Was it a Grand Deceiver—a creator of a Terror—as Lord Carlston feared? If something like that was after her, then surely she had justification to use the miniature.

Darby arrived with a cup of morning chocolate and a gift that she had made overnight: a small cream silk bag with a drawstring long enough to hang around the neck or tie around the waist. "It's for the miniature, so you can wear it close by without getting a headache," she whispered. "I figured you'd not want to let it out of your sight now." She looked at the closed door and then pulled the portrait out from under her bodice, lifting the riband over her head. With an anxious smile, she passed it back.

Helen caught her hand. "Thank you," she said, feeling an absurd desire to cry.

Not long after, Aunt bustled into the room with another bouquet. "Look, aren't they pretty?" she said, waving the arrangement of peonies at Helen, who was back in bed, demurely sitting up against a pyramid of pillows. "Admittedly, they came via Selburn's footman, but it is only eight o'clock, and one can hardly expect a Duke to be up before ten." She handed the flowers to Darby, then paced to the window and back again, pausing at the end of the bed to smile uncertainly at Helen. "I know your uncle is yet to visit you, my dear, but do not think he is unconcerned." She lifted the tassel that hung from the corner of the bed canopy, smoothing out the thick gold thread. "He does not think it seemly to visit you in your bedchamber, but he asks for reports upon your health whenever I see him. I am sure that once you are able to manage the stairs to the drawing room, he will take the first opportunity to sit with you."

She was, of course, lying. Helen had no doubt that her uncle was still too furious to be in the same room as his wanton, disobedient niece. She knew there would have to be an interview with him at some point, and just the thought of it made her innards tense into a hard knot.

During his promised visit, Dr. Roberts pronounced her recovered enough to dress and sit on the chaise longue. It had been set by her bedchamber window for the light and view, displacing her writing desk to the other side of the room. Dr. Roberts even suggested opening the window, but Aunt felt that was going a little too far. Helen, feeling wretched about missing Millicent's ball, asked him if she could invite her friend to visit. The doctor agreed: after all, the enlivening company of a good comrade was essential to convalescence, as long as the young lady did not stay too long.

Millicent, escorted by her manservant, arrived at the same time as the Duke, delivering another hothouse posy himself. Naturally, His Grace could not ascend to Helen's bedchamber, but he sent his warm wishes with a wide-eyed Miss Gardwell, and the posy of rosebuds in Darby's tender care.

"The Duke of Selburn?" Millicent said, seating herself on the end of the chaise longue and pulling at her bonnet ribands. "You sly thing! Coraline Pritchard will be devastated." She took off the bonnet—a pretty confection of brown silk, coffee-colored lace, and pink feathers—and passed it to Darby.

"Coraline Pritchard?" Helen inquired. She patted down the wool rug across her legs. "She is in her second Season, is she not?"

"Yes, and not one proposal yet. She has set her cap at the Duke. Hasn't a chance, of course—squints, poor thing." Millicent held out a package wrapped in Gunter's distinctive paper. "Fruit jellies. I know they are your favorite." She passed the gift, pressing Helen's hand for a fervent moment. "I am so glad you are better. When the news came, I was beside myself. I could not believe Circe threw you. Whatever happened? Did she hit a hole?"

Helen licked her lips, unprepared to conjure such detail. "I was galloping her at the morning ride, and she must have shied at something. I am not sure what—I cannot remember." She hurried onto a new topic. "I am so sorry I missed your ball."

"You could hardly help it, could you?" Millicent said. She leaned forward. "But I did miss you. I was so nervous. And, of course, we had the most horrific storm. Did anyone tell you?" At the shake of Helen's head, she continued. "At about half past eight, just as the first guests were arriving, the whole sky went dark, and then the most terrifying thunder and lightning started. All very dramatic. I swear, Mother thought it was divine retribution for choosing the cheaper champagne."

Helen laughed, rocking hard against the back of the chaise. As she finally subsided into a few giggling hiccups, it occurred to her that it was the first real laughter she had enjoyed in weeks.

"So, tell me about the Duke," Millicent said, working off her gloves. "It seems a lot has happened since our promenade together. Your aunt told me he asked you to go riding along Rotten Row, and has sent you at least eight posies since the accident. Do you think . . ." She allowed the sentence to trail off dramatically, her arched eyebrows posing the question.

"I don't know. Perhaps."

Millicent clapped her hands. "And do you like him?" She waved away the question. "How could you not? He is *charmant*! And, of course, the catch of the Season."

"I do like him. Very much," Helen said, but all she could see was an image of Lord Carlston's dark head tilting toward her own. What would Millicent make of such a situation? Of course, she could not share that exhilarating, confusing moment with her friend. Or anyone, for that matter. Not even Darby. Besides, Lord Carlston had betrayed her, and it was possible—no, probable—he thought that moment had been a mistake. With a bright smile, she lifted the box of fruit jellies. "Shall we have one?" At Millicent's enthusiastic nod, Helen tore the paper from the box.

"I have a little bit of news myself," Millicent said as she considered the selection. Her fingers hovered, then struck, digging out a jelly in the shape of a pineapple. "Lord Holbridge has been rather assiduous in his attentions. We danced twice at my ball, talked the whole way through, and he took me into supper."

Helen remembered the young Viscount. Nice-looking in a milky kind of way, with a good sense of humor. She chose a strawberry jelly. "Describe everything that happened," she said, sinking back into the pillows and the safe, easy excitements of her old life. "I want to hear every detail."

HALF AN HOUR later, Millicent rose to take her leave, insisting that if she stayed any longer, she would expire from too many fruit jellies. As the door closed behind her friend—under the escort of Darby—Helen rose from the chaise longue to walk around the room and work some of her own queasiness from her body. Five fruit jellies were definitely beyond her limit too. In fact, she needed something far more vigorous than a mere walk.

She started a series of *jetés*, the leap from one foot to another getting faster and higher. Muscles stretching, blood pounding, the room a blur of increasing velocity, every part of her working in perfect harmony. Such a glory to move with so much confidence and unearthly speed—another thing that would go if she used the miniature. The knock on the door caught her spinning into a wild pirouette. She stopped, breath coming in short, sharp gasps.

"Who is it?" she called.

"It is your uncle, Helen. I wish to speak to you."

Helen clamped her hand over her mouth, trying to calm her breathing. She ran to the chaise longue and dropped onto it, yanking the rug across her legs.

Dragging in a deep breath, she called, "Of course, Uncle."

The door opened. He stood in the doorway, snuff-stained nostrils flared as if he could smell the abandon in the room.

"I believe you are well enough to receive me," he said.

Without waiting for confirmation, he strode in, waving her back onto the chaise as she prepared to rise and curtsy. His mouth had folded into lipless disapproval, his face suffused with a purple choler that made the broken veins across his cheeks bulge into violent blue chasing.

Helen pulled the rug up to her chest—a soft, woolen shield—and waited for her uncle to speak. He paced across to the secretaire, and stared down at the posies displayed across its top.

"I cannot even imagine what could have compelled you to do something so unwomanly, so *disgusting*, as to attend a hanging by yourself." He swung around to face her, voice rising into brimstone and fire. "To go forward into the world unescorted and available—like a common whore." He sucked in a hissing breath between his bared teeth. "Do you realize that strange men could have touched your body as you were carried from that crowd?"

Helen found herself leaning back, away from his words. She straightened her spine. She would not cringe.

"Your brother is extremely upset," Uncle said. "To be so embarrassed in front of his friend the Duke. If it were not for His Grace, you would have brought even further dishonor to the family name. I am sorry to say that you are, truly, your mother's daughter."

Helen clenched her jaw, holding back the truth. She was her mother's daughter in more ways than he could ever count.

"The Duke has just left," he said. "He has applied to me for your hand. You can expect a proposal. For some reason, he believes your spirit is merely lively, not pernicious, and that it needs only to be directed into more womanly activities."

"The Duke wishes to marry me?" Helen drew back, confused. Why would he want her after she had disgraced herself so thoroughly?

"Yes, you *should* be amazed," her uncle snapped. "You are lucky you have forty thousand pounds, girl. I have a feeling your lively spirit would be far less attractive without it."

Helen stared down at the rug, fists bunched around the wool. Her uncle was mistaken: the Duke was not a venal man. He was far nobler than that. Her eyes blurred with tears. Was it possible that he cared for her? He had shown some particularity, that was true, but there had been nothing ardent in his manner before. Perhaps it was just a convergence of suitability, timing, and a gallant nature. Did it matter? The match would bring everything her family expected: rank, protection, honor. And he was such a kind man. A union with him brought every prospect of happiness and a safe life.

"You are indeed fortunate," Uncle added. "If knowledge of your shame was to spread further amongst our acquaintances, you would be unmarriageable: your mother's taint and your own disgraceful behavior would prevent any decent offer." He crossed his arms high on his barrel chest, the points of his shirt rising up around his jowls. "As it is, the Duke has used his wide influence and rank to stop the papers printing any reports of your conduct. He has placed only one condition upon such generosity. He feels that Lord Carlston has some kind of sway upon you. As a gentleman, he refused to elaborate, but I shudder at what he could mean. He has asked that we no longer accept Carlston's claim on our family. Considering his own history with the man and what he is doing to save you from your own nature—what he is doing for this family by taking you—I have no qualm in cutting that connection." He strode to the bed then swung around to face her, his mouth curled in disgust. "Is there truth in what he says? Do you have some kind of base attachment to Carlston?"

Helen raised her chin, but she felt heat coloring her skin. "No."

He pressed his hand over his eyes. "A liar as well as a wanton. Your capacity for deceit is sickening." He strode across to the chaise longue and shoved his face before her own. "You will accept the Duke. Do you understand?"

She turned away from the spray of vehement spittle. At the corner of her sight, she saw his hands clench. No need for Reclaimer calculations to know that if she hesitated too long, she would feel his fist. For one fierce moment she knew she could pick him up and throw him across the room if she wished. And, God forgive her, she did so wish. She closed her eyes, letting the frightening rise of savagery pass.

Even so, she had no reason to hesitate or refuse. "Yes," she said. "I understand."

"From now until your ball, you will stay in the house. You will attend only those appointments I deem necessary for the preparation of that event. Do you understand?"

"Yes."

He drew back. "I will withdraw Lord Carlston's invitation to your ball and make it clear to him that his claim on our family is at an end."

Helen kept her face blank. Surely she should be relieved that his lordship would not be at the ball or have any claim upon her again. Why then did she feel so hollow?

"You should spend your days praying in the hope that you can, at least, offer the Duke a clean soul, free of the thoughts of another man, and free of those base female desires that no decent woman would propagate."

"Yes, Uncle."

"Start now." He grabbed her shoulder and wrenched her off the low chaise, pushing her onto her knees. "Give thanks that Selburn will have you." He released his hold upon her shoulder, the brutal dig of his fingers remaining on her flesh. "I shall certainly be giving thanks that you will soon be another man's problem."

He turned and strode from the room, leaving the odor of old snuff and sour breath.

Helen stayed on her knees until she heard his footsteps descend the stairs. Slowly, she pulled herself back onto the chaise and dragged the wool rug around her shoulders.

What if she refused the Duke? Her uncle would almost certainly try to impel her to marry him. Or if the Duke would not agree to a forced marriage, she would no doubt be quickly wed to the next who offered—perhaps the meat-loving Sir Reginald. Helen shuddered. Uncle could incarcerate her at his estate, Lansdale, until she "saw sense" or was free of his guardianship—and his control of her money—seven years hence. Seven years! It was even possible that in his fury he would cast her out and refuse her access to her fortune. She would be forced to rely upon Andrew's charity.

Helen shook her head. She was tormenting herself for no reason. Now that her mind had calmed and cleared, she could see that her uncle's brutal manner had set up a false resistance within her. For goodness' sake, she liked the Duke! She just did not want to do what her uncle demanded: a humiliatingly childish response. She could not allow such a contrary reason to rule the most important decision in her life.

The Duke was a good man. An enlightened man. A man of enormous wealth and influence. But, above all that, he was a man worthy of admiration and respect. If she married him, she would be the Duchess of Selburn, below only the Queen and Princesses in rank. There would be grand salons and parties and travel, and life at the very pinnacle of society; the life that she had been trained to lead, and that she had thought was no longer possible. It was the life that her mother had *wanted* her to live. She had no reason to hesitate. After all, she had already resolved to strip herself of the alternative, and once that was done, there would no longer be any danger from Deceivers for herself or anyone in her life.

The decision was made: she would accept the Duke.

She pulled the rug tighter around her shoulders. Why, then, did doubt still flutter within her chest like a trapped bird?

~

A LITTLE BEFORE the dinner hour—as Darby arranged a small table for Helen's meal—a soft knock sounded on the door.

"Who is it?" Helen called from the chaise longue.

"Lily, my lady."

Helen met Darby's eyes. *Lord Carlston's spy.* She had expected some kind of communication from his lordship, and Lily was the obvious conduit. Yet, now that it was here, she was not sure what she wanted. An explanation? An apology? Or maybe some kind of absolution for the sin of wanting a normal life. Except that she was not a Papist, and surely it was not a sin to want safety and protection.

"Come," Helen said. She swung her feet to the floor and faced Lily's arrival. Darby came to stand behind the chaise, a reassuring presence. "Close the door," Helen said as Lily curtsied.

With their privacy secure, the maid ventured further into the room. Her watchful eyes flicked from Helen to Darby, then back again. "I have a message from his lordship, my lady." She pulled a letter from her apron pocket and delivered it into Helen's hand. "He has asked me to return with an answer."

The packet was thin. Two sheets at most. "I will call you if I need you."

Lily bobbed another curtsy and turned to leave. Helen pressed her fingertips upon the wax seal.

"My lady?" Helen looked up. Lily had paused at the door. "I wanted to tell you that I have still not found any sign of a Deceiver within the household."

Helen smiled. "Thank you, Lily."

With a nod, the maid turned the handle and, with a quick look right and left along the hall, departed, closing the door behind her with a soft click.

"Check it," Helen said.

Darby opened the door a crack, nodded, and closed it again. "Do we not trust her, then?"

"I don't know," Helen said. "I don't know who we can trust now."

Darby eyed the letter. "Shall I leave you to read?" Helen nodded. "Then I'll just be in the dressing room, my lady."

Finally alone, Helen slid her fingertip beneath the seal and worked it free. With a deep breath, she unfolded the pages, smoothed the creases from them, and began to read.

St. James's Square. 21 May 1812

Lady Helen,

It was with great relief that I received Lily's communication that you have fully recovered after the events of 18 May. It is those events that I now wish to clarify and, I hope, bring some understanding to you about my actions.

Your surmise was correct that Mr. Benchley had proposed that he and I transfer the darkness within our souls into your own. I swear, I did not know that he had used your mother in that way so many years ago. Naturally, I refused his proposal. It was a heinous suggestion, but one that I knew would not readily leave his mind. I therefore invited Mr. Benchley to Newgate Street in order to demonstrate to him your extraordinary abilities—particularly with your mother's miniature—and your importance to our cause. It was, I believed, the only way to stop him from thoughts of transferring his darkness to you, and thus stop him from continuing to be a threat to your well-being.

Helen shook her head. She did not believe anything would stop Mr. Benchley. But at least his lordship had refused.

Of course, we both know the course of events from when you entered the Newgate Street room. I have only ever read one mention of a Colligat in my studies, and so I did not readily recognize your mother's portrait as that ancient and terrible creation, even when its effects became apparent on Jeremiah. I condemn myself for such ignorance.

Your Colligat is one component in a three-part alchemical abomination called a Trinitas that can render all Reclaimers dead. The danger of such a creation is obvious, but at least we can be assured that the Vis—the power source of a Trinitas—is currently within safe Reclaimer hold and cannot be replicated, unlike your Colligat or the third component, another alchemical device called a Ligatus. Thus the threat of your Colligat is great, but it is not immediately lethal to our kind. I admit that the reaction of Mr. Benchley and myself to the discovery of what you held was, perhaps, overly strong and poorly managed. I hope, however, you now find it understandable.

Helen did understand. She held something that frightened a man as brave as his lordship.

I am painfully aware of the other use of your Colligat. You now have a real choice of destiny. I cannot force you to join us and never sought to do so. Standing against the Deceivers is something that must be done from the heart. It demands a sense of duty and responsibility, a belief in the cause that will carry the Reclaimer through the danger and darkness of our calling. As you are aware, I feel certain that you are here as a sign of the coming of a Grand Deceiver, and also as that creature's nemesis. I know that you also saw the disturbing development of Deceivers working together in the crowd outside the prison. That development is, I believe, another sign that some creature strong enough to pull them together has appeared in our world. They were, undoubtedly, hunting your Colligat, and I fear there will be another attempt to obtain it.

Unnerved, Helen looked over her shoulder. She was, of course, alone. Yet his lordship was right: the Deceivers would want the *Colligat.* She could still feel the brutality within the demimonde Deceiver's grip around her throat and hear the creature's soft words: *He is coming for you.* Her fingers found the silk drawstring around her neck. She gave a small tug, feeling the weight of the portrait in its bag. To have it upon her person was the only assurance of keeping it safe until her ball. Until she used it to escape all this horror.

I trust that your mother made you aware of the dangers of using the Colligat to strip yourself of your destiny: what you may lose of yourself along with your abilities. It is a risk-laden venture even during the strong earth energies of a full moon. Your mother, I am sure, had your best interests at heart, but you are no longer a child. Nor are you beholden to a memory. I have learned that lesson myself from hard experience.

I ask you to join us and to give the Colligat into my care so that I may properly destroy it. You once said to me that all I offer you is danger and threat. That is true. However, I also offer you extraordinary importance and purpose. You and I have been called into the service of mankind, and I can conceive of no greater honor. I hope that you will answer that call, Lady Helen. You can be assured I will stand beside you as your mentor, and that ranged behind us will be the brave men and women of the Dark Days Club. Together I believe that we can be a formidable force against a Grand Deceiver, the madness of Mr. Benchley, or whatever may threaten the souls and lives of the British people.

I do not believe easily, Lady Helen. You and I share a philosophical bent and, in particular, a respect for the evidence of our eyes. I have watched you discover your abilities and with them the knowledge of our hidden world. There is one other thing that I now firmly believe. You have far more courage than you think you do.

William Standfield

Helen sat still, her throat aching from the faith in his final words. She touched the scrawl of his name. William. He had signed it *William.*

Slowly, she stood, feeling as if every joint in her body had stiffened into misery. She walked across to the fire that burned in the grate. William Standfield, the Earl of Carlston, was wrong: she was not courageous at all. She leaned over and held the letter above the glowing coals, the heat stinging her fingertips. It was time to be done with his world. To be safe. The sting sharpened into a burn, the paper sending up a curl of preparatory smoke.

No.

She snatched back the letter and pressed the singed edges between her fingers. She could not destroy his words. Not yet.

You have far more courage than you think you do.

She unlocked her writing desk and reached for *The Magus*. It had been his gift, after all. On the shelf above, her father's face looked out fearlessly from its gold frame. Yet courage had not been enough for him. Nor for her mother. Even love had not been enough. She pulled the leather-bound book from the shelf, slid the folded letter between its pages, and pushed it back into place.

With the hatch safely locked again, and sufficient distance between her and the writing desk, Helen called Darby back into the room.

"Find Lily," she said.

Darby's curious eyes rested for a moment on Helen's empty hands, but she said nothing. With a curtsy, she left in search of the maidservant.

Helen lowered herself onto the chaise longue, hands clasped in her lap. She looked up at the knock on the door.

"Come."

Darby entered first followed by Lily. They both curtsied.

"Shall I stay, my lady?" Darby asked.

"Yes." Helen could not keep the brittle tone from her voice. She saw Darby note it and move to stand behind the chaise again.

Lily observed them with shrewd eyes, large square hands folded at the front of her apron. *A phlegmatic woman,* Helen thought. She wished she had such stoic calm.

"You wanted to see me, my lady?" Lily finally prompted.

Helen met her expectant gaze. "You may tell Lord Carlston that there will be no answer."

Twenty-Six

Saturday, 23 May 1812

SATURDAY MORNING BROUGHT Dr. Roberts on his final consultation. He drew back from his inspection of Helen's head with a pleased, if slightly perplexed, smile.

"I see no reason why you cannot resume normal activities, including your ball," he said, glancing at Aunt. "But do so gently, Lady Helen, and keep in mind that you have been very lucky."

With a supplementary draught prescribed and a final bow, the doctor departed, with his apprentice trailing stolidly behind.

"Well, then," Aunt said, rising from the chaise longue, "we are back to normal. I shall expect you to join me in the drawing room in half an hour." She took in Helen's high-collared muslin morning gown and wrinkled her nose. "But first, dear, do change into your green velvet. You are still a little too peaky to wear white so close to your skin. You need some color to enliven your complexion."

Although Helen felt that her complexion had quite enough liveliness in it for a morning spent sewing beside her aunt, she obediently returned to her dressing room to make the change.

"The neckline will be too low for the miniature, my lady," Darby whispered, holding up the little silk bag against the gown's bright velvet bodice. "You will need to tie it around your waist."

The best method of doing so took some low-voiced discussion, but finally the drawstring was threaded through the lowest eyelet of Helen's stays and the bag secured. Dutifully garbed in the ensemble, her workbag ready, Helen opened her door to find Philip outside it, hands clasped behind his back, with an air of having stood there for quite some time.

"Why are you outside my door, Philip?" she asked. "Surely you are needed downstairs for the ball preparations."

He cleared his throat, a flush spreading up from under his crisp white stock. "Lord Pennworth has ordered that a footman always be outside your room or any room you are in, my lady."

Helen felt heat rise to her own cheeks. But unlike the young man before her, it was not from embarrassment. It was from fury. Her uncle had set guards upon her as if she were a criminal. "I see," she said crisply.

"I am sorry, my lady," Philip murmured.

Helen gave a short nod of acknowledgment, but did not trust herself to say more. He followed her downstairs to the drawing room, no doubt taking up a position outside once he had closed the doors.

Aunt was not seated alone on the yellow silk sofa. At the opposite end, Andrew sat reading *The Morning Post,* his legs crossed, one booted foot jiggling. He looked up from the spread of paper. "How are you feeling today?"

"Very well," Helen managed. She stalked across the room to an armchair. "Aunt, did you know that I am under guard?"

Aunt opened her mouth to answer, but Andrew cut in. "You can hardly be surprised, Helen."

She glared at him. "You agree that I should be watched?"

"I think lately you have forgotten you are a grown woman," he said, his voice uncharacteristically hard. "If you are not careful, you'll lose Selburn to a chit who has some sense of propriety."

"Andrew, do keep in mind that your sister has just risen from her sickbed," Aunt said over her tambour frame. She turned her attention to Helen. "Sit down, dear. This footman business is your uncle's will, and you must abide by it."

Helen sat and opened her workbag to give her hands something to do other than clench into fists. She pulled out a length of linen destined to be hemmed into a cravat. For her brother. She sent a malevolent look in his direction and stuffed it back into the bag.

"Is there some poor work?" she asked.

Aunt nodded to the basket beside the hearth. "There are some sheets and infant gowns that need hemming."

Helen was about to rise when the doorbell rang. "Who is that?"

Even as she said it, the answer came to her in a rush of panicked certainty: it was the Duke. He had come to offer. She had not expected it to be done so quickly. She'd not had enough time to become accustomed to the idea or to settle into her decision with any sense of ease. She looked wildly at her aunt—*It is too soon*—but Aunt merely smiled and nodded encouragingly as she pushed aside her tambour frame.

"A visitor at this hour?" Andrew complained. He folded the paper, placing it on the small table by his elbow.

At the soft knock, they all rose to their feet. The doors opened to admit Barnett, who announced with some ceremony, "His Grace, the Duke of Selburn."

The butler stepped to one side and bowed as Selburn entered. Always a particular dresser, the Duke had outdone himself that morning with a rich brown tailcoat and olive striped waistcoat of fine silk. His gaze swept the room and settled on Helen, the warmth in his eyes dissolving the embarrassment that had frozen her into unmoving discourtesy. She felt the room swirl and realized she was holding her breath. Drawing in a gulp of air, she sank into a belated curtsy.

"Devil take it, Selburn, this is a bit early for you, ain't it?" Andrew said, rising from his own bow. "I thought, oh—" He stopped, clearly coming to a late understanding of the situation.

"Duke, how lovely to see you this morning," Aunt said into the awkward silence. "Pray, take a seat."

"Thank you, Lady Pennworth."

The Duke strode to the other armchair. Helen glanced at Andrew. He was grinning like a fool.

"It is a fine morning out," the Duke remarked as they all sat. His eyes cut to Helen. "Good weather for riding," he added blandly. Helen looked down at her hands. It would have been funny if she had been in any fit state to be teased.

"Quite," Aunt said. She turned to face Andrew. "I do believe there is something urgent I must discuss with you regarding the arrangements for the ball. Would you accompany me to the ballroom for a moment or two?"

"Of course, Aunt," Andrew said solemnly.

They all rose, the exchange of curtsies and bows done in heavy silence. Aunt led Andrew from the room, her dignified exit only slightly compromised by the stifled smile upon her face and the backward glance of triumph she sent Helen.

As the door closed behind them, Helen lowered herself into her chair again, eyes upon the carpet. What was she to say? Selburn remained standing. He did not seem to be in any hurry to break the silence.

Helen finally looked up at him, falling back upon the safety of convention. "Thank you for all the lovely posies."

"I am glad you like them."

"I do, very much." Helen gathered her courage. "I would also like to thank you for your"—she sought the right word—"*assistance* on Monday morning."

He gave a small bow. "It was my honor. I am just glad that you have recovered so well." It seemed he, too, was taking refuge in the well-worn paths of courtesy.

"Thank you." She wet her lips. "You must be wondering what I was doing in Newgate Street."

He shook his head. "Not at all. I presume you were there for the same reason as everyone else. To view the hanging."

She met his eyes. There was no condemnation in them. Quite the contrary: the intensity of his expression brought a flush to her cheeks.

"Yes, the hanging," she murmured. "Will you take a seat, Your Grace?"

He sat in the chair opposite. "Lady Helen, I think you know why I am here," he said, grave formality once more in his voice. "I have applied to your uncle, and he has given me permission to address you." He leaned forward, and she smelled the scent he wore, fragrant with cloves. "I would very much like you to be my wife."

Helen looked steadily into his earnest face: it did not have the heart-stopping symmetry of another face that rose too readily to mind. Nevertheless, there was wit and kindness within its long bones and thinner features. It occurred to her how perverse it was that she should know every line and contour on the face of a man who was already married—albeit to a ghost—and yet she barely knew the face of the man she was destined to wed. All that illicit time spent with Lord Carlston, and little more than three hours strung together with the Duke. Then again, most girls accepted an offer on little more than a Season of shared dances and chaperoned meetings. Why should she be any different? All she had to do now was say one word and bring joy to her family and an end to so many struggles. Just one word.

"Why?"

Not the word she should have said.

He drew back slightly. "Do you mean, why do I wish to marry you?"

"Yes."

"Well, that is easily explained," he said smiling. "I wish to marry and start a family with a worthy woman of my rank. Yet, for the last three Seasons, the young ladies whom I have met all seem to mistake loudness for vivacity, interrogation for intelligence, and obstinacy for strength. Or they are so compliant that they can barely voice an opinion. Lady Helen, you do not fall into those traps. Your vivacity is natural and born from quickness, your intelligence honed through curiosity, and your strength is built from reason. I believe we could deal well together. We share a love of art, of riding, of literature, and I can imagine that our tastes will coincide in other matters as well. You also have a great deal of spirit, a most attractive quality."

She had never heard herself rhapsodized with such warmth. She returned his smile and saw something else flash across his face. She had seen it in Lord Carlston's eyes too: the desire for her flesh as well as her spirit. For a moment she was left breathless. It would not be a cold marriage, then. "My uncle would not agree with you about my spirit," she said.

He leaned across and took her hand. "Admittedly, it has recently led you into some unfortunate episodes, but with some gentle guidance, I think you would readily direct it toward more worthy pursuits. Would you not?"

Helen stared at her hand sweetly trapped in his grasp, the touch of his skin hot upon her own. He admired her quickness, her intelligence, her reason. Yet, in just a few days, all of these admirable qualities could be gone or damaged when she unleashed her mother's *Colligat*. He was asking the Helen-of-now to be his wife, but what if he did not admire the Helen-who-was-to-be? She could not, in all decency, accept his offer under such fraudulent circumstances. Yet if she did not, her uncle's fury would shake the earth and she would be at his mercy.

All she had to do was say one word.

"Do you think people can change?" she asked. "I mean, *essentially* change, at our very core."

He gave a perplexed smile. This was obviously not how he had imagined the course of his proposal. "Well, I think that, at our core, we have natures that stay the same."

"What if my nature were to change—if I were not so quick or intelligent or had such spirit?"

"Then I suppose you would not be you." He stared at her for a long moment, a searching expression upon his face, and then gave a light laugh. "But that is not likely to happen, is it? Come, this is not a time for philosophy. You have not yet given me your answer."

Helen pulled her hand free. What she was about to say was a risk, but it was for his own sake. "If you do hold me in such esteem, Duke, will you grant me an indulgence?"

"An indulgence?"

"Will you allow me to delay my acceptance until after my ball?"

"You accept?" A bright fire burned in his face for a moment.

"I *will* accept—after my ball," she said, feeling a small ache as she saw the flame of his joy gutter into confusion. "I ask that you visit me on the morning after, and sit with me and talk for a while. Then, if you so desire, you can ask me again, and I will accept."

He stared down at his steepled hands for a moment, clearly trying to comprehend her strange request. "Is it that you do not wish to be engaged for your presentation ball?" He looked up. "I assure you, if we were to be engaged now, I would not interfere in any of your enjoyments."

"No, it is not that." She shook her head, counting herself a fool for denying such an easy explanation. But she did not want him to think she was frivolous.

He licked his lips. "Is there . . ." He paused, then straightened. "Do you have another attachment? Lord Carlston?" He almost spat the name.

"No!" Helen leaned forward, her hands raised to block his line of questioning. "It is not that."

"What is it then?"

She groped for a reason—any reason—that would stop the look of pained outrage building in his eyes. "The day of my ball is the anniversary of the day when Andrew and I were told of our parents' deaths," she said. "You will think me sentimental, but I would not want this time of memorial to be swept away by happier news. Nor for my joy to be forever linked to my sadness. If we could wait until after the ball . . ."

"Yes," he said. "Yes, I understand." He nodded with the abrupt quickness of a man convincing himself. "A most worthy sentiment." He drew a breath and released it. "Yes, I can wait four days." He gave a small smile, obviously trying for lightness. "But only if you promise me the first two dances at your ball. And the supper set? It will be remarked upon, I know, but that does not matter, does it? We will be announcing the following day."

Helen allowed him to take her hand between his own again, the gentle warmth of his enclosing hold bringing a sting of tears to her eyes.

~

The Duke left the room soon after. With her Reclaimer hearing strained to its very edges, Helen followed the subsequent events in the foyer downstairs. She heard the Duke's short description of the interview, the muted response from her aunt and brother, and the departure of His Grace. She heard her uncle emerge from his library, her aunt's careful explanation, and then no Reclaimer hearing was required for Uncle's comments about her monstrous nature. At some point, Andrew coaxed him into the library again, too far for even Helen to make out the words within the screaming rant. Finally silence fell.

She gripped the edge of the sofa seat and braced herself, watching the closed door. *If it comes to it, I will use my strength. Break Uncle's arm if he raises his hand.*

It was Andrew who entered. He stood for a moment, fury and disappointment writ large upon his face. He closed the door.

"You are lucky I am here to stop Uncle," he finally said. Helen bowed her head. "What game are you playing?"

"I am not playing a game. I swear." How she wished she could explain it to him.

"Then why did you not accept him now?" He strode across the room and stood over her, one hand kneading the other. "Selburn says you want to wait until after the ball. Whatever for? I do not believe this nonsense about our parents, and I don't think he does either."

There was nothing she could say.

"What if he changes his mind?" Andrew demanded. "I would not be surprised—why should a man of his rank and importance tolerate such treatment? What do you think Uncle will do then?"

She shook her head, although she had a fair idea.

"He is talking about *madness*," Andrew said.

Helen lifted her head, the word striking cold into her heart. "I am not mad!"

Her brother paced across the carpet. "There are some who say our mother was mad, Helen, and all I can see at present is my sister showing the same kind of strange, irrational behavior that I remember in Mamma's nature. And it is all that Uncle is willing to see." He stopped walking for a moment, as if what had come to mind was far too terrible to voice. "I am frightened for you, sprite."

"Mother was not mad!" Helen said vehemently. "She was brave and strong."

"Mother is not at issue here," Andrew said. "It is your own behavior. You used to be so eager to do what is right, but now you seem to be constantly seeking ways to step outside propriety."

Helen hunched her shoulders at the unfair accusation. What was right and wrong was no longer so easy to determine. "It is just a delay," she said.

"It is a delay now, but what if this goes awry and Selburn backs away?" Andrew asked. "I cannot gainsay Uncle's rulings upon you. He is your legal guardian until you are twenty-five, not I. If you have some kind of notion that I can make him give you access to your fortune, and then see you set up in my house or your own, you are wrong." He drew in a breath. "You are at his disposal, Helen, and we both know what he is like."

Helen closed her eyes, but all she could see was an image of herself locked in a madwoman's cell. Her friend Delia probably had such images in her mind too. She opened her eyes again.

"He said yesterday that he would give thanks that I would be another man's problem," she whispered. "He might want you to take over my care."

"That was yesterday. Now I think he would prefer to punish you," Andrew said. "Why don't you just write to the Duke? Accept. I will take it to him myself. Please, Helen."

For just an instant she felt herself sway. It would be easy to put pen to paper and seal her future. No, she could not accept the

Duke's proposal as the woman she was now, and then marry him after she had been reduced to something else. It would not be fair. He must have the opportunity to withdraw his regard.

"The Duke will offer again after the ball, as he said he would," she said, looking away from the fading hope in her brother's face. "He is an honorable man."

Just as she was an honorable woman.

⁓

HELEN'S FAILURE TO see reason resulted in her being confined to her room, with Philip stationed at her door and Darby her only company. She slept for some of the day—a restless dozing brought about by the high emotion of the morning—and woke in the gloom of the early evening, the room cold and bereft.

"Darby?"

No answer.

The shutters had not yet been closed for the night, and the last of the sunset cast an orange glow upon the low clouds. A silk shawl had been laid across her as she slept, and Helen pulled it around her shoulders as she rose stiffly from the bed. The weight of the miniature dropped on its drawstring and bumped against her thigh. Safe. Rubbing a crick from her neck, she crossed to the window for the last moments of daylight and a glimpse of the wider world beyond her room.

She leaned her hands on the windowsill and looked down into the street. A man and woman hurried across the road in front of a gig pulled by a sweet-stepping black horse, and a professional-looking gentleman strode purposefully along the pavement opposite. As she followed his progress, Helen's sharp eyes caught a shadow moving from a gap between two houses. A man stepped out onto the pavement. Dun-colored greatcoat and black beaver, his face turned upward. Even from such a distance and in the poor light, Helen recognized the strong angles and classic contours. Lord Carlston. Although she could not see the detail of his dark eyes, she knew his gaze was fixed upon her own.

Her breath locked into her heartbeat.

What was he doing standing out there?

She heard the hallway door of the dressing room open and close, the clink of the porcelain pitcher against the side of the washbasin, and the rush of water being poured. Darby. Yet Helen could not take her eyes from his lordship's face.

You have far more courage than you think you do.

Footsteps across the carpet heralded her maid's approach.

"You are awake, my lady." At the corner of her eye, Helen saw Darby's sturdy figure lean into the space beside her and look out of the window at the street below. "Ah."

"You knew he was there?"

"It was Mr. Quinn this morning. I think they are guarding us, in turn, from the Deceivers."

"And from Mr. Benchley," Helen said. Her skin seemed to tighten at the thought of the mad Reclaimer out there—somewhere—waiting.

Darby's silence beside her was full of alarm. "From what you have told me, he is a desperate man," she finally said. "If you will allow it, my lady, from this night onward I will sleep here on the chaise. Two sets of ears and eyes are better than one."

"Yes, a good idea," Helen said. "Thank you."

His lordship still stared upward. She bunched her hands on the sill, quelling the impulse to run downstairs and into the street. To stand before him, smell the clean strength of him, watch his mouth curl into that irritating half smile, and explain that she was not a coward. That a woman's duty was to her family. That her mother had wanted her to have a normal life.

"Did you speak to Mr. Quinn?" she asked.

"No." Darby drew back. "What is there to say?"

The sadness in her voice pulled Helen's gaze away from the window. "You liked him, didn't you?" she said. "I am sorry."

"I am sorry too, my lady," Darby said.

Helen turned back to the window. The pavement was empty. His lordship had already stepped back into the shadows.

Twenty-Seven

Sunday, 24 May 1812

THE FOLLOWING TWO days were full of preparations for the ball.

On Sunday morning, on the way to church, Aunt had pointed out to Uncle—with her customary relentlessness—that she required Helen's assistance for the final arrangements, and he must allow his niece out of her room for more than just meals and Sunday service. Why, they had not even decided upon the ball's finishing dance, not to mention what was to be done in the event that the Prince Regent made an appearance, or whether they should delay supper another half hour, as Lady Drayton had last month. The later suppertime had seemed to work quite well, although that ball did go past four in the morning, which was probably an hour too long really, don't you think, Pennworth?

Helen was allowed out of her room.

Although he had conceded that privilege, Uncle would not budge on the question of visitors, and so on Sunday afternoon Helen watched from the drawing room window as Millicent, Lady Margaret and her brother, and other well-wishers were turned away for the sake of her "delicate health."

Aunt had not been exaggerating about the amount of preparation still required. Although Helen's heart was heavy, she did find some relief by focusing upon candle and mirror placement for maximum light, the number of maids in the women's retiring room, and whether to serve a fashionable ice just before the final set—perhaps the new parmesan cheese flavor—or would punch *à la romaine* be more exciting? After all, such domestic arrangements and decisions would be the main responsibility in her life as the Duchess of Selburn.

Before that could happen, however, another set of preparations had to be finalized.

Late Monday evening, before Darby took her post on the chaise longue, Helen picked up the silver candle holder by her bed and went to her secretaire. Aunt had positioned Mr. Brummell's posy in pride of place upon the top, and Helen now shifted it to one side, noting that the edges of the blue irises had begun to curl into death. She slid the candle holder next to it, along with a small fruit knife that she had kept from her dinner. The desk was unlocked in the space of a heartbeat, the hatch pulled open.

The flickering candlelight caught the gold lettering on the spine of *The Magus* and brought a gleam to the glass front of her father's miniature. She pulled the book from the shelf and fanned the pages, the momentum stopping at Lord Carlston's letter. She touched the singed edges of the parchment, fighting an overwhelming impulse to read his words again. William's words.

No, that was not why she was here.

Another fan of the pages brought her to her mother's letter. Smoothing out the thick paper, she scanned the elegant writing and, once again, read her mother's instructions for the use of the *Colligat*.

She had already collected most of the objects for the ritual and hidden them in the desk, at the back of the top shelf. The vial of sanctified water from the church font had been the most difficult to obtain. She gave a grim smile, remembering the strange look she had received from the verger. Next to the vial stood the small silver bowl that usually housed her washing sponge—soon to be used for burning the hair and mixing the solution—and a chased silver tinderbox containing all the makings of a flame. She picked up the little fruit knife, its blade thin enough to prise open the glass back of the miniature, and set it in place on the shelf. Now she had everything ready for tomorrow evening. For the last stroke of midnight.

Her eyes slid down the last page, to the paragraph after the instructions.

> *There is one other warning I must give you, and which you must consider alongside the danger you face. I do not know how much of our natures are linked to our Reclaimer gifts. It is probable that as they are stripped away, you will also lose some aspects of yourself that you treasure.*

What would it be like to lose intelligence or curiosity, or even her wit? Fear rose into her throat. Maybe she would not even realize she had lost them, but just live in a smaller, duller world. Or maybe she would know, forever mourning who she had been. Uncle would, no doubt, welcome a duller Helen, but what about Aunt and Andrew and Millicent? It would be unbearable to lose their respect or see their regard turn into mere toleration. And, of course, there was the Duke. At least she could give him the chance to reconsider his offer.

Still carefully ignoring the other letter, she refolded her mother's missive and slid it into *The Magus,* quickly returning the book to its place on the shelf. She shut the hatch and firmly turned the key, as if locking away something wild and savage.

~

THE NEXT MORNING—the day of the ball—the house was already in an uproar when Helen descended the stairs for breakfast. She peered into the drawing room as she passed. The double doors had been opened into the saloon beyond, transforming the two large spaces into one huge ballroom. The furniture had already been removed, and two of the footmen were rolling up the rugs, exposing the handsome parquetry that would become the dance floor. The other saloon had been transformed into the supper room, a troop of servants hauling up baskets of cutlery and porcelain from the butler's pantry.

Her aunt was already at work at the breakfast table, perusing a list as she sipped her tea.

"Good morning, my dear," she said, raising her eyes to cast a keenly assessing glance over Helen. "Did you sleep well?"

"Well enough, thank you," Helen lied. She had not slept at all. Her mind had conjured grim image after image of madness and idiocy, and the Duke's good-natured face turning away from her, only to become Lord Carlston's stern countenance.

Aunt put down her cup with a click of authority. "My dear, I can see you hardly got a moment—you've rings under your eyes and no color. You must rest as much as you can before Monsieur Le Graf comes at three to do your hair. After that, it will be time to dress, and resting will be out of the question. You must try to recover some of your bloom."

"Yes, Aunt." Helen took a warm roll from the basket.

"If you do not, we may have to resort to the rouge pot," Aunt said.

A knock sent Barnett across the room. He opened the door, his subsequent whispered conversation lifting Helen's eyes from her plate just as he stepped back and announced, "Mrs. Grant wishes to speak to you, my lady."

The housekeeper stood at the threshold cradling a plain deal box.

Berta's box.

Helen's hand clenched around her butter knife.

"What is it, Mrs. Grant?" Aunt called. "Has Gunter's not delivered the sweet course yet?"

The housekeeper dropped into an awkward curtsy. "Gunter's *has* delivered, my lady. This is about something else. Earlier, I pulled out the box belonging to Berta, the maid who ran away, and it has been broke open." She held up the evidence.

Helen stared at the splintered wood around the lock. The awful memory of it cracking apart resounded in her head.

"This is hardly the time to be bringing it to my attention," Aunt said. "We have a ball this evening."

"I know, my lady. I just thought that since we are having all the plate out tonight, you should know that there may be a thief among the staff."

Aunt gave a small grunt of irritation. "Well, let us have a look at it then. Although how we will be able to determine if something has been taken is beyond me." She waved Mrs. Grant over. "At least, Helen, you will be able to look for some way of contacting the girl's mother, as you wanted." Aunt stopped, her eyes narrowing. "You wouldn't know anything about this, would you, my dear?"

"No," Helen said with a little too much force.

Thankfully, her aunt's focus was upon the box. Good Lord, what if she found the obscene cards in *The Lady of the Lake*?

Barnett swiftly shifted a plate and knife as Mrs. Grant placed the box between Helen and her aunt, and then stepped back. Aunt opened the lid, letting it rest back on its hinges.

Everyone peered inside.

"It is not packed very neatly," Aunt remarked. She pulled out the white chemisette, placing it on the table.

"Rifled by a thief, madam," Mrs. Grant said firmly.

Helen felt as if all eyes turned upon her, but when she looked up, everyone was still inspecting the box.

"I cannot see why Berta would leave this behind." Aunt held up the blue dimity dress length. It followed the white chemisette onto the table. The heart-shaped tin box was next. Aunt opened the lid. "Just coins." She studied the remaining items. "There do not seem to be any letters."

"I'm not sure Berta could write, my lady," Mrs. Grant said.

"There are books here," Aunt said. "She could obviously read." Helen held her breath as Aunt reached into the box again. "Maybe one of them will have some clue for you, Helen. An address or a letter between the pages."

She nodded. Finally her aunt pulled out the leather-bound Bible. "Ah, perhaps we will find an inscription in here."

Helen breathed out again. "I'll take the other book, shall I, Aunt?"

Without waiting for a reply, she leaned over and levered out the copy of *The Lady of the Lake*, laid flat on the bottom. Just where she had left it. She turned slightly away and fanned the pages. They flicked smoothly through to the end. Where were the cards? She fanned the pages again. Nothing. She took the book by the thin spine and shook it over her lap. Nothing dropped out. The cards were gone. Had she misremembered? Left them in the Bible? She glanced across at her aunt, flicking through the first few pages of the Holy Book. No, she had definitely jammed them into *The Lady of the Lake*.

Someone else had taken them. A lascivious servant?

The other possibility hardened into icy alarm. Another Deceiver.

"Is there anything in that book, Helen?" Aunt asked.

Helen shook her head, unable to speak.

"Nothing in this Bible, either. Surely if a thief had broken into the box, he or she would have taken the coins. Perhaps it has simply been damaged somehow, Mrs. Grant."

"Perhaps, madam." Mrs. Grant's disbelief was thick in her voice.

"May I have a look at the Bible, Aunt?" Helen croaked. She had to be sure.

With a tiny shrug, Aunt passed it over. Helen fanned the pages, knowing even as she did so that it was fruitless.

"Take it away, Mrs. Grant," Aunt said, gesturing for the housekeeper to pack away the meager belongings. "We will think what to do with it all after the ball."

"Yes, madam." Mrs. Grant deftly stowed the belongings, clearing her throat to gently prompt Helen to return the Bible. Helen handed it back, feeling as if she were handing over a last hope. It went into the box, atop the chemisette, and the lid was closed with a soft, final thud.

~

FINALLY RELEASED FROM the breakfast room, Helen made her way upstairs, weaving around the busy servants. Huge arrangements of flowers were being heaved into place, oil lamps trimmed and hung from sconces, and large mirrored trifold screens set up in corners to reflect the light of the extra crystal candelabra. She passed faces she knew and a few she did not, every one of them a potential Deceiver.

Back in the safety of her bedchamber, she called for Darby. Her maid appeared at the dressing room doorway, her arms full of linen. "Yes, my lady?"

"Come over here." She motioned Darby across to the chaise under the window, as far away from the door and its ubiquitous guard as possible. "Aunt just opened Berta's box, and the cards are missing."

"Missing?" Darby's eyes widened with horror. She lowered her voice into barely a breath. "You think they were taken by another Deceiver?"

Helen blessed her maid's quick understanding. "I don't know. Perhaps it was just one of the footmen looking for money and finding obscenity instead."

"Is the money gone too?"

"No."

Darby's nose wrinkled. "A footman would have taken the money as well."

"Yes," Helen said, her vain hope defeated by logic.

"What will we do, my lady?"

Helen stared fiercely at the roses on the carpet, trying to marshal her thoughts. If there was a Deceiver in the house, then there was a good chance it was after the *Colligat*. Her hand found the small pouch beneath the layers of her clothing. Some of the Deceivers obviously knew she possessed it. Only a fool would ignore the possibility that news of the *Colligat* could have been passed along to other Deceivers, including one secreted within her household. If that was the case, she had to assume that a Deceiver now knew of the weapon, and that it would be intent upon stealing it. But the creature could not know she intended to use it that night. All she had to do, then, was keep the miniature safe. Then she could use it to strip her powers, destroying the weave of hair and its magic, and it would no longer be of any use or interest to the Deceivers. Or a threat to the other Reclaimers. Just as she would be of no use or interest or threat to either party.

Helen gave a sharp nod. Her reasoning was sound. Still, it would not hurt to have someone search for the Deceiver in her house.

"Find Lily," she said.

Darby dropped the linen on the chaise longue and hurried from the room.

Helen paced to the door and back again, unable to stand still. She crossed to the window and looked down into the street. Her eyes found the gap between the two houses, her heart lifting as she saw a man leaning against the wall. Too big for his lordship. Quinn, then. Helen pushed away the absurd disappointment.

A soft knock, and the door opened again. Darby and Lily entered. It did not take long to apprise Lily of the very real possibility that there was another Deceiver in the house.

She rubbed her mouth, considering. "I've truly seen no sign of one, my lady. If it has eluded me, it must be very canny."

"If there is one, why does it not strike?" Darby asked. She glanced at Helen. "Sorry, my lady."

"No, it is a good question."

Lily gave a small shrug, not offering much reassurance. "There could be many reasons. It may not be in communication with others. Or perhaps it is collaborating, and searching for the *Colligat*. That would take some time, I can assure you. It is not easy to find something in a household as big as this." Darby nodded her emphatic agreement. "Is the piece safe, my lady?"

"Yes," Helen said. A new caution stopped her from adding its location.

"The safest place for it would be on your person at all times, my lady," Lily said. "A Deceiver would only strike, I think, if it had glutted and built whips. To me, it seems unlikely that one would attempt to glut and risk being discovered by you. Without weapons, no Deceiver would risk attacking a Reclaimer. Even such an untrained one as yourself, my lady."

Helen nodded, although she was taken aback by the idea that

a Deceiver would consider her a danger. Hard on the heels of the surprise, however, came a fleeting sense of fierce power.

Lily straightened into new purpose. "I'll keep searching, my lady. And I'll try to get a look at the belongings of the other maids and the footmen. See if I can find those cards."

"There is something else you can do, Lily," Helen said. "I know Mr. Quinn is out front—"

"And Mr. Bales at the back," the girl interjected.

Helen had not known that, but let it pass. "Go out and tell Mr. Quinn the news so he can take it to Lord Carlston. Perhaps his lordship or Sir Jonathan will have some new idea who the Deceiver could be."

Although the expression on Lily's face told her it was not likely, the girl nodded. "I will, my lady." She curtsied and withdrew.

"Anyone could be a Deceiver," Darby said as the door closed. "There could even be more than one."

"I know," Helen said, trying to keep the hollow fear from her voice. "We just have to keep my mother's miniature safe until midnight."

Twenty-Eight

HELEN GLANCED AT the small gilt clock on her dressing table. A quarter before ten. In less than fifteen minutes, her first guests would start to arrive. She could hear the musicians tuning their instruments in the drawing room-turned-ballroom, the twang of a fiddle and a snatch of "Juliana" from a flute. The smell of the sumptuous supper, particularly the game pies and roast fowl, permeated the whole house.

"Don't move, my lady," Darby said softly, poised to replace a diamond pin that had come loose from her coiffure; Helen had touched the elaborate braids and curls once too often since Monsieur Le Graf had departed. Darby pushed the pin into the twisted knot at Helen's crown, exhaling with relief. "There." She stepped back, judging the result. "No harm done."

Helen kneaded one gloved hand with the other, her eyes upon her own reflection in the mirror. Ringlets fell rather becomingly on either side of her face, and another longer curl from the back of the coiffure had been arranged over her left shoulder. An emerald diadem curved across the front of the high-set hair, her drop earrings and necklace matching the gleaming headpiece. It had been a gift from Aunt, from her own jewels.

"I will come up at about ten minutes to midnight," she said, meeting Darby's eyes in the mirror.

"What if it is in the middle of a dance, my lady?"

"If necessary, I will say I need a few moments to rest." Helen wet her lips. Every part of her felt parched. "You saw how long it took Lord Carlston to mix the alchemy for Jeremiah—no more than a few minutes. I will prepare everything and then wait to drink at the stroke of twelve."

Darby nodded, but her face buckled into itself as if she were trying to hold back tears. "And if you cannot go out to the ball again, I will find your aunt and make your excuses." Her voice held the flat tone of rehearsal. Or perhaps it was dread.

"Too much excitement combined with my injury: she will believe that," Helen said. She forced some brightness into her tone. "All will be well."

"Will it, my lady?"

Darby was right to be doubtful. No one knew the full effects of using the *Colligat*. Not even Lady Catherine, and she had created it.

Helen took her maid's hand. "I don't know what I will be when I—" She stopped, not sure what she wanted to say. An apology, perhaps, for whom she might be afterward?

Darby closed her other hand over Helen's. "I just hope you don't become like Lady Anton," she said.

Helen gave a dry laugh. Lady Anton was renowned for throwing things at her servants.

"Are you sure you want to do this, my lady?"

"It is what my mother wanted. I don't want to go mad or be hunted forever."

She turned back to her reflection, finding refuge from her own doubts in the fierce contemplation of her gown. Madame Hortense had outdone herself. The pleated cream bodice sparkled with brilliants, and the band around the high waist was thick with spring-green embroidery and pearl flowers, the lustrous gems also sprinkled across the sheer overskirt. The sleeves had been caught up at the center of each shoulder with a pearl-and-diamond *fleur-de-lis,* exposing a delicate lace half sleeve beneath. It was a suitably magnificent gown for her last night as her true self.

A rap on the dressing room door made her jump. Lud, her nerves were as tight as fiddle strings.

She turned as Darby opened the door to Philip, dressed in his formal red-and-gold livery, a freshly powdered wig upon his head.

He bowed to Helen. "Lady Pennworth requires you in the ballroom, my lady."

"Thank you." Helen stood and smoothed her skirt. Once again Darby had secured the little bag with her mother's miniature—her mother's *Colligat*—between her chemise and petticoat, tied to her stays. She was ready.

~

HELEN DREW AN appreciative breath as she walked into the ballroom. The mirrored screens against the walls reflected the hundreds of candles set into crystal and silver candelabra, creating a soft but brilliant light. Arrangements of cream roses, to match her gown, stood in lustered vases, a riot of the blooms filling the fireplace. The floor had been chalked, ready for dancing, and small groups of gilt chairs stood in the corners.

Aunt was making one last critical circuit, the scarlet feathers in her turban swaying as she appraised every detail. The musicians dipped their heads as she passed, visibly relieved when she nodded her approval. Two liveried footmen stood at the doors, and four more were stationed at the corners of the room. Helen studied the face of each young man, their politely blank expressions—a requisite for their role—taking on a new menace. One of them could be the Deceiver.

Aunt turned from her scrutiny of a candelabrum, saw Helen at the doorway, and bustled across the room. "How are you feeling, my dear?" She peered into Helen's face. "Did Darby use the rouge? You still look pale."

Helen touched her cheek. "She used a little."

"Well, we cannot risk too much. We don't want you looking like a trollop."

The sound of orderly commotion downstairs halted her aunt's scrutiny. "Ah, I think our first guests are arriving." Her voice vibrated with excitement. "Come, let us take our places to receive them."

Aunt had decided to have the receiving line in the foyer, just before the stairs. Uncle would greet the guests first, then Aunt, and then Helen. Guests could then move up the stairs to the ballroom or, if they were not inclined to dance, to the small chamber behind the supper room set aside for cards.

Uncle stood ready, resplendent in his bottle-green evening tailcoat and tight satin breeches. He eyed Helen critically as she took her place beside her aunt. "I hope you realize what a concession this is after your recent behavior," he said.

She was saved from answering by Barnett's announcement of the first guests, Lord and Lady Southcoate. The ball had begun.

Millicent and her parents arrived soon after. The Gardwells had traveled by foot, rather than carriage, so they were not caught up in the long queue of coaches along Half Moon Street.

Helen raised her hand in a small wave as Millicent made her way into the library—now doing duty as the ladies' retiring room—to change from half boots to dancing slippers and discard her silver cloak. It seemed to take an inordinate amount of time, Helen thought as she smiled and greeted a number of other guests, but then Millicent was never quick about such things. Finally her friend emerged in a delicate gown of pink gossamer net over white satin, made her greetings to Uncle and Aunt, and stood across from Helen.

"I am so glad to see you," she said, catching both of Helen's hands in her own as they rose from their curtsies. "I didn't know what to think when I was turned away on Sunday. Are you sure you are well?"

"Very well," Helen said, managing a genuine smile.

Millicent looked down at her hem. "Look, I tore my lace on the walk over. It took forever for one of your girls to mend it, and I don't think it will last. I shall be in rags by the end of the first set."

"I am sure Lord Holbridge will not complain about that."

"He is coming?" At Helen's nod, Millicent beamed, quickly shifting her expression into a more suitable, demure smile. "You are a *very* good friend!" She glanced at the ever-growing line of guests. "I shall see you in the ballroom, yes? We'll manage a few sets together!"

With one last squeeze of Helen's fingers, she headed toward the stairs where a young gentleman, hovering hopefully at the bottom step, offered his arm for the onerous journey to the first floor. Helen watched them ascend, Millicent laughing at a whispered comment from her admirer. She was such a dear, and a good friend. Helen had to admit that over the past few weeks, she had not been a particularly good friend in return. *After midnight that will change,* she vowed, and turned to greet the next guest. She would not have to lie to Millicent anymore. She would be just a girl again—albeit not the same girl—full of breathy excitement over balls and assemblies and the latest gossip. That would not be so bad, would it?

From then on, the queue was relentless. Helen curtsied and murmured greetings, a smile fixed upon her face as lords and ladies and misters and misses paraded past. Pug Brompton came through, dressed in a dubious shade of orange crape, and scolding Helen for allowing her horse to trip in the park. As Helen reassured her that Circe was unharmed, she caught a glimpse of a familiar, vivid face further down the line: Lady Margaret, her brother at her side. Helen's heart quickened. Perhaps they had a message from his lordship.

"Well, that is good news," Lady Elizabeth said. "I've always liked that mare of yours. Sweet temper. Thank the Lord and all his angels that she's all right."

On that benediction, Pug barreled toward the stairs, bringing the brother and sister one step closer. A curtsy and a murmured greeting to Sir Egmont and his lady, and then another to the very sweet Miss Taylor, finally brought Lady Margaret opposite Helen.

They curtsied.

"How lovely to see you again," Helen said. A slight rise of her eyebrows asked: *Has he sent a message?*

"We have all been so worried about you," Lady Margaret answered. *Yes.* She took Helen's hand, leaning closer as if to share a laughing confidence, the two matching gold bracelets over her glove clinking together. "His lordship said to tell you that he would be here soon," she whispered.

He was coming? But she had heard Uncle instruct Barnett and the footmen at the door to deny entrance to Lord Carlston. She shook her head. "He will not get in."

Lady Margaret gave a tight-lipped smile. "Yes, he will." She drew Helen even closer. "You put all of us in danger," she hissed. Helen tried to pull away, but the angry grip tightened. "You are throwing all these gifts away."

"It is my choice," Helen said through her teeth.

"Choice?" Lady Margaret's contempt was clear. She released Helen's hand and, with one last penetrating look, moved on, making way for her brother's elegant bow.

"May I have the honor of a dance this evening, Lady Helen?" he asked.

She regarded him dourly. "Yes, but only if you promise not to berate me as your sister does, Mr. Hammond."

He glanced at Lady Margaret, waiting for him at the stairs, with a calm smile upon her face and her gloved hands clenched. "Be assured that I, like his lordship, believe your calling must be by choice. It cannot be forced."

Helen curtsied. "Then I would be delighted to dance the third with you, sir. Thank you."

"Do not be too hard upon her, Lady Helen," he murmured. "She is worried for him."

Helen smiled politely. He was a very good brother, but Lady Margaret did not have a monopoly on worry. "Does his lordship think Mr. Benchley is a threat tonight?" she asked.

"We have not been able to find him since the hanging," Mr. Hammond said softly. "But be easy: his lordship has posted more men around your house tonight. You are secure."

She nodded, but she did not feel secure at all.

A murmur of greetings broke through the hubbub. Helen glanced down the line. The Duke and her brother had arrived. His Grace's tall, impeccably dressed figure had drawn some of the other young gentlemen into a cluster around him. He looked over their heads, searching the receiving line. She knew the moment he saw her: his face lit with a smile. She smiled back, then had to glance away, unable to meet the possession in his eyes. By the time she had regained her composure, he and Andrew had already moved toward the men's cloakroom to deposit their hats and canes.

It was not long, however, before she was curtsying to the Duke and trying to shake off the chill of her brother's perfunctory greeting received just a moment before. Andrew was, clearly, still annoyed.

"You must forgive your brother's curtness," the Duke said, his voice pitched for privacy. "He is most eager for your happiness, and I don't think he understands your delay."

They both looked at Andrew, who stood by the stairs, wearing an uncharacteristic frown of discontent.

"And you must forgive me for saying that I wish this night was over," the Duke added, smiling. "I wish it were already tomorrow morning, in your aunt's drawing room."

She looked up at him and tried to match his lighter tone. "Does that mean, Your Grace, that those sets you have solicited me to dance will be a chore?"

"A terrible chore," he said. "But one that I would not give up for the world. And please, call me Selburn."

She drew a sharp breath, hoping no one had heard the untoward invitation. It did not seem so, although her aunt had an odd smile upon her face as she turned to greet Lady Melbourne. "You honor me, sir, but you know I cannot."

The Duke bowed. "Not *yet*. I look forward to the terrible chore of dancing the opening set with you, Lady Helen." With a last smile, he joined her brother at the stairs.

"My dear," Aunt said sharply. "Lady Melbourne is waiting for you."

Helen turned back to the line, curtsying to the venerable lady. Almost all the guests had arrived, and it was not long before her aunt gave instructions to Barnett to bring any latecomers to the ballroom. With a satisfied survey of the crowded landing above, she ushered Helen upstairs to lead the dancing.

"I saw you talking closely with the Duke," Aunt said as they ascended. "Is everything well there?"

"Yes," Helen said shortly. She paused on the threshold of the ballroom, her heightened senses momentarily overwhelmed by the chattering crowd and the heat.

Aunt looked around with justifiable pride. "I heard Mrs. Harris already call it a 'sad crush.' We cannot have asked for a better attendance. Unless, of course, Mr. Brummell arrives. Then it will be complete."

"And the Prince Regent," Helen added, amused.

"Yes, him too," Aunt said.

Helen searched the groups of people and found Millicent near the fireplace, fanning herself and talking with Lord Holbridge under the short-sighted gaze of her mother. Helen smiled. That, at least, was going well. Lady Margaret and Mr. Hammond stood side by side, silently watching the proceedings, no doubt in expectation of his lordship. A futile wait. Helen followed her aunt further into the room, murmuring greetings to Sir Giles and Lady Gardwell, and nodding a general greeting to the blur of faces, all of them turning toward her with genial expectation.

"Call the dance, my dear," Aunt prompted. "Everyone is eager to take to the floor."

"Ladies and gentlemen," Helen said, raising her voice to penetrate the low hubbub. She waited as the quieting ripple of her call reached the end of the long room. "Pray, take your partners for 'Lady Caroline Lee's Waltz.'"

It was one of the best-known of the country-dances: a good choice to start the evening's entertainment. She looked across at the musicians. Their leader, the fiddle player, bowed his head in acknowledgment. The room shifted into motion as those guests who had no partner or did not dance drifted to the walls, while those engaged for the first formed two long columns.

The Duke appeared before her, bowing. "I am here for my onerous duty," he said. He took her hand, leading her to the top of the dancers, closest to the musicians, and delivering her into the first lady position. With a smile and an illicit wink, he took his position opposite.

The first note drew out into the honors—curtsies and bows exchanged—and then it was time for Helen to start her ball. With spine straight and arms curved, she began.

The Duke danced well, she noted. Not quite as athletic or elegant as his lordship, but then the Duke did not have the benefit of unearthly balance or strength. She smiled as he took her hand for the lead down the middle, their skipping steps a beat too fast for the music.

"The disadvantage of our long legs," he whispered as they slowed to match the tempo.

Helen laughed at the wicked comment, allowing the moment to push the specter of midnight into the back of her mind.

For the most part during the first two dance sets, the specter stayed subsumed; a raw presence that only pushed its way into her mind when she was not caught up in the dancing and conversation. Or when she happened to glimpse the clock upon the mantel.

Half past ten brought a sense of cold unease.

Eleven o'clock settled heavily within her chest.

Twenty after eleven wrapped icy fingers around her innards, the gilt clock face squarely in her vision as she advanced into the last figure of "La Vinetta." She quickly looked away, but panic spread through her body. Only half an hour to go. She rose up on her toes and returned to the side of the square, catching sight of Hugo searching the room with a worried frown.

Something was wrong.

He edged over to where her uncle sat, and bent to whisper something in his ear. The effect was astounding. Uncle sat bolt upright, his color changing from a flushed red into dark purple, brows angled into fury. He asked a question, the answer rocking him back in his seat as if he had come to a frustrating conclusion. He stood and gave a nod, sending Hugo out of the room at a quick pace. With a violent wave, Uncle called over one of the younger footmen, a curt command in the boy's ear sending him toward the musicians.

What was happening? A lesser dancer would have broken the figure, but Helen's reflexes and hours of practice kept her placed in the square. She watched the young footman sidle up to the fiddler and deliver the message. The man's heavy black brows rose, although he did not miss a beat.

The quadrille was coming to the final promenade. Just as everyone turned to begin, the sound of wood knocking upon wood halted the music, causing confusion on the dance floor and drawing everyone's attention to the doorway. Helen craned her head to see.

Barnett stood on the threshold, another bang of his long staff shifting people back and quieting the room. "Ladies and Gentlemen," he announced, "His Royal Highness, the Prince Regent. The Earl of Carlston, and Mr. Brummell."

He stepped aside, bowing as a portly figure in immaculate evening clothes strolled through the door, shadowed by two taller men, one fair and one dark. The arrogant tilt of the dark, shorn head was unmistakable. Lord Carlston.

Helen sank into a curtsy, the Viscount beside her making a graceful Court bow. From the corner of her eye she saw the sea of bent heads and knees and elegantly spread skirts, the silence broken only by the tick of the clock. She fixed her eyes upon the scuffed floor and tried to calm her racing heart—not caused by the presence of Royalty, but by the sheer audacity of Lord Carlston. The man had actually used the Prince Regent to gain entrance! No wonder her uncle was livid: he could not deny a member of the Royal entourage.

"Rise," His Royal Highness said.

Helen rose, alongside everyone in the room, to see the Prince Regent still at the doorway, his quizzing glass raised to his eye. Although he was soon to be fifty, there were still traces of the pretty looks that had made him Europe's premier chevalier in his youth. His skin was still fair, his hair brushed and curled carefully, and the plumpness of his cheeks added an eternal boyishness to his face. A few of the younger ladies giggled under his smiling scrutiny.

Helen looked beyond His Royal Highness, seeking the dark eyes that she knew would be searching for her own. Lord Carlston was scanning the other end of the room, forehead furrowed in concentration. *This way,* she called silently. *I am here.* As if he heard her, he turned, his expression warming into gladness. Her own smile locked into his gaze, the silent conversation between them read in the barest lift of a brow, flicker of an eyelid, the slow curve of a lip.

You are here. She did not try to hide her relief.

Did you doubt me?

Her gaze dropped for a moment. She had indeed doubted him. Perhaps she still did.

A tilt of his head accepted his part in that lost faith. *I gave my word I would keep you safe, and I will.*

Even though I choose . . . ?

Yes, even though.

"Now, where are our good hosts, Lord and Lady Pennworth?" the Prince Regent inquired, strolling into the room with an amiable smile.

Mr. Brummell touched Carlston's arm, drawing his attention back to His Royal Highness. A few strides and they had caught up with him, Mr. Brummell meeting Helen's eyes in cool acknowledgment. It seemed he was of the same mind as Lady Margaret. Helen felt a crimsoning of shame.

Aunt hurried forward to greet her Royal guest and sank into another curtsy. Uncle was not far behind, in arrival or in obeisance. "Your Royal Highness, you do us great honor," he said.

"Ah, Lord Pennworth, delighted. Absolutely delighted. I have heard much about your charming niece from Carlston here. It would please me greatly to be introduced," the Prince Regent said.

Uncle shot a venomous glance at Carlston. Aunt, meanwhile, looked wildly around the room, finally finding Helen. With a frantic hand, she gestured her over.

Helen had, of course, seen His Royal Highness many times from a distance, but up close he was a strange mix of intimidating Royal presence, stout geniality, and—dare she think it?—childish petulance that could be seen in the slight droop of his mouth and the obvious enjoyment of her uncle's and aunt's unease. It was well known that Mr. Brummell's influence had reined in the Prince Regent's love of ostentation, but an abundance of jeweled fobs still hung from his white waistcoat.

"Your Highness, may I present my niece, the Lady Helen Wrexhall," Uncle said, and Helen heard the clipped fury within his voice.

She dropped into a curtsy, praying she did not wobble on the way back up.

"Charming, charming," the Prince Regent said. His eyes were fixed upon her décolletage as she rose. She had heard about that regretful proclivity, but she gritted her teeth and smiled.

"Carlston tells me you are an accomplished dancer, Lady Helen," he said, finally lifting his eyes to her face.

"I am sure Lord Carlston is merely being kind, Your Highness," Helen managed.

The Prince Regent gave what could only be called a snort. "I doubt it, Lady Helen. He is most reticent with his approval. I, however, am eager to approve. Nothing gives me more pleasure than to see an exhibition of well-executed dancing. Do you have a free dance for his lordship, by chance?"

Helen had, in fact, no free dances. She wet her lips, not quite knowing how to respond to such a veiled Royal command.

"Of course she does, Your Highness," Aunt said brightly then added ruthlessly, "The next, I believe."

"Excellent," the Prince Regent said. He waved Carlston forward. "Well, go to it, man."

With a bow to his monarch, Carlston stepped forward and offered his arm. "May I, Lady Helen?"

She curtsied. "It would be my pleasure." She placed her hand on his forearm and felt a flat, hard curve of leather beneath his coat sleeve. He had come armored.

"Call the dance, Helen," her aunt instructed.

It was meant to be Lady Elizabeth's call. Casting Pug an apologetic look, Helen cleared her throat and announced the first that came to mind. "Pray take your partners for the 'Fairy Dance.'"

She closed her eyes, mortified. She had called one of the simplest country-dances: hardly a showcase for accomplishment. Still, she doubted that His Royal Highness actually wanted to see her dance. More likely, his lordship, or Mr. Brummell, had somehow inveigled the Prince Regent to request it. Perhaps under the guise of mischief—he dearly loved pranks and capers. Or perhaps His Royal Highness knew of the Reclaimers, as his mother did, and was disposed to help. Whatever the case, the reason was clear: Lord Carlston thought to persuade her to give him the *Colligat*.

She allowed him to lead her toward the musicians, people all around them hurrying across the floor to stand at the edges of the room or to take a place in the two columns. "It will not work," she whispered to him. "I am determined."

"You know I must ask," he said, his face earnest. "Please, give it to me. Allow me to destroy it."

"It is my way out of this nightmare," she said.

Lord Carlston stopped abruptly, people still swirling around them. Helen's eyes fixed on the tall, furious reason for their sudden halt. The Duke of Selburn blocked their way, standing an inch too close to his lordship. She looked down. His hand gripped the Earl's arm. Good God, Carlston could kill him with just one blow.

"What do you want with Lady Helen?" The Duke's voice was low, a false smile on his face. "Her uncle has made it clear you are not welcome here."

"I am about to dance with her, at the Prince Regent's request," Carlston said. "I do not see any objection from her uncle. What is your objection?"

"My objection is to you."

Carlston smiled. "Do you have an objection that I would give a damn about?"

"I have received her uncle's permission to address her. She is to be my wife."

Helen saw Carlston's jaw clench. He turned to look at her, his eyes completely black. "Lady Helen, is that true?" he asked tightly.

"Yes."

"You are betrothed?"

"No," Helen said, too quickly. Selburn caught his breath, as if she had delivered a blow.

Carlston turned back to Selburn, his teeth bared in his own false smile. "When you are betrothed, Duke, then I'll give a damn. Until then, you are on the dance floor without a partner." He looked down at Selburn's hand on his arm, a palpable warning in the slow glance.

The Duke released him. With his fist clenched, Carlston led Helen past him, toward the top of the column. She looked back at the Duke. His narrow face was white with fury.

"Do you really intend to marry him?" Carlston demanded, his voice pitched to a savage whisper.

"If he asks me again," she said coldly.

"Again?"

"I asked him to wait until tomorrow, in case—" Why was she even explaining it to him?

"In case of what?"

She lifted her chin. "In case I am a completely different person tomorrow. After I use it."

He looked at her for a long moment, then shook his head. "Lady Helen, you have far more honor than he does."

They had reached their place at the head of the column. Only nine other couples stood in line, somewhat less than usual. Perhaps dancing before the Prince Regent was too daunting for some. His lordship led her into position, then took his own. The musicians immediately struck up the first notes of the lively tune. The exchange of honors was made, and then, with unquiet eyes fixed upon one another, Carlston and Helen took three traveling *chassé* steps to Mr. Duncannon. The young man eagerly took their hands for the circle.

"It is a most excellent ball, Lady Helen," he said as they side-stepped to the beat. "I wish to—"

"Are you really going to refuse your duty?" Carlston demanded over him. "Your responsibility to humankind?"

Helen smiled sweetly at Mr. Duncannon. "I am glad you are enjoying the evening," she said.

They released the young man's hands and crossed to his partner, Miss Harris, who received no joy when she attempted to smile at his lordship.

"Are you going to ignore the question?" he asked Helen roughly.

"I thought you believed that this duty could not be forced, that it must be a choice," she hissed. "Well, this is my choice."

They released the goggling Miss Harris's hands and returned to the center.

"If that is your decision, then I ask that you do it in my presence," Carlston said, clasping both of Helen's hands, the grip a little tighter than decorum decreed. "So that I am sure you are safe and it is completely destroyed."

They began the skipping journey down the middle of the column.

"And you will not try to stop me? On your word?" Helen asked.

"On my word."

She drew in a breath. There could be no greater guarantee. "It must be done at midnight. I have arranged with my maid to be upstairs in my bedchamber at ten minutes to twelve."

He gave a nod. "Do not go up there until I am with you, do you understand?"

"I understand," Helen said as they held hands and skipped back up between the clapping dancers.

On the final note of the dance, Helen glanced at the gilt clock. Twenty minutes to midnight. She closed her eyes for a moment, gathering her courage, then sank into the finishing curtsy. Then another curtsy to His Royal Highness, who was pleased to incline his head before returning to the attentions of Lady Southcoate. His lordship rose from his own bow, a swift step bringing him to her side.

"I must find my aunt," Helen said, clapping politely alongside the other dancers. "Do you see the time?" She laid her hand on his offered arm. "I must tell her I will be retiring upstairs for a few minutes."

"She is over there with your brother and Lady Melbourne," he said, indicating the group seated in a corner, conversing. Helen heard her aunt's loud laugh ring out, and saw Andrew wince at the sound. Carlston sent a searching glance around the room. "Come, before your future husband appears in all his righteous fury."

Despite the sarcasm, his lordship had a point: the last thing she needed was the Duke to delay her retreat. They threaded between the knots of people gathering for the rest between dances and the cooling glasses of punch *à la romaine* offered by the footmen.

"My Lord Carlston? I have a message for you."

Helen and his lordship turned to see Hugo, a silver salver in his hand. He bowed and offered up the scrap of paper laid upon it. "From a large gentleman downstairs," he added. "He says he is your man."

Carlston took the offered missive. "Thank you." He unfolded it. Helen caught a glimpse of the writing: it was in no language that she had seen before. His eyes flicked across its contents, the only reaction a convulsive tightening of his fingers. "There will be no answer," he said, his voice flat.

Hugo bowed and retreated.

"Is it Mr. Benchley?" Helen demanded.

"No." The alarm deep in his eyes sent a jolt of fear through her body. "Brace yourself. Do not let any reaction show."

Helen nodded, her breath suspended into terrible foreboding.

"Quinn has found Bales, Lily, and one of your other maids dead in the alley beyond."

Helen felt the room lurch. *Lily dead? And Bales?* "Which other girl?" She gasped and grabbed his arm. "Darby?"

"Control yourself," he hissed. "Quinn knows Darby. He would have used her name."

Yes, true. She took a shaking breath. "Who could have killed them?"

"He says their bodies have the hallmark of a Deceiver glut." He caught her elbow. "Steady now. Smile." As she obeyed, he added softly, "I must search the house for the creature. Do not go to your chamber until I return."

"No—do not leave me here!"

"It will not try anything in this crowd. You must stay." He reached for his fob and pulled out the touch watch, the diamond arrow set upon the blue enamel case almost at the quarter-to-twelve mark. "The creature has glutted, so it will be easy to see." He took her arm, drawing her forward. "Come, I will take you to Lady Margaret and Hammond. You must stay with them for safety."

The brother and sister stood beside the fireplace, Lady Margaret fanning herself in slow arcs. Even her pale skin had a flush of pink from the warmth in the room. Her face brightened as she saw his lordship approaching, her pleasure shifting into concern as they drew closer. She could see something was wrong, yet her smile of welcome did not waver. Helen stood rigidly as his lordship apprised them of the events. Lady Margaret's hand tightened around her fan, and Mr. Hammond drew an outraged breath, but otherwise they showed no sign that a deadly creature had infiltrated the house.

"Shall I go with you, sir?" Mr. Hammond asked, squaring his shoulders.

His lordship shook his head. "Stay with Lady Helen." He bowed and started to work his way toward the door. Helen saw him flip open the touch watch and start to assemble the lens.

"Michael, fetch her some punch," Lady Margaret said, looking worriedly into Helen's face. "I think she is in need of refreshment."

Mr. Hammond snagged a glass from one of the trays carried by a passing footman and pushed it into Helen's hands. She did not want it, but Lady Margaret gently took her wrist, urging her to lift it to her mouth, and so she took a sip of the creamy iced punch. The rum within it burned her throat and jolted her from her shock. On the mantel, the hands on the gilt clock shifted to ten minutes to midnight.

She was going to lose her chance. Perhaps this was some kind of ruse by his lordship to stop her from stripping her powers. Helen shook her head. He could not have manufactured the alarm she had seen. But what if he was wrong about Darby? She took another, fevered sip, trying to calm herself. No, he was right: Quinn would have named her in the note. A worse thought made her cough as she swallowed the burning liquor: What if the creature was in her chamber? Where Darby waited. Oh God! Darby could already be dead!

She shoved the glass into Mr. Hammond's hands, the man grasping it in reflex as she spun on her heel and walked quickly into the crowd. She smiled and nodded at the faces that turned at her indecorous speed, forging past the claims on her company. A glance back showed both Mr. Hammond and Lady Margaret in pursuit.

"Lady Helen," Sir Egmont said, bowing. "It is such a—"

"Lovely," Helen said, sidestepping him and his wife, their surprise flashing by. She ducked into a clear space and looked back again. Mr. Hammond was gaining upon her; he would be at her side in just a few steps. She quickened her pace and saw salvation standing in the doorway.

"Duke," she said, dipping into a curtsy before him.

"Lady Helen. I see that you have finished dancing with his lordship." There was a frigid edge to his voice.

"Under His Royal Highness's order," she said bluntly. She had no time for fragile feelings. She drew a breath, trying to moderate the urgency in her voice. "Would you be so kind as to escort me to the stairs? I am not feeling well, and would like a few moments' respite before the next set."

No gentleman could refuse a claim of frailty.

"Of course." He offered his arm.

She glanced back again. The brother and sister stopped, the strain on Mr. Hammond's face giving Helen a sharp moment of guilt.

The Duke cleared his throat. "I would like to apologize for my behavior earlier." He gave a grim smile. "I am afraid Lord Carlston brings out the worst in me."

"I think you are not alone in that," Helen said as they reached the staircase.

She nodded to the footman posted to discourage guests from ascending into the private rooms. He moved aside with a bow. In the ballroom behind them, Lady Elizabeth's strident voice called, "Pray take your partners for the 'Scottish Reel.'"

"I do not like to see you in his company, Lady Helen," the Duke said. "What he did to Elise—" He stopped. "Well, you are aware of what he did."

"I am in no danger from him," Helen said quickly. She had to get upstairs.

"You have my guarantee of that," the Duke said. He lifted her hand to his lips in the old courtly gesture. "I look forward to the supper dance."

"Yes, of course. I am looking forward to it too." She withdrew her hand. Smiled. Took the first step, and the second, and the third, forcing a sedate pace that almost made her scream in frustration. Finally she reached the first landing, gathered her skirts, and took the next set of stairs two at a time, her breath shortening. *Dear Lord, keep Darby safe.*

Twenty-Nine

THE DOORS TO her dressing room and bedchamber were shut. Not unusual. She paused for an instant outside her chamber, listening for any sign of Darby. Or something else. No sound within, although her straining ears could hear the start of the lively music for the reel two floors down. She turned the handle and pushed.

The room was deserted. The candelabrum upon her writing desk cast a soft glow, and another had been placed on the mantel above the dying fire. The adjoining door stood open, the dressing room beyond shadowed and gloomy as if lit by only one candle.

"Darby?" she whispered, closing the door behind herself. "Darby, are you there?"

No response.

"Darby!" her voice rang shrilly into the ominous quiet. "Answer me!"

"My lady?" Darby appeared in the dressing room doorway. "I am here."

Helen gave a soft sob of relief. Unharmed, thank God.

"Has something gone wrong?" Darby said, hurrying into the bedchamber. "We have only five minutes until midnight."

"The Deceiver has killed Lily and Mr. Bales and one of the housemaids."

"What?" Darby pressed her hand to her chest. "Which housemaid? Not Tilly?"

"I don't know." *Good Lord, don't let it be little Tilly.* Helen crossed to the desk, stripping off her gloves. "His lordship is looking for the creature. It has glutted."

She threw the gloves on the chair, then felt along the desk for the key compartment. It did not matter if Darby saw her now.

"Glutted?" Darby's horror propelled her to Helen's side. "What are we to do?"

Helen unlocked the hatch and pulled down the desk. "Get the things out, Darby. They are on that top shelf. I shall get the miniature."

She sat on the edge of the bed, drawing up her skirts and petticoat, and freed the silk bag from the layers of her gown. As she pulled it open, a clink made her look up. The vial of sanctified water had chimed on the side of the silver bowl, set next to the tinderbox and knife. Darby turned to her. "All done, my lady."

Helen stood, holding the miniature. Darby's pale blue life-force flared out around her body. "Good work," Helen said. "Give me the knife."

"Give me the miniature," a man's voice said.

Helen whirled around to the adjoining door, the soft voice and bright Reclaimer glow registering as Mr. Benchley a moment before she saw his seamed face and pale gray stare.

"How did you get in the house?" She saw the answer in his attire: full evening dress.

He entered the room, pointing a sleek dueling pistol straight at her chest. "Through the kitchens. Just another inebriated guest wandering into the basement by mistake. A pretty little housemaid helped me back upstairs to the ball."

Somewhere within her shock, she noted he must have come in alone. No Mr. Lowry looming behind. She tightened her hold on the miniature. For an instant she considered throwing it to Darby. The girl was so close to the door, she could escape with it. But Benchley had Reclaimer speed and no conscience.

Abandoning that idea, Helen chose the alternative. "Darby, run!"

Her maid leaped for the door.

"Stay where you are, girl, or I will shoot your mistress!"

Darby froze. Slowly, she took her hand from the knob.

Benchley motioned her away. "Stand against the wall and do not move."

With a glare, Darby obeyed. "Further away," he ordered. She sidestepped until she stood near the desk. "That will do." He walked to the center of the room. "Lady Helen, you realize I cannot let you destroy your talents and my chance for redemption, don't you? Not to mention the power of that *Colligat*. Put it down on the bed."

Helen frowned. "You want the *Colligat* for its power? I thought you wanted to destroy it."

"Everyone wants the *Colligat*, my dear, and I can assure you no one wants to destroy it. Not even Carlston. Put it down on the bed like a good girl."

Helen slowly placed the miniature on the velvet bedcover, her mother's challenging gaze pointed to the heavens. The blue glow dropped away from Benchley and Darby.

A knock on the door wrenched everyone's attention around.

"My lady, are you in there?" It was Philip's voice. Helen felt a flash of hope, yet what could the young footman do against a seasoned Reclaimer? "Your aunt wishes you to come back downstairs."

In a few strides, Benchley was beside Darby, his hand closed around her jaw. She gave a small gasp. "Tell him to go," he said softly to Helen. "Or I will crush her."

Helen swallowed, her throat drying with fear. "Leave me, Philip," she croaked. "I am not well."

The door handle turned. What was he doing?

"I am sorry, my lady, but your aunt was insistent."

The door opened. Philip entered, the candlelight picking up the burnished copper in his hair. For some reason, he was no longer wearing his powdered wig. His eyes widened at the violent tableau at the writing desk.

"Shut the door," Benchley ordered, gesturing with the pistol.

Slowly, Philip pushed the door closed. He moved further into the room, his body lowering into an animal crouch.

"So," he said calmly. "You must be Benchley."

For an instant Helen was caught in the roar of her own confusion and the pounding of her heart. How could Philip know Benchley?

Good God! The rush of comprehension propelled her across the bed. She grabbed for the miniature. As her hand closed around the gold frame, a brilliant blue Deceiver glow leaped around Philip's body, three long, writhing whips curled above his head.

"He's the Deceiver!" she yelled.

The middle whip came slashing down. She rolled, flailing, off the side of the bed, the covers and mattress sliced into an explosion of feathers and burned velvet. She scrabbled backward along the carpet, her shoulder hitting the wall so hard, it sent hollow pain into her chest. Coughing, she squinted through the swirling dust and feathers. Benchley must have dived for cover too—he was nowhere to be seen. She saw Philip's liveried figure run forward, two of his three bright blue whips slicing downward. The sound of splintering wood and a low curse from Benchley pressed Helen harder against the wall. One of the candelabra arced through the air, a whip knocking it into the far wall with a ringing clank, its candles extinguished by the velocity. The light dropped into a murky gloom.

Where was Darby? Had she escaped?

She heard the slamming thud of whips hitting wood. Plaster spun through the air, and a plume of heavy dust burst into the room. Surely someone would hear them over the music and dancing.

She crawled back to the shelter of the bed, her legs catching in her gown. Wresting the skirt and petticoat out from beneath her knees, she gathered them into an unseemly bundle around her middle and inched forward. Philip had his back to her, whips poised above his head. With hammering heart, she risked a glance around the bedpost.

A pile of wood and torn paper lay where her secretaire had stood, and a hole had been punched into the connecting wall of the dressing room. Benchley lay on his back, white waistcoat soaked with blood, Philip standing over him. Helen gasped as two of the whips plunged down. Benchley rolled, dodging one whip, the other clipping his arm, slicing open his coat and shirt in a surge of fresh blood. He cursed, the momentum of his roll bringing him up on his knees.

Darby was nowhere to be seen, but the door was ajar. She had got out: thank God. And she would bring help. In the distance, the first deep toll of midnight struck.

Philip glanced over his shoulder. The middle whip slammed down in front of her, slicing into the carpet. She ducked behind the bed, biting her knuckles to keep from screaming. An awful realization pushed her further back: she was wearing so much metal. She ripped the diadem from her hair, yanked out the earrings, then feverishly undid the necklace, letting it drop to the floor. There were no pins in the gown, but the miniature was surrounded in gold. Hide it? No, she had to keep it safe and with her, or she would lose her chance.

Over the edge of the bed, she saw Benchley lunge, slashing at Philip's right whip with a glass knife, both men staggering and crashing to the floor. The bed frame shuddered as they slammed into it over and over, grunts breaking into low curses. Helen tried to gauge their position. Could she make it to the dressing room? To safety? She crawled to the end of the bed again. They were barely two yards away. Philip had straddled Benchley, the three whips and a pulsing blue-black tentacle all buried in the Reclaimer's chest—in his heart—his torso lifted from the ground. Blue power pulsed from the older man's body, his face contorted, his back arched in agony.

Helen reeled back. He was being drained!

Panting, she peered around again. Benchley writhed under the attack, pink foam bubbling from his mouth, his eyes wide. He reached a bloodied hand toward Helen.

"Help me," he gasped.

Help him? He had killed families. Murdered a baby. He had nearly destroyed her mother!

"Stay back," Philip snarled.

One of his whips uncurled from Benchley's body and snaked toward her, ready to strike. She ducked away. The other two drove down deeper into Benchley's chest, the tentacle sucking more violent blue power. He convulsed again.

"Help me." His voice was a wet whisper.

He clawed at the wood, dragging himself an inch toward her, the effort clear in his agonized eyes. She crept to the edge of the bed again. A whip slammed into the floor a finger's length from her face. She rocked back, momentarily blinded. Her vision cleared to a horrific sight: Benchley's bloodied eyes bulging, every vein bright with the energy being dragged out of him, his lips drawn back over yellowed teeth in a silent scream. His head pounded the floor, arms flailing. His whole body lifted into one huge convulsion that wrenched his torso upward for a moment, then dropped him back to the floor, dead.

Helen stared at the lifeless face, that final agony set into the wide-open mouth and bulging eyes. She pressed her palm over her own mouth, a rush of bile burning her throat. No time for sensibilities. She had to escape. Drawing a hard, panting breath, she forced the shock back down into her body.

The distant clock tolled again.

She had lost count. She waited for another strike, her ears straining—but heard only the rumble of carriage wheels, the calls of late revelers, and the beat of the reel below, the thud of the dancers' feet keeping time.

Midnight had come and gone.

Philip pulled his whips from Benchley's body, the tentacle retracting into his back. He turned to Helen. The three weaving whips were eye-achingly bright. Full of Benchley's life-force. "Give me the *Colligat*."

She clutched the hard oval frame. There would be another full moon next month—if she could keep it safe that long. If she could stay safe that long. She saw the glint of gold amidst the ruin of her writing desk. Her father's miniature. "It was in my desk," she said. "You can see it over there."

Philip shook his head, smiling. "A good effort, my lady, but I can sense it on you."

She clenched her teeth: of course he could. Yet why did he not attack and take it? Even as she thought it, she remembered the slam of his whip into the floor, driving her back behind the bed. He could have easily attacked her then, but he had not. Nor later. He did not mean to kill her at all. At least, not yet. "Are you the Grand Deceiver?"

He took a step closer. "Me?" He gave a harsh laugh, the three whips curling above his head again, undulating in a slow, obscene manner. "I am merely his vassal." He held out his hand. "Give it to me."

Behind him, the light in the dressing room flickered as if someone had opened the door and sent a draught across the candle. Helen drew in a breath, a prayer upon it. *Please God, let it be Lord Carlston.*

"I thought you creatures did not work together," she said quickly. "Why do you bow down to another of your kind?"

"He is not of my kind." Philip advanced another step.

"What kind is he?" she asked sharply. He was tilting his head, listening. "What does he want?" She must keep his attention upon her, not the doorway.

"I am not here to explain my lord's plans," Philip said. "I am here for the *Colligat*."

"He is a lord?"

"Not in the way that you think."

A sudden blur of speed erupted from the dressing room doorway. Philip spun, his whips slashing at the crouched figure that ducked and rolled. For a moment Helen saw Carlston's face, set into the hard lines of the hunter, then she leaped for the bed, dragging herself across its ruined linen. She dropped onto the other side, a trail of feathers rising behind her.

"Lady Helen, get out!" his lordship yelled.

A whip lashed against the door, slamming it shut. On hands and knees, miniature clenched in her fist, Helen lunged to the corner of the bed. His lordship grabbed one of the whips and wrapped it around his arm, dodging the other two as they sliced at his head. One connected with the wall, reaming a gaping hole, sending down a shower of plaster. Carlston leaped for the other, his hand closing around air as the lashing end flicked away.

He was trying to take all three!

"No!" Helen yelled.

He wrenched at the whip he held, staggering backward as the momentum jerked Philip off balance. Carlston hit the wall, Philip ramming into him. A moment of winded silence held them both still, then Philip's swollen feeder snaked out toward Carlston's chest. His lordship heaved Philip off him, grabbing the second whip as he rolled away from the groping tentacle. Roaring with rage, Philip yanked at his captured weapon, but Carlston grimly kept hold of the writhing end, doggedly wrapping it around his forearm as he ducked the slicing attack of the last whip.

She had to stop him from taking it. All three would kill him.

The third whip cut through the air again, the low buzz of it like a thousand angry bees. Carlston threw himself sideways, the blue lash carving a red pathway across his chest. Philip flailed, pulled behind him, stumbling over Benchley's leg. The two men staggered and hit the mantel, Carlston falling to his knees.

Helen saw a dark shape on the ground. The pistol! She jumped, her fingers clawing for the wooden butt, the miniature sliding from her hand. The blue glows disappeared. She grabbed the gun and swung around, ramming her finger into the trigger ring. She aimed at Philip's back and fired. Nothing. She stared at the pistol, frantically trying to remember what Andrew had shown her on the estate. The hammer. The hammer was not cocked. She wrenched it back. Aimed again and pulled the trigger. A crack. A flash of fire. She felt herself flung backward, the smell of smoke and gunpowder sharp in the air.

She blinked. Had she hit Philip? But he and Carlston had turned at the explosion, their struggle suspended in surprise. She had missed; a new hole punched through the wall above them.

The music downstairs faltered and stopped.

His lordship recovered first. Although Helen could no longer see Philip's whips or feeder, she saw Carlston's hand twist as if winding something around his wrist. He had caught the third whip! His other hand groped for the glass knife that lay near Benchley's head. His fingers connected and curled around the handle. Philip jerked back, slamming his elbow into Carlston's shoulder, desperately trying to loosen his grip. His lordship swung around and, in one savage stroke, sliced the glass blade across Philip's shoulders at the base of the three whips.

Philip screamed and dropped to the floor.

Carlston looked at her, panting, his body rigid as he tried to hold the whip energy that Helen knew was wrapped around his arm.

"Take the *Colligat*. Go!" he rasped.

Behind her, Helen heard the commotion of arrival. His lordship threw back his head and lifted his arms. She had seen that stance before, at Vauxhall Gardens: he was going to take the power into his body, the violent blue energy that had brought the terrifying smile of madness.

"No!" she cried.

She saw his arm plunge, his eyes widen as the power of the three whips slammed into his chest, arching his back into a rigid bow of agony.

"No! My lord, no!" A huge figure burst into the room—Quinn.

Darby stumbled in close behind him. "My lady!"

Twenty seconds. Before the energy consumed Carlston. Before it killed him. Twenty seconds to get him down three floors to the ground. To discharge the terrifying power ripping through his body.

"Get him out, Quinn!" Helen yelled. "Get him to earth!"

Quinn kicked his way through the debris on the floor and dropped down beside Carlston, trying to gather him into his arms.

"No!" Carlston gasped. He convulsed. "Too far up, too many people. Get her to safety."

"No, no, I can do it. I can do it," Quinn said through his teeth, but Helen could hear the defeat in his voice. "I can get you down."

"No," Carlston rasped. "My order. Do it!" He convulsed again, his veins bright bulging lines beneath his skin. The smiling madness was already in his face.

Bowing his head, Quinn released him, tears running down his cheeks. "I'm sorry," he said to Helen.

"No!" Surely, she could do something. What was the use of all this power if she could not save his life? *Save his life*—Lady Margaret had said as much in the Gardens. *One Reclaimer can absorb whip energy from another,* she'd said. *It would save his life.*

Absorb the energy. But how?

She saw movement out of the corner of her eye and swung around. Philip had hauled himself to his knees, his focus on the miniature she had dropped. He looked up, their eyes connecting for a frozen moment. She could see the savage determination, the fierce need. He had one aim: to take the *Colligat* for his master. Unless she stopped him. But Carlston was running out of time.

Helen gathered herself, ready to lunge. But which way? If she saved the miniature from the Deceiver, Carlston would surely die. If she leaped for Carlston and risked madness, the Deceiver would steal the *Colligat*—her way back to a normal life—and all that power would be in the hands of a Grand Deceiver.

Sometimes there is no good choice. Just the choice that has to be made.

Helen propelled herself across the floor. She hit the solid muscle of his lordship's chest, the impact slamming him on to his back, her body sprawled across him. As she clung to his shaking shoulders, she saw Philip dive upon the miniature. The Deceiver hauled himself to his feet and ran.

"Stop him!" she yelled, but he had already pushed past a gawking footman at the door.

Gone. The *Colligat* was gone. She felt it go, as if part of herself was being ripped away.

Sobbing, she grabbed for Carlston, blind instinct screaming that it had to be skin to skin. That she must touch him to save him. She pressed her tear-wet face to his, her mouth on the blood and sweat that smeared his cheek. He wrenched his head around, panting with pain, his lips against her throat, her jaw. Her lips. For an instant she froze—a reflex—then pressed into the taste of him: salt and brandywine, her breath hard against his gasp.

A jolt of energy arced between them, every nerve stripped raw, exploding into pain that edged into some strange, agonized delight. His lordship's arm locked around her back, their bodies seeking more contact, every touch bringing more and more power. She felt a savage joy, a spiraling triumph. It peaked: a breath-stopping moment of irreversible change that lifted her from herself into glorious exaltation and then plunged her back into her mind and body. Back into the ruined room and the sensation of his lips against her own.

Gasping, she raised her head, his lordship's stunned dark eyes upon her.

"Are we mad?" she said, panting. "I don't feel mad." Everything felt different—brighter—but not mad.

"No." He drew in a deep, shaking breath. "I think we are unharmed. I'm not sure how, but the energy is gone."

Gone. Like Philip and the miniature. "The Deceiver got the *Colligat*," she said. "He will have escaped the house by now. They will have its power. What should we do?" She frowned. "Why do you smile so?"

His lips had curved upward into some kind of elation. "Because, Lady Helen, you are a Reclaimer. You are truly one of us now." It was a statement. An announcement. A jubilant celebration. And she could not help but smile back.

"Helen!" Her uncle's voice cut through the sweet moment, the shock of its harsh disgust rolling her away from his lordship's body.

Lord Pennworth stood at the doorway, aghast. Barnett and two footmen peered over his shoulder. "Get out," he barked at them. They rapidly retreated.

He stared around the devastated room. "God's Blood, what has happened here? What are you doing? On the floor with a man. Like a whore. A *whore*!" He gripped the doorframe. "You," he spit, his eyes on Carlston. "Corruptor. Devil. What have you done to her?"

Carlston moved to rise but fell back, panting. Quinn caught his arm and braced him.

"He has done nothing wrong," Helen said. She climbed to her feet, the power still singing in her blood. "It is not as you think!"

"You defend him?" Uncle pushed past Darby and strode across the room. "We have His Royal Highness in the house, for God's sake. And the Duke." He grabbed Helen's arm. "Have you run mad? No. No, you are not mad"—his grip tightened into bruising punishment—"you are *evil*. I do not know what foul corruption you are part of, but you are no longer my niece. Leave my house, and never show your face again. Do you understand?"

Helen looked down at his brutal hold. *No more*. Very slowly, she peeled his fingers from her flesh. He strained against her strength, but inexorably, she lifted his hand away. With a snarl, he tried to yank himself free. Once, twice. But her grip did not yield.

Panting, he stared at her, a sudden, confused fear in his eyes.

"Yes, I understand," Helen said, and finally released him.

He backed away, clutching his hand. Now he understood too.

Thirty

Thursday, 28 May 1812

Two days later Helen sat alone in the morning room of Lady Margaret's town house in Caroline Street, pen in hand, the opening lines of a letter abandoned as she stared out of the window. Beside the inkwell stood a small stack of completed letters folded into neat packets, ready to be delivered. She watched as a mud-spattered carriage passed by, drawn by a very wet pair of bays. For the last two days, every grinding wheel on the road had brought a rise of expectation. But none had brought Lord Carlston, and now all she felt was a dull ache of uncertainty and guilt.

Her uncle's threat of dispossession had not been hollow. Nor had it been slow. He had insisted on her leaving the house that night, and had sent her belongings to Caroline Street the next day along with a curt note that dismissed Darby from his household. However, Helen knew that was not the end of it. He still had control of her money, and Andrew's silence did not bode well for any kind of mediation. She rubbed her breastbone, the ache of that estrangement like a dull counterpoint to her heartbeat.

She still did not know how the ruin of her room had been explained, or Mr. Benchley's body, or the disappearance of Philip;

Lady Margaret and Mr. Hammond had hurried her from Half Moon Street before the guests had departed. Apparently, everyone had been told that the excitement of her own ball had tragically caused her to relapse from the effects of her fall. She had not even had a chance to speak to Aunt.

She touched the letter on the top of the stack, addressed to Lady Pennworth. Of course it could not hold any true explanation, but she hoped Aunt would read the love and gratitude within the lines. Darby was in the midst of packing their traveling trunks, but as soon as that was completed, Helen would send her around to Half Moon Street again to place the letter directly into Aunt's hands. Otherwise, it would end up in Uncle's fireplace.

Darby had discovered that dear Tilly had not been the third victim of Philip's glut. It had been a kitchenmaid, the poor girl barely sixteen.

With all the death and mayhem, it was a marvel that no story had appeared in the papers, particularly since the Prince Regent had been present. Helen wondered how that feat had been managed, for this time it could not have been the Duke. Perhaps the Home Office had been called in by his lordship: obscured facts and vanishing corpses certainly had their touch upon it.

Yet Carlston had stayed away. Was it because she had lost the *Colligat*?

He had said nothing to her in the aftermath. Instead, when Uncle had retreated from the room, his lordship had risen from the floor and taken command, dispatching Darby to fetch Lady Margaret, and Quinn on errands that followed whispered instructions and the supply of coin. It seemed unlikely that he would now stay away from her in anger. Even so, she could not shake the fear that she had, somehow, failed.

She turned back to the unfinished letter on the desk and reread what she had written:

Caroline Street, London. 29 May 1812

My dear Delia,

It is with great pleasure that I write to you again. Although I cannot go into any detail at present, I find that my circumstances have changed to such a degree that I believe we can resume both our correspondence and friendship with impunity. I am to go to Brighton in the next few days with my friend the Lady Margaret Ridgewell and her brother, and will stay there for the summer season as their guest. Thence I am not sure where I will travel, but my hope is that we can soon meet again. Perhaps in Brighton, or if that is not possible, over Christmas once I am settled.

I also have another reason for writing, dear friend. I wish to reassure you that those events that you saw in that squalid room on that regrettable day were not figments of your imagination nor a sign of madness. I have good reason to believe they were real, and one day I hope to be able to explain to you what you saw. For now, however, be assured that you are sane, and that I

A knock lifted her eyes from the letter. "Yes?"

The door opened to admit Garner, Lady Margaret's butler. "My lady, Lord Hayden awaits below. Shall I show him up?"

Helen slowly put down the pen. "Yes."

As Garner withdrew, Helen took a deep breath and rose from her chair. What had Uncle told Andrew? No doubt something that cast her in a heinous light. But at least her brother had come.

"Lord Hayden," Garner announced. Andrew entered and stood watching her, unsmiling, as the door was closed behind him. He had not removed his greatcoat; the capes glinted with a sprinkling of raindrops. A short visit then. And, it would seem, not a friendly one.

"Hello, Andrew," Helen said, finally breaking the silence.

He crossed his arms. "Who are these people you are staying with?"

"Friends."

Andrew shook his head. "Aunt says that you have known them for only a few weeks."

"Yet they are kind enough to take me in."

He walked to the fireplace. "What happened, Helen? All Uncle will say is that Carlston has ruined you, and that he will not have you in his house again." His open face sharpened into savagery. "By God, if that is true, I will kill Carlston."

"It is not true," Helen said quickly.

"Uncle said you would defend him." Andrew's voice was heavy. "He has hinted that he found you on top of—" He stopped and turned his face away. "That is not true, is it?"

Helen clasped her hands, feeling the heat rise into her face.

"Good God." Her brother's eyes widened. "What has come over you? Do you think yourself in love with him?"

"No!"

"Yet you blush. I think you are lying to yourself as well as to me, Helen. Even if one could overlook his black heart and his crimes, he is still *married* by law!" Andrew paced a few angry steps. "You cannot stay here. You must come to Deanswood. Now! At least there I can make sure you are safe from him."

Helen clutched the back of her chair. "No, Andrew. I will not be hidden away."

"You have no choice. Uncle will not free your money. Do you propose to live on the charity of these so-called friends?"

"If that is what must happen," Helen said stonily. "But I had hoped you would help me."

"To your own destruction? Are you mad?" His jaw tightened. "Uncle thinks you *are* mad, like Mother. Tell me he is not right."

"Uncle's mind is always bent to the worst," Helen said. "You know as well as I do that Mother was not mad."

"Perhaps not, but she was selfish and wanton. I thought I would never say this, but I see her within you."

"Then I am glad."

Andrew shook his head. "If I cannot control you, Helen, Uncle will step in. He will force you into compliance."

Helen remembered the fear in her uncle's eyes. "No, I don't think he will." She met Andrew's hard gaze. "Will *you* force me, brother?"

The pained anger in his face shifted into resignation.

"No," he said. "You know I will not."

She stepped forward. "It will be all right, Andrew. Trust me. I am going to Brighton with Lady Margaret for the summer. She is taking a house for the season. She is a widow, a suitable chaperone. Every propriety will be observed." How easily subterfuge came to her lips now.

Andrew gave a reluctant nod. "You know you are causing Aunt enormous grief," he said.

Helen bowed her head. "I know." She reached for the letter addressed to Lady Pennworth. Even with all his anger and disapproval, she knew her brother would deliver it safely. "Will you pass this straight to her—when Uncle is not nearby?"

"Of course I will." Andrew crossed the floor and took the packet. He turned it over in his hands, his gaze upon it but his sight clearly inward. He was coming to some decision. "If you are to stay here," he finally said, "I will not have you living on the charity of others. I will make you a small allowance, but you must stop any contact with Lord Carlston. For the sake of your future." He slid the letter into his pocket. "The Duke has asked me to inquire if he may call on you."

For a moment Helen saw a sharp, terrible image of the Duke and Carlston arriving at the same time. "No, not here," she said. "I know he has a right to the interview, but not here."

"You misunderstand me, Helen. He does not want to withdraw his suit. Quite the contrary."

She shook her head, nonplussed. "You must be mistaken."

"No. He said to me that he would not stand by and let you suffer the same fate that befell Lady Elise. He lost one woman he loved to Carlston. He is determined it will not happen again."

"His Grace is acting from misplaced nobility and honor," Helen said quickly. "Please, tell him to expect a letter from me. I will release him from his obligation."

"He is acting from deep regard for you and your safety. I can assure you he is a determined man. For goodness' sake, girl, he still wants you."

"You must persuade him otherwise, Andrew."

"I certainly will not. Look me in the eye and tell me that you no longer have any regard for him."

"It is not that at all."

"I thought as much," her brother said. "Anyway, I agree with him. You need to be protected from Carlston."

Helen looked away, fighting back the impulse to tell him the truth about Lord Carlston. But she was part of the Dark Days Club now, and that world—including his lordship's honor—had to be hidden. Besides, if she started to talk of Reclaimers and Deceivers and alchemy, Andrew would surely think her mad.

"When do you leave for Brighton?" he asked.

"The day after next."

"Then I'll write to our lawyer today and arrange for the allowance."

"Thank you."

He gave a brusque nod and bowed. "I'll take my leave." He paused at the door and looked back. "I am still worried for you, sprite. Perhaps if you are good and quiet in Brighton, Uncle will have you back, and everything will be as it was." His smile was full of boyish hope.

The door closed behind him. Helen stood, her eyes upon the vacated space, transfixed by a sudden understanding. Her brother had not yet learned that, in the end, nothing ever stayed the same. Least of all, people.

~

THE NEXT MORNING she was writing the last of her letter to Delia when the sound of a carriage drawing up stopped her pen. Lady Margaret, seated near the window with her embroidery, peered out.

"He is come," she said. The excitement in her voice and the flush to her cheeks could only mean one particular arrival. Lord Carlston.

Helen laid down her pen, wretchedly aware of the ink stains upon her fingers. No time to wash them. And, despite all the waiting and wondering, no time to gather herself.

"Lord Carlston, my lady," Garner announced.

Lady Margaret stood and smoothed the front of her gown. "Show him in."

Helen rose, feeling a little light-headed. What if his lordship was angry after all? A *Colligat* in the hands of a Grand Deceiver was no small matter.

Lord Carlston entered. He had removed his gloves and coat—a long visit. Lady Margaret would be glad.

"Good morning," he said, bowing to their curtsies. He held a small flat box in one hand.

"It is such a pleasure to see you, Lord Carlston," Lady Margaret said.

"I am sorry I have been so long in calling upon you," he answered, but his eyes flicked to Helen.

"Are you well?" Lady Margaret took a few steps toward him. "Lady Helen says she is without effect, but you took those three whips—"

He held up his hand, halting her concern. "I am well, thank you. Is Hammond already in Brighton?"

"Yes, as you ordered."

"Good." He gave a short nod. "I wish to speak to Lady Helen alone. Would you be so kind as to leave us?"

Helen saw Lady Margaret's gaze snap across to her, then back to his lordship: she did not like being excluded. "Of course." She curtsied again and withdrew, her glance staying upon Carlston as she closed the door.

Helen cleared her throat. They were alone, but propriety no longer mattered. Not now.

"Are you truly well?" he asked.

"Yes, thank you." She lowered her eyes, trying to suppress the sudden image of lying astride the length of him. The taste of brandywine. "And you?"

He nodded. Of course, Lady Margaret had already inquired about his health. The pause lengthened into awkwardness.

"Would you like to sit down?" Helen asked, motioning to the two armchairs before the small fire.

They sat.

Helen clasped her hands in her lap, staring at the ink stains along her fingers. If she looked up, she would remember the touch of his mouth upon hers, and surely he would see it in her face.

"I am sorry for the grief you must be feeling regarding the estrangement from your family," he began.

"It was my choice, sir," she said, cutting in. "I only hope you do not blame me for letting that creature take the *Colligat*."

He shook his head. "Lady Helen, let me assure you that I respect your choice." He paused, his half smile arriving with a soft laugh. "Especially since it saved my life."

Today that smile did not seem so irritating.

"I am not sure how you did it though," he continued. "By rights, the energy we shared should have still required release into the earth. But it did not. Nor do we have any perceivable effects from keeping it. At least, I do not."

"Nor I," she said, adding a silent prayer of thanks.

He nodded, as if expecting her answer. "It is all unusual. But then, you are a direct inheritor. Your power is unusual."

"Even so," she said somberly, "it is my fault that the *Colligat* is in the hands of the Grand Deceiver."

"At least we now know that the Grand Deceiver is a true threat. From this time on, he must be our focus. He has one part of a *Trinitas*; we cannot allow him to collect the other two." He gave a sigh. "I cannot mourn for Benchley—he was no longer the man I once knew—but I mourn for the knowledge that he took with him."

"Did he not keep any written record?"

"No, not that we know of." He looked down at the case in his hands and then held it out. "This is for you, Lady Helen." The smile lifted his lips again. "As an appreciation of your courage."

She took the box, neither its weight nor the gold-embossed

stamp upon the green leather giving any clue as to what it held. She unhooked the two brass catches and lifted the lid. Nestled in a swath of white silk lay a sea-green touch watch. The central arrow was made of diamonds, like his lordship's, but the twelve markers around the edge were beautifully cut emeralds. The light from the window played upon the glossy green enamel, sending a shimmer across its surface, like a breaking wave.

"If you open it," he said, urging her to take it from the box, "you will see that inside, it has the same lens configuration as my own. I had two made, in case one was damaged." He reached for it. "Please, allow me."

Their fingers touched as the watch passed between them. The memory of that dizzying jolt of power flashed across Helen's skin, sending an echo of delight through her body. He felt it, too: she knew it from the catch of his breath and the flare of his eyes, their centers completely black. Now she understood why he did not want to release the Deceiver energy. Why he fought Quinn to keep it.

"A beautiful gift," she finally said, looking away from the lock of his gaze. "Thank you."

"It does not replace the power of your mother's miniature, of course," he said, his voice a little rough. "You will have to use the lens to see the Deceivers." He leaned over and replaced the unopened watch within the silk as if it burned his fingers. "Your training will start in earnest in Brighton, but I thought perhaps this morning we could review the use of the lens and the energy breaker within it." He glanced at the desk. "I see, however, that you are writing letters. If you would prefer to continue, I shall take my leave and return later."

"I am finished for now," Helen said.

After Delia's letter, there was only one more to write. Her first and last letter to the Duke of Selburn. Words of apology and regret—*sincere* regret for any pain caused—and, finally, words of adamant release. But for now, those words could wait.

She picked up his lordship's gift again and ran her finger across the diamond-studded arrow. It pointed to twelve o'clock.

"I do not think we have a minute to waste, Lord Carlston," she said, and held out the watch to him. "Show me how to use it as a weapon."

END OF BOOK ONE

Author's Note

I had an obscene amount of fun researching Lady Helen's world and the Regency era. There is some difference in opinion about what period in history is considered the Regency, but I sit firmly in the "true Regency" camp—1811 to 1820—when Prinny was acting as his father's Regent.

I have worked hard to make the London of 1812 and its social milieu as accurate as I possibly can, as well as maintaining a strict eye on the actual events that occur in the background of the action. I checked the historical weather reports, read military and crime accounts in *The Times*, made notes on the phases of the moon, perused the fashion plates in *La Belle Assemblée*, studied numerous eighteenth- and nineteenth-century museum exhibits, consulted Regency experts, walked along Rotten Row and the streets of Mayfair, watched countless documentaries and Jane Austen–inspired films and miniseries, collected and wore a wardrobe of Regency gowns and stays, learned how to dance in the Regency style, tried Regency recipes for food and drink, and read, read, read everything I could get my hands on about the era. I am now, officially, a Regency bore.

Even so, after all that research and those vows to remain historically accurate, there are a few editorial departures from fact that I want to mention:

Vauxhall Gardens did not open until June first in 1812, due to renovations, but I have merrily opened it in early May because I really wanted to set those important scenes in the Gardens and the deliciously named Dark Walk.

Lord Byron did attend a party at the Howards' on the night of Sunday, May 3, but it appears to have been much smaller than the one I depicted. In addition, there is no documentation that Lady Caroline Lamb also attended; although, in my defense, she did often follow him around.

To my knowledge, there is also no documentation that supports the assertion that Napoleon Bonaparte was a Grand Deceiver . . . but you never know.

A number of the minor characters are my interpretations of real historical figures: the Prince Regent, of course, as well as Queen Charlotte and Princesses Mary and Augusta, Beau Brummell, Lady Jersey, Lord Byron, Lady Caroline Lamb, Lord Perceval, and John Bellingham. The events around Lord Perceval and Bellingham are also true—Bellingham did assassinate the Prime Minister—and my depiction is entirely based on newspaper and magazine reports from the time, as is my description of the terrible Ratcliffe Highway murders. The scandalous love affair between Byron and Caro Lamb is well documented too, although I have given it my own slant. A number of other real people are also mentioned: the artists Sir Joshua Reynolds, William Turner, and Sebastiano Ricci; the Berry sisters; David Brewster; the aforementioned Napoleon Bonaparte; Bishop Meath; Annabella Milbanke (who would later marry Lord Byron); Messrs. Haggerty and Holloway; and Lord and Lady Cholmondeley. Pug Brompton, however, is not real. She is inspired by some of the romping aristocratic girls depicted in *Love in a Cold Climate* by Nancy Mitford, and my delving into the lifestyles of the twentieth-century "between World Wars" rich and horsey.

A few extra things you may find interesting:

The touch watch is modeled on a real timepiece: a magnificent watch that Napoleon Bonaparte gave his brother-in-law as a gift. You can see it, as well as other beautiful jewelry, Regency fashion, and ephemera on my Pinterest page at www.pinterest.com/alisongoodman.

The pornographic cards that Helen and Darby find in Berta's lockbox are actual illustrations by Rowlandson and an unknown artist. They are, however, *not* on my Pinterest page.

The simultaneous lighting of the lamps at Vauxhall Gardens was one of its advertised "spectacles." In a world where only candles and oil lamps supplied artificial illumination, it must have been a spellbinding experience to see darkness suddenly driven away by such a blaze of light.

Mr. Hammond is described as having a respectable fortune of 2,000 pounds a year. (It was thought that a genteel lifestyle in Regency London required a minimum of 1,000 pounds annually.) Today, 2,000 pounds would be roughly 67,900 pounds or 110,700 dollars—a very respectable yearly amount indeed! Helen, with her inheritance of 40,000 pounds, would have had over 1.3 million dollars to her name.

All of the books, newspapers, and magazines mentioned, including *The Magus, Debrett's Peerage,* and *Old Moore's Almanack,* are real, and some of them (such as *Debrett's* and *The Times*) are still being published today.

Because of the beginnings of industrialization and a rising middle class, shopping came into its own in the Regency period as a leisure activity. (The Prince Regent loved to shop, and I mean *really* loved to shop, racking up a debt of approximately 75,000 pounds every year.) The first arcades and department stores were established, and I have mentioned some actual shops and businesses of the time, including Gunter's, the confectioners; Farrance's, the pastry shop; and the Lamb Tavern (which still exists).

To ensure that my 1812 London was as accurate as possible, I relied upon *The A to Z of Regency London*, published by the London Topographical Society. It is a series of maps based on a survey taken by Richard Horwood from 1792 to 1799, which was then updated by William Faden in 1813. A truly fabulous find.

I've listed the newspapers, magazines, books, films, documentaries, and exhibits that I used to create Helen's Regency world in the research section on my website at www.darkdaysclub.com. You can also see some pictures of me in my Regency garb. Prodigious good fun!

—Alison Goodman, January 2016

Acknowledgments

I would like to thank Ron, my brilliant husband, for his steadfast support and belief, and his excellent research, scientific, engineering, philosophical and cooking skills. Huge thanks also to my best friend, Karen McKenzie, who is my trusted first reader and whose insight and writing knowledge are invaluable to me, as is her friendship. And I am always grateful to my loving and beloved parents, Doug and Charmaine Goodman.

I feel very lucky to be working alongside some wonderful people who are friends as well as business associates. At the top of that list are my fabulous agent, Jill Grinberg, and my rock star editor/publisher, Sharyn November: a big thank you to them, and to their hard-working, enthusiastic teams.

I am a big believer in the value of a writing group as a way of refining work and surviving the ups and downs of the strange life that is fiction writing. Big thanks to my two gangs: The Y. & J. Writers, and Clan Destine, a group of madcaps who lighten the load. I'd like to give a particular shout out to Chris Bell, who generously read and commented on a large section of the book while moving house. My thanks also to Sean Williams for his kindness, generosity, and wise words.

I did an enormous amount of research for this book and loved every minute of it. One of my most favorite research moments was attending the Jane Austen Festival of Australia (JAFA) where

I learned to dance the Regency quadrilles and country dances that appear in the book. A big thank you to John Gardiner-Garden for his excellent dance instruction and historical dance books, and to Aylwen Gardiner-Garden, who organizes the fun, dance-filled JAFA every year.

Recreating Regency London was both a challenge and a delight, and I was privileged to have Jen Kloester, author of *Georgette Heyer's Regency World,* read my manuscript and check my Regency world. Jen also generously and promptly answered some very strange questions on the hop, for which I am very grateful.

My sincere thanks also to the two back specialists who kept me upright while I wrote the book: my chiropractor Dr. Warren Sipser, and my physiotherapist Natalie Szmerling.

Finally, I must acknowledge the sweet hound from hell, Xander. His loud snoring, stubborn Jack Russell demands, and random barking are an integral part of my writing workday.

Keep reading for a bonus
Dark Days Club novella
from Alison Goodman

Regency London, 30 April 1812

St. James's Palace

LORD CARLSTON STUDIED the thronging State Room, every part of his body focused on finding one unnatural gesture or expression in the flow of humanity. It was the first Queen's Drawing Room since the King's madness had descended two years ago, and Carlston had no doubt that the thrum of nervous energy in the crowd had tempted at least one of the creatures. Any kind of sharp arousal attracted them—sexual energy was best, but fear and anticipation could work almost as well.

He had positioned himself in front of the huge marble mantelpiece, the best place to view the room, but it was going to be nearly impossible to spot a mistake amongst the human distractions. All was in motion: nodding ostrich plumes in the women's hair, the sway of hooped skirts, fans carving arcs through the humid air, officials darting through gaps, and the dips of curtseys and bows. Even so, Carlston was patient. If a mistake was going to be made, he would see it.

It was an instant of unnatural stillness that caught his attention: a man no older than his own twenty-six years, standing in a patch of sunlight by the window that looked out across the royal gardens. Well-fitted green silk tailcoat, dress sword at his waist, tow-colored hair brushed forward into a competent *à la Brutus*, and a sharp-planed face set with a moment of utter blankness. Then it was gone, replaced by the fluidity of a human smile. A Deceiver. Carlston felt the certainty of it in his gut.

From habit, his toes bunched, body tensing forward for the fight. Not that he could do anything in a Royal Drawing Room. And more to the point, he was there to meet and test the girl, not confront Deceivers.

He eased his body back, noting the man's companions. All human and all oblivious, of course. But there was something else about the creature. Something familiar in the way he held his head. Carlston frowned. Had he encountered this one before? He flexed his hands, unsettled by the lapse in memory.

"She is standing with her aunt by the blue urn. Not quite what I was expecting, but then I have no firm idea of what one looks for in a Reclaimer."

The voice at his shoulder, soft and mocking, brought a half smile across Carlston's disquiet. He had not heard that voice in over three years. Yet he did not immediately turn to face its owner, instead switching his attention to the subject of the remark: an overly tall girl across the room, somewhat awkward in the old-fashioned hooped dress still required for presentation to the Queen. Lady Helen Wrexhall: the focus of all his hope.

On first glance, the chit was disappointing. Unremarkable dark hair built up into the high coiffure needed to hold the regulation ostrich feathers, brown eyes that were bright enough but held no particular fire, and a very decided jaw. He had last seen her when she was ten years old, but there was very little of that soft child left in the bold bones of her eighteen-year-old face. Definitely not a beauty in the classic, rounded way of fashion, yet she had presence. And, it seemed, a sense of humor, for her mouth struggled to suppress a smile as the girl beside her bumped her own ridiculous hoop into a gallant and almost knocked him over. Yes, a clever, knowing smile that brought its own kind of loveliness. Not unlike Elise.

He bowed his head, waiting for the pain of his wife's loss to pass. It seemed he was to be haunted at every turn in this damned country.

"It is fortunate, then, that I know what we are looking for," he said, finally turning to face George Brummell.

"My lord." The Beau's bow was as elegantly tailored as his plain blue velvet coat and white silk breeches. Although Court dress still demanded embroidery and lace, he remained unadorned. "It is remarkably good to see you again, William."

Carlston inclined his head. "And you, George."

His friend had not changed in face or manner: as sardonic as ever, and immaculate from his curled fair hair to the soft black leather of his buckled shoes. Not so himself—Carlston knew the years had bitten hard into his soul. The grief and anger were writ into the lines on his face.

The State Room was now so crowded with guests that some of the early arrivals had been edged up against the long line of red velvet swagged windows. The afternoon sunlight shimmered across satins, silver embroidery, and layered diamonds. Yet even with the hot, perfumed press of so many people, a wide half circle of space had been left around him. Society had a long memory. Every eye he encountered held either cold dislike or shocked curiosity. The wife killer was back; a dark fox amongst the virginal chicks in their white spangled tulle.

"Even after three years, the prodigal son is not welcome home," he said. "Are you sure you wish to stand here with me?"

Brummell gave a soft snort. "I lead society, William. Not the other way around."

Carlston bowed slightly, acknowledging the truth of his friend's words. Not even the Prince Regent had more influence on fashion and society than Beau Brummell.

"Prinny invited me to the theater two nights gone, and I have been summoned to the entertainment tonight. Your doing?"

George nodded. "His Royal Highness just needed a small push. In his own fashion he has always supported you."

"You have done a good job keeping him safe."

"Safe, but alas still wearing those foul embroidered waistcoats."

Carlston's sharp laugh brought the unfriendly regard of a nearby older man in regiment red—someone he remembered as once being a friend of his late father, the fifth Earl. The old man shook his head, murmuring a comment to his gray-faced companion. Even through the din of shrill conversation, Carlston's Reclaimer hearing caught the word *murderer.* No formal charges had ever been laid against him, but his countrymen had gone ahead and convicted him in the broadsheets, clubs, and assembly rooms anyway.

Christ's blood, why had he returned? Although Bonaparte still rampaged across Europe, the Continent at least held anonymity. But he knew why he was back, and there was no getting around the duty. Or the responsibility.

He glanced at that duty again. Lady Helen was talking to her aunt, a woman with a similarly thin build and angular face, who had taken her and her brother in after the death of their parents. It had been ten years since the Earl of Hayden and his wife had drowned off the coast of Cornwall, their bodies unrecovered, but Carlston still mourned the loss of Lady Catherine, one of their best Reclaimers. It pained him that such an honorable woman had died with the label of traitor sullying her name.

It was his hope—his desperation—that Lady Catherine's Reclaimer abilities had emerged in her daughter too. She had once mentioned that the girl showed a cleverness beyond her age, but did that point to the child being a Reclaimer?

L

exchange
Lobster
puppy

Calamity
Drooping
Program
Dirty

The unlikeliness of it sat like a stone in his gut. The talent was *lusus naturae*: a whim of nature, not an inheritance. He was proof of it. None of his ancestors had been burdened with the talent, yet here he was, built for strength and reflex and killing. So much responsibility, and so few Reclaimers in the world to maintain the uneasy Pact between human and Deceiver. Only the chance that Lady Helen was one of his kind had brought him back. One Reclaimer to train another. God willing. Nothing else would have made him return to England.

She suddenly looked over her shoulder at him, eyes alight with curiosity. What had prompted such attention? Perhaps she already had enhanced hearing.

He tucked in his chin; he must stop indulging in hope and get proof, either way. Of course, if she was a rare direct inheritor of the gifts, that brought a whole new swathe of problems. The arrival of a direct inheritor could mean the arrival of a Grand Deceiver—an even stronger foe to fight. They were damned if she was and damned if she wasn't.

The aunt had noticed his interest and turned her back, the obligatory low-cut bodice of her lilac gown showing bony shoulder blades like extended wings. It was a courageous gesture on her part, considering he stood beside Brummell, the one man who could destroy social success with the flick of an arched eyebrow. Nevertheless, her cold shoulder did not change the fact that she was his second cousin by marriage; a useful connection that would bring him greater access to the girl. In a few minutes, the old hen was going to have to welcome a very unwelcome member of the family.

The thought of her discomfort brought a moment of wry amusement. He pushed it away. *Schadenfreude* was not an impulse he admired.

"Have you heard news of our latest literary genius?" Brummell asked.

"I presume you mean Byron?"

Carlston adjusted the *chapeau bras* tucked under his arm. Carrying the flat crescent hat was one of the more irritating requirements of Court, along with the lace and velvet, but at least the dress sword was useful. The ceramic blade sheathed at his side might not be quite what Her Majesty had in mind, but if it came to close quarters with a Deceiver, it was good for one heart thrust.

"Yes, the darling of the ladies. And"—Brummell lifted his quizzing glass, a handsome monocle set in blue enamel, to survey a stripling dressed in canary yellow—"a surprising number of the men. Caro Lamb is so smitten she is not taking any care to hide it from her husband or the polite world. Lord Byron is fêted wherever he goes. I've not seen anything like it. And the vain fool is constantly courting more adoration."

"He can hardly know the consequences of it," Carlston said. Despite the half circle of space around them, it was still devilishly hot and airless. He shifted his shoulders, feeling the damp linen of his shirt catch on the nearly healed gash across his back: a recent burn from the energy whip of a Deceiver. "Are we in immediate danger? Are they grouping?"

"Perhaps. We may not have your talent for finding them, William, but we know they are circling. There is an extraordinary hysteria around my Lord Byron and they are lapping it up. They have already prompted two brawls with one fatality."

"Then Byron must be guarded. We cannot allow his energies to be sapped; we must find a way to defuse the hysteria that is drawing so many to him."

George raised his quizzing glass again and studied the room. Even his forehead was sheened with sweat from the oppressive fug. "Do they know about our young hope yonder? Are they circling her too?" he asked.

"I believe I have found one so far: the fashionable buck over by the far window." The slightest of nods pointed George's scrutiny toward the tow-haired man. "Whether he is here for Lady Helen or his own needs remains to be seen."

At that instant, the man turned his head and stared at them. A long, searching gaze followed by a smile of insufferable collusion.

A jolt of recognition fired through Carlston. He knew where he had seen the creature before: at Southampton when he had docked four days ago. That same smile had been in the doorway of a tavern as he passed. And he'd wager that the creature's earlier moment of blankness had not been a mistake, after all.

Perhaps he was an assassin. If so, a strange one to boldly show himself and court his target's attention. It was more likely he was interested in the girl. But what could he do here? Any direct action would result in what both sides were trying to prevent: knowledge of the Deceivers' existence by the populace.

This strange collaboration had been formalized in the Pact: an agreement for mutual survival. If George thought there was hysteria around Lord Byron, it would be nothing compared with the mayhem if it became general knowledge that Deceivers lived amongst them. Everyone would become a demon hunter, and everyone a potential demon. And the government's mortal fear of the mob—born from the Terror in France, and fed by the latest Luddite riots in Nottingham—would only add to the chaos and slaughter.

"Do you know who he is, George?"

"Count Piotr Solanski. Polish. Aide to the ambassador."

Of course George knew his name and position. He knew everyone and everything that happened in society. It was what made him so valuable to the Dark Days Club.

"Has he any connections here?"

"No English ancestry. Jonathan has confirmed that he has only two infant offspring. Both in this country."

Carlston grunted. It was hard to map the legitimate and baseborn children of a Deceiver, but Sir Jonathan Beech was a diligent Tracer. He rarely made mistakes, not after the debacle in Exeter five years ago.

Solanski lifted his chin, an insolent acknowledgment of Carlston's regard. Although the man looked to be only in his third decade, the creature inside would have arrived centuries ago, like all the others. And like its fellow hunters, it would have survived hundreds of years by stealing the bodies of its own human offspring.

Yet this Deceiver had only two infant children. An unusual lack of progeny.

Carlston felt the battle energy rise in his body again, tightening him like a hair trigger. If he reclaimed the children back to whole humanity, he could destroy this Deceiver. It was not often he could deliver *Mors Ultima*, the final death. And infants were easy to reclaim. They had not yet manifested the appetites that came from their Deceiver dam or sire.

He lightly clasped his forearm over the soft velvet sleeve, feeling the last tenderness in a near-healed stab wound that ran from wrist to elbow. A memento of the Deceiver offspring he had reclaimed a week ago: a seven-year-old girl in Calais, mothered by a whore and already vicious from the Deceiver energy—the vestige—that her sire had embedded in her soul. It had been a hard extraction, the girl slicing open his arm with a candle spike as he struggled to rip the vestige from her spirit. But he had finally reclaimed her to full humanity: an untainted soul, and a body that could no longer be her sire's next lifespan.

Still, Carlston knew she was only one of the creature's many offspring. That particular Deceiver had whored his way across France, and there were many other children for him to possibly colonize when his current body died. All of them embedded with that spark that formed a pathway to their flesh. He tightened his grip around his forearm, trying to contain the call to battle that hammered through his veins.

"Are there any others in the room besides Solanski?" George asked.

"None have shown themselves."

"We have sorely missed your keen eye, William. It has been a hard road without you." Brummell touched Carlston's shoulder, a fleeting contact.

The Reclaimer reflex was upon Carlston as fast as an indrawn breath. They both looked down at the small black-handled knife in his hand, the tip of its glass blade pressed lightly against the white silk of George's waistcoat. Another shift of his weight and it would be in his friend's heart. He could almost feel George's pulse through the knife.

To the room at large, he had merely leaned in to whisper a comment, his hand on Beau Brummell's shoulder.

"I would have chosen an ivory handle for the occasion," George drawled, but Carlston heard the quaver in his voice.

A few years out of polite society and he had turned savage. Or was it the beginnings of the vestige madness? If a Reclaimer saved too many offspring, took too much Deceiver vestige into his soul, it eventually ripped away his sanity. No, it could not be the madness. He had years of reclaiming to do before he had to confront that possibility.

"I beg your pardon, George." He drew back, pushing the blade up into his sleeve until he felt the reassuring lock of the silent, spring-loaded mechanism. "From all I hear, you have done well without me."

Brummell met his eye, a moment of hard blame in his face. "Not as well as we would have if you had been here. Benchley is no longer the leader he once was, William. I've heard he is reclaiming again. I've heard that he is *affected* by it."

Had George somehow picked up on his fear of the vestige madness? No, that was impossible, and yet here he was saying that Benchley—Carlston's Reclaimer mentor, the man who had been more of a father to him than his own unlamented parent—was heading toward that grim fate.

"Unlikely," he said, voice clipped. "Before I left, Benchley gave me his word he would stop. Besides, he is well aware of the danger if he continues. He would not risk his sanity."

"I know you live by *your* word, William"—Brummell lowered his voice—"but that does not mean everyone around you does the same. I've heard disturbing stories, and it cannot be denied that Benchley has failed as a leader. He has not kept the other Reclaimers united, and Pike, from the Home Office, has stepped in."

"Pike?" Now there was a man without honor.

"Yes, and as you may imagine, he is more concerned with politics and his own power than maintaining the Pact."

Carlston saw where this was heading. "I will not be staying, George," he warned.

"What if Lady Helen is like her mother? Will you stay then?"

"You know it is unlikely she has the talent. Her brother does not."

Brummell's mouth quirked in shared disappointment. "Nor has he the stuff to join our ranks."

Carlston nodded his agreement. Andrew Wrexhall, the current Earl of Hayden, was a pleasant enough young blood, but he lacked guile and discipline.

"So, you will stay if Lady Helen is what we need? And if she is not, you will return to your search for Elise?"

"Yes."

"Elise is gone, my friend." To the untrained eye, Brummell's customary sardonic expression was in place, but Carlston saw the tiny shift into entreaty. "There is no evidence that she is still alive.

You can do nothing about what happened. We need you here."

True, there was no evidence. Yet he had found the ruby signet that had been her wedding ring on the floor of the blood-spattered bedchamber. The ring was engraved on the underside with an interlocking W and E. WE: always together; the little pun a foolish, shared delight. Why had she taken it off? He spread his bare fingers, feeling the ghost weight of his own ring.

Solanski was on the move. Carlston watched him bow to his companions and slowly weave through the clusters of young women and their sponsors waiting to be called into the Grand Council Chamber and the presence of Queen Charlotte. The man was smiling again, this time with pleasure. How he must be soaking up the women's nervous anticipation, wallowing in the energy wash from their sweating, bound bodies. He would be glutted with power before long, and at his most dangerous.

George's focus was back on the girl. "What if she is what we need, but will not join us? Or does not have the necessary courage?"

"Then she becomes a liability." Carlston eyed his friend, challenging any judgment. "You know she will be a target for them. They must not have access to Reclaimer energy."

"Is that how it is now? We dispatch innocents as well?"

"I have had some practice in the area." Carlston kept all expression out of his voice, although self-disgust clogged his throat.

"Good God, man."

"We can safely say that God has nothing to do with it."

Yet if he still had any right to pray, he would beg that Lady Helen was her mother's daughter; as brave and talented, and as willing to step outside the confines of society as Lady Catherine. Then perhaps two souls would be saved: hers and his own. If indeed he had enough grace left in his soul for any kind of redemption.

George shook his head. "William, that young man in Exeter

was as much Sir Jonathan's mistake as he was yours. You cannot take all the blame for his death."

Carlston raised his hand, silencing the protest. "I believe our friend is making his way toward Lady Helen, and we cannot allow that. Introduce me to her aunt, George. It is time to start."

Brummell masterfully carved a pathway through the tightly packed room with a touch to a shoulder here, a bow there, and a raised quizzing glass at a particularly intransigent Lady Pembroke. Carlston kept his eyes on their objective, ignoring the low murmur that followed their progress, the slowly converging figure of Solanski always at the edge of his vision.

The aunt saw them coming and clasped the girl's gloved forearm in warning. If the situation had been less serious, he would have been vastly entertained by the woman's warring expressions of delight at Brummell's approach and dismay at his own.

She received George's bow with a jerky tilt of her head, the plume of long lilac ostrich feathers dipping and shivering. The woman had made liberal use of lavender water, but underneath it was a strong earthy scent of powder, clammy skin, and hairdresser's grease.

"Mr. Brummell, how lovely to see you again."

"It is always a pleasure, madam." George bowed again and with an elegant flourish of hand made the introduction. "Lady Pennworth, may I present the Earl of Carlston."

She bent her neck in cold acknowledgment. "Lord Carlston."

He inclined his head. "Madam."

Beside the old hen, the girl gathered an object at the base of her fan and closed her hand around it. A neatly executed maneuver, but he was attuned to subterfuge. She was hiding something. Had she brought contraband to her own presentation? Perhaps the girl had something of her mother's daring and initiative, after all. Or was he just clutching at straws?

With some attempt at grace, the Viscountess said, "My dear, allow me to present the Earl of Carlston and Mr. Brummell. Gentlemen, this is my niece, the Lady Helen Wrexhall."

Carlston studied the girl as he bowed, intrigued to see that she watched him just as closely. She kept her expression well controlled, but his impassive face was clearly causing her some frustration. She was used to reading people with ease. He bit down on the tiny hope that it was a first sign of a Reclaimer.

"Lord Carlston," she said, rising from her curtsey with creditable control of the hoop. Her cool glance also took in George. "Mr. Brummell. I am pleased to make your acquaintance."

She was tall for her sex: past his chin, when most women, and a good number of men, hovered well below. If it came to sword and knife training, it could be an advantage.

"Lady Helen, it is indeed a delight," he said. "Particularly since we are related."

"Distantly," Lady Pennworth said, mouth small.

Carlston smiled his Earl's smile. "And yet irrefutably."

The aunt subsided.

George cleared his throat, alerting him to the fact that Solanski was getting closer. Carlston gauged the man's approach. He was not quite mid-room and still had to make his way through the denser part of the crowd. But George was right—they would need to intercept him soon.

He turned his smile to the girl and targeted her most obvious point of weakness. "Lady Helen, I see that you carry a Vernis Martin fan."

He had once given Elise such a fan; there could be no mistaking the maker's high lacquer on the painted sticks. At the remark, the girl's jaw tensed and she touched the damp, flushed skin on her throat: definitely hiding something, and a little afraid of him too.

"I am a great connoisseur of fans," he added.

"Really? Of fans?" She kept a tight hold on her own. "And do you have much cause to use them?"

Carlston felt George's shoulder twitch with a suppressed laugh.

The aunt's eyes widened in warning at her charge. "Helen, dear, I am sure Lord Carlston merely has an interest."

"I do, madam," Carlston lied. "Would you allow me to inspect your example, Lady Helen?"

"It is nothing out of the ordinary, Lord Carlston," she said with a delightfully false smile. "I'm sure it can be of no interest to such an expert."

"A Vernis Martin is always out of the ordinary, Lady Helen." He held out his hand.

She met his gaze but did not move. Such a look in those brown eyes: a mix of stony stubbornness and hunted animal. He almost wanted to step back and save her the ordeal.

"Helen, show Lord Carlston your fan," the aunt ordered.

"I cannot believe you are serious, sir," she said, attempting the coquette. "I feel sure you are funning with me."

There was some native charm in her manner, but it would have to be brought out more if she was to be as effective as her mother.

"You will find that I am always serious, Lady Helen," he said.

"Show him, my dear," Lady Pennworth hissed, her real message clear in the tilt of her head: *Show him the fan so that we may be rid of him.*

He used the small diversion to track Solanski. The man was still mid-room, called to the side of Lady Conyngham. He would be held there for a few minutes at least; the famous beauty would not be rushed through the required admiration.

Lady Helen still hesitated. Carlston extended his hand further, the gesture forcing her into either unforgivable discourtesy or compliance.

With her chin up, the girl passed him the closed fan, the riveted head turned to his palm. Her stiffened fingers pushed something round and heavy at its end into his grasp, her expression schooled into indifference. But his training saw the tension around her mouth—dread and a little bit of fury—and the shift of her jaw. A quick mind playing out possible strategies. His hope lifted.

A flick of his wrist opened the carved ivory sticks, her secret locked under the crook of his fingers and shielded from all other eyes.

"A very pretty fan," he said, pretending to study the pastoral scene on the varnished ivory.

Attached to the rivet on a short blue riband was a miniature portrait of her mother, Lady Catherine. Good God, no wonder she was hiding it. She was about to carry a memento of a suspected traitor into the Queen's presence. Not to mention what was hidden inside the gold frame: Lady Catherine's Reclaimer glass. She had shown it to him at the start of his training, and he now had one himself, concealed in the pocket watch on the chain at his waist. Did the girl know what she had hanging by that riband? Perhaps not. Whatever the case, she would not have it much longer, and he would see how she dealt with unforeseen events.

He looked up and paused so that all attention was fixed on his next words. The girl stood as motionless as a hare circled by hounds. He released the knife, sliding it from its sheath up along his palm.

"Was this represented to you as an original Vernis Martin?" he asked.

Calculated words that brought the desired effect: a bantam spine-straightening in the aunt. As she gathered herself for protest, he tilted his hand until the razor-thin glass blade sliced through the riband. He gripped the untethered frame more firmly under his fingertips.

"I will have you know that the fan was a gift from her uncle, Viscount Pennworth," the aunt said, nostrils pinched.

"A lovely gift."

He pressed the blade back into its sheath and passed the fan to Lady Helen, the miniature already hidden in his other hand. He watched her reaction.

A quick glance down, a heavy swallow, and a tightening of her fingers around the closed fan, but nothing else. Such control; and she was not giving anything away in the level gaze that rose to meet his own. He almost smiled but fought the impulse to acknowledge their complicity. For an instant, fury narrowed her face—she had seen his enjoyment. His mask was not so foolproof, after all.

"I believe we must make way for others who wish to make your acquaintance, Lady Helen," he said, bowing. "It has been a pleasure."

"Lord Carlston, I do hope you will visit us," she said, stopping his deft withdrawal.

Beside him, George paused in his own bow, eyebrows lifting at the girl's audacity.

"I mean," she continued, ignoring the rustle of horror from her aunt, "will you do us the honor of calling on us tomorrow? Since we are *family*."

Clever girl, turning his own tactic against him.

"Helen!" Lady Pennworth was almost quivering at the girl's abandonment of propriety. And, no doubt, at the idea of furthering their acquaintance with him.

"Since we are family, Lady Helen," he said, "I would be delighted to call tomorrow. As would Mr. Brummell."

The aunt could not refuse a morning call from Beau Brummell.

George rose gallantly to the call to arms. "Yes, a pleasure, madam. Until tomorrow, then."

"Tomorrow," Lady Pennworth said faintly.

They withdrew, their different notorieties easing their side-by-side passage through the crowd.

"Really, William," George said, pained, "a call tomorrow? I had planned a visit to Hoby's for a new pair of boots."

"Lady Helen wants her miniature back." He opened his hand.

George's mouth pursed. "Is that what I think it is?"

Carlston nodded, closing his hand around the portrait again.

"Does it mean she has her mother's talent?"

Carlston heard the hope in his friend's voice. "Maybe." He looked back at Lady Helen as he slid the tiny gold frame into his waistcoat pocket, alongside his watch. Through the undulating stands of ostrich plumes, the girl was watching him, her strong jaw mutinous. She held the fan clenched in her hand, and it was clear she wanted to club him around the head with it. "I will know more after tomorrow's visit. That is, if you can divert the aunt and give me a moment alone with the chit."

George nodded. "Consider it done." He tilted his head at Solanski, freed from Lady Conyngham and heading toward them with purpose writ on his face. "It seems you are his target, not Lady Helen. What do we do?"

Solanski's behavior was baffling. If he was intent on assassination, he was possibly the worst assassin in the world. No, he must have some other goal.

A terrible thought took shape as he glanced around the State Room. So many diplomat guests: the American *chargé d'affaires* with a wondering smile upon his face, the more jaded Spanish and Turkish ambassadors conversing with their Sardinian and Neapolitan counterparts. And those were just the ones he recognized. The Queen's Drawing Room had brought the world to St. James's Palace. Was suicide Solanski's plan? Did he intend to display himself in the energy light show that was a Deceiver's death and destroy his brethren's hidden existence?

Carlston flexed his wrist at his side, sliding the knife back into his grip.

No, there would be no benefit. For all their lack of cooperation with each other, the Deceivers shared an ultimate goal: to survive like every other creature in existence. If Solanski brought them to the notice of the world, they would be slaughtered in the hysteria, along with countless humans.

For a moment, Carlston was reassured. A short-lived comfort; there was still no good reason for Solanski seeking him out.

"We will improvise," he said.

"Excellent," George said dryly. "I had forgotten how thrilling it is to be around you." He lifted his quizzing glass and watched the approach of the Deceiver.

"Lord Carlston," Solanski said, bowing with a militarist snap of his heels. "What a delight it is to meet you again. Please forgive me for bringing business to such a grand occasion, but I have some information for you that is to your advantage."

Carlston met the steady gaze, his heightened senses feeling the prickle of energy from the man's overcharged body. He had, of course, never been introduced to Solanski and could rapidly escalate the situation by refusing to accept the claimed association. Yet the possibility of information stopped him. Deceivers were not in the habit of contacting their enemy.

He bowed slightly and said, "Count Solanski, a pleasure to meet you again."

The man's eyes flickered with relief.

"May I present Mr. Brummell," Carlston added.

The two men bowed to each another.

Carlston fingered the smooth wooden handle of the knife still in his hand. "What is this information?"

"It is to be heard only by you, my lord. Perhaps we could step someplace that affords more privacy?"

George shifted uneasily. He was right, of course—it was an invitation to a trap. But it would get Solanski out of the crowded

State Room into a more manageable space. Especially since the Prince Regent was due to make an appearance.

"You will want to hear what I have to say," Solanski added.

Carlston had to admit he was curious. "Do you know the whereabouts of the Chapel Royal?"

"Yes."

"I will meet you inside."

The chapel was at the west side of the great gate and would be relatively deserted on such a secular day. It was also full of wood and stone. Insulators.

With a bow, Solanski withdrew and started to thread his way toward the center of the three doorways that led to the Grand Staircase. It seemed he did not want witnesses either.

"William, do you think this is wise?" George said, lowering his voice.

"Wise? When has any of this been wise?"

George frowned. "I will go with you."

Carlston briefly gripped his friend's shoulder, heartened by the offer. It felt good to have the resources of the Dark Days Club behind him again. Nevertheless, violence was not George's natural habitat.

"No. I trust you to stay here and make sure that events do not cause any"—he paused, taking in the *beau monde* around them—"unwanted revelations. I will collect Quinn on my way through."

He waited for George's reluctant nod, then walked into the tight pack of people. Heavy hooped skirts were pulled back and men stepped away, opening up a pathway before him. There were some benefits to being a pariah.

Even with infamy easing his progress, it took some time to make his way down the Grand Staircase. It had become a solid block of gawking onlookers, guests caught in the jam leading into the State Rooms, and Yeomen of the Guard attempting to keep order. Solanski must have made excellent headway or taken a different route, for Carlston did not see him on the steps or in the passage that led to the grounds.

Outside, on the palace's front portico, Carlston took out his touch watch. The blue enameled case was edged with twelve diamonds that stood for the hours, and a diamond arrow was set in the center, affixed to the workings inside. In the dark, he could read the time by feeling the position of the arrow in relation to the circle of gems. A side button opened the enameled cover to reveal a normal fob watch for daytime use. Carlston flicked open the cover now, but not to check the time. He pressed a tiny hidden catch at the bottom of the face, twisting it left, then right. The frame of the watch swung out on an axis to allow three gold-mounted prisms to rise from under the workings: two of solid glass and one of Iceland spar. He fitted them together—the spar in the center—and locked them into place. Newton's famous light prisms reworked into a Reclaimer glass.

Holding the device hidden in the cage of his hand, he walked down the steps and into the bright afternoon sunshine. First he would collect Quinn, and then they would make their way to the chapel and Solanski.

Carlston felt an old discordance. In the library at his country seat he had hundreds of historical papers that called these creatures demons, but he had never come across one that had been perturbed by entering a house of God or by facing any of the old exorcisms.

Quinn stood waiting with the carriage, broad shoulders leaned back against the polished side of the vehicle. A circle of other servants stood around him, gawking at the fiercely angled lines and swirls tattooed upon his dark face. Quinn ignored them, seemingly at ease, but Carlston could see he was primed for either curiosity or attack.

He straightened as Carlston approached, the spectators scattering back to their own equipages. "Trouble, my lord?" he asked, dipping his head into a bow.

Seven years as Carlston's Terrene—his guard and aide—had attuned Quinn to his every expression.

"I have been approached by a Deceiver. An offer of information. Most likely a trap."

"And you intend to walk into it?" Quinn said flatly.

He fell in beside Carlston, clearly not expecting an answer. They had walked into many worse situations on the Continent.

"Perhaps it really does have information."

Quinn grunted. "Anything it says will be a lie." He glanced sideways, voice dry. "The clue is in their name."

Carlston smiled. An old joke.

They quickly made their way through the various inner palace courtyards. Carlston was relieved to see the number of spectators diminish rapidly as they moved farther away from the State Apartments. Quinn made one sweep of Color Court, the closest yard to the chapel, but all was quiet, and so Carlston led the way through the final archway to the Chapel Royal.

The entrance to the small church was still within palace bounds, but the building's far wall stretched along Cleveland Row near St. James's Street and the racket of carriages from that busy thoroughfare was loud enough to reach him. Good. If events in the chapel escalated, he would need the cover of that street noise.

Both of the chapel's oak doors were closed. He handed his *chapeau bras* to Quinn, then drew the ceramic dress sword.

"Ready," he said.

Quinn pulled one of the heavy doors halfway open. With an eye to ambush, Carlston peered inside.

The chapel was dim and cool, the only light coming from three high windows and a line of sunlight through the opened door. The famous wooden ceiling was decorated with carved octagons and crosses, white paint picking out the shapes in stark outlines. A bank of wooden box pews stood along each wall, a single central aisle between them. The Royal balcony box was set high on the left wall, opposite the pulpit and the darker rectangle of an open vestry door. If he recalled correctly, that side chamber also held an exit to the street. Another escape route.

"Lord Carlston, do come in," Solanski called. "Or do you intend to remain in the doorway?"

The Deceiver stood near the pulpit with another, slighter man in black vestments. A priest. Or more to the point, a hostage.

Ignoring the jibe, Carlston lifted the Reclaimer glass to his eye and looked through the line of prisms. The priest's body was surrounded by the soft corona of pale blue light that belonged to all humans. Beside him, the violent ultramarine of Solanski's body pulsed with a long energy whip curling out from his left shoulder. Only one, but at least four feet long and bright with charge. The priest absently scratched his thin shoulder, unaware that the itch came from the lethal energy whip hovering above him.

"Damn," Carlston breathed. The distance between him and the Deceiver was too great. If Solanski attacked the priest, he'd not get there fast enough.

"How many whips?" Quinn asked quietly, squaring up.

"Only one."

Even so, it was going to be difficult with just a glass knife and ceramic sword to hand. Carlston palmed the prisms and the workings back into the case and pocketed the watch, its metal clinking against the girl's miniature.

"Is that your man Quinn behind you?" the Count called, stepping closer to the priest. "I really must insist that he stay outside, my lord."

Quinn shifted uneasily. Carlston gave a small shake of his head. He could not risk the priest.

"Quinn will stay back," he said, then stepped fully into the chapel, allowing the door to thud shut between him and his Terrene.

The Count gestured toward the priest. "Allow me to present the Reverend Alexander."

"My lord." The priest bowed, his thin pale face matching his slight frame. "Count Solanski tells me that you are both interested in the history of the chapel." His voice held a note of doubt but he pressed on. "I have a pamphlet you may find illuminating. The ceiling above us, for example, is attributed to Holbein."

"Reverend, leave us," Carlston ordered. He gathered himself, ready to spring into Reclaimer speed. "Count, I swear if you harm him—"

"Harm?" The priest stiffened. "What do you mean?"

"Go, Reverend!" Carlston roared. "Now!"

Perhaps God did look after his own, for the man jumped as if Carlston had shot at him and rapidly backed away through the side door that led to the vestry.

Solanski made no move. "I had no intention of harming him," he said mildly.

Carlston forced down the clamoring call in his blood. "You have built a four-foot whip," he said, walking slowly up the aisle. "In my experience, that holds a great deal of intention." He stopped a pew box away from the pulpit.

"Your reputation precedes you, my lord. I would be a fool to come without defense."

"You approached me. What do you want?"

"I have come to make a bargain."

Carlston snorted. "Again I say, with a whip?"

Solanski paced into the center of the aisle, his blond hair catching the soft light. He was giving himself room.

Carlston casually leaned his hand against the pew box door

beside him. It shifted slightly toward him. Box doors that swung out: a veritable line of insulating shields.

Solanski took in a deep breath. "I will discharge into the ground if you vow, on your honor, to listen to me without attack."

Discharge? Carlston studied him. What was his game? He had never come across a Deceiver who wished to parley, let alone one that offered to weaken itself as a sign of good faith.

"Discharge then."

"On your word as a nobleman?"

Did he want to give such a solemn bond? Yet he could not walk away from the possibility of information.

He held up the ceramic sword and placed it across the corner of the box pew. "On my word. I will not attack."

With a nod, Solanski squatted and slammed his hands against the tiled floor. Carlston did not need his Reclaimer glass to see the energy driving into the ground. The rumbling force sent up spinning stones and tiles. He ducked as they clattered back to the ground and drummed a short tattoo along the wooden pews. Dust plumed into the air, bringing shape to the shafts of sunlight across the ruined floor. The air smelled of dirt and the strange clean odor that came after lightning.

Carlston held his breath and listened for shouts of alarm. There were none.

"It will not have been remarked," Solanski said. He stood and brushed dust off his green silk coat. "The ground has swallowed most of the noise."

Carlston straightened. This was all uncharted territory. A slight movement in the vestry caught his attention: the priest peered from behind the door, hands clasped over his mouth. At least the man had the sense to stay there.

Carlston took out his watch and deftly reassembled the Reclaimer glass. He held it to his eye. The three prisms confirmed that Solanski's energy was no longer the bright ultramarine of glut, but had been reduced back to the same pale blue corona as a human. And the whip was gone.

"So we have both kept our word," Carlston said, clicking the instrument back into the watch case and sliding it into his pocket. "What is this bargain?"

Solanski wet his lips. "I have been delegated by some of my kind to speak to you."

"Your kind do not work together."

Solanski inclined his head. "That is true. This agreement did not come easily to us. However, if centuries of living in flesh have taught us one thing, it is the value of cooperation."

Carlston tightened his hand on the smooth edge of the pew box. Deceivers cooperating with each other was the last thing the Dark Days Club needed. "So what do you want to say?"

"You have a reputation for upholding the Pact with rigor and fairness. Is that still true?"

"Of course. It is a Reclaimer's sworn duty."

"Yet one of your kind is breaking the agreement. Killing us beyond the allowances of the Pact. All we want is to live our lives in peace, so here is the bargain, Lord Carlston. I ask for your intervention, I ask you to stop him; and in return I will give you information about your Dark Days Club. About the danger you are in."

"Who is breaking the Pact?"

Solanski met his eye. "Your fellow Reclaimer Samuel Benchley."

Carlston gave a sharp laugh. "That does not tally with the man I know."

And yet George had just been hinting that something was awry with his old friend.

"I assure you I am speaking the truth, my lord," Solanski said. "Just as I am speaking the truth when I say Benchley is also killing humans."

Now he knew Solanski was lying.

"That is ridiculous. There is no bargain to be had here."

"Ask your people about Ratcliffe Highway."

"Do not try to place that horror upon Samuel Benchley. I assure you I will not believe it for a second."

The Ratcliffe Highway murders were the worst killings in London in recent memory. Seven innocent people slaughtered in their homes, hammered to death with a maul for no apparent reason. One of them an infant.

"I tell you, Benchley is the perpetrator, and your people know it. There is something rotten at the core of your Dark Days Club, Lord Carlston."

"What reason could he have for such a heinous crime?"

"He thinks he is preparing for a Grand Deceiver."

Carlston stepped forward. Here was a chance for real information. "Has a Grand Deceiver arrived in England?"

"That is what I hear."

"Who is he?"

"I do not know."

Carlston shook his head—that was no answer; but Solanski showed his palms, an insistence of sincerity.

"A Grand Deceiver has many faces. I swear upon the lives of my offspring, and thus upon my own existence, that I do not know." Solanski laughed; a hollow sound. "You have no idea what is coming your way. A Grand Deceiver is not like us. I have heard your kind called *lusus naturae*, because of your speed and strength that matches our own. Well, a Grand Deceiver is our *lusus naturae*. As normal humans are to you, weak and slow, so we are to a Grand Deceiver. Can you conceive of that kind of power? Are you ready to battle it?"

"Stand aside, man, I wish to enter!" A woman's voice, outside the oak door.

Damn, they had company.

"Lady Drummond, please!" Quinn's voice. "There has been an accident within. It is not safe."

Lady Drummond: one of the more pious courtiers.

"Will you keep your word, Lord Carlston?" Solanski asked, skirting the hole in the floor, heading toward the vestry door. "Will you stop Benchley?"

"I will inquire," Carlston said.

Solanski nodded, a last sideways glance meeting Carlston's own. For an instant, that strange unnatural stillness wiped the humanity from the man's face, then it softened back into smiling bonhomie. He quickened his pace through the side door, the little priest holding up his cross and flattening himself against the wall as the Count passed.

Carlston slumped back against the pew. Did he believe Solanski? Perhaps it was just a sophisticated Deceiver trick to undermine the Dark Days Club. Yet if a Grand Deceiver had arrived and was as powerful as Solanski claimed, it was going to take much more than a united Dark Days Club to defeat him. It was going to take a Grand Reclaimer.

One of the oak doors swung open, sending a shaft of sunlight across the ruined floor.

"Lud!" Lady Drummond stood in the open doorway, the gold silk of her gown flaring in the bright light. "What has happened here?"

Carlston straightened and bowed. "An unfortunate collapse of the foundations," he said hoarsely. "You should withdraw, Lady Drummond, for your own safety."

The woman stared at him for a hard moment, then backed away. The door closed again and the sound of her shrill astonishment receded.

"Collapse?" The priest was at his side, staring at the hole in the floor as if it were a doorway to Hell. "I saw what happened, my lord. What was that creature?"

"I think it best that you stay with the story of an accident, Reverend. I am acquainted with your Bishop, and he will agree. I shall, of course, recompense the chapel." He pulled the diamond pin from the folds of his cravat. It would be at least two years' income for the man. "Here, take it. For yourself."

The priest hesitated, then reached for it. "I will take it for the poor," he said fiercely.

"Very worthy," Carlston murmured, but he liked the little man for his hesitation and unexpected backbone.

Holding the pin away from himself, the priest asked, "Do you know what diabolic forces you are dealing with, my lord?"

"It is not what you think." Then again, he thought tiredly, maybe it was. He pressed the heel of his hand into his forehead.

The priest crossed himself. "Did he harm you?"

"No."

Dear God, if Solanski was telling the truth, there was no one in the Home Office he could trust. Surely that was a lie?

The priest took a step closer. "I shall pray for your soul, my lord."

Carlston pushed himself upright and picked up the sword. He walked stiffly to the chapel entrance and opened the heavy door. A bright shaft of sunlight barbed his eyes.

He squinted back into the dim chapel at the lone figure in the aisle. "Don't pray for me, Reverend. Let your prayers be for a girl. Pray that she is everything she needs to be."

"What girl?"

Carlston stepped out of the chapel and let the door shut behind him. "Lady Helen Wrexhall," he said softly. "Pray for Lady Helen Wrexhall."

Turn the page for a preview of the sequel

One

Friday, 3 July 1812

At Lord Carlston's bidding, Lady Helen Wrexhall studied the gentleman walking rapidly toward them up the rise of Brighton's Marine Parade. Even at such a distance she could see that he was a thin, bitter-faced man in a sober blue coat rather badly cut across his stooped shoulders, and an unfashionable tricorn hat drawn low over his brow.

"Can you really see him in detail from this far away?" Mr. Hammond asked, squinting at the tiny figure. "He is little more than a blur to me."

"Of course she can: it is part of the gift," his sister said. "Do stop making comments, Michael."

"I can even see his expression, Mr. Hammond," Helen said across Lady Margaret's rebuke. The woman was forever criticizing and correcting. "I can report that the gentleman's countenance is quite sour. Probably a bad kipper for breakfast."

Mr. Hammond laughed. "Bad kipper. Did you hear that, Margaret?"

"Quite," his sister said, her expression as sour as the one under discussion.

Lord Carlston thumped the ebony tip of his cane into the dirt path. "Lady Helen, focus. What do you notice about his gait?"

She smothered a sigh. So it was to be another lesson on manly pedestrianism. His lordship was adamant that she perfect a male disguise; their duties, he said, would take them into taverns and the like, and she must convince as a man. Clearly, however, she had not yet mastered her understanding of the masculine stride.

She studied his lordship from the corner of her eye. Today he looked older than his twenty-six years, weary and distant, the bold angles of his face set into stern command. The forbidding expression was becoming all too familiar. Ever since she had been cast out of her uncle's house four weeks ago, she had watched Lord Carlston retreat from the strange energy that leaped between them when they touched, pushing it behind his new role of instructor. It felt as if a shared pulse was slowly being extinguished. Yet what could she say? Nothing between them had ever been voiced, could *ever* be voiced. He was, by law, still married. She must quash the energy, too, although she did not know how. Whenever he guided her arm through a sword stroke or showed her how to punch, it felt as if her body were aflame.

He had noticed her scrutiny. She saw something flicker in his eyes—that pulse perhaps, not totally quelled—and then a lift of his dark slanted eyebrows called her to the task at hand. She shifted her parasol, taking refuge behind the green silk shield—*Dear God, do not let him see the flush upon my cheeks*—and returned her attention to the fast-approaching figure.

"He moves his arms with vigor," she ventured. "And keeps his eyes to the fore."

"No, forget his eyes and arms. Do you see how each pace is at least this long?" Lord Carlston's cane plunged into the dirt again, measuring a good length from the toe of his right Hessian boot. "And despite those rounded shoulders, there is confidence in his upper body. You must take up more space when you walk and move with greater purpose."

Space and purpose. Helen took an experimental step alongside the flimsy fence that safeguarded the sheer drop to the beach. The hem of her promenade gown brought her up short, the sudden halt causing her touch watch to swing out on the end of its silk neck-cord and slap back against her ribs. Despite its compact size, the watch was no small weight—a product of the hidden crystal lens folded inside—and its impact left a definite sting, even through her layers of muslin and lawn. She gathered up the green enameled case and cupped it in her palm, the diamond arrow at its center pointing to the large emerald set at the eleven o'clock mark. Lord Carlston had given her the watch to replace the miniature portrait of her mother that had contained its own lens, which she had lost to the enemy. A most forgiving gesture on his lordship's part, considering the alchemy built into the miniature, and how dangerous it was to them all.

"Lady Helen?" Lord Carlston's voice sharpened. "Do I have your attention?"

She jerked her head up and let the watch drop back to the end of its cord. "Of course. More space and purpose."

She had no difficulty with the idea of more *purpose.* Surely that was just a matter of taking a longer stride—something that would be far more achievable when she was clad in breeches. Her long, lean measurements had already been given to a London tailor to sew her a pair of buckskins and all the other gentlemanly accoutrements. She was to be a fine young man, at least in the cut of her clothing. Her manner, however, was not so easily stitched into masculinity. According to his lordship, she still needed to deepen her voice, be less careful with the placement of her arms and legs, and now also take up more *space.* No easy task, since she had spent most of her life learning to control any excess gesture or movement. Nevertheless, she gathered up the hem of her gown, squared her shoulders, and rocked forward onto the balls of her feet.

"For goodness' sake, you cannot go striding around with your skirts up," Lady Margaret hissed. "Someone may see."

"It is not as if she is galloping along the seafront in her chemise, my dear," Mr. Hammond said.

"That may be so," his sister replied, her delicate features pinched beneath her straw-chip hat, "but it is past the breakfast hour, and we are in full view of everyone's drawing rooms."

They all looked across at the row of houses that lined the Parade. Most of them were still shuttered, but enough had their windows exposed to the bright June morning to give credence to Lady Margaret's alarm.

"I doubt that one or two steps will bring us undone," his lordship told her, "but your caution is exemplary."

Helen let go of her skirts and turned toward the sea to hide her pique, her eyes fixed upon a three-masted war-sloop no doubt making its way to Plymouth before joining the newly declared war with the United States. Perhaps it could aim its cannons at Lady Margaret and her *exemplary caution* instead, Helen thought, then immediately felt churlish. The woman was irritating, but she and her brother had been valued members of the Dark Days Club for over five years, whereas Helen had only just joined the secret order that protected mankind from the Deceivers. And although Lady Margaret and her brother were not *Reclaimers* like herself and Lord Carlston—rare warriors born to fight the hidden creatures—it could not be denied that they were also placing themselves in great danger. Not to mention the fact they had been kind enough to take her in after she had been expelled from her Uncle Pennworth's house.

"You must weigh and consider every action now," Lady Margaret added, her severe tone drawing Helen around to face her again. "One slip and you will—"

"I am aware of it." Helen smiled through clenched teeth. "But I am obliged to you for the reminder."

Lady Margaret regarded her warily, clearly recognizing the strain in her voice. They had been confined together over the past four weeks in a rented town house in German Place, not without some sharp words from both sides. The unhappy incarceration had been ordered by Lord Carlston, as it was imperative to the Dark Days Club that Helen start her Reclaimer training in earnest. It was a time-consuming project, and his lordship had insisted that they establish a reason why such a well-connected young lady staying in Brighton would be absent from many of the town's social delights. Convalescence was the most believable excuse, and so Helen had stayed indoors alongside Lady Margaret and feigned poor health. She had also braved a visit from the proprietor of Awsiter's Baths with his foul elixir of seawater and milk, and engaged the services of Martha Gunn, a sturdy old woman who dipped young ladies in the sea for their health—both clear indicators to society that she had come to the seaside resort for her constitution and not for the busy Season.

When she had asked his lordship why they had not gone to a quieter town instead—to her mind, a perfectly reasonable question—he had merely given her an endless shark-eyed stare. One of his more maddening traits. At least her *convalescence* story was now established to his satisfaction, and this morning he was permitting them to unobtrusively walk into town to sign the subscription book at Donaldson's Circulating Library: the very hub of fashionable Brighton life and, according to Lord Carlston, its center of illicit information.

Helen felt her gaze drawn to him again. He was back to watching the progress of the man walking up the hill, the clean lines of his profile set and unyielding. He reminded her of one of the Roman centurion statues she seen in Bullock's Museum, forever waiting for the enemy. Yet she could not forget that beyond those noble features she had seen a deep darkness within his soul. At first, she had thought it was the black mark of his wife's murder—a crime that he had never denied—but now she knew it was a slow poisoning from the Deceivers' foul energy. Every time he reclaimed a Deceiver's offspring back to humanity, the blight he ripped from its soul took root within his own. Helen knew that every Reclaimer had to eventually retire from saving souls, else it would send them mad. Yet Mr. Hammond had said his lordship refused to stop.

"I believe we are about to receive a visit from the Home Office," Lord Carlston said dryly, his attention still fixed upon the approaching figure. Helen looked back at the stooped man: his intention was now clearly aimed at the four of them.

Mr. Hammond tilted back the brim of his beaver hat. "By Jove, is that—?"

"Ignatious Pike," Carlston said. "I recognized him when he started up the hill. Hard to mistake that deplorable Whitehall style."

Helen saw a fleeting frown tighten Mr. Hammond's face, and knew he felt as exasperated as she did. If his lordship had known it was the government man all along, why had he not offered the information? He kept his own counsel too much. It was even more maddening than his shark-eyed stare.

"What is he doing here?" Lady Margaret asked.

"I would hazard a guess that the new Home Secretary has finally been informed about the Dark Days Club," Carlston said.

It was near two months since the Prime Minister, Lord Perceval, had been assassinated in the House of Commons. After much mayhem, His Royal Highness the Prince Regent had finally ratified a new government on the eighth of June, and along with it a new Home Secretary, Lord Sidmouth, who would, among other duties, oversee the clandestine Dark Days Club.

"Well, at least we do not have Ryder over us anymore," Mr. Hammond said.

Carlston nodded his agreement. "They could not keep him, not after he covered up Benchley's involvement in the Ratcliffe murders."

Just the mention of Lord Carlston's old Reclaimer mentor sent a crawling sensation across Helen's nape. It was Samuel Benchley who had forced her mother to absorb the Deceiver darkness within him, and it had all but killed Lady Catherine's soul. He had planned to do the same to Helen, but her mother had bequeathed her a *Colligat*—an alchemical way to strip herself of her Reclaimer heritage—hidden in the miniature portrait alongside the Reclaimer lens. Benchley had attacked Helen in her uncle's house, bent on stealing the miniature and its power, but had been killed by the Deceiver hiding as a footman in the household.

Even in the bright sunlight and warmth of the Brighton morning, Helen shuddered at the memory of Benchley's bulging eyes and popping veins as he died at the Deceiver's hands. The creature would have attacked her as well, but Lord Carlston had intervened and absorbed all of its lethal whip energy. The Deceiver had then grabbed for the *Colligat*, and Helen had been forced to make a terrible choice: leap for the *Colligat* herself and protect her only way to a normal life; or absorb half of the whip energy raging through Lord Carlston and save his life but lose the *Colligat*.

She had flung herself atop the Earl, and the intensity of that moment still sang in her blood. There had been so much power between them as their bodies locked together in an intimate embrace, which, if she were honest, had not been fueled only by the overwhelming hold of the Deceiver energy. Even now, standing on the road above the beach, the memory of his arms around her brought a wave of heat across her skin. She found the lever on her parasol and pulled down the canopy, trying to distract herself from the disturbing images. Had she not just vowed to reject these wayward emotions?

With the parasol folded and her composure back in place, she turned her attention to the arrival of Ignatious Pike. He was taller than she had expected—the downhill perspective must have skewed her reckoning—and if he had stood straight, he would have been almost Lord Carlston's commanding height. He did not, however, have the Earl's breadth of shoulder nor his air of strength. Still, his breath was unhurried even after his rapid climb, and he moved with some agility. The man was more athletic than his spindly, round-shouldered frame suggested.

He bowed to Carlston. "My lord." A cool glance took in Helen. "My lady, we are not yet acquainted. I am Ignatious Pike, Second Secretary to the Home Office."

Helen stared at him, taken aback. Was he grossly ill-mannered, or did his position allow him to sidestep the conventions of polite introduction? She looked across at his lordship, knowing he would see the question in her eyes. His answer came in the flick of one eyebrow and a wry cast to his mouth: *Acknowledge him.* So it was the latter: the man had some kind of status.

"How do you do, Mr. Pike," she said, and found his gaze had narrowed into a shrewd gaze of evaluation.

Two could play at that game: she met his close scrutiny with her own. It was difficult to place an age upon him. His face had a wizened quality, but his cold blue stare was bright, and his pasty skin still had the tautness of youth. No more than thirty, Helen guessed, and that was all she could glean from his sharp features.

Usually she could read a person's truth within their face—it was one of the Reclaimer abilities—but this man was even more closed than his lordship.

He allowed a wintry smile of triumph to touch his lips: he had seen her attempt *and* her failure.

"Mr. Pike, I believe you are already acquainted with Lady Margaret and Mr. Hammond," Lord Carlston said.

"Yes." Pike afforded the brother and sister a quick nod, before turning back to his lordship. "No doubt you know why I am here. You are requested to return to London immediately to meet with Lord Sidmouth. He has now been apprised of the Dark Days Club and its activities."

"Hopefully he will not be as corruptible as Mr. Ryder," Mr. Hammond said.

Pike turned a hard look upon him. "Mr. Ryder made the necessary decisions to contain the damage created by Benchley and to protect the Dark Days Club from public knowledge." The hard look traveled to his lordship.

"I think we all know that those *necessary* decisions were more yours than Mr. Ryder's," Carlston said. "You certainly know how to survive, Mr. Pike."

"Your lordship gives me credit that I am not due."

Carlston made a small sound of disbelief. "Has our new prime minister been fully apprised of the Dark Days Club as well? *And* the current situation?"

Pike let the question hang between them for a moment, his icy smile appearing again. "Lord Liverpool has been fully briefed, and I assure you, he gives Lord Sidmouth his full support."

"I would not have thought otherwise."

Although Carlston's tone was pleasant, Helen heard the draw of steel within it. The two men, it seemed, were stepping back into an old battle.

Pike crossed his arms. "Neither of them is convinced by your evidence that a Grand Deceiver has arrived in England."

"Not convinced?" Helen exclaimed. "But the Deceiver who attacked me *said* he served a Grand Deceiver."

"They are Deceivers, Lady Helen," Pike said with a note of condescension in his voice. "They manage to live as humans and fool us all. Deception is their nature."

"And yet we saw a number of them working together at Bellingham's hanging," Carlston said. "You know that is out of the ordinary."

"It is," Pike allowed. "But nothing in the archives even hints that such an occurrence points to the arrival of a Grand Deceiver."

Carlston drew a breath through pinched nostrils. "Then what about Lady Helen herself? She is a direct inheritor; the Reclaimer daughter of a Reclaimer mother. That, at least, is documented."

The wave of a thin hand dismissed his lordship's words. Or, Helen thought, maybe it dismissed such a *female* lineage.

"If I remember correctly, that archive only states that a direct inheritor has powers beyond a normal Reclaimer, to stand against all that may come." Pike looked inquiringly at Helen.

She felt obliged to shake her head: she had not yet exhibited any extra powers. A small mercy, in her opinion; she was having enough difficulty with the ones she already had.

"To stand against all that may come," Pike repeated. "Not a Grand Deceiver in particular; such a creature is never named. We cannot chase phantoms, Lord Carlston, especially with the Luddites rioting through the country and Bonaparte across the channel." He drew himself up. "You are expected at Lord Sidmouth's house to dine this evening, my lord. I suggest you start your journey back as soon as possible."

He gave a small bow, his eyes meeting Helen's again for an odd, intense moment, then he turned and walked back the way he had come, looking neither to the left at the sea, nor to the right at the handsome row of houses. Mr. Pike, it seemed, had not the time or inclination for a beautiful view.

Lady Margaret lifted her shoulders as if struck by a sudden chill. "Horrid man."

"Why does he not believe you?" Helen asked Lord Carlston. A jab of pain in her hand drew her attention to the fact that she was holding her parasol like a club, the lever biting into her palm. She eased her grip.

"Because it is I who brought the news," he said acidly. "Ignatious Pike is the bureaucratic heart of the Dark Days Club and its senior officer, yet he just delivered a summons that could easily have been carried by one of his underlings. So why did he make the journey?"

"Good point," Mr. Hammond said. "Perhaps it was to acknowledge you as new leader of the Reclaimers."

"No, he is here on some other business," his lordship said. "But what, I wonder."

Mr. Hammond pulled his fob watch from his breeches' pocket. "He is right about one thing. If Sidmouth expects you tonight, that does not give you much time to get back to Mayfair. It is already near eleven thirty."

Helen calculated the journey. It had taken her and Lady Margaret seven hours to travel to Brighton, but that had been in a coach-and-four, using the ill-matched teams that went for hire at the posting inns. His lordship had driven down in his curricle, a far lighter equipage, and he kept his own thoroughbreds stabled at the inns for each change. He could possibly make it back to London within five hours. Still, it would mean he would most probably not start his return to Brighton until the following morning.

The thought brought a small slump of disappointment. She

had begun to look forward to her training. The long hours under his lordship's tutelage were never easy—he gave no quarter—but the challenge was exhilarating, and it took her away from Lady Margaret's *reminders* of her duty.

Now he would be away for a day. Probably two.

Two days without the chance of touching him.

She coughed, shocked by the thought. Could she not even last five minutes without her mind taking a lascivious path?

"I shall make London by evening, and return Sunday afternoon," Carlston said, confirming her estimate. Yet she heard something in his tone that made her observe him more closely. He was uneasy in a way she had not seen before.

He turned to address her, once more the stern instructor. "While I am away, I want you to start reading the Romford book on alchemy—pay particular attention to the binding rituals—and practice your male disguise. The pitch of your voice is coming along well, but your gait needs a lot more work. Mr. Hammond, I trust you will assist Lady Helen and deal with any other issues that arise?"

Mr. Hammond straightened. "Of course, sir."

"I take my leave, then." Carlston bowed, then plainly bethought himself of something else and turned back to Helen, his eyes finding the touch watch around her neck. "When I gave that to you, I am sure I told you not to wear it on your person."

"You said not to wear it on a chain." She hooked the cord around her thumb. "See, it is on silk. And you said the enameling was made of glass and would insulate—"

"I said the enameling *may* insulate the metal underneath from creating a pathway for a Deceiver's whip-energy. But do you really want to take the chance?"

"No."

"I thought not." His tone sharpened. "Carry it in your reticule, and listen more carefully."

Helen pulled the cord over her head, opened the tiny purse, and dropped the dangling watch inside. "You wear yours," she muttered. Even to herself she sounded like a sullen child.

"I wear mine in a specially prepared leather-lined pocket in my breeches. As far as I know, ladies' gowns do not have pockets. Until they do, or you are wearing your own breeches, carry the watch in your reticule. For once, do as you are told."

Helen stiffened at the unfair criticism; she did everything she was told.

He pressed his fingers hard into his forehead. "I beg your pardon, Lady Helen. Forgive my ill humor. I clearly misled you regarding the effectiveness of the enameling." With that, he strode away in the direction of his lodgings.

They watched his progress up the hill, each silent and unmoving as if his departure had somehow suspended them. At the corner of Camelford Street, he paused and looked back at them, then was gone.

"He is far more ill-tempered than usual," Mr. Hammond said.

"It is just weariness," Lady Margaret said quickly. "They place too much upon him. It is a strain."

Helen glanced at her: she was half-right. Lord Carlston *was* weary and strained, but not only from the burden of his responsibilities. It was also the constant battle against the Deceiver darkness that shadowed his soul. She had seen the canker within him, had felt its corruption spreading, sapping the light from him, creeping a little deeper into his heart every time he reclaimed another Deceiver offspring. Yet he would not stop. Was it duty that compelled him to such risk, or something else?

She laid her hand on her chest where the touch watch had hung.

There was only one known way to cleanse a Reclaimer's soul: by pouring the darkness into another Reclaimer and destroying them instead. It had been Benchley's despicable solution, but neither she nor his lordship would ever resort to such a heinous act.

She turned her gaze back to the empty street corner where his lordship had stood only moments before. Yet what would happen if Lord Carlston finally descended into the tormented madness of a poisoned soul?

She closed her eyes. Yes, what then?

Read Alison Goodman's
New York Times bestselling duet

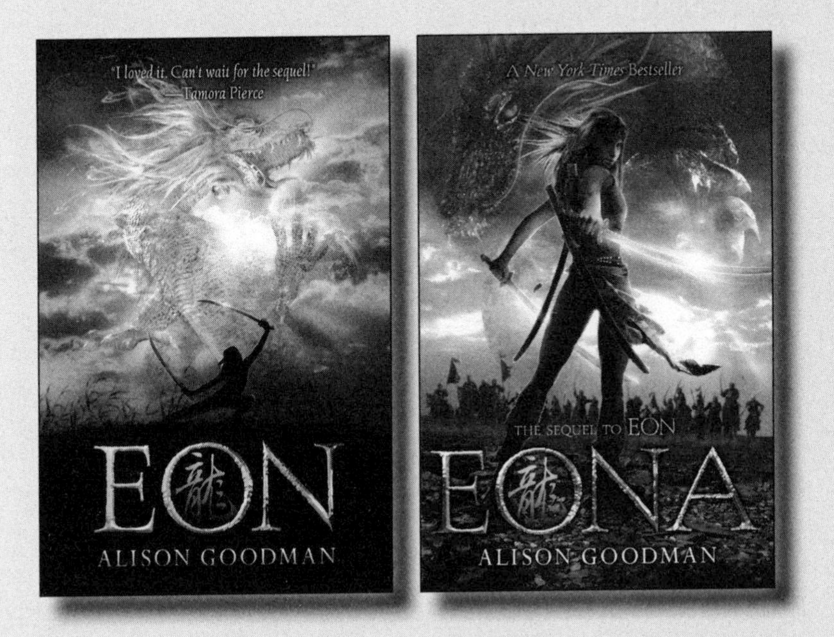

Check out Alison Goodman's genre-bending adventure

ALISON GOODMAN

is the author of the internationally bestselling and award-winning *Eon/Eona* duology, as well as the YA science fiction thriller *Singing the Dogstar Blues* and an adult novel, *A New Kind of Death* (originally titled *Killing the Rabbit*). She was a D. J. O'Hearn Memorial Fellow at Melbourne University, holds a Master of Arts, and mentors emerging writers.

She is on Twitter @AlisonGoodman and keeps a constantly growing Regency treasure trove at pinterest.com/alisongoodman.

Alison Goodman and her husband live in Victoria, Australia, with their irrepressible terrier, Xander.